Miscarriage of Justice

Miscarriage of Justice

A NOVEL

Kip Gayden

CENTER STREET

New York   Boston   Nashville

Center Street
Hachette Book Group USA
237 Park Avenue
New York, NY 10017

Visit our Web site at www.centerstreet.com

Center Street is a division of Hachette Book Group USA, Inc.
The Center Street name and logo is a trademark of Hachette Book Group USA, Inc.

Printed in the United States of America

First edition: February 2008
10 9 8 7 6 5 4 3 2 1

Library of Congress Cataloging-in-Publication Data
Gayden, Kip.
    Miscarriage of justice / Kip Gayden.—1st ed.
       p. cm.
    ISBN-13: 978-1-59995-687-9
    ISBN-10: 1-59995-687-X
    1. Triangles (Interpersonal relations)—Fiction. 2. Trials (Murder)—Fiction.
3. Tennessee—Fiction. I. Title.

    PS3607.A98575M57 2007
    813'.6—dc22   2007012536

Acknowledgments

Two people to whom I am forever grateful for their energy and enthusiasm in directing this novel into its finished form are my editors, Thom Lemmons and Christina Boys.

For other forms of research, advice and counsel, I am grateful to Mike Morgan, my friend and agent, as well as Jade Rogers Mayberry, Tonna Heath, Gary Webb, Mike Zibart, Walter Sills, Kenneth Thomson, Natilee Duning, Etheridge Dodson, Chancellor Claudia Bonnyman, Chester Campbell, Allen Haynes, Dr. Michael Montijo, Kimberly Allen, Hamilton Gayden III, Claiborne Gayden, Whitney Lawson, and my dear wife, Paulette Gayden.

The Ides of March

Nashville, Tennessee
March 15, 1913

WHEN THE PHONE RANG, Sidebottom gave it an annoyed look. It jangled on its cradle twice, and he just stared at it, chewing on the cigar he always carried, but never smoked. Finally, rolling his eyes at the ceiling and giving Christian a sad little shrug, he yanked the earpiece from its hook and leaned toward the phone.

"Sidebottom."

Paul Christian could hear the faint squawking of the person on the other end of the call, and from the way Sidebottom scowled, he began to hope that lounging around the police station on this overcast Saturday afternoon hadn't been a waste of time after all. He reached for his notepad and waited to see what he could pick up from Sidebottom's part of the conversation.

"It's on Broadway, you say? Jackson's Barbershop? Yeah, I know the place." He was scribbling on a scrap of paper. "Suspect in custody, yes. Witnesses?" He scratched some figures on his paper. Christian couldn't read them from where he was, but he had already noted the place and street.

"What do we know about the victim?" Sidebottom asked. Christian perked up even more. A juicy headline involving violent crime would sell more papers than yet another round of harrumphs about the suffragette march and convention that had started in Washington, D.C., twelve days before. Christian certainly wasn't any fan of the women's movement, but even he was getting tired of reading stories in the *Tennessean* about the crazy women in their white dresses and yellow sashes—and he had written his share of them.

"Has anybody called a doctor?" Sidebottom said. He listened a few seconds, grunted, and shook his head. "Well, the suspect better hope you're wrong. Get an ambulance over there as quick as you can. I'm on my way." The detective shoved the earpiece back onto its hook and heaved himself up from his chair.

"Sorry, Paul, got to run," he said as he swept his derby and jacket from the coat tree behind his desk. Detective Sidebottom strode out of the room without giving Christian another look.

The reporter thought about following Sidebottom down to the crime scene but decided instead to just make his way over to the booking room, where the suspect would be brought anyway, once placed under arrest.

He wasn't disappointed. Not only did he see the suspect, but he was also able to get an exclusive interview, including a full confession.

That was when everything started to change, though Christian didn't fully realize it at the time.

He called his editor and told him what he had. "I think it's page one, boss," he said. "You name it, this story's got it: adultery, society folks, eyewitnesses, a shooting in broad daylight—and we just found out the victim died. It's a murder charge, now."

Christian didn't exactly have to twist his editor's arm.

"Get over here as soon as you can, Christian," he said. "We've got an hour before deadline, and I want your story for the lead."

PART ONE

The Crime

1

Red Boiling Springs, Tennessee
Summer 1896

W HEN WALTER DOTSON volunteered at the Red Boiling
Springs Christian Camp, just before his final year of medical
school, he had no idea he would meet the woman destined to become
his wife.

He came from a religious and educated family, and couldn't remember a Sunday when he and his brothers and sisters, along with
their parents, weren't on the second pew from the front at the Westmoreland, Tennessee, Christian Church. Walter grew up around
Bible reading, music, and literature, and all three had continued to
shape his life and interests. At the camp, in addition to teaching Bible
study classes, he conducted elective sessions on Shakespeare and was
responsible for organizing the camp orchestra. Walter himself played
the tuba and was becoming fairly proficient with the violin.

Walter was standing with the other counselors in front of the camp
assembly building, taking his turn at greeting the newly arriving
campers when a gig, pulled by a dusty, lathered sorrel, rolled slowly
to a stop in the red gravel of the assembly yard. He watched as a girl

stepped down, stretching her back and arms after the long drive on the rutted roads from the railroad station.

Later, Walter was fond of remarking that nothing about her silky blonde hair, her striking blue eyes, or her slender neck and perfect features had caused him to saunter over and introduce himself. "I was just doing my job," he'd say, as Anna would roll her eyes in obvious, practiced skepticism.

In fact, Walter first approached the man stepping down from the carriage, presumably the young woman's father.

"Hello, sir. I'm Walter Dotson, one of the counselors here. I'd like to welcome you and your family to the camp."

"Pastor Dennis. Pleased to meet you. I'm the minister at Lafayette Christian Church in Lafayette, Tennessee. This is my daughter, Anna. She'll be here at the camp."

"Pleased to meet you, Miss Dennis," Walter said, offering his hand. Anna squeezed his fingers politely and gave a little curtsy. Her eyes never wavered from his as she said, "It's nice to meet you, too, Mr. Dotson."

It was a couple of seconds before Walter remembered the clipboard tucked beneath his left arm. He ran his finger down the list of names. "Yes, Miss Dennis, you've been assigned to Cabin Four, just up this hill and on the left. If you like, I'll carry your bags."

"Better see how many she brought before you offer that, young fella," her father said with a chuckle.

Walter grinned. He went to the rear of the buggy and gripped the handles of the two suitcases he found there. "Right this way," he said, motioning with his head. Anna Dennis and her father started up the hill ahead of him.

As they walked, Walter found himself studying the young woman's figure. She carried herself with a surety and a possession that seemed beyond what he would have expected of a sixteen-year-old, as he guessed Anna to be. She laid a hand on her father's arm as they went, and the skin of her hand appeared to Walter to be as flawless and soft as that of an infant. She laughed at something her father said, and the sound was completely enchanting to Walter. Then he realized the path of his thoughts and gave himself a little silent lecture. She was likely to be at least five or six years his junior. No, it wouldn't do; he'd have to take strict control of his thoughts where young Anna Dennis was concerned.

Later that afternoon, when the parents had departed and the campers had stored their belongings in their cabins, the entire camp assembled in the main building. Walter sat on the dais with the other counselors and camp staff and listened as the camp director addressed the campers, sitting in rows before him. Without really meaning to, Walter searched the upturned faces until he found Anna's. His eyes shied away, then returned, again and again. Each time he looked at her, he started a fresh sermon in his head.

Like any healthy young man, Walter hoped and expected to some-day find a woman with whom he could start a home and a family. And, as he thought on it, he realized there was no shortage of young ladies back in Westmoreland who had let him know in various ways that they weren't averse to the company of a tall, slender fellow with a strong chin and an intelligent look about him—at least, that was how Walter's mother summed it up. But there was a proper way to go about things, as Walter knew very well. Courting, or even thinking about courting, a young girl who was away from the watchful eyes of her parents was strictly not on the list of proper behavior.

The director welcomed them all and announced the basic schedule for each day, which consisted of Bible study in the morning, followed by elective activities ranging from athletic pursuits to more intellectual options in the afternoons. Evenings would be devoted to various entertainments and social activities.

When the director outlined the camp rules, Walter found himself cringing with guilt; one of the director's first topics was the prohibition of fraternization between campers and staff. "This is a camp dedicated to the nourishment of the soul, mind, and body," the director said. "It is not a social club. Young ladies, if any of my counselors behave improperly in the least, I expect you to let me know, and I'll deal decisively with the matter." Walter hoped he wasn't blushing, and he kept his eyes studiously averted from Anna Dennis's vicinity during this part of the presentation.

The director asked each of the counselors to make a brief personal introduction and give a description of the elective courses he would be teaching. When Walter's turn came, he did his best to be persuasive about the merits of Shakespeare. He also made a brief pitch for the camp orchestra. As he was finishing, he allowed his eyes to drift in Anna's direction. That blue gaze was fixed on him; he had to work hard to keep from stammering his concluding remarks.

The next morning, the counselors received listings of those who would be in both their Bible classes and electives. When Walter came to the D's he slowed, hoping and at the same time thinking it would be better for all concerned if . . .

But there she was, "Anna Dennis," subscribed both in his Shakespeare class and as a member of the orchestra! Walter was thrilled—despite knowing he would need to say a lot of prayers for forgiveness over the course of the camp session.

The first week of camp progressed, and Walter soon knew he was in trouble. When he and his students read from *Taming of the Shrew, A Midsummer Night's Dream,* or *Romeo and Juliet,* Anna's face drew his eyes like a magnet. During the discussions, she rarely took her eyes from his. Walter didn't have to work too hard to convince himself that she could be imagining herself as Katharina to his Petruchio, Hermia to his Lysander . . . or even, he dared to suppose, Juliet to his Romeo. In music classes, she stated a desire to learn the violin. Before long, she was staying after the rest of the group had left. Walter demonstrated the position of the instrument and coached her on fingering and bowing technique. As he touched her wrist to correct an angle or nudged her fingers toward a better position on the strings, it was as if fire flowed into him from her soft skin. In the evenings, after the close of the day's events, Walter spent a great deal of time rereading the Ten Commandments and the Sermon on the Mount—especially Matthew 5:28: "...But I say unto you, that whosoever looketh on a woman to lust after her hath committed adultery with her already in his heart."

By the middle of the second week, Walter had to admit to himself that he was thoroughly besotted. Anna Dennis was his every thought, waking and sleeping. He only hoped that the other students in his classes hadn't noticed the way he looked at her. And it wasn't just her attractive appearance; Anna was intelligent and perceptive. In Shakespeare class, she often asked the question that plunged to the very heart of the Bard's meaning for the passage. Sometimes, it seemed to Walter that she had somehow looked inside his mind to see how he intended to guide the class, then made the very comment that propelled the discussion in his intended direction. He had never experienced anything like it. And if he smiled and congratulated her on her insight, she returned his smile with a cocked, knowing expression that seemed to say, "Of course. What else would you expect?"

Walter found himself wishing he could empty his soul to her, longing to tell her things he had never wanted to tell anyone before. And the maddening thing was, she gave every evidence of wanting to hear! But how on God's green earth could he permit himself such intimacies with a camper in his charge? It was impossible. So he stewed in his own juices, growing more deliciously miserable each time he saw her.

On the final Saturday, the last day of camp, everyone had free time in the afternoon. Walter was sitting on the back steps of the counselors' cabin, looking at the spectacular sunset and moping, because tomorrow after the campers left he wouldn't see Anna again, probably for the rest of his life. He heard footsteps on the path beside the cabin and his heart went a-scramble in his chest when he realized she was walking toward him.

"Hello, Walter," she said. "I hope I may call you 'Walter'?"

"Uh, yes," he said, rising awkwardly to his feet and brushing his hands on the seat of his pants. "But . . . Miss Dennis, are you certain you should be here?"

She gave a quick glance over her shoulder, then back at him, and the expression on her face made Walter's pulse race even faster. "I'm quite certain," she said, "that I want to be here."

They stared at each other for several seconds. "There's . . . there's a bit of a cliff just over there, through the woods," Walter said. "Quite a view, actually. We could . . . we could watch the sun setting."

"Yes. We could." She smiled at him. "Will you show me the way?"

Walter willed his breathing to slow. *Collect yourself, Dotson, for pity's sake!* He offered her his arm, and she placed her hand in the crook of his elbow.

They reached the small clearing that opened onto the cliff. Walter dusted at a convenient boulder with his hand and gestured for Anna to sit. They stared out across the forestscape as the sunset limned the trees with gold.

" 'Shall I compare thee to a summer's day?' " Walter said, half to himself.

"What?"

"Oh, it's . . . just some Shakespeare."

"Something we read in class?"

"No, one of the sonnets."

"What's the rest?"

"Oh, I—"

"Please! I'm sure you know it."

"Actually, no."

"Well, you must know a little more anyway. Won't you humor me, Walter?"

Walter cleared his throat, feeling a bit foolish reciting poetry like a hero in a dime novel romance. But then, he reminded himself, this was no different from reading a passage from *Macbeth* in class to his students.

> *"Shall I compare thee to a summer's day?*
> *Thou art more lovely and more temperate:*
> *Rough winds do shake the darling buds of May,*
> *And summer's lease hath all too short a date . . .*

"That's all I can remember," Walter said.

"It was beautiful." She stood, holding his eyes in her crystal-blue stare, then leaned forward and kissed him. Walter pulled back, surprised.

"I'm sorry," she said. "I'm afraid I'm rather impetuous. It's a fault I've had since birth, my father tells me."

"I'm . . . not sorry at all." Giving in at last, Walter drew her to him and kissed her deeply.

2

ANNA DENNIS watched over her shoulder as she and her father drove away from the camp. Walter's tall, straight figure was visible, gazing after her, until a bend in the red-dirt road took him out of her sight. She turned around in the seat and stared ahead, trying to fight down the lump in her throat and the tears stinging the corners of her eyes.

It wasn't fair! She had only just discovered the love of her life, and now he was taken away from her. She wanted to tell Papa to stop the buggy. She wanted to run back to Walter and throw herself into his arms, swearing never to be apart from him for the rest of their lives.

Anna wanted to look at Papa, to see if he had taken note of the way his oldest daughter was pining for the handsome counselor—probably still standing in the yard of the camp, longing for her return! She hoped Papa did notice. After all, Papa couldn't think she was still a little girl who didn't care about things like true love. She was sixteen! She was practically a grown woman, and it was time Papa and Mama knew it.

ANNA SPENT THE REMAINDER of that summer wishing she had gotten an address from Walter—or at least the name of his hometown, for goodness' sake!—so she could write to him of her undying love. For all she knew, he was back at college, courting the older girls and forgetting all about her. The thought of it made her want to weep and throw herself across her bed, to shut herself in her room for a week and eat nothing but stale bread, like the heroines of those stories she'd glimpsed in Mama's issues of *Godey's Magazine*.

Fall approached, and Anna began her eleventh year of school. She was a bright girl and a good student—if "a little too liberal with her opinions," as some of her teachers put it. Her favorite subject was literature, despite the fact that some of the stories the teacher assigned were as dry as last year's bird's nest. That year, *Julius Caesar* was on the curriculum. That wasn't too bad, but Anna would have very much preferred *Romeo and Juliet*, or at the very least *A Midsummer Night's Dream*. She would have preferred something with a little romance in it, at any rate. Still, each time in class when they read aloud from Shakespeare, her thoughts went flying back to the camp at Red Boiling Springs, and to handsome Walter, sitting so straight and proper at the front of the group, wearing his clean white shirt and reading in his strong voice. She thought of his clear brown eyes and his perfectly combed hair, and the way his smile tipped slightly higher on one side than the other. She thought of his hands, the fingers so sensitive, yet so strong. Each time he'd shown her how to hold the violin or touched her wrist to adjust her hand position, all she could think about was wishing he'd cradle her in his arms and tuck her head under his chin . . . Oh! It was almost enough to make a girl desperate.

The Christmas holidays came around, and following the high school principal's recommendation, Anna applied to do volunteer work at Lafayette City Hospital. She had volunteered there during the previous summer, and with her bright disposition, eagerness to learn, and utter lack of reticence at trying new things, she soon won the hearts of the nurses and other hospital staff. The director of nurses quickly made a place for her on the volunteer roster. Anna looked forward to going back to the hospital, and she hoped that her past experience would qualify her to help more with patient care, which she especially enjoyed.

On her first day at the hospital, Anna was assigned to the front desk in the main reception area, greeting patients and their families and helping with room assignments. Anna saw a paper on the desk that listed doctors on duty for the months of December and January. As she idly scanned the list, she saw the name, "Dotson, Walter." Her pulse quickening, she also noted that someone had written beside the name, "Arr. Wed., Dec. 23." Two days from now! Was it possible?

A few minutes later, the director of nursing happened by. She smiled at Anna and walked over to her table.

"So glad to have you back with us, Anna. Are you getting settled in?"

"Yes, Nurse Hawkins, thank you very much. I'm glad to be back." Anna took a deep breath, reminded herself to keep her tone casual, and said, "I noticed a name on the doctors' list that I don't remember from last summer. It's a . . . Dr. Walter Dotson?"

"Oh, yes. Dr. Dotson is actually an intern from Nashville. He's in his final semester at Vanderbilt Medical School, and he has been assigned to our hospital for four weeks, beginning—" She glanced at the list. "—next Wednesday, it appears." She looked at Anna. "Why do you ask?"

"Oh, nothing," Anna said. "I just . . . didn't recognize the name, that's all." She said a silent little prayer, asking God's forgiveness for the fib.

"Well, let me know if you need anything, all right, Anna?"

"Yes, Nurse Hawkins, I will."

As the director walked away, Anna had to concentrate on taking slow, deep breaths. Walter Dotson, a medical student from Nashville! It *had* to be her Walter, it just had to be! He had remembered where she lived, and he had requested assignment to this hospital for his internship, just so he could see her again! It made Anna want to weep and dance in the hallway, by turns. Walter was coming for her!

Anna had a mischievous thought: Walter had no idea she was volunteering at the hospital. Wouldn't he be surprised if he were to walk in here on Wednesday morning to be greeted, ever so coolly and professionally, by the girl of his dreams? For the rest of the day, almost everyone who passed her desk asked Anna what she was smiling so broadly about. But she wouldn't tell.

Anna barely slept at all Tuesday night. She got out of bed when the first hint of dawn seeped around the edges of her bedroom curtains. She agonized over the best way to arrange her hair, and over which of her dresses to wear beneath the pink hospital volunteer pinafore.

She hurried down the front steps of her house, disregarding the curious stares of Mama and Papa, and was at her desk well before her usual time. Whenever the hospital door opened, her head would swivel eagerly toward the new arrival, only to be disappointed over and over again when it proved to be someone other than her Walter.

But finally, he walked in, and Anna had to actually grip the edges of the desk to prevent herself from rushing toward him. He was even more handsome than she remembered—especially now, when he was wearing his crisp, spotlessly white physician's coat. He approached her desk, but he was studying a piece of paper as he walked, and he barely glanced in her direction. Anna was practically holding her breath by the time he stopped in front of her.

"Yes, Miss, I'm Dr. Walter Dotson. This is my first day on call, and I need to find Room 117. Can you help me?"

"Dr. Dotson, you said?"

"Yes," he muttered, still poring over his paper.

"Dr. Walter Dotson?"

"Yes, that's me, Walter Dotson. Where can I find Room—"

"Dr. Walter Dotson, interning from Vanderbilt Medical School, who was formerly a counselor at Red Boiling Springs Christian Camp?"

His head bobbed up then and his eyes went wide as he looked at her. "Anna? Is that you? What are you—"

She leaned forward and extended her hand. "Anna Dennis, Dr. Dotson. I'm a volunteer here at Lafayette City Hospital. How may I assist you?"

He stared at her for perhaps a full five seconds before he collected himself. "Anna, I . . . I don't know what to say."

"You might start by telling me why you came to this hospital in the first place."

"Well, isn't it obvious? I saw 'Lafayette, Tennessee' on the list of openings for internships, and I snapped it up. Did you really think I'd forgotten you?"

Anna actually managed a bit of a pout; she was so proud of herself! "How was I to know? All those weeks, then months, and no word from you . . ."

"Oh, Anna, dear Anna! I—" He seemed to remember where he was, and lowered his voice. He leaned toward her, still keeping a respectful distance. "I've thought of nothing and no one but you since the moment we—since I watched you and your father driving away from the camp. I had to at least try to find you. I was so hoping that while I was here for my internship I might be able to locate you . . . and here you are!"

"I'd say it was a favorable sign, wouldn't you?"

They knew they couldn't continue their conversation in the hospital lobby. Anna directed Walter to Room 117 and made sure he learned that she left at four o'clock that afternoon. He asked to walk her home and she was thrilled to agree—though she tried not to let him see just how thrilled.

The hours until four o'clock crept by like tortoises wearing stone shoes. But at last, Walter came and offered Anna his arm as they went toward the front door. Anna was sure tongues were wagging behind their backs, but she didn't care. Her Walter had come for her, and nothing could ever separate them now.

Anna removed her hand from Walter's arm as they neared the Dennis home, and he grew very quiet as they walked toward the front steps. Anna guessed he was feverishly composing a speech aimed at convincing her father of the honor of his intentions toward her. Well, he didn't need to worry; if he couldn't convince Papa, Anna would see to it, herself.

Walter opened the door, and Anna's father was standing in the entry hall, a confused look on his face. Walter stuck out his hand, but before he could speak, Anna said, "Oh, Papa! You remember Walter Dotson, from camp last summer, don't you? He's a doctor, Papa, and he's interning at the hospital during the Christmas vacation. Isn't that grand? I insisted that he walk me home so you could see him again."

Papa, his eyes flickering back and forth between Anna and Walter, extended his hand and took Walter's in a firm grip.

"Well, then . . . what a coincidence," Papa said.

"So pleased to see you again, Pastor Dennis," Walter said.

"Yes, well . . . yes. And you were . . . at the camp?"

"I was a counselor there, sir. I met you and your daughter on the first day, when you arrived? Carried the luggage?"

"Oh, yes."

Mama came from the kitchen, drying her hands on her apron. Papa turned toward her. "Mother, this is Dr. Dotson. He's a . . . a friend of Anna's, from the hospital."

"Walter Dotson, Ma'am," Walter said, taking Mama's hand.

"From the hospital?"

"We met at the camp last summer, Mama," Anna said. "Walter taught Bible classes and Shakespeare." She smiled up at him. "He's a wonderful teacher."

"I daresay," Mama said. Anna didn't miss the look she gave Papa.

3

IN LATER YEARS, Anna would say that the thing most instrumen-
tal in bringing about her marriage to Walter was the influenza out-
break of the winter of 1896–97.

Of course, it also didn't hurt that Walter made sure he was in attendance at Lafayette Christian Church every time the doors were
open. He sat with their family and listened closely to her father's
preaching, never failing to discuss the main points of the sermon on
the walk back to the house. Anna was pleased when Mama invited
Walter to Sunday lunch. At first, Anna's younger brother, Bobby,
gave Walter a wide berth and a baleful look, but Walter's courtesy
and knowledge of so many interesting things soon won the boy over.
Flora, naturally, was no problem at all; four years younger than Anna,
she was hopelessly smitten with the dashing Walter from the first
moment she laid eyes on him.

When Walter would leave to go back to the room he rented at the
home of one of the local doctors, Anna would endure the quiet, yet
urgent, questioning of her parents: Had Walter ever behaved improperly toward her? Wasn't Anna concerned about the difference in their
ages and experiences? She had known him only a short period of time;
how could she be sure what sort of person he really was? Anna kept a

strict rein on her tongue and gave Mama and Papa the answers they wanted to hear, as much as she could, and used her best powers of persuasion at all times. She also told herself that things like proper behavior, age, and character were in the eye of the beholder. Anna was already thinking of certain behaviors that she longed to pursue with Walter, and they extended considerably beyond last summer's kisses.

On a cold morning just after New Year's Day, Anna went to the hospital, only to find a sign on the front door that read, "Quarantine: No Admittance Except for Hospital Staff." In front of the sign was a uniformed constable. As Anna approached, he held up a hand. "Sorry, Miss Dennis. Only doctors and nurses."

"But . . . I'm supposed to work." *How would she see Walter if she couldn't get into the hospital?*

"You're a volunteer, Miss. I can't allow you inside, on orders from the hospital superintendent."

As Anna pondered what to do, the director of nursing approached. The policeman stood aside and opened the door for her. As she was about to go in, a haggard nurse emerged from inside.

"Nurse Hawkins, I was watching for you. I don't know what we're going to do. The influenza has spread to the staff; we have so many nurses sick now that we're having trouble assisting the doctors."

Nurse Hawkins gave a worried look; Anna saw an opening. "Nurse Hawkins, can I help? It sounds like you're shorthanded."

Nurse Hawkins looked at Anna, then the constable. "I don't know, Anna. This influenza is bad; you could become very ill."

"I don't care. I want to help, and even the doctors can't do anyone any good if they don't have adequate assistance."

The other nurse nodded her head. "We're really in dire need."

Anna decided to press her advantage. She strode toward the door. "All right, then. I'm coming in to help, just until the situation improves." She walked right past the constable and Nurse Hawkins, and that was that.

For three days Anna never left Walter's side. It was heartbreaking to watch the suffering of the old and the infants, those most susceptible to the disease's effects. Walter hardly slept; with the other doctors and nurses, he was attending patients around the clock, trying to help as many as possible to gain strength enough to go home in order to free up beds for the dozens still arriving each day.

An unexpected advantage of the quarantine was that it prevented Papa from dragging her away from Walter, back to the house. Even the minister of the Christian Church wasn't allowed into the hospital. Despite her growing fatigue, Anna was happy to be able to be with Walter, performing the nursing tasks required to support his efforts.

About halfway through the second day, Walter tried to convince her to go home. "You'll get sick, Anna. I couldn't bear that. Why don't you go home and get some rest?"

She refused. Anna knew that once she was outside the doors of the hospital, she was back in Papa's control and, worse, shut away from Walter. "Besides, what if you get sick?" she said. "I'm staying here with you until the epidemic is under control."

He gave her a long look, and a slow smile spread across his weary features. "You're a stubborn little outfit, aren't you?"

"I am when it's something I believe in."

"All right then, Miss Dennis. I guess I'll just have to remember that."

"You'd do well to."

THE EPIDEMIC EASED and life returned to normal, more or less. But the day came when Walter's internship ended, and he had to return to Vanderbilt. Unlike the previous summer, Anna was scrupulous about getting his address and giving hers in exchange. She extracted promises from Walter to write her every single day, promises he seemed more than eager to give. Going through the grueling experience of the influenza epidemic had done nothing but increase Anna's admiration for Walter and her determination to have him for her own. She also believed he was looking at her differently: less as a young girl and more as a potential helpmate. Anna reasoned that if she could stand up to the rigors of the influenza crisis, she could manage the day-to-day business of life as a doctor's wife. At least, that was what she told Mama and Papa.

She and Walter bid a long farewell at the train station. True to his word, letters bearing his handwriting began arriving at the Dennis home on a daily basis, and Anna reciprocated. And then, on a rainy afternoon in late March, Anna read the words she had been longing to see.

> *Dear Anna,*
>
> *It must surely be apparent to you that my heart is yours and yours alone. Accordingly, I want to tell you that I intend, upon the next convenient occasion, to request from your father the honor of your hand in marriage. That is, of course, if you are of similar mind. I think that you are, and I fervently hope that you are, but I shall await word from you. Please write soon, for I fear that the anticipation and worry over your response may interfere with my studies, so great is my feeling in this matter.*

Anna clasped the letter to her and twirled around her room. She ran downstairs to Papa's writing desk and scrabbled for paper and pen. She dashed off her rapturous response—"Yes, my darling Walter, yes, a thousand times yes!"—and practically ran to the post office to put it in the mail with her own hands.

They agreed that Walter would come to Lafayette during Vanderbilt's Easter break, by that time only two weeks away. During those intervening days, Anna took every opportunity to speak to Mama and Papa about Walter, about how well he was doing in medical school, about all the wonderful opportunities that were sure to open to him upon his graduation. She dropped barely veiled hints that they had serious intentions for their relationship. One day, she even asked Mama if she could borrow the latest issue of *Godey's*, since she'd noticed the front fashion plate was of a bridal gown in the latest style. By the time Walter arrived on the Tuesday after Easter and sat down with Mama and Papa in the parlor, dry-mouthed and swallowing after every other syllable, Anna knew very well that her parents had no reasonable choice but to consent to her marriage to Walter Dotson.

THEY MARRIED THE FOLLOWING JUNE. At Walter's request, Anna's father officiated. All of Walter's family and many friends from Westmoreland came to Lafayette for the ceremony. Combined with the high standing of the Dennis family in the community, there was hardly an empty space in the church by the time the wedding started.

The newlyweds departed the church in a hired carriage, amid a flurry of waving handkerchiefs, flung rice, blown kisses, and shouted admonitions. They drove to the railroad station and boarded a train for Nashville, where Walter had rented a room at the luxurious Maxwell House Hotel for their wedding night.

Anna knew some things about what to expect, and had guessed many others. That night, after a delicious dinner largely spent in long gazes into each other's eyes, they went upstairs to their room on the fourth floor. Anna gave Walter a long, lingering kiss and went into the washroom, promising to emerge not long after. She undressed, then put on the nightgown trimmed in white lace Mama had bought for her. She unpinned her hair and brushed it until it was smooth and silky. She applied some of the new French perfume bought for her by the ladies at the Christian Church, blushing as she recalled some of the shockingly bawdy remarks that had accompanied the gift. She looked in the mirror and assured herself that she was ready, then quietly opened the door to go to her husband.

Walter was standing in the dark, wearing his nightshirt. His clothing was tossed on a chair in the corner. When Anna came to him, he folded her in his arms and kissed her, then kissed her some more. Their breath mingled, coming quicker and quicker as hands explored above clothing, then beneath, moving more urgently by the moment. Walter cupped her breasts and smoothed his palms across the small of her back, the globes of her buttocks; Anna gripped his shoulders and pulled him into her, feeling the hardness of his body and longing for him, hungering in an immediate way in which she had never before suspected she was capable.

They fell back onto the bed and made love intensely, their bodies knowing what to do better than they would have ever guessed. They didn't bother turning down the coverlet, so great was their need. Walter reached his peak a bit sooner than Anna expected, but it was all right; yes, it was all right, all right. She held him as his breathing slowed, said "yes" with a fond smile when he timidly asked if "it" was agreeable to her. He was her husband, and they were joined as one flesh, just like the Bible said, and nothing would ever be wrong again.

IN JULY, Walter and Anna moved to Chicago so he could take up his postgraduate internship at the Cook County Hospital. Chicago was the farthest either Walter or Anna had ever been from home, but Anna was excited by the prospect of finally traveling beyond the borders of north-central Tennessee and southern Kentucky. They rented a two-room flat in an apartment building on the borders of Hyde Park, near the University of Chicago. Anna began volunteering at the Rush Medical School hospital, which was also near their apartment.

It was here, among the hardworking nurses, that Anna first began

24

hearing about the growing women's suffrage movement. Though entirely new to her, the ideas behind the movement intrigued her. Anna had always been independent of mind, and the notion that women ought to be allowed a greater say in the conduct of their own affairs—and the nation's—made intuitive sense to her. She became more and more interested in current events, and often read the day's *Tribune* from end to end before Walter came home from his rounds. She tried to discuss with Walter what she was reading, but he was often either too tired or seemed impatient at some of the notions she expressed. In the interest of greater harmony, Anna soon began keeping her political opinions mostly to herself.

Walter's yearlong internship in Chicago was succeeded by the offer of a residency at a prestigious hospital in New York. From there, the young couple traveled to Vienna, Austria, where Walter had been invited to pursue specialized studies in ear, nose, and throat medicine. During those busy days, Mabel was born, and the young family began to coalesce around the nucleus of caring for the needs of a baby. As much as Anna loved being Walter's wife, she adored being a mother even more. Every time she looked into her daughter's face, she felt her heart swelling with a fearful pride for the new life that had been entrusted to her care.

At the end of the Vienna residency, Walter and Anna faced an important choice: Would Walter accept one of the several lucrative offers he had received to practice his specialty with a doctor's group in a large city like New York or Chicago, or would they move back to Tennessee to be nearer the extended families they both missed so much? After much thought and discussion, they reached the joint decision to return to Tennessee. Walter found an opening in a small town not far from either his hometown of Westmoreland or Anna's family in Lafayette. And so, in the late summer of 1906, Walter and Anna Dotson moved to Smithville, Tennessee, where Walter began what would become a very successful family practice.

Smithville welcomed the little family of three with open arms. A young doctor moving to town was always a positive thing, and Walter soon had a thriving general practice. Six-year-old Mabel was the darling of her Sunday school class; Walter was soon teaching Bible classes at church and had even been invited to join the Masonic Lodge. Whenever Anna went anywhere in Smithville, folks greeted her by name. Looking back from years later, Anna would realize that these had been the best days of their marriage.

Unfortunately, worse days would follow soon enough.

After two years, Walter began wishing for opportunities to practice his specialty. He told Anna that he wanted to look for a place closer to Nashville, the nearest city of any size, where he would at least have the chance to attract some patients who required his expertise. Eventually, he settled on Gallatin, about twenty-five miles north of Nashville, and only seventeen or so miles south of his hometown of Westmoreland. And it was an easy half-day's train ride from her parents in Lafayette, he told her.

Anna felt thoroughly at home in Smithville, but Walter seemed so certain things would be better for them in Gallatin. And she really did want him to have every chance to make a success for their family. So, in 1908, the Dotsons—who now numbered four with the recent birth of Walter Scott Dotson Jr.—loaded their belongings onto a drayman's rig, boarded the train amid a crowd of regretful well-wishers, and headed northwest toward their new home in Gallatin.

IN NO TIME AT ALL, the Dotsons were strongly integrated into the civic and social fabric of Gallatin. Walter's reputation as an ear, nose, and throat specialist was spreading. He was deeply committed to those under his care, and he was also a skilled physician. Soon people were coming from all over central Tennessee to consult with him. Many were the nights Anna tucked Scott, as Walter Jr. was called, and Mabel in their beds, then retired alone, waiting for Walter to return from a late consultation with one of the wealthy patients who could afford to have him come to their homes.

Walter maintained his interest in music and literature, joining the Gallatin Commercial Club Band and the Greater Gallatin Reading Circle. He also remained active with the Masons, often serving as a lecturer for the evening meetings of lodges in outlying areas.

Anna was also far from idle. Her outgoing personality and sense of style soon endeared her to the ladies of the town, and she found herself plied with invitations to all sorts of gatherings. When they moved into their handsome new two-story home on North Water Avenue, Anna soon made it a popular gathering place for all sorts of women's groups.

Anna was still interested in the suffrage movement, though she could tell Walter didn't entirely approve. He wouldn't discuss the cause with her, but he never strictly forbade her from keeping herself informed.

Anna wasn't quite sure when she began to notice that she and Walter had lost the joy of their early days as man and wife. But in the winter of 1909, she suffered a miscarriage, requiring some months for her to recover. Somehow, after that, things were different. Walter was solicitous of her during her convalescence, certainly, and no one could say that she didn't have everything she needed to encourage a full recovery. But after losing the baby, Walter's attitude toward her underwent a subtle shift. His physical attentions, which had tapered off to some degree after Scott's birth, now became virtually nonexistent. Anna wondered if he was afraid she might become pregnant again, and so avoided intimacy with her out of concern for her health. She tried to talk with him about it, but he simply denied any cause for concern existed, maintained he loved her as always, and advised her not to fret herself. "I am a doctor, after all," he would say. "I think I might know something of what I'm talking about, don't you?" Meanwhile, he busied himself more than ever with church, Masonic, and civic activities, as well as the ever-present demands of his growing medical practice.

4

Gallatin, Tennessee
December 1910

GALLATIN STATION, FOLKS. Arriving in Gallatin Station."
Hearing the conductor's singsong announcement, Walter turned to Anna. "Home again, home again," he said with a tired smile.

Anna nodded without looking at him. If he noticed the distance in her manner, he said nothing. He pulled himself up out of the seat and began gathering their things.

The medical convention in Chicago had been a success, she supposed. Walter had attended a number of sessions and had made, by all accounts, a fine presentation on a topic concerned with his specialty. A professional success, maybe, but Anna's personal hopes for the trip to Chicago had been woefully disappointed.

Anna followed her husband out of the railroad car onto the platform of the Gallatin station. Her back was stiff; the five-hour ride from Louisville had seemed longer to her than the whole rest of their journey from Chicago.

Walter was waving at someone. Anna peered through the crowd

and, seeing her brother Bobby, hoped he had brought the Winton Six. It was only two blocks from the station to their house, but at that moment the thought of walking was positively hateful to her. As she waited, Anna couldn't keep her thoughts from turning to the French nightgown nestled in her suitcase, carefully folded among her underthings. Anna had held such high hopes for the nightgown.

She had felt daring and independent when she bought it. She had tried it on, right there in the store, thrilled by the chance to shop in all the places she hadn't been able to frequent when her husband was a poverty-stricken medical student. It was one of the reasons Anna had been so eager to accompany Walter to his medical convention. Now, after a few years and Walter's success as an ear, nose, and throat specialist in the Nashville area, the boutiques of downtown Chicago beckoned her with an irresistible call. Walter spent his days attending seminars and lectures, and Anna spent hers on the sidewalks of Michigan Avenue and State Street, going from shop to shop.

It felt like fate when she saw the display in Madeleine's on the very last day. She had immediately recognized the styles from the advertisements in her latest issues of *Vogue*. Anna had so admired the nightgowns pictured there—especially the one with the revealing neckline and back—and had torn the page from her magazine and brought it with her on the trip.

"Good afternoon, Madame," the female sales clerk greeted her immediately in a French accent. "How may we help you?"

Anna dug the folded magazine page out of her handbag. "Do you have this style?" She held out the illustration for the clerk's inspection.

"Ah, *oui, Madame*, we certainly do. Right over here." The clerk helped her select her size and showed her to one of the mirrored dressing rooms.

The effervescent silk slid across Anna's skin like a caress from an invisible lover. She admired her figure in the dressing room mirror, pleasing herself with the realization that two babies and a miscarriage hadn't stolen her attractive shape. The material was sheer enough to allow translucent glimpses of her legs and body. The back of the gown dipped daringly near the cleavage of her buttocks, and Anna felt a flush of excitement merely from seeing herself in such a revealing garment.

Anna had been longing for the physical intimacy she had enjoyed with Walter during the early days of their marriage, an intimacy that had been sorely lacking for much too long. She knew she was still attractive; she could tell from the way men's eyes roved her upon greeting, or when they thought she wasn't looking. She didn't understand why her husband couldn't see her that way, or enjoy her feminine charms, as was his right. But every night, when he'd finished his "chores" in the bathroom that joined their two bedrooms, he retired to his own chamber. Seldom did Anna hear the knock on her door that she was wishing for.

Maybe the French nightgown would change all that. After his last lecture, Walter had promised her a romantic, candlelight dinner at the café of the Hotel Chicago. When they went up to their room, Anna decided, she would put on the nightgown. She would display herself for her husband and surely he would respond to her. He would take her in his arms and crush her mouth with kisses, like the men in the *Argosy* serial romances. He would carry her to the nearest bed—or couch!—and ravish her. They would fall asleep in a tangle of limbs and cast-off clothing, sighing with the tired satisfaction of lovers who have drunk their fill of each other's charms.

Dinner was wonderful, and as they went back up to their room, Anna leaned near her husband. "I have a surprise for you, dear."

"Really? What is it?"

"Oh, I can't tell you. I have to show you," she said in the silky voice of a seductress.

He smiled at her in that amused, offhand way he had, but said nothing else. Anna had to stop herself from becoming infuriated. Did the man have no imagination whatsoever? Was he completely immune to the desire she was trying to kindle in him, to the fleshly anticipation of pleasure? He just plodded along down the hall, fishing in his pocket for the room key. But Anna schooled herself to patience. She would go into the toilet and change, and when she came out in the French nightgown, nature would have no choice but to take its course.

They went in, and Walter, yawning, began shrugging out of his tuxedo jacket. Anna went into the lavatory and retrieved the package from Madeleine's out of the drawer above the vanity where she had secreted it. She removed her dress, petticoats, and stockings, then slid the nightgown over her head and let it settle like mist around her lower calves. Anna unpinned her long blonde hair, running her tortoiseshell brush through it until it hung like a veil over her bare arms. Giving herself a final, critical glance in the mirror, she quietly opened the door.

"And now for your surprise," she said, smiling as she stepped into the room for Walter's inspection.

He was asleep on the bed. He lay on his back with his mouth open, and he was snoring softly.

Anna considered trying to wake him, then realized she didn't want to. She didn't want to try to create something that obviously wasn't there. If he woke up and saw her, she guessed, he'd probably either want to know how much the nightgown cost or give her a disapproving look for wearing something so risqué. Walter had very strict opinions on what was proper for women.

Anna lay down on the bed, right beside Walter. Her pulse was pounding with frustration, with the excitement of the French nightgown, with knowing what she was about to do. She reached between her thighs and used her fingers, trying to tease out and rub away the thought of Walter's wooden insensitivity toward her. In her mind's eye she saw the men in the *Argosy* stories, with their dark, smoldering eyes and fierce smiles. She watched Walter, half-hoping he would wake and see what she was doing and perhaps feel an instant of remorse—but his breathing never changed, his eyelids never so much as flickered.

And when the moment came, when she reached the crest and then lay quiet in the pooling, dim light of the electric bulb on the wall sconce above the bed, she realized that the emptiness in her heart was even greater than before.

WALTER HELD THE DOOR FOR HER. She stepped up into the backseat of the Winton Six and waited for Bobby to crank the automobile. Anna could see the twin turrets of their home, rising above the roofline of the single-story train station. The car coughed, then caught, belching a puff of black smoke from its exhaust. Bobby hurried around to the driver's seat, fiddled with some knobs and levers, then put the car in gear and pulled away from Gallatin Station.

They drove up to the front gate, on North Water Avenue, two blocks north of the Gallatin town square. Walter helped Bobby gather the valises and other luggage, while Anna went up the walk to the front steps and onto the wide porch that wrapped all the way around the first floor of the large, clapboard-sided house. She opened the front door and called out, "Mabel! Scott! Mama and Daddy are home!"

Mabel, their eleven-year-old, came bounding from her room and down the stairs, grinning with delight. She ran into Anna's outstretched arms and buried her face in her mother's skirts.

"Hello, my darling! I've missed you so much. Have you been a good girl for Uncle Bobby and Aunt Flora?"

Mabel nodded vigorously.

"Where is your brother?"

"He's asleep. He has a cold and hasn't been feeling so good."

Anna immediately began climbing the stairs. Part of her mind told her to calm herself, but another part could scarcely bide the time it took to reach her son's door and go inside to check on him. Ever since her miscarriage, Anna had been more solicitous than ever of her children's health—to the point of obsession, Walter would sometimes say. "I'm a physician, Anna. Do you think I'd let something happen to one of our children?" But Walter didn't know everything. He hadn't been able to save their unborn child, had he?

Anna went quietly to Scott's bedside and laid a hand on his forehead. No fever. She let out her breath and said a quick prayer of thanks. His breathing was slow and regular and his skin felt normal. Anna motioned to Mabel, who had followed her up the stairs, to be quiet. She tiptoed out of the room and softly closed the door.

"Let your brother sleep, all right? And later I'll show you some of the things I got while Daddy and I were away."

"In Chicago?"

Anna nodded. The rapturous look on Mabel's face made her laugh. "You're going to be fashion-crazy someday soon, aren't you, sweetie? Just like your mama."

Mabel trailed Anna to her room at the other end of the upstairs hallway. Bobby was just setting down her luggage. He smiled at his sister, then his niece.

"How was the weather in Chicago?" he asked.

"Cold as anything. When the north wind comes off Lake Michigan, they say it cuts like a knife, and I believe it."

"We had a pretty cold night or two here," Bobby said, "but no snow."

"Oh, I do hope it snows for Christmas," Mabel said.

"Well, I better get downstairs and help Walter with the rest of the bags," Bobby said. "Welcome home, Sister."

She squeezed his arm as he passed.

Anna tugged one of her suitcases onto her bed and opened the latches. "Now, let's see here . . . what can I find?"

Mabel plopped herself in the middle of Anna's bed and gazed at the brightly colored fabrics her mother was pulling from the suitcase.

Anna showed her daughter the blouses, the scarves, the dresses. She even showed her the new silk stockings she'd found at a boutique on Wabash Avenue. But she decided she wouldn't show her the French nightgown. It just didn't seem right. The nightgown would stay hidden for now.

"Oh, Mama, I'm so glad you're home."

Anna looked at Mabel and smiled. "Me too, sweetheart. Me too."

Just as Anna had finished putting away the last of her clothes and new things from the trip, Scott came padding into her room in his stocking feet, rubbing his eyes with balled-up fists.

"Well, hello there, young sir," Anna said. "I'm so glad to see you up! I came into your room as soon as Daddy and I got home from the station, but you were like Little Boy Blue, under the haystack fast asleep."

Scott came to her and raised his arms to be held. Anna hoisted him up and clasped him in a hug. She kissed the side of his neck with loud, smacking sounds. He giggled and squirmed away from her.

"It tickles, Mama."

Anna carried Scott to her bed and sat him down on the edge. "Now, you have to tell me everything you did while Daddy and I were away. Don't leave out a single thing."

Scott looked around her room. "Did you bring me anything?"

"Maybe I did, and maybe I didn't. You'll just have to wait and see. Christmas is coming, you know."

"Mama!"

"Patience, young man."

"'Patience, thou young and rose-lipp'd cherubin,—'" quoted Mabel, standing in the doorway.

"Oh, your father and his Shakespeare," Anna said, shaking her head at her daughter.

"Mama, can we go downtown and see the Christmas decorations?" Mabel said. "In an hour or two, they'll be turning on the lights. I want to see it, don't you?"

"Me, too!" Scott said, standing up on his mother's bed and jumping up and down.

"No more monkeys jumping on the bed," Anna said, grabbing him round the waist and swinging him in a wide arc down to the floor. "All right, you two. Shall we go for a stroll?"

"Yeeeeeeeeessssssss!" the children shouted.

"Can Daddy come?" Scott said.

Anna realized she hadn't seen Walter since she got out of the automobile. "I think Daddy went to his office to check on his patients. Maybe we can walk by there to see, all right?"

She bundled her children and herself in coats and scarves against the December air and went to the kitchen to tell Gertrude, their maid, where she and the children were going, in case Walter came home before they did. Then, holding Scott's hand on one side and Mabel's on the other, she went out the front door and down the sidewalk to the gate, turning right toward the town center.

The Dotson home fronted North Water Avenue, sitting on the west side of the town's main north-south thoroughfare, close to where Railroad Street intersected. Across the street, situated in the V of the intersection, sat the Keystone Hotel, with its large, wraparound porch that provided a gathering place popular with many of Gallatin's downtown merchants and workers—especially the young, unattached men. Sometimes Anna would see Bobby there after his working hours, sitting at a table with some of his cronies, drinking cider—at least, that's what he told his big sister he drank—and holding forth on the topic of the day. He wasn't there now, though, as far as she could see. Most likely he'd had to get back to the store and make up for the time he'd spent seeing them home from the station.

As Anna strolled past the Keystone on the opposite side of the street, she did see someone watching her: a fellow with a slender, muscular build and black hair. He wore a black derby and he didn't look away, even though Anna was certain he knew she noticed him watching her. He sat at a table with three other men, and after another second or two, turned to say something to one of his companions. Anna wasn't sure whether to be annoyed at his impudence or complimented by the interest he'd shown—if that was what it was. Then Mabel started tugging her toward the decorated windows of the shops on Boyers Avenue, and Anna had to pay attention in order to guide her children safely across the busy intersection.

They trudged up Water Street, climbing the hill toward the town square, dominated by the Sumner County Courthouse, its white trim stark against the red brick of its walls. Walter's medical office was on the town square, along with many of the town's most prosperous business establishments: Person's Barbershop, the Jennings Art Gallery, a beauty salon, a druggist with a soda fountain, and Whitehead's Hardware and Dry Goods, where Bobby worked.

Anna pulled open the door to Walter's clinic and held it for the children. Scott went straight to the bureau drawer where Walter kept sweet treats for his youngest patients. He extracted a small packet of horehound candy wrapped in white paper and looked a question at his mother. She gave him a smile and a nod, and he swiftly popped one of the dark, brown lozenges into his mouth.

"Daddy?" Mabel said, stepping through the front parlor toward the short hallway that connected the two small surgeries.

"Back here, darling." Walter's voice had come from the far right end of the hallway, where his private office was located. The children and Anna went down the hall and stood in the doorway. Walter sat at his oak rolltop desk; papers of various sizes spread all across the desk in front of him.

"Trying to catch up on all the correspondence from while we were gone," he said.

"The children wanted to see the Christmas windows. Can you come with us?"

He gave them a regretful little smile. "Oh, no. Far too much to do here, if I want to hit the ground running with my patients in the morning. You all run along and have a good time. Maybe I'll finish early enough to catch up with you before you go back to the house."

"All right, children, let's get out of Daddy's way," Anna said, motioning Mabel and Scott back down the hallway.

"Daddy, will you be home for supper?" Scott said. "I want to show you the sword Uncle Bobby helped me make."

"A sword, is it? Well, I might just have to see that," Walter said, smiling. "Go on, now, and mind your mama."

"Try not to be too late," Anna said in a lower voice as the children walked toward the front parlor. "They've missed you."

"I'll do my best," he said. To Anna, his tone sounded much the same as the one he'd used with Scott.

"Why don't we go say hello to Uncle Bobby?" Anna said. The three of them walked down to Whitehead's. Anna was pleased to see Scott tug open the door and hold it for her and Mabel. "Why, thank you, sir," she said, smiling at her son as they went inside. "Where did you ever learn such lovely manners?"

Bobby was handing a sales ticket to a customer when they came in. He looked up and saw them.

"Hello, Sister," he said. He came out from behind the counter and stooped down to receive Mabel, grabbing her in his arms and giving her a big hug.

"I don't think I ever actually thanked you for picking us up at the station," Anna said.

"No trouble at all. How was Chicago?"

"Fine. Scott, don't touch the lamps, please."

"How did Walter's presentation go?"

"Oh, I'm sure he was wonderful, as always." Her tone was a little sharper than she intended, and her brother gave her an odd look.

"Uncle Bobby, can I have this?" Scott was holding a cork gun.

"You'll have to ask your mama," Bobby said.

"Mama, please, can I?"

"Absolutely not, Scott. I've already told you once today that Christmas is coming. Now you just put that right back where you found it." Scott hesitated, and Anna gave him a look that suggested obedience as the best choice. Heaving a dramatic sigh, Scott put the toy back on its shelf.

"You ought to be ashamed, putting things like that where young boys' fingers can be tempted," Anna said to Bobby in a low voice.

Bobby grinned. "Well, now we have to help Santa along somehow, don't we? Your mama's right, Scott," he said in a louder voice. "Old Santa Claus is coming pretty soon. I'll try and remember to tell him you had your eye on that popgun, all right?"

"Come on, children. Let's go see Mrs. Jennings and look at some paintings."

Mabel smiled happily and skipped toward the door, while Scott shuffled more slowly, his hands shoved in his pockets, still sending longing glances at the cork gun.

"Thank you again, Bobby," Anna said. "Why don't you come over for supper tomorrow night?"

"That'd be nice. Thank you, Sis."

They went out, then around the square to the Jennings Art Gallery. Anna was delighted to see Elizabeth Jennings behind the counter, talking with another woman. Like Anna, Elizabeth kept up with the suffrage movement, and was one of the younger ladies in the informal gathering Anna met with weekly over tea. Elizabeth would catch Anna up on all the local gossip that had accumulated while she was away. Anna gave her friend a wave and waited, looking at the displays of oils and watercolors with the children, until the other woman left.

She told the children to look, but not touch, and went over to where Elizabeth waited. The two friends hugged in greeting.

"When did you get back from Chicago?" Elizabeth said.

"Oh, an hour or two ago. The children wanted to see the Christmas things, so . . ."

"Was it all just wonderful?"

"Chicago was nice. Lots of good shopping."

Elizabeth's eyes widened. "I want to see."

"Isn't it my turn to host the tea next Tuesday? I'll show you everything."

"I can hardly wait. Where did you stay?"

"The Hotel Chicago, where the convention was held. It's very nice."

"Was it just so romantic?"

Anna felt a little pang. "It was lovely, yes. Our room was very nice. So . . . what's the latest news around here?"

Elizabeth filled her in on the goings-on around Gallatin: The wife of the Presbyterian minister had hosted a coming-out for her niece, a rather plain girl from some little crossroads in Trousdale County; Mrs. Olmstead and Mrs. Baskerville—both of whom were members of the weekly tea group—were mortified when they both showed up wearing the identical dress.

"I'd have thought they'd have communicated better beforehand," Anna said.

Elizabeth shrugged. "They're both dears, of course, but also both a little vain. You and I would've just laughed it off." Then she told Anna about the current, big public debate in Gallatin over the proposal before the Board of Aldermen to raise the speed limit for horseless carriages from five to eight miles per hour. "I expect the car owners will be bending Walter's ear, now that he's back in town, trying to convince him to vote for raising the limit."

"Oh, I can't imagine Walter doing something so daring," Anna said.

Elizabeth gave her a quizzical, amused look. "But I've saved the most interesting news for last," she said. "At the next Board of Aldermen meeting, we're planning something a little more exciting than speed limits. Several of us from the local association are planning to address the aldermen about the cause."

Anna gave her a surprised look. "How on earth did you get that on the agenda?"

"Oh, we didn't. We're just going to show up, in full regalia, with our Tennessee Equal Suffrage Association banner, and demand to be heard. What do you think?"

"I think you'd better hope Tennessee men are more tolerant than those mobs in London."

Elizabeth's face fell. "Good point. The papers make it sound awful over there."

"It's one thing when they holler 'she-male' at you on the street. It's something else when they pelt you with stones and drag you off to jail."

"Are you losing interest in the cause? You signed the petition, didn't you?"

"Of course I did, and no, I still believe in the cause. I'm just . . . frustrated, I suppose. After all, every woman in the United States could sign the petition, and it still wouldn't matter as long as the men don't give their approval. They're the only ones who can vote, the only ones who can be elected, the only ones who can . . . do anything. My name isn't even on the title to our home since there's a man available for the job."

Elizabeth looked at Anna, then put her hand on her arm. "You've got the blues, haven't you, dear? I'm sorry. Is anything wrong?"

Anna took a deep breath and found a smile to offer her friend.

"No, not really. I'm fine, Elizabeth. Maybe I'm just tired from the long trip back."

Anna heard Mabel scolding Scott. "I think Scott is getting restless," she said. "I'd better go. It's so good to see you again. I'm looking forward to Tuesday."

"Me, too. Glad you're back safely, dear friend." Elizabeth waved at Mabel and Scott. "'Bye, children. Bring your mother back soon, all right?"

5

PERSON'S BARBERSHOP looked crowded. Walter was disappointed; he was hoping to be able to pop in, get his trim and shave, and hurry back to his office before his afternoon appointments.

There were three barber chairs and, facing them, a dozen seats for waiting customers. Walter knew most of the downtown merchants and businessmen in the shop. He went down the line, shaking hands.

"Kinda full up today, Doc," said J. P. Person. He was lathering the face of a patron. "You in a hurry?"

"Oh, a little, I guess, J. P. Wanted to tidy up before the Board of Aldermen's meeting tonight."

"I hear some a them she-males are planning something for tonight," one of the waiting customers said.

"Give 'em the vote, next thing, they'll want to drive automobiles," someone else muttered.

"Now, fellas," Walter said, "not all women are suffragettes."

"You sure?" one of the others said. "My wife won't leave me alone about it."

"I wish the legislature would hurry up and vote," someone else said. "The whole country's crawling all over Tennessee's business.

The sooner we get it over with—one way or the other—the better, is what I say."

Walter noticed a barber at the third chair he hadn't seen before—a new man in town, maybe? He went over and stuck out his hand. "Walter Dotson. Don't believe I've seen you here at J. P.'s before, have I?"

The barber shifted his scissors to the other hand and gripped Walter's outstretched palm firmly. "Pleased to meet you, Walter. I'm Charlie Cobb. Just moved here a few weeks ago, from Big Rock."

"Hey, Doc, you want to give Charlie a try?" one of the men said. "I'm next with him, but if you're in a hurry, you can go in front of me."

"Fine with me," J. P. said. "I got three more waiting."

"You're a doctor?" the new man said, combing and clipping expertly at the hair of the man in his chair.

"Yes, my office is just over there, on the other side of the square."

Cobb nodded. He had dense, curly black hair, and was of average height, with a strong, wiry build. He certainly looked like he knew what he was doing with the scissors.

"Well, fine, then—that is, if you're sure, Will," Walter said, looking at the man who'd made the offer.

"Be my guest," he said. "Besides, if those she-males come busting in tonight at the aldermen's meeting, you'll want to look nice for the papers."

Some of the men laughed.

"I'm almost finished here, Dr. Dotson," Charlie Cobb said. "Just give me a couple more minutes."

"Call me Walter," he said, finding an empty seat.

Someone down the line made a disgusted noise and threw down the newspaper. "Taft is an idiot," he said.

"He's a Republican," someone else said. "That's the same thing, ain't it?"

Several of the men were grinning at Walter, waiting to see what he'd say.

"Now, fellas," he said, "how about laying off all that, for once? I just got back in town, after all—"

"I thought things around town had been going smoother than normal," J. P. said with a smirk. "Sure enough, Doc, you *have* been gone, haven't you?"

Some of the others chuckled.

"You can always tell a Republican," J. P. said, "you just can't tell him much."

A bigger laugh, this time.

"Now, J. P., is that any way to talk to one of your best customers?" Walter said.

"You better watch out, J. P.," someone said. "Doc is friends with President Taft. He's liable to get you shut down if you're not careful."

"I wouldn't say we're friends," Walter said. "But if you Democrats don't leave me alone, I may try to get the President to at least give you a good talking-to."

"I wish he'd give Congress a talking-to and shut down some of these she-males," someone said. "Wonder what they're going to try tonight at the meeting?"

"Hey, Charlie," J. P. said, motioning toward the new barber. "What do you think about all this women's suffrage stuff?"

Charlie Cobb was unpinning the towel from his customer's neck. He swept the covering aside with a practiced motion as the man got up from his chair. He motioned toward Walter, then looked around at the other men. "I think a woman's place is at home, taking care of her children and keeping her husband satisfied," he said.

"Keep 'em between the sheets, eh?" J. P. said. Everyone laughed.

Walter sat down in Cobb's chair. He was smiling along with everyone else, but he was feeling less than satisfied with the prospect of facing a bevy of demonstrating suffragettes at tonight's Board of Aldermen meeting. He knew Anna was interested in the question, and he wasn't quite comfortable with that, but so far he hadn't seen fit to forbid her involvement.

Not that forbidding something to Anna would solve the problem; Walter knew that from the influenza epidemic at the Lafayette hospital. Once his wife got something in her head, you couldn't argue it out. Over the years, Walter had most often found it easiest to leave her alone as much as he could.

"You live close to here, Walter?" Charlie asked as he pinned the towel behind Walter's neck.

"Just over on North Water Avenue," Walter said. "Right across the street from the hotel."

"Yes, I've been staying there," Charlie said. His comb was moving through Walter's hair; Walter could hear the scissors clicking. "My wife and daughter will be joining me here pretty soon. We've rented a little place on the north end of Railroad Street."

"It'll be good to get your family back together, I guess."

"I reckon." Charlie Cobb fell silent for a moment; his hands moving deftly over Walter's scalp. "So, is your house the nice two-story with the two turrets on the front, right there close to the intersection?"

"Yes, that's it," Walter said.

"I think I saw your wife and children the other day, walking toward downtown. Girl and a boy?"

"Yes, that was probably them," Walter said.

"You've got a real nice family there, Walter."

"Thank you."

Charlie finished trimming Walter's hair and then mixed a cup of shaving lather. He spread the warm mixture on Walter's face and began stropping his straight-edge razor on the leather strap hanging down the back of the chair. Walter leaned back, enjoying the relaxing warmth on his face. The razor moved smoothly over his skin. When Charlie was finished shaving him, he wiped off the traces of lather with a warm cloth, then reached for a bottle on the shelf above the mirror behind the chair. He dashed some bay rum into his palm, rubbed his hands together, then applied the tonic to Walter's face and neck. It was cooling and soothing after the shave. Cobb unpinned the towel from around Walter's neck.

"All done, Walter." He spun the chair around and held a hand mirror behind Walter's head so he could inspect the entire haircut. "Look all right?"

"Fine, Charlie. Just fine."

"All right, then." He spun the chair back around. "Two bits, just like they say."

Walter got out of the chair and put some coins in Charlie's palm. "Keep the change, Charlie," he said. "And thanks for working me in so quickly."

"Thank you very much. Come back anytime."

Walter made his farewells to J. P. and the other men, with a few repeats of some of the earlier joshing. He went out, tugging his watch from his vest pocket. He flipped open the cover: a quarter to one. He might actually have time to get a quick bite at the drugstore before he started on his afternoon patients. He rubbed his face. Charlie Cobb had done a real nice job. Walter decided he'd start asking for him when he went in J. P.'s place.

CHARLIE COBB MOTIONED for the next customer. As the man sauntered toward his chair, Charlie peered out the window in the direction Walter Dotson had gone. He wished he'd thought to ask Walter his wife's name. She was a handsome woman, and no mistake. And the other day, when he'd admired her from the porch of the Keystone Hotel, he'd had the feeling she didn't at all mind his appreciation of her figure. It was something to keep in mind.

THE MEETING ROOM at City Hall was full, and as Walter looked out from his seat on the dais, he feared the attendance wasn't just because of the Board of Aldermen's announced intention to take up the issue of the speed limit for horseless carriages. Apparently, the local suffragettes had let it be known that they intended to bring the national debate over the proposed Nineteenth Amendment to the U.S. Constitution right into Gallatin, Tennessee.

Mayor Brown had just called the meeting to order when the back doors slammed open and a parade of women in the trademark yellow-sashed, white dresses marched down the center aisle, waving plac-ards and shouting slogans about the repression of women. For the few heart-stopping seconds it took him to scan their ranks, Walter was terrified that Anna might be with them. But no, she wasn't. He breathed a little easier. The next few moments might be uncomfort-able, but at least he wouldn't be personally embarrassed in front of the whole town of Gallatin.

Apparently, the Jennings woman was their spokesman. That wasn't good; Walter had heard Anna mention her often.

"Mayor Brown, we, the women of the Gallatin and Sumner County chapter of the Tennessee Equal Suffrage Association, have drafted a resolution calling for—"

"This demonstration is out of order!" shouted the mayor. "You women will leave this instant, or I will call the police and have you arrested."

"Mayor Brown, this petition has been signed—"

"I don't care if it's been signed by the President of the United States," Brown said. "You have no right to be here."

"Precisely, Mayor! We have no right to address this Board of Alder-men, just as we have no right to vote in the election of its members. We have no right to own property in our own names, rather than our husbands'; we have no right to do anything except bear children, raise them, and sweep the floors in our houses. But change is com-ing, Mayor. It is sweeping across this land and we, the women of the Equal Suffrage Association, are announcing its arrival. We will not be denied, nor shall we be moved!"

The other women in white gave a loud cheer, soon swallowed up in a roar of protest from many of the men—and some of the women—in the hall. Mayor Brown pounded his gavel, but it was some moments before the din subsided enough for him to make himself heard.

"Enough! That is enough, I say! Madam, will you leave now?"

Elizabeth Jennings turned and said something to one of the other women. They began passing up and down the rows of the audience, handing out printed handbills.

"We have prepared a draft resolution for the Gallatin Board of Aldermen. We urge—no, demand—that the leaders of this community pass a resolution calling upon our elected representatives in Nashville to vote in favor of the ratification of the Nineteenth Amendment. It is time to step out of the paternalistic, tribal past and join the modern world. Give women the right to vote!"

The other suffragettes began a chant: "Right to vote! Right to vote! Right to vote!"

Just as Mayor Brown appeared ready to leap upon Elizabeth Jennings and do her bodily harm, Aloysius Hix, one of the aldermen, stood and said, "Your Honor, I move that this board approve the draft resolution as presented by these ladies."

Brown wheeled on the alderman. "Have you taken leave of your senses, Aloysius? What are you trying to do?"

Hix just stood there, staring at the mayor.

"Well? What are you going to do, Mayor?" the Jennings woman said. "One of your own aldermen has made a motion."

"There is no second," the mayor said, staring fiercely at the rest of the aldermen. "Since there is no second, the motion may not be considered."

"You can kick my motion out if you want, your Honor," Hix said, "but this question isn't going to go away. You know it won't."

"May I offer an alternative?" Walter said. Everyone looked at him. "I propose that this question be remanded to a subcommittee of the board for further study. The committee will then make a recommendation to the full board."

Mayor Brown stared at Walter for a few long seconds, then began nodding slowly. "Yes, maybe that's a good idea. No sense doing something in haste."

Walter knew the mayor was probably hoping that stringing the question along would draw out its venom, as it were. Then, the board could quietly veto the notion, out of the public limelight. He wasn't sure he didn't agree with the mayor, but he also wasn't sure he didn't agree with Aloysius Hix. Mainly, he wanted to get past this evening's awkward impasse.

Hix, looking thoughtfully at Walter, said, "I withdraw my motion in favor of that presented by Dr. Dotson. I second his motion and I volunteer to serve on the subcommittee."

"All right, then," Mayor Brown said. "We have a motion and a second. All in favor?"

All five aldermen raised their hands. The suffragettes applauded loudly. Elizabeth Jennings gave Walter a measuring look, but she appeared mollified, at least, by the turn of events.

After the board adjourned and the crowd dispersed, the aldermen lingered. Mayor Brown observed, "Walter, you ought to think about it. We need a man like you as mayor. I will not be running for reelection. And maybe, someday . . . who knows?"

Walter tried to ignore the flutter of excitement under his breastbone. He gave the mayor a little smile and a shake of the head. "Now, your Honor, I'm just a simple country doctor, trying to serve this community as best I can. I've never entertained aspirations for mayor."

"Before you get that piece of humble pie all the way in your mouth," Alderman Hix said, "you ought to listen to the mayor. The way you handled that situation this evening with the suffragettes was very smooth, Walter. You showed some good instincts."

"Yeah . . . even if I'm still not sure why you did it," Brown said. "Or what it's going to accomplish, with those she-males."

"Walter, you're the only Republican I know in these parts who could actually get himself elected to something," Hix said. "You ought to think about that, too. You could do your party some good."

Walter stared out the window. He had to admit he'd been thinking lately about what it would be like to hold an office with a little more reach. And why shouldn't he run for mayor? He was a respected member of the business and professional community. He was a leader at his church. He was even a part of the community's cultural fabric, through his activities with the town orchestra. And Anna had her place, too, with the town's leading women.

Anna . . . Walter felt a shadow of guilt fall across the rosy visions he was painting for himself. He wasn't sure how she'd feel about his getting more active in politics. He hadn't missed the long silences that seemed to be getting longer, lately. Especially noticed was the inevitable chill when he told her he'd be home late from a patient appointment, or from a meeting at the church, or from a band re-hearsal, or a Masonic lecture.

Certainly, a man had to do what he had to do, and his wife's place was at home with the children, but something still tugged at a corner of Walter's mind on those occasions, like now, when he allowed himself to dwell on what might lie behind those lengthening silences.

"Well, fellas, that's something to think about, I guess," he said, extracting himself from his reverie. "I sure appreciate your confidence, and all, but, right now . . . I don't know . . ."

"Give it some thought, Walter," Mayor Brown said. "You and I don't always see eye to eye on everything, but we still respect each other. That's the kind of thing not every man can say. People listen to you, Walter. You could accomplish things. That's all I'm saying."

Walter nodded. "I'll think about it, Mayor, I really will."

"Glad to hear it." The mayor tugged his watch out of his vest pocket and thumbed it open. "Well, I'd better go."

The other aldermen nodded at Mayor Brown as he made his way to the front door.

"I guess I'd better be going too," Walter said. "Good day to you all."

Hix stood with the others to leave, and shook Walter's hand. "And to you. I really hope you'll give it some thought."

"Yes, I will. It's just that right now . . . Well, anyhow. I'll study on it."

Walter felt a lightness in his step as he crossed the Gallatin town square toward home. It was nice to be thought of as an up-and-comer by men like Brown and Hix. Walter's future seemed to be opening up in front of him, just there for the taking.

And then, he thought again of Anna. What would she say, or, maybe worse, not say?

If he tried just a little, Walter could remember those heady early days of their marriage, when he felt like he could just about eat her up with a spoon. He couldn't get enough of her then; the look in her eyes in those moments repaid his attentions a thousand fold.

When was it he first started thinking of her in terms of the limitations she represented, rather than the opportunities?

The miscarriage was part of it, he guessed. Certainly, there was a time when the idea of another pregnancy made him tend toward circumspection in his physical attentions. But then, after a while . . . it just seemed other things interested him more: his career, and getting established in Gallatin, and figuring out how things worked in this community, this part of the state . . . Walter supposed it was part of the natural stages of a responsible man's life. When you were young, you tended to be more romantic. Maybe that was God's plan, after all—to encourage mankind to be fruitful and multiply, as scripture said. But wasn't there a time when a man needed to take care of other things? Maybe Walter was just in that time of life.

He didn't think Anna understood that, though, and the thought of trying to talk to her about it made him uncomfortable. He wasn't sure he could explain to her that he loved her as always, just in a different way.

Come to think of it, he wasn't sure he understood it himself.

Yes, a man had to do what he had to do. Surely Anna would understand.

6

"GOOD MORNING, MRS. OLMSTEAD," Anna said as she opened the door. "Gertrude," she called over her shoulder.

The minister's wife nodded. "Good morning, Mrs. Dotson. Nice to see you." She stepped inside and began unbuttoning her black, woolen outer coat. Gertrude came from the kitchen and took Mrs. Olmstead's coat and muffler, then stood quietly, waiting for Anna's guest to finish unpinning her hat.

"Mrs. Baskerville, Mrs. Bate, Mrs. Oldham, and Mrs. Pardue are already here," Anna said. "We're waiting for Mrs. Hix and Mrs. Jennings. I believe Gertrude has seated them in the parlor. Please make yourself at home."

Mrs. Olmstead gave Anna a serene smile and walked through the vestibule toward the parlor, where the other women were sitting primly on the edges of the mahogany Queen Anne settee and chairs, waiting for everyone to arrive.

Anna was the youngest member of the group, five years Elizabeth Jennings's junior, but she had never felt the least bit intimidated by the older women. When she and Walter had moved to Gallatin, she had assumed her place in the social circle with as much aplomb as if she had received an engraved invitation. The women got together every week; they took turns hosting the group. All of them lived within the same four-block area, a convenient walking distance. They drank tea, exchanged gossip, discussed local events, and talked about the latest styles.

When Elizabeth Jennings and Alma Hix arrived, walking together, Gertrude showed them into the parlor, then quickly brought the tray from the kitchen and began filling the porcelain demitasse cups with steaming tea. Anna brought a silver tray into the parlor. "Here are some cookies, ladies. Please help yourselves."

Anna had been looking forward to today's meeting; it was the first since the raucous Board of Aldermen's session that had been interrupted by the suffragettes, led by Elizabeth Jennings. Anna guessed it was no coincidence that Elizabeth had come in the company of Alma Hix, whose husband had made the motion calling for the aldermen to endorse the proclamation in favor of women's suffrage. Anna was especially interested to find out about Walter's initiative for the subcommittee. Of course, he hadn't said a word to her about the matter, but talk was all over town. Anna could hardly believe safe, stolid Walter would stick out his neck on such a controversial issue. She wondered what other surprises Walter might have in store.

"Mrs. Dotson, you must show us some of the things you found in Chicago," Elizabeth said, as soon as Anna had set down the cookie tray. "We're all just dying to see what you brought back."

"I was hoping you'd ask," Anna said. She got up and lifted her skirts halfway to her knees, displaying the pair of stockings she'd decided was her favorite: sheer black, with little diamond-shaped sequins sewn on either side of the seams that ran all the way up the backs of her legs. The women gasped or gave shocked little chuckles as Anna pranced and twirled, making sure everyone in the room had a chance to see the stockings from every angle.

"Oh, Mrs. Dotson, you naughty thing!" said Mrs. Bate. "But aren't they lovely?"

"Wait, I've got more," Anna said. She went over to the burled-walnut bureau and took down a brightly colored sack with "Madeleine's" printed on the side. One by one, she removed the filmy silk stockings and passed them around the circle of women, who oohed and ahhed satisfyingly.

"Aren't these like the ones in *Vogue*?" someone asked.

"Yes. In fact, I wrote down the style numbers, if anyone's interested. You can order them by mail from Madeleine's. I've got the address."

"Well, I don't know," said Mrs. Olmstead. Her husband was the minister of the Christian Church, which all the ladies except Mrs. Hix and Mrs. Bate attended. "They sure are pretty, but if Mr. Olmstead ever caught me with a pair of these on, I don't know what he'd say."

"You never know, Mrs. Olmstead," Anna said, grinning. "Reverend Olmstead might take a whole new interest in staying home nights."

Mrs. Olmstead gave Anna a wide-eyed, shocked look. Elizabeth Jennings giggled into her tea napkin.

"Mrs. Dotson, I hardly think that's the sort of thing we ought to be discussing," Mrs. Pardue said.

"Oh, I don't know," Elizabeth said. "Why shouldn't we wear what we please? Why should our husbands control that, too?"

A long silence limped past. The women sat, looking everywhere except at Elizabeth, taking dry, little sips of their tea.

"Mrs. Jennings, not all of us share your political views," Mrs. Baskerville said, finally.

"Your husband is a lawyer, Mrs. Baskerville," Alma Hix said. "Surely he can't believe that laws shouldn't be changed once in a while?"

"My husband and I do not talk about such matters," Mrs. Baskerville said.

"Mine either," Anna said. "But maybe we should. Maybe we all should be talking to our husbands about . . . things. We have brains in our heads, after all. We have ideas."

"Exactly right," Elizabeth said. "But that's what most men don't want to hear. Like those ruffians in London, with their mob tactics."

"If the women of London were at home, where they belong, they wouldn't have anything to worry about," said Mrs. Pardue. "If you ask me, women should just mind their own business and run the household, and let the men worry about running the country. A nation is only as strong as its homes, after all."

"But if a nation ignores half its citizens, treating them as if they were invisible—" Mrs. Hix said.

"Invisible! That's exactly right!" Elizabeth said. "We can't vote, we can't serve on juries—"

"Why on earth would any woman want to do those things?" Mrs. Bate said. "Sitting around all day at that horrid courthouse—I can't imagine a bigger waste of time."

Elizabeth started to say something else, but Mrs. Olmstead's voice rose above the growing hubbub. "Ladies, ladies! Let's not forget ourselves. Surely we aren't going to let this political question ruin our friendship. One way or the other, a decision is going to be made about all this. And when it is, we'll all still be here, living in this community, doing the best we can. Why don't we let this suffrage matter be for a while, and talk about something else?"

After a long pause, Mrs. Baskerville said, "My husband says there's a new barber down at Person's. A nice-looking, intelligent fellow, he says."

"Is he the one I've seen walking toward downtown, mornings? Broad-shouldered, slender? Wears a black derby?" Mrs. Hix inquired.

Anna's memory flashed to the day she and the children had walked downtown, to the man who'd eyed her from the porch of the Keystone Hotel. He had been wearing a black derby, hadn't he? Of course, there were probably at least a dozen men in Gallatin who wore them.

"I hear he came here from somewhere over in Stewart County," Mrs. Hix said. "He's rented a room at the Keystone Hotel."

"Does this barber have a name?" Anna said.

The women looked at each other and shrugged.

"Well, maybe we can talk to our husbands about that, at least," Elizabeth Jennings said. "That is, if Mrs. Baskerville approves." Mrs. Baskerville gave her a hard look.

The ladies agreed that after the first of the year—just two meetings away, now—they would begin discussing plans for their summer gala, a community-wide event to raise money for the local hospital. After a few more minutes of chitchat, the meeting began to break up. Anna went to the door and handed each guest her wrap, taken from the stack held in Gertrude's arms. She wished them a good day, and they all expressed their enjoyment of the morning's tea. Anna smiled to herself. She was fairly certain Mrs. Baskerville, Mrs. Pardue, and the other traditionalists had enjoyed today's little set-to much less than they were willing to admit, but manners dictated not mentioning one's true feelings in such situations.

Elizabeth Jennings hung back until the last, as Anna had hoped she would. She wanted to bend her friend's ear a little bit more, out of the hearing of the others.

"Well, you certainly won some points today, dear," Anna said when she'd closed the door behind the last of the other guests.

"Oh, Anna! I get so frustrated! As if it weren't bad enough that the men pretend we don't exist, even the women, who ought to understand how important the cause is, seem so, so . . . blind and stupid!"

"I'm sorry, Elizabeth. It's hard when you can't seem to make yourself understood on a matter so important, isn't it?"

Elizabeth nodded. "At least I can talk to you, Anna. I think we're kindred spirits, in many ways." She took Anna's hands in hers. "You needed cheering up the other day, in my shop, and now I need you to return the favor, don't I?"

Anna smiled at her. "Can I show you something? I didn't dare let the other women see it. They'd have either died from the shock, or had me arrested and tried as a bad public influence. They barely managed the stockings."

"What is it?" Elizabeth said, her voice dropping near a whisper.

"Something I bought in Chicago. Come up to my room, all right?"

They went upstairs. Anna asked Elizabeth to wait in one of the overstuffed chairs in her room. She went to her armoire and retrieved the French nightgown from its place at the bottom of one of the drawers, then went into the bathroom. She stepped out of her shoes and removed her dress, underthings, and stockings, and slipped the nightgown over her head. She went back into her room and relished the look that instantly appeared on Elizabeth's face—something between shock and awe.

"That is...the most daring...it's beautiful!" Elizabeth said. "Wherever did you find it?"

"At Madeleine's, the same place I bought the stockings. Isn't it something?" Anna twirled, so Elizabeth could see the plunging back.

"How can I get one?" Elizabeth said.

Anna gave her friend a surprised look. "Elizabeth! Are you sure? What will Wallace think?"

"I don't know," Elizabeth said, creasing her brow. "But I must have one of these. Even if nobody ever sees it but me."

"I hope you have better luck with yours than I did," Anna said. She told Elizabeth about her failed attempt at seduction in Chicago. "And there he was, asleep on the bed. I felt like a perfect fool."

"Oh, Anna. That must have been such a . . . disappointment."

Elizabeth appeared to be blushing slightly.

"I'm sorry, Elizabeth. Have I embarrassed you?"

"No. That is . . . well, maybe a little. You always surprise me, Anna. I never know what you're thinking. Here I am, the bold suffragette, and you're more free to express yourself than I ever thought to be."

"Well, if it's any consolation, I'd trade my freedom of expression for a bit of romance from my husband."

Now Elizabeth was looking at her with something like pity. "So that's why you were so sad the other day."

Anna nodded. She wanted to get out of the nightgown; it was bringing back memories she didn't want right now. "I'll be right back," she said.

She dressed and put the nightgown away. Then she sat on the edge of her bed, facing Elizabeth. "In a way, my trouble with Walter is part of the whole problem the cause is trying to address: Men don't recognize that women have feelings, opinions, and needs of their own, besides just running a household and doing the knitting. They either treat us like porcelain goddesses, up on a pedestal, or they use us for pleasure and undesirable chores. Either way, they don't see us as we really are."

"But surely Walter has at least some sympathy, Anna. He's the one who broke the deadlock with the aldermen and the mayor."

Anna shook her head. "I still haven't puzzled that one out. Walter is the last person I'd ever expect to do anything daring, much less controversial. Maybe he's just trying to buy some time until the fuss blows over."

"That thought had occurred to me," Elizabeth said. "But I don't intend to let the issue die."

Anna looked at her friend. "Well, good for you, Elizabeth. At least one of us is going to get what she wants from Walter. Oh, dear, I've done it again; you're blushing."

Elizabeth shook her head. "I do declare, Anna Dotson! Whatever shall we do with you?"

7

CHARLIE ALLOWED HIMSELF a little private grin; there was no mistaking that build, that posture, that walk, or that face. Anna Dotson had just walked past the barbershop, and he thought he could guess why. Things were definitely getting more interesting. He decided it was time to do a little more research.

When Walter Dotson came in for his next haircut, Charlie was all smiles. The shop was not too busy right then, which suited Charlie's purposes just fine.

"Good afternoon, Doc. Nice to see you."

"Hello, Charlie."

"Anything special you need today?" Charlie dusted off his barber chair and twisted it toward Walter, motioning for him to take a seat.

"No, just the usual, I guess." Walter settled himself and leaned back easily into the leather cushions. Charlie started combing Walter's hair, preparatory to beginning the trim.

"Been busy, I guess?" Charlie said.

"Oh, always, Charlie. Always. Too much to do, and too little time."

"I know what you mean. Some days, by the time it's five o'clock here, I'm about ready to drop."

Walter gave a little laugh. "Five o'clock? Friend, I wish I could count on going home at five every day."

"Sure enough?"

"Yes. Some days, by the time the last patient walks out the front door of my office, it's nearly seven."

"You don't mean it?" Charlie made a *tsk* sound with his tongue. "And then, I guess you have meetings a lot of evenings, don't you? Aren't you on the city council or something of that sort?"

"Board of Aldermen, yes."

Charlie was amused by the resigned, weary tone Walter was using. *You love it, though, don't you, old sport? And that pretty wife of yours home all alone, just waiting . . .*

"I guess all this suffrage business is giving you lots of trouble, these days," Charlie said. "I'm sure glad my wife hasn't gone in for all that."

"Well, Charlie, count your lucky stars. I wish I could forget about it, or let somebody else deal with it. But I've got myself right in the middle of the whole mess, I'm afraid."

"Too bad, that's for sure."

"Charlie, where do you and your wife go to church?"

Charlie was caught a little off his guard by the question. "Well, we haven't placed our card anywhere, just yet. Daisy and Alice have only been here for a little while, so we're still looking at that, I guess."

"Well, we'd love to have you come and visit at the Christian Church. I'm an elder, and we've got a real fine group of people meeting there."

"Well . . . thank you, Walter. I'll give that some thought, I truly will. Daisy was raised Baptist, but . . . By the way, Doc, somebody told me you were some kind of specialist. That right?"

"Well, I am, as a matter of fact, Charlie. I specialize in otorhinolaryngology."

"Oh-to-what?"

Walter gave a little chuckle. "It means diseases and treatments of the ear, nose, and throat."

"Do tell! I've never heard of that."

"Well, I guess it's fairly new in this country. They've been practicing in places like Austria since at least the 1870s."

"Is there much call for that in a little town like Gallatin?" Charlie had finished Walter's hair; now he fussed about with the doctor's sideburns and eyebrows. These were the little touches that kept his customers coming back.

"Well, not too much. But we're close enough to Nashville that I get a good many referrals from physicians there."

"Mmm-hmm. But I guess that must mean more travel time for you?"

"Sometimes. I don't mind it too much, though. The folks who can afford my services can generally make it worth my while."

And I don't mind it either, Doc.

Charlie levered the back of the chair, placing Walter in a semi-reclining position. He took a towel out of the warmer and wrapped it around Walter's face and neck. He swished his lather brush in the cup, stirring warm water in with the soap, then spread the creamy mixture on Walter's face. He ran his razor over the strop a few times, then began the shave.

"Well, I'm glad I'm just a barber, I guess," he said as he worked. "Though from what I've read, fellows in my line of business used to be in your business, too. When the barber was the only one in town with a good, sharp blade, he got to do some doctoring too, it seems. But not anymore, is it, Doc? No, I'll leave yours to you, as long as you leave mine to me. And we'll both be happy."

Walter made a sound of agreement.

Charlie toweled Walter and patted bay rum on his face. He spun his customer toward the large mirror on the back wall.

"Looks good," Walter said, rubbing first one cheek, then the other. "Your usual excellent job, Charlie."

"Thank you, Doc. I aim to please." Charlie gave him a little smile.

ANNA STARED OUT the parlor window, toward the porch of the Keystone Hotel. He wasn't there, and hadn't been for the past three days. She didn't know what to make of it.

She didn't even know his name. These last few days, she'd been trying to figure out a way to learn more about her mystery man. She could have just asked Walter, of course. He'd surely know, since he was a regular patron of J. P. Person's establishment. A few times she'd considered doing that, but something held her back. She wasn't ready to share her "secret," as she thought of it. Besides, it would be just like Walter to suddenly take an interest in things she was thinking—an interest that could lead to questions she wasn't quite ready to answer.

Small footsteps on the stairs behind her interrupted Anna's musings. She turned from the window; it was Scott. "Mama, can I have a cookie?" He came over to her chair. "Please? I've been home from school for almost an hour. I'm getting hungry."

"But what about the supper you won't eat if I give you a cookie?" she said, running her fingers through his soft, straight blond hair. Mabel had her father's coloring, and Scott had hers.

"I'll eat my supper, I promise," he said. "Please, Mama. Just one cookie."

She ruffled his hair, then stood. "Well, young sir, since you've promised."

They went into the kitchen and Anna asked Gertrude to give Scott one—"just one, mind you"—of the fresh oatmeal cookies she'd baked that afternoon. "And a small glass of milk, if we've still got some left." Gertrude nodded and reached into the cupboard for a small saucer to hold Scott's snack.

Anna ruffled her son's hair one more time, then had a thought: it was about time Scott had a haircut, which he despised more than nearly anything. Anna herself thought J. P. was becoming a little rougher and less patient as he got on up in years. Maybe this new barber would be just the thing for Scott. And she could even ask Walter what he thought of the idea. That would throw him off the scent, for sure.

Not that there was any scent, she reminded herself. She just wondered about the man, that was all. He was a newcomer to Gallatin. Maybe he had a wife—that was possible, wasn't it? Even likely? A new woman in town who'd want another woman to talk to.

Last night, she'd tried again with Walter. The children were already in bed. She and Walter sat in the drawing room, Walter reading Shakespeare and Anna looking through her latest issue of *Argosy*. She was reading a story about a woman in love with the keeper of a lighthouse on a lonely, rocky coast. The woman could never seem to attract the attentions of the handsome, distant lighthouse keeper, though she brought him pies and fresh bread she baked herself. She despaired of his ever returning her love. One night, in a melancholy mood, she rowed out in a small dory to watch the play of the moonlight on the water. The tide began to carry her out to sea, past the promontory on which the lighthouse stood. She began to despair of her life, watching as the glow from the lighthouse grew smaller and more distant. Then, from the darkness, a dinghy hove near. The lighthouse keeper had seen her distress and put out to rescue her. His strong arms drove his craft through the water; he came alongside and asked her what on earth she was about. She told all, professing at the same time her love and her despair.

"Dear woman," the keeper said, "how foolish we've both been!"
"Whatever can you mean?"
"For as long as I've seen you in your little cottage by the cliff, I've loved

*you. How I longed to tell you! But I knew a poor man such as myself
could never be worthy of you! And so alas! I resigned myself to silence."*

The last sentence found them locked in a rapturous embrace, rocking in their boats on the moon-washed sea. Anna brushed aside tears as she closed her magazine. She looked at Walter, sitting in his favorite chair with his Shakespeare open on his lap. If only he could see her as the keeper finally came to see his admirer!

She went over and kneeled down beside his chair. He looked at her aslant, and put his book aside.

"Walter, I love you."

"I love you too, Anna. You know that."

"Dear, I wonder if . . . That is, I'd like it if we could . . ."

She tried to say the words, but the puzzled expression on his face worked past her intentions, past her sentimental wish for a romantic marriage, past most of her reserves of patience. She would have to do everything, say everything herself—Walter would be no help. He truly, honestly had no idea of the passion locked in her, the tide of desire that beat against her day and night.

Still, she decided to forge ahead. She found a slow, seductive smile somewhere; she pressed her hand against the inside of his knee, then slid it slowly upward. "Does this remind you of anything?" she whispered. "The Maxwell House Hotel, maybe?"

Walter grabbed her hand and pulled it away from his leg, giving a horrified glance at the stairs. "Anna! What if the children were to wake?"

It was no use, absolutely no use at all. Her husband might as well be made of brick. Anna got up and dusted her dress. "You're right, of course, Walter. As always."

She went away from him, toward the stairs. Maybe he watched her go, maybe not—Anna didn't care. He would never have the slightest understanding of her needs.

She had gone to her room and undressed for bed. After a few seconds of thought, she went to her armoire and dug out the French nightgown. She put it on and lay on her bed. She would pleasure herself as best she could, she had decided. She had formed a picture in her mind of the handsome stranger in the black derby, imagined him coming to her door in the middle of the day, finding her in the house alone, wearing nothing but the French nightgown . . .

8

M AMA! OUCH! You're squeezing my hand!"

"I'm sorry, darling. Come along, though."

"I don't want to! I hate getting a haircut."

"Your father says the new barber is very good. He says you'll barely know he's there."

"I still don't want to."

Anna pushed open the door of Person's Barbershop. J. P. and the men in the waiting chairs looked at her askance, but the man standing behind the empty chair nearest the window had on a smile as welcoming as a spring sunrise.

"Hello, ma'am. Does this young fellow need a little trim?" he said.

"Yes, if you please. I believe you're Charles Cobb, the man who cuts Dr. Walter Dotson's hair?"

"Why, yes, ma'am, that's right." He stuck out a hand. "But my friends call me Charlie. You must be Mrs. Dotson."

Anna extended her gloved hand to take the ends of his fingers. "Pleased to make your acquaintance, Mr. Cobb."

"And what is your name, young sir?" he said, leaning over and offering a hand to Scott.

"Walter Scott Dotson Junior." Scott gave Charlie Cobb's hand a diffident shake, looking everywhere except at the barber.

"Now, that's a fine name, young man. Did you know there was a famous author named Sir Walter Scott?"

Scott nodded. He was giving Charlie Cobb a look of cautious interest. "Yes, he's one of my daddy's favorite book writers."

"Well, then, Walter Scott Dotson Junior, you'd better climb up in this chair here." Charlie reached behind the chair and picked up a board about three feet long and nine inches wide, which he laid across the chair's arms. "There we go, a little extra height. Now, then, Mrs. Dotson, why don't you tell me exactly what you want?"

"Maybe I ought to just stand beside him and make sure he sits still," Anna said, moving closer to her son.

"Mama, I won't wiggle."

"I think that's a fine idea," Charlie said, pinning the cloth around Scott's neck. He turned toward the counter behind the chair and selected a comb and a pair of clippers from his glass equipment case.

Anna guessed Scott would probably behave. He was almost unfailingly cooperative, even when having to do something he didn't want to do, like get a haircut. She should probably sit in one of the chairs for the waiting customers ... but she didn't want to. She wanted to stand closer to Charlie Cobb; she wanted to know as much about him as she could.

"He has a double cowlick," she told Charlie, motioning at the crown of her son's head. "He nearly always has a rooster tail."

Charlie smiled. "Well, there's only so much we can do to fight nature, you know."

His eyes twinkled at her, and Anna hoped he didn't notice the tiny catch in her breath. "You're so right about that," she said, and allowed a shy little smile to show. "Leave it a little longer in front; it's easier for me to comb it over."

"Yes, ma'am." The clippers began to chatter. "Now, Mrs. Dotson, don't you have a daughter, as well?"

"Yes, Mabel."

"I'll bet she's as lovely as her mother, isn't she?"

"Mr. Cobb. You'll embarrass me."

"Oh, I beg your pardon. I sure wouldn't want to do that. But didn't I see you walking with Scott, and his sister, back before Christmas?"

"Well, I don't know. Where would you have seen us?" It was a bit of a fib, but Anna hadn't actually made complete eye contact with him—that first time, at least.

"I believe I was sitting on the porch of the Keystone Hotel. That's right across the street from your house, isn't it?"

"Yes, it is. I suppose you could have seen us walking by. We often take little strolls downtown."

"Yes, ma'am. Say, Mr. Scott, can you hold your chin up just a little bit for me? There you go. Yes, I believe that's when it was."

"Are you . . . still staying at the Keystone?"

"No, ma'am. My family and I have a little house up on Railroad Street, north end. Not too far from your place, actually."

"Oh, really? You're married, then?"

"Yes, ma'am. Daisy is my wife, and our little girl is named Alice."

Anna wasn't sure whether she felt relieved or disappointed. "Daisy. That's a pretty name. And how old is Alice?"

"She's not quite three."

"Mabel is eleven, but I'll wager she and Alice could have some fun playing dolls. She has always been good with little ones."

"I'm satisfied you're right about that. I'll tell Daisy. She's been wanting to meet some people here in Gallatin. She and Alice have only been here since just after the first of the year."

"I see. Are you and your family attending church anywhere?"

Charlie laughed. "Funny thing, Mrs. Dotson—your husband asked me the same thing, last time I cut his hair. This is sure one church-going community."

"Well, I was raised as a minister's daughter, so . . ."

"Oh, I see! At church every time the doors open, I take it?"

He was looking at her in a way that seemed somewhere between mocking and teasing. Anna felt a blush creeping up the back of her neck. She looked away.

"We . . . try to do our part."

"Yes, ma'am, I'm sure you do. Hey, there, sport, can you lean your head that way just a fraction? There you go, perfect. Well, Mrs. Dotson, I think that's grand, I really do. The family that prays together stays together, I always say."

"You always say that, do you?" Anna could hardly believe the words had come out of her mouth. *Listen to the sass I'm giving him, right back! I ought to be ashamed of myself.* But she wasn't. He was looking at her differently: more respectfully, somehow, and more playfully too. She was an equal, not to be trifled with—a worthy opponent in this little verbal fencing match. Anna hadn't felt this way, talking with a man, in a long time. She'd forgotten how much she enjoyed it.

Charlie made a few more passes at the back of Scott's head, combed the hair this way and that. "Well, what do you think?" he said finally, standing back a little. Anna inspected Scott, tilting her head and studying him from several angles. "It looks good, Mr. Cobb. Very nice."

Charlie rotated the chair to let Scott look in the back mirror. "Okay with you, Mr. Walter Scott Dotson Junior?"

Scott gave a bored glance at the mirror and shrugged. "I guess so."

"Well, then," Charlie said, spinning the chair back to the front. He unpinned the cloth and removed it with a quick, snapping motion. "There you go, young man. All done."

Anna dug in her pocketbook and found three quarters and a dime.

She handed the coins to Charlie. "Thank you, Mr. Cobb. He looks very nice."

"Thank you, ma'am. I hope we'll be seeing each other again, real soon."

Their eyes held for just a fraction longer than necessary.

"Yes, well . . . Good day to you, then, Mr. Cobb."

He gave her a little bow. "And to you, Mrs. Dotson." He stuck out a hand at Scott, who gave him another halfhearted shake. "Very nice to meet you, young man. You were a perfectly well-behaved customer."

"What do you say?" Anna said softly.

"Thank you."

Charlie watched them go out. He stared appreciatively at the way Anna's skirts swayed as she walked away down the sidewalk, holding her son's hand. He smiled to himself as he reached for the broom and began sweeping up the clippings around his chair. Anna Dotson liked him; he was reasonably sure of that. And she hadn't backed away one iota. He was pretty sure she was receiving all the messages he was sending. When the opportunity presented itself, he'd see where else matters might be persuaded to lead.

THE WINTON SIX backed down the drive, backfiring noisily. Walter Dotson let it roll into the street, then shifted into first gear, hauling mightily on the steering wheel to bring the automobile's front end around. With a few jumps and pops, the Winton Six headed off down North Water Avenue.

From his seat on the Keystone Hotel porch, Charlie watched the car drive away. He took out his watch and thumbed open the cover. This time of a Sunday afternoon, he was guessing the good doctor was on his way to a meeting at his church. Charlie judged he'd most likely be gone for an hour, at least.

Charlie dropped his watch back into his vest pocket. He leaned back in his chair and tipped his black derby forward on his head. He was willing to bet that Mrs. Dotson had looked out her windows at least once, and if she had, then she'd have seen him. He'd positioned himself to make sure of that.

He'd told Daisy he had to go downtown to look at a customer's horse for him. He'd heard Charlie had some blacksmithing experience, Charlie told her, and the horse was favoring his off front leg. "I said I might be able to tell what was wrong. He asked me if I could come take a look." Daisy had looked at him a few seconds, then shrugged and nodded.

Charlie watched the front of the house and sipped at the lemonade he'd bought inside at the bar. It was a sunny, late March afternoon, but still a bit chilly, strictly speaking, for a glass of lemonade. Still, Charlie didn't think it would do for him to be seen drinking beer on a Sunday afternoon, right out on the street. Might hurt his business. So, the lemonade would have to do.

Someone was standing beside him.

"Mind if I join you, Charlie?"

It was Avery Upshur, one of his regulars. "Good afternoon, Avery. Not at all, have a seat." Charlie pushed a chair back from the table and motioned for the other man to sit down.

"Nice day, isn't it?" Avery said, taking off his hat and mopping his forehead. Charlie had noticed that Avery was always sweating, seemingly without regard for the temperature.

"Sure is." Charlie kept his eyes on the front of the Dotson house as he talked. "What brings you around?"

"Oh, just getting out of the house for a little bit. Wife's holding an afternoon tea party with some of her suffrage friends. Little too hot at home, if you know what I mean."

Charlie laughed. "Well, I don't blame you."

"I'll sure be glad when all this women's foolishness is over with," Avery said. "What do you reckon the legislature'll do? Will they vote to ratify?"

"Oh, I don't know, Avery. I reckon I don't follow it all that closely."

"Is that so?"

Charlie shook his head. "No, I don't guess I much care if a woman votes or if she doesn't—just as long as she does what I need her to do, if you take my meaning." He gave Avery a conspiratorial wink.

Avery snickered.

At that moment, the front door of Anna's house opened and she walked outside, holding in front of her what looked like a newspaper or a magazine. She sat down in a wicker chair that faced the street. Her face was angled down for a moment, as if she was reading, then she looked up. Charlie gave her a friendly wave. Her face immediately returned to her reading.

"Isn't that Anna Dotson?" Avery said, looking in the direction Charlie had waved.

"Mmm-hmm."

"How do you know her?"

"I cut her husband's hair. Her son's, too."

Avery nodded. "Don't guess she saw you, though."

Charlie smiled, keeping his eyes on Anna. "Oh, yes, she did. Excuse me a minute, will you, Avery?" He got up from the table and crossed the street. He went to the front gate, then called out, "Good afternoon, Mrs. Dotson. Lovely day, isn't it?"

For a second, he thought she was going to ignore him. Then she looked up from whatever she was reading. She gave him a little wave.

"May I come in?" he said, his hand on the gate latch. He could hear the children's voices carrying from the backyard, but they were conveniently out of sight.

"I . . . suppose so."

He opened the gate and went up the sidewalk, keeping his eyes on her and holding onto a friendly smile. *Just like working with a high-*

74

strung horse: no sudden moves, keep your voice nice and easy, and pretty soon
you can do whatever you want.

Charlie stopped when he reached the porch steps. She was staring at him as if she were afraid of what he might do. He motioned
toward the thing she'd been reading. "I don't suppose that's today's
newspaper, is it? There was a story I heard about, and I wanted to see
if it was in there."

"No, it's not a newspaper, it's . . . a magazine."

"Oh, really? Which one?"

"<i>Argosy.</i>"

"No fooling? The one with the stories in it?"

"You've heard of it?"

"Well, sure! I've read some of those stories; some of them are pretty
good. I like some of the poetry, too."

Her eyes widened. "Really?"

He nodded. "Any good ones in this issue?"

She looked down at the magazine, thumbing the pages. "I like this
one," she said, handing him the periodical.

"<i>A River Apart</i>," he read. He scanned the first few sentences. "Looks
interesting," he said, handing the magazine back to her.

"Why don't you keep it?" she said.

"You sure you don't mind?"

"No, not at all. It's a back issue and I've already gone through it.
Read it, if you like. I'd be interested to hear your thoughts on it."

"Is that so? Well, all right then, with your permission." He folded
the <i>Argosy</i> and tucked it under his arm. He touched the brim of his
derby. "Nice talking with you, Anna."

She didn't flinch. "Enjoy the magazine, Charlie," she said.

He gave her a wide smile and went back the way he'd come, letting
himself out the front gate. He crossed the street and returned to his
table. Avery was watching him.

"What was all that about?"

Charlie made a dismissing wave. "Oh, nothing to it. Just asking her how her son was liking his new haircut." He looked at Avery. "Taking care of my customers is all."

Avery nodded, but he was looking at Anna Dotson, still sitting in her chair, her head tipped back, as if she were taking the afternoon sun.

9

ANNA SAT ON HER PORCH for about another ten minutes, then went inside the house. She went to the kitchen to see if there was anything left of the chess pie Gertrude had made on Friday. Chess pie was her favorite, since childhood. Sure enough, there was a single thin sliver remaining, resting on a tin plate covered with cheesecloth. Anna didn't bother with a fork; she picked up the pie with her hand and downed it in three quick bites. She licked her fingers, looking through the kitchen windows into the backyard. The children were still playing with her sister Flora, who had come to visit.

Charlie Cobb was trouble; she couldn't pretend otherwise. But then he'd come up to her front porch a little while ago—so careful to stop just short of gross impropriety, the careful rascal!—and looked up at her with those hazel eyes, wearing that dimpled, sneaky smile of his. Her mind took off like a spooked horse, trampling through all sorts of places it had no business going. When he called her "Anna," there was a secret place inside her that rolled over like a lap dog, then sat up and begged for more.

She wasn't really planning to give him the magazine; that just sort of happened as she was trying to think of things to say. But now that she had, she could see the usefulness of it, even the justice. She'd been reading a story in *Argosy* when she'd made her disastrous blunder with Walter—her last blunder with him, she told herself. Walter sitting over there, high and mighty with his Shakespeare, too good to trouble himself for one moment about her feelings, except to worry about being discovered by Mabel or Scott. Far be it from Walter to talk with her about a story she'd liked and that had made her weep, both with joy for the lovers who'd discovered each other in the nick of time, and for the utter absence of any such chance in the world outside the magazine's pages, where Anna was doomed to live.

Let Walter keep his Shakespeare, his dusty-dry literature that matched his dusty-dry heart! Charlie Cobb knew how to talk to a woman. He was interested in what interested Anna. He wasn't too good to cross the street and pass the time of day, nor too proud to think that he might enjoy something that amused her.

And besides, who said anything was going to happen with Charlie Cobb? Anna was a free and independent woman—in mind, anyway, if not before the law. She'd decide for herself whom she would and wouldn't converse with, thank you very much!

"ALL RIGHT, THAT TAKES CARE of the menu. Mrs. Pardue, we are so very appreciative of all your careful thought. And now, the entertainment." It was Tuesday, and the ladies had gathered at the home of Mrs. Olmstead.

They all looked at Anna, as she'd known they would. "I'm sure the band will be happy to play," she said. "I'll speak to Dr. Dotson about it."

"Oh, I do hope they've learned a new Sousa march," Mrs. Baskerville said, in the overly dramatic way Anna found so annoying. "I'm so dreadfully tired of hearing 'The Washington Post' and 'The Liberty Bell,' year after year. I was in Nashville a few weeks ago, and one of the municipal bands there played the most delightful march. It had tunes from *The Mikado* . . . Oh, and now I've forgotten the name.

Mrs. Dotson, dear, couldn't you speak to your husband and see if he couldn't find out—"

"I doubt Dr. Dotson is interested in my opinions on the band's repertoire, Mrs. Baskerville. But maybe you'd like to speak to him yourself?" Ignoring Mrs. Baskerville's open-mouthed stare, Anna said, "I suppose it will be about the same as in years past: music before and during the dinner, then a short program afterward, followed by dancing?"

"Ah, yes, that is what I presumed," Mrs. Oldham said, glancing nervously at Mrs. Baskerville. "I'm sure that . . . whatever the band plays will be fine."

"Thank you," Anna said. Elizabeth was looking at her strangely. Anna just rolled her eyes.

The Spring Gala and hospital fundraiser was three weeks away, and the ladies in the tea group seemed all atwitter about it. Anna found herself rather bored with the whole thing. The first few years it had been somewhat enjoyable, helping with the arrangements and getting to know the ladies in the process. Walter had been only too happy to commit the Gallatin Commercial Club Band to provide the evening's music, even though he had rather strict views on dancing. "Not in public," he'd say, and Anna would laughingly demand what other sort of dancing he might imagine engaging in. "A minister's daughter ought to know better," he'd say, finding no humor at all in her comment. Despite his moral reservations, though, he always managed to provide a satisfactory program, mixing in the latest waltzes, fox-trots, and even the odd one-step—though he always appeared nervous when the band played something so avant-garde.

Still, though the Gallatin Spring Gala might be the social event of the season, Anna's enthusiasm was sorely lacking this year. She even only came to the teas now to see Elizabeth.

The discussion ground on, in excruciating detail. Mrs. Oldham, the chairwoman for this year's event, meticulously covered each item on her list: the decorations, the invitation list, the evening's program—including the precise time of each planned activity—and the exact makeup of the head table.

"Now, we simply must have at least three of the city aldermen there," Mrs. Oldham said. "Mrs. Hix, your husband plans to attend, doesn't he?" Alma Hix nodded. "And Mrs. Dotson, your husband will certainly be there, since he'll be performing with the band. That still leaves one." She looked around the room. "Which of us knows one of the others and will take responsibility for inviting him?"

"Speaking of the aldermen . . . Mrs. Dotson, when is your husband's subcommittee going to make its recommendation to the mayor?" Mrs. Bate said. She took a dainty sip of tea, then said, "It's been, what? Over three months, now?"

Anna wouldn't look at Mrs. Bate. "I wouldn't know. Dr. Dotson and I don't discuss civic matters any more than we do Sousa."

"I see," Mrs. Bate said, after an awkward pause. Mrs. Baskerville was still sitting with her lips pinched together.

"Why don't we keep our attention on plans for the Gala?" Elizabeth said, glancing worriedly at Anna. Some of the other women gave her a surprised look. Usually, Elizabeth needed far less excuse to expound on the cause.

"Thank you, Mrs. Jennings," said Mrs. Oldham. "But I believe we've just about taken care of everything on my agenda for today, except for making sure we have a majority of the aldermen there. It's very important for our event to enjoy the support of our community leaders, you know." Several of the women nodded.

The meeting broke up. Anna gave an obligatory thanks to Mrs. Olmstead, the hostess for the gathering. She was nearly to the sidewalk in front of the house when she heard Elizabeth Jennings's voice behind her. "Anna! Wait!"

Anna turned and waited as her friend hurried toward her. "I wanted to walk with you, Anna, if I may?"

Anna shrugged and turned to continue on her way.

"What's the matter, Anna? You were all out of sorts at the meeting today."

"Oh, I don't know, Elizabeth. For some reason, lately everything we talk about at our teas seems so . . . silly. A waste of time. I don't know. I'll try to be in better spirits next week."

"Is that all it is? Are you sure?"

"Certainly. What else would it be?"

Elizabeth watched the sidewalk in front of her feet. "I don't know, exactly. But for some reason, I wonder . . . is everything all right between you and your husband?"

Anna looked at her sharply. "Why would you say such a thing?"

"Please don't be offended, Anna. I'm not trying to pry. I just . . . want to help, if I can."

"Well, there's nothing to help about," Anna said. "Walter and I are fine. Our children are fine. Everything is fine. All right?"

They walked several paces. "I was just trying to be your friend," Elizabeth said, finally.

"I'm sorry, Elizabeth. And I appreciate your concern, I really do. But I'm all right."

"Very well, let's say no more about it."

By the time they reached Anna's front gate, they were chatting easily. Elizabeth had to go to the gallery, she said, and they parted. Anna went into the yard and up the walk toward her house.

The fact was, she *was* irritable. Charlie Cobb had not spoken to her a single time since she'd given him the magazine, over two weeks ago. She watched him walking to work each morning, sauntering along down North Water Avenue like the Sultan of Samarkand, smiling and waving to all and sundry. He'd even tip his hat to her if she happened to be sitting on the front porch. And in the evenings, he would pass again on his way home.

Anna knew very well that he was taking a less direct route from his house to work, if he lived, as he said, on Railroad Street. He was troubling himself to detour sufficiently to stroll past her front gate, morning and evening. But would he stop? Would he ask permission to come into the yard? Would he as much as mention whether he'd read "A River Apart," or how he liked it? He most certainly would not.

Anna was becoming thoroughly annoyed about the whole matter. What was he about? Had he forgotten about her, about their conversation? Was it all just a joke to him, leading her on with his winning smile and his veiled hints, then treating her as if she were a stranger?

Anna wondered if, somehow, his wife—Daisy, was it?—suspected something and forbade him to speak to her again. If she had, then Anna hated her, and hated Charlie for paying attention to her silly demands.

She fretted over it all that morning and past noon, then decided she could bear the suspense no longer. She would walk downtown, to Elizabeth's art gallery, and on the way, she would pop in at Person's Barbershop and see about having a word or two with Mr. Charlie Cobb. Why should she wait for him? He was only a man, after all, the same as Walter and the others. How could she expect him to take any trouble about her feelings?

Climbing the hill toward the town square, Anna had an amusing thought: She tried to imagine what Mrs. Baskerville would think of her, walking by herself, going downtown to speak face-to-face with a man who wasn't her husband. *That would be a new tune to march to, wouldn't it, Mrs. Baskerville?* Anna felt bold and reckless. She laughed out loud and didn't care if anybody heard her or what they thought about it.

When the striped pole of Person's came into view, Anna felt her confidence falter the slightest bit. But she stiffened her backbone and kept right on going. She was going to show Mr. Charlie Cobb that the world didn't wait on him. She wanted to know something, and she was going to find out, all on her own and without anyone's permission.

Her entrance into the barbershop was an eerie re-enactment of her first time, except that today she didn't have the camouflage of her nine-year-old son's presence. The men in the waiting chairs and the barbers stared at her as if she were covered with blue fur.

Except for Charlie Cobb. Just like before, he was smiling at her as if he'd been expecting her all day. "Oh, yes, Mrs. Dotson. I've got it right here," he said, excusing himself from the customer in his chair. He opened a drawer in the counter, reached inside, and retrieved the folded issue of *Argosy* Anna had given him.

"Thank you again for loaning me that article," he said. "Daisy thought it was very interesting. And thank you for picking it up on your way, today. That was very convenient, and I appreciate it."

She stared at him for a few seconds, then managed, "Of course, Mr. Cobb. You're . . . welcome. Both of you."

He smiled at her, then went back to combing and clipping.

10

OUTSIDE, ANNA COLLECTED HERSELF as she continued on toward Elizabeth's gallery. Charlie Cobb was too clever by half! Not only had he thought about her taking matters into her own hands, he'd counted on it. He'd handed her the magazine as if it were nothing special, passed off their encounter as something casual and prearranged—known to Daisy, even!

He was playing her like a fish on a hook. And the trouble was, as hard as she tried to be offended, Anna was enjoying it.

It was exciting to think that Charlie had spent time considering her possible reactions, thinking up strategies. It had been so long since Walter had taken any trouble about her whatsoever that the notion of this handsome, well-spoken man holding the thought of her in his mind was thrilling. It was dark and secret and delicious, like the last piece of chocolate in a hidden box.

As she opened the door of the Jennings Art Gallery, Anna again felt audacious and capable, like a pirate or a highwayman. She would take what she needed, no matter the consequences.

"Hello, Elizabeth," she said, turning around, then realized it was Wallace, Elizabeth's husband, who stood behind the counter.

"Oh, I'm sorry, Mr. Jennings. Elizabeth told me she was coming down here, and I just expected to see her."

"Hello, Mrs. Dotson. Elizabeth was here, but the school sent word that one of the children needed her. I told her to go on. Anything I can do for you today?"

"No, I suppose I— Wait." Anna walked toward a canvas hanging on the wall of the gallery, a depiction of a woman in white, reading in a garden. "What is this?"

"That's by an American artist, Mary Cassatt. I'm not sure about her. She goes in for all this strange new French nonsense. One of our dealers recommended her, and we took this painting just to see, but, I don't know—"

"It's stunning," Anna breathed. She moved closer. With her eyes two feet from the canvas, she could see the small sweeps of blue against the white of the woman's dress, the hints of it beneath her eyes, in the hollows of her cheeks. At this range, the composition had a misty, unfinished look—as if the artist had painted the woman from an image in her mind, rather than as a simple study of some model. And yet, to Anna, it seemed perfect. The woman in the picture reminded Anna of herself, sitting on her porch and reading her stories, waiting for Charlie Cobb—or something, at any rate—to enter her life with some understanding, some romance, something to deliver her from her everyday prison of polite conversation, tea, and empty stretches of hours devoid of all passion. This woman could be her, Anna decided. She was reading, imagining worlds beyond. She was in her chair in a garden, but her soul was roaming the universe, searching for its meaning, its consummation, its mate.

"I'll take it," Anna said, turning toward Wallace Jennings.

"Pardon?"

"I said I want this painting. Can you have it delivered to my house?"

He looked surprised. "Well, I suppose so, but wouldn't you like for Dr. Dotson to—"

"No! Send it to my house. Have it framed with . . . that," she said, pointing to a thick, gilded framing sample, done in leaves and vines.

"Are you sure, Mrs. Dotson? That frame alone probably costs—"

"Yes, quite sure, Mr. Jennings, if you please."

He shrugged and started making notes on a pad. "Very well, then."

"Good. Thank you very much, Mr. Jennings. And please tell Elizabeth I came by."

"Yes, ma'am."

Anna left the shop, feeling more exhilarated than she had in a long time. She knew exactly where she would hang the painting: above her bed. It would remind her; it would give her hope.

Anna was halfway home when she remembered the *Argosy* in her hand. The Cassatt painting had quite knocked it out of her head, but as soon as she remembered, she walked a little faster. She should have time, she calculated, to look through the magazine before the children came home from school.

She went inside and tossed her hat and parasol on the table in the vestibule. She went to the parlor and settled herself on the Queen Anne settee and spread the magazine in her lap. By the time she had turned two pages, she could already tell she was going to be enthralled.

In the margins, in a neat, small hand, Charlie Cobb had written notes to her. She didn't even need to turn to the story she'd mentioned to him; the notes started within the first five pages, next to a poem entitled "Hearts Aflame":

This poet has captured me entirely, dear Anna.

A bit farther down, apparently as an afterthought, he had written

Daisy, of course, would never understand why.

Anna felt a fierce smile spread across her face. Of course she wouldn't. She and Charlie were linked somehow, in some primal way that Anna herself didn't understand.

She flipped the pages until she came to the story, "A River Apart," about the woman from a wealthy family who had fallen in love with a man who lived on the "poor side of the river." Near the beginning of the story, Charlie had written

> *Loneliness is truly a curse, and it knows no boundaries of class.*

A bit later on, near a paragraph describing Diana, the story's main female character, she found some lines in Charlie's hand:

> *She walks in beauty, like the night*
> *Of cloudless climes and starry skies;*
> *And all that's best of dark and bright*
> *Meet in her aspect and her eyes.*
> *. . . Byron speaks for my heart, too. —C.*

Anna felt her heart marching in quickstep. Charlie's words plunged into her like an arrow dipped in honey—it was as if he could read her innermost thoughts.

The clock in the hall chimed the quarter-hour. Mabel and Scott would be home soon. Anna went upstairs, to her room. She put the magazine in her armoire, beneath the French nightgown.

Later that evening, after the children were in bed, she told Walter she was tired, that she was going to bed a bit early. She went upstairs and got the *Argosy* from her armoire and scanned it from cover to cover by the gas lamp beside her bed, reading and analyzing each of Charlie's handwritten comments. She got some scissors from her bureau and clipped out all of Charlie's notes, then tossed the magazine in the trash can. Anna placed the clippings in an envelope and slid the envelope back into the bottom of the drawer in the armoire, beneath the French nightgown. Briefly, she ran her fingertips across the nightgown, enjoying its suppleness, its smoothness.

Then Anna found her latest issue of *Argosy*, and carried it to her writing desk. She opened it and began making her own notations in the margins. When the opportunity presented itself, she would give this issue to Charlie. It wasn't quite the same as having a real, face-to-face conversation—but it also wasn't as risky.

The next morning, as Anna sat at the breakfast table in the kitchen, sipping a cup of coffee and staring out the window, Walter came into the kitchen.

"Your light was on rather late, wasn't it, dear?"

"Oh, yes. I decided to do a little reading in bed, before I turned down the light."

"What were you reading?"

"Just one of my periodicals."

He gave a little smile and shook his head. "More of those stories?"

Anna took another sip of coffee and kept her eyes out the window.

"I wonder, dear, whether you might have plans for tomorrow evening?"

She set down her cup and looked at him. "Friday night?"

Walter nodded. "I was hoping we could have a little dinner party here for a family that's new to town."

"Really? Anyone I know?"

"Yes, matter of fact. You and I were talking about him the other day: my new barber, Charlie Cobb."

At hearing Charlie's name on her husband's lips, Anna had the fleeting thought that she'd been discovered, but realized that was ridiculous. Walter could know nothing because . . . there was nothing to know. She'd loaned Charlie a magazine, and he'd given it back. That was all there was.

"Yes, he seems like a nice man. He did a wonderful job on Scott's hair."

"I'm pretty impressed with him, too. As a matter of fact, I think he'd make a good Mason. I'd like for us to get to know the family a little better. They have a little girl."

Anna caught herself before saying, *Yes, her name is Alice.* Instead, she gave Walter an interested look and nodded. "That sounds fine, Walter. Will you make the invitation, or shall I?"

"I'll talk to Charlie today, on my way to the office. I think seven o'clock or so, don't you?"

"Fine."

"All right, then. Thank you, dear. I think we'll enjoy the Cobbs' company."

Anna suppressed the giggle that tried, beyond all reason, to burst from her lips. "If you say so, dear."

Walter gave her a surprised look. "My! You're certainly agreeable, this morning."

"Why wouldn't I be?"

"Oh, no reason, just . . . Well, fine, then."

They heard the sound of feet on the stairs.

"Sounds like the children are ready for school."

"Yes, Walter. I'll walk with them."

"Well, then." He stepped across the kitchen to her table, leaned over, and gave her a chaste peck on the forehead. "Have a good day, dear."

"You, too."

He went whistling down the back steps, just as Mabel and Scott, faces washed and in their school clothes, came shambling into the kitchen, with Gertrude bringing up the rear.

"You want me to walk them to school, Missus?"

"No, Gertrude. I'll walk them, today."

"Yes'm."

Anna picked up the brown paper sacks containing the children's lunches, prepared by Gertrude and waiting beside the stove. She put the sacks into their satchels and kissed Mabel, then Scott, on the crown of the head.

"All ready for another day?" she said.

The children made mumbled replies.

"All right, then, here we go."

As they marched down the front steps and into the bright April sunshine, Anna thought about the interesting twists and turns life could take. On the way downtown today, she was going to drop off the *Argosy* so Charlie could read her messages. And tomorrow night, he and his wife and daughter would be her dinner guests.

Very, very interesting . . .

"MAMA, CAN I SHOW the little girl my dresses?"

For the tenth time today, Anna had to suppress the urge to say, "Her name is Alice." *I don't know her name, don't know her name, don't know her name . . .* "Why, certainly, darling, I don't know why not. I think the two of you are going to have a whole lot of fun playing together. Can you fold those napkins and help Gertrude put them on the table, please?"

"Yes, ma'am. Oh, I hope she likes books! I want to read her some of my stories!"

"That's very sweet, Mabel. I think she'd like that."

"Yes, it's such fun to be read to," Mabel said. "I love it when you read to me."

Anna had the fleeting image of herself and Charlie Cobb, sitting in the arbor swing in the side yard, reading aloud to each other from the stories in *Argosy*.

"Well, sweetheart, when Alice gets here—"

"Who?"

Anna turned away so her daughter wouldn't see her wince. "Alice. I . . . think I heard Daddy say that was her name." *Careful! Careful, careful, careful . . .*

"Oh. Alice. That's a nice name. Maybe we could play that she's my baby sister. Wouldn't that be fun?" She chattered on, but Anna wasn't listening. Mabel would have had a sister about Alice's age. Or it might have been a boy. Walter had never said either way. Perhaps it was best not to know.

"Do you think so?" Mabel was looking at her expectantly.

"Yes, dear. Could you please help Mama set out the silverware?"

The Cobbs arrived almost at the stroke of seven o'clock. Anna looked out the front window and saw them coming through the front gate.

"They're here, Walter," she called over her shoulder, then hurried outside, making sure she was the first to greet them.

"Hello, hello!" she said, smiling broadly as they came up the walk. "It's nice to see you again, Mr. Cobb. And this must be the wife and daughter I've heard so much about." Daisy Cobb had an uncertain air about her, like someone trying to play a game she'd never seen before. Her dress was clean, but frayed at the neckline. And her hat had clearly seen better days . . . many days ago. Charlie touched the brim of his black derby. "Good evening, Mrs. Dotson. It's so good of you and Dr. Dotson to have us over. This is Daisy, and this is our little girl, Alice."

Anna squeezed Daisy's offered hand, then put her hands on her knees and leaned down to speak to Alice, a mousy little thing with her daddy's curly black hair and her mother's watery blue eyes. "Well, hello, there, Miss Alice! There is a little girl named Mabel who can hardly wait to see you!"

Alice took her finger out of her mouth long enough to give Anna a hesitant smile.

"Well, come in, come in. Dinner is just about ready, and I believe Dr. Dotson is on his way down."

At that moment, the front door opened and Walter came down the steps, holding out his hand to take Charlie's. "Hello, Charlie! So glad you could come. And this must be your family."

As Charlie made the introductions to Walter, Anna studied Daisy. She was a shrinking violet, all right—not at all what she pictured for someone as dashing as Charlie. Still . . . he'd married her, hadn't he? Oh, well. Marry in haste, repent at leisure, the saying went. Anna knew it all too well.

11

THEY WENT INTO THE HOUSE and into the dining room, just as Gertrude was setting the meat platter on the table.

"I hope you like pork chops," Anna said.

"I sure do," Daisy said.

Anna directed each of them to a seat. She and Walter were at opposite ends of the table, as was their custom. Scott, looking bored, dressed in his church clothes and with his hair plastered down, sat at Walter's right. Daisy was to Anna's right, with Charlie next to her.

When they were all seated, Walter turned to Charlie. "Mr. Cobb, would you do us the favor of offering thanks for our meal?"

They all bowed their heads, and Charlie gave a reasonably fluent prayer; he even remembered to ask a blessing on "our gracious host and his family." At the amen, Gertrude picked up the meat platter and offered it to Charlie Cobb.

"Daisy, how do you find Gallatin, so far?" Anna said.

"Oh, it's real nice, real nice. We like it here. Charlie's doing real good."

Why can't she look me in the eye? "I'm so glad to hear it. My husband has really enjoyed having Mr. Cobb as his barber, and I have to say, he does so much better with Scott than J. P. Person. I think J. P. is getting a little old to be cutting youngsters' hair."

Daisy smiled as she forked a chop off the platter held by Gertrude.

"Now, Daisy, we simply must get the children together," Anna said, nodding toward Alice and Mabel. "I think they'd have a good time."

"Yes. That would be nice for Alice, I know."

"Good, then it's settled."

"Mrs. Dotson and I have been hoping we'd see you and your family at church, Mr. Cobb," Walter was saying.

Charlie smiled and ducked his head a little. "Yes, Dr. Dotson, I know. We really need to do something about that."

"No time like the present," Walter said, smiling. "How about this Sunday?"

"Well, let me talk it over with Mrs. Cobb," Charlie said. "We certainly need to join somewhere. Daisy here was raised Baptist, but..."

"We read the Bible to Alice every night," Daisy said.

The meal passed pleasantly. Anna and Walter kept up a steady flow of conversation, mostly with Charlie. Daisy just didn't seem to be much on making social talk. But Charlie more than made up for her lack, smiling and answering questions and darting off along the path of a story he was reminded of by some chance comment or other. He had Walter roaring with laughter when he recounted an incident from his horse-shoeing days with his father, a comical confrontation with a tobacco sharecropper from southern Kentucky whose mule, he swore, had been rendered deaf by the shoes Charlie's father had put on him.

"When I say 'gee over,' he haws, and when I say 'haw,' he gees," Charlie said, imitating a backwoods accent.

"And then my dad told him, 'Why, shoot, Amos, that mule ain't deaf. I just put his shoes on him backwards, is all.'"

Walter nearly had tears in his eyes; Anna hadn't seen him laugh so hard in years. She realized she was having the thought that Charlie Cobb was good for her husband's temperament. The notion made her uncomfortable for reasons she couldn't strictly account for.

After dessert and coffee, Mabel took Alice upstairs to her room, while Scott slouched off, still in a foul mood. The adults went into the parlor for a little more conversation.

"Charlie, have you ever thought about being a Mason?" Walter asked, leaning back expansively in his cabriole chair. By now, they were all feeling comfortable enough to use first names.

"That's an interesting notion, Walter. No, I can't say I ever have."

"Well, you ought to give it some thought. I'm with the lodge here, even do a bit of lecturing for some of the smaller lodges out in the countryside. Sometime, I'd love to have you visit one of our meetings—the public part, of course. Meet some of the fellows, see what you think."

"Charlie never runs out of something to say," Daisy said. "He never met a stranger."

Anna smiled at her. *Poor thing; you're hopelessly out of your depth, aren't you?* "I'd like you to meet some of the ladies, too, Daisy."

"That'd be nice, I reckon."

Anna nodded. "Oh, I know just the thing! In a week, we're having our Spring Gala. My ladies' group sponsors it. Walter will be playing with our local band; there will be food, and dancing—it will be just a grand evening. I can get you invitations. It's being held at the Keystone, right across the street. Alice could stay right here with Mabel and Scott, so you wouldn't have to worry about her. What do you think? It would be so nice for you to come."

Anna felt a little guilty for bringing it up; Daisy would likely look ridiculous at such a "high-society" affair, and Charlie might not have much experience in those circles, himself. Of course, he had his native gifts of personality and easy conversation, but Daisy had no such advantages. Still, the offer was out in front of everyone. Anna decided to see what would happen.

"That's mighty kind, Anna," Charlie said.

"I don't have nothing to wear to something like that," Daisy said. Anna thought there was an edge of panic in her voice. An awkward silence followed.

"Well, we can think about it," Walter said, finally.

After another spell of quiet, Charlie looked at his wife. "You think it's about time we got Alice home to bed?"

Daisy nodded—a little gratefully, Anna thought—and the four of them stood. Anna went upstairs to call Alice, while Walter made conversation with the Cobbs. When she came back downstairs, Mabel and Alice trooping along behind her, she felt her daughter tugging at her skirts. She leaned down to listen to Mabel's whispered words.

"She wants to know if Alice can come over and play tomorrow afternoon. Would that be all right? You could come too, Daisy. We could visit a little more."

"Well . . ." Daisy looked at Charlie. "I guess, if it's all right with Charlie."

"Why not, dear?" he said. "Do you good, I think."

Anna didn't miss the way his eyes flickered in her direction, even as he was speaking to his wife. Butter wouldn't melt in his mouth.

SITTING AT HIS TABLE on the Keystone Hotel porch, Charlie leafed through the *Argosy* Anna had given him the previous Thursday morning. He smiled to himself. She was interested, for sure. Beside a poem titled "A Lark at Sunset" she had penned the words, "Sharing a sunset with someone you love is a special gift." Hardly a comment a woman would make to someone she regarded as a casual acquaintance. Beside the opening paragraphs of the continuation of the story "A River Apart," Anna had written, "If their love is true, the difference in their stations shouldn't matter." An unmistakable encouragement of his attentions, Charlie thought.

And then, on the last page of the magazine, the jackpot. Anna had written, in the bottom right corner of the magazine, "I'm usually alone on Thursday afternoons, until the children come home from school."

It was quite amusing to him, thinking back on the dinner last Friday night at the Dotsons. There he was chatting cozily with Walter, and Daisy, doing her best to imitate a woman of quality, in conversation with Anna. And all the time, he was looking at Anna and thinking about his next opportunity to talk to her, to have one more chance to solidify his claim on her mind, her emotions, her darkest fantasies.

Charlie knew he couldn't yet be sure where things were going with Anna Dotson—and that very uncertainty excited him. He had visions of being with her, of making love to her and hearing her cries of passion and pleasure. But they were a long way from that, at this point in the game. The game—that was what he loved. The notion of adding a society woman like Anna Dotson to his list of conquests was very gratifying. And it didn't hurt anything that Anna cut a luscious figure, with her thin waist and her swaying hips, her soft-looking blonde hair and those blue eyes that seemed to drink Charlie in each time they talked. Charlie wanted Anna Dotson as he had never before wanted a woman. Maybe it was the challenge, or the thrill of sexually owning something far too expensive for him to obtain any other way. Whatever it was, Charlie thought about it almost constantly. He was determined to see this little story through, all the way to its end.

So Walter wanted him to join his church, join his Masonic lodge. The good doctor wanted to get cozy with Charlie and Daisy. That suited Charlie just fine. The way he saw it, any time he was around Anna Dotson was a chance to keep things moving in his direction.

And if Walter was foolish enough to leave his lovely wife alone on Thursday afternoons, that was all right, too.

Today was Tuesday. He decided to talk to J. P. Person about taking an afternoon off each week—preferably Thursday. He folded the magazine and tucked it under his arm. He drained his glass of lemonade and, giving a final glance across the street at the Dotson house, got up from his table to start the walk home.

ANNA WALKED INTO THE LOBBY of the Keystone Hotel, her hand on Walter's arm. She was wearing her favorite ball gown, a light blue satin taffeta with an overskirt of royal blue velvet. She fancied the blue set off her eyes to good advantage. The sleeveless bodice showed off her upper arms; her long white gloves covered everything else, starting just above her elbows.

Her hand rested gently on Walter's arm as they promenaded into the ballroom, where much of Sumner County's polite society was already gathered. Walter would make a quick tour of the ballroom in her company, meeting and greeting the other attendees, before hurrying over to the bandstand and getting the evening's music underway.

Anna was having thoughts about Charlie Cobb. She hadn't seen him walking by the house since the first of the week, when he sent his and Daisy's regrets by way of Walter. They wouldn't be attending the gala, he said. Not that Anna was surprised. She really shouldn't have said anything about it to them. Now, she was afraid she'd embarrassed or angered Charlie somehow, that he wouldn't want to speak to her anymore—he certainly wouldn't take up her tacit invitation to drop by on Thursdays for a visit.

Anna imagined how Charlie would look if he were here, wearing one of the smart, black tuxedos and crisp, starched shirts like the rest of the men. Anna thought about dancing with him—surely someone as suave as Charlie Cobb wouldn't have views against dancing—circling the floor with him, gazing always into those mesmerizing hazel eyes. She imagined slipping away with him during the gala, up to some private place: a prearranged room in the hotel, maybe. They would rush together and kiss, then he would take her, still fully clothed except for the underthings he would savagely tear away.

"Anna, dear? Are you all right? You look a little flushed."

"Oh, yes, Walter. I'm fine. I think we might have walked a bit fast on the way across the street. Just let me sit for a moment, if you please."

Elizabeth and Wallace Jennings walked toward them, Elizabeth smiling and extending a hand to Anna. "Oh, Anna! Wallace showed me the Mary Cassatt painting you ordered. It's exquisite! And the frame is absolutely perfect for it."

"Painting?" Walter said.

"Should be ready for delivery sometime tomorrow," Wallace said. "I'll send a bill with it."

"That will be fine," Anna said.

"Bill? Painting?" said Walter.

"Never mind, dear, I'll tell you all about it later. The saxophone player is waving at you; you'd better go over and get the band started, hadn't you?"

Giving her a final, quizzical look, Walter hurried off toward the bandstand.

"Anna," Elizabeth said, "you look radiant tonight. Blue is certainly your color." She tilted her head and looked at Anna. "I'm so glad to see you in good spirits. I can see the change in your face."

Anna smiled. "Well, thank you. Why don't we find a table?"

12

ANNA WAS TRYING TO DECIDE if she was angry or sad. It was nearly two o'clock on a Thursday afternoon, and she had seen no sign of Charlie Cobb.

It was a beautiful May afternoon, and she was sitting on the arbor swing in the side yard, idly flipping through the pages of her latest *Vogue* fashion magazine, but not really seeing any of the pictures. She kept telling herself she ought to just give up and go inside the house, get busy with something and take her mind off Charlie, but she kept thumbing back and forth through the magazine, wishing her handsome barber would show his face.

She heard a whistle from the back fence, and looked up. Charlie Cobb was leaning a bicycle against the gate. He had apparently ridden down the alley behind the house, approaching from a direction she hadn't expected. She had the urge to jump up from the swing and hurry toward him, but she counseled herself to patience. She stayed where she was and waited as he crossed the backyard, smiling at her as if he were a pirate and she were the treasure.

"Good afternoon, Mrs. Dotson. Lovely day for a swing, isn't it?" He touched his hat and gave her a little bow.

Her reserve melted. "Charlie Cobb, I've a good mind to throw you off this property! It's been nearly two weeks since I gave you that magazine and as good as invited you to come on Thursdays, and here you are, dragging in like . . . I don't know what, and all you can give me is 'Good day, Mrs. Dotson'?"

He gave her a shocked look, like a schoolboy wrongfully accused. "Why, Anna. To speak to a man so! I hardly know what to say." Then he grinned at her and sat down on the swing, right next to her. She could feel his thigh against hers, through the layers of her dress and petticoats and his trousers. She thought about ordering him to get up, or getting up herself—but she didn't really want to do either one.

Anna was a little nervous; the side yard was not exactly hidden from the street, and passersby could see them if they cared to look in this direction. But a part of her also relished the danger, as well as Charlie's brashness. He was so different from Walter, so much more adventurous . . . and maybe a little dangerous. Yes, that was it: The danger in him hummed in her veins, vibrating within her in a way that was becoming more and more irresistible.

Without thinking, she pushed off and set the swing going, and they soon fell into an easy rhythm. "What did Daisy think about the *Argosy*?" she said, sliding him a mischievous look. "I'd have written something a little different if I knew you were going to share it with her."

Charlie laughed. "Well, I don't tell Daisy everything I do."

"I'm glad to hear it."

"Sure. A man's got to have a little mystery in his life. Keeps him young. It works for women, too."

"And how would you know that?"

"Oh . . . I hear things."

"And who tells you these things?"

"Mystery, Anna, mystery." He whispered the words, leaning

close to her ear. She could feel his breath on the side of her face. She closed her eyes for an instant, surrendering to the pull of it, then stopped herself. She scooted as far away as she could—which wasn't much, confined as they were by the wooden arms of the swing on either side.

"Charlie, we must be careful. We're both married, and we have responsibilities. We've made promises before God. We can be friends, but nothing more than that."

Charlie pulled away from her. "Well . . . certainly, Anna. You're right. I don't think there's anything at all wrong with a man and a woman being friends. Discussing literature, poetry, that sort of thing. What is this you're reading, for example?" He motioned toward the *Vogue* in her lap.

"Oh, this . . . it's just a fashion magazine I was looking at while I was . . ."

"Waiting for me?"

"Charlie, I mean it!"

"Sorry, sorry." He held up his hands in a surrendering gesture. "So, what sort of fashions do they put in magazines?"

She handed him the *Vogue*. "Here. See for yourself."

Charlie flipped through the pages, making interested noises. Then he paused for a long time. Anna looked over his shoulder. "Charlie, those are pictures of lingerie!"

He gave her a guilty smile. "I'm sorry, Anna. I don't mean to shock or embarrass you. But I can't help . . ."

"What? You can't help what?"

"I oughtn't say."

She grabbed the *Vogue* away from him, looked at the page where he had lingered. "What is it? Charlie, tell me."

"I just . . . well, Anna, I can't help looking at these pictures and thinking of how beautiful you'd look, wearing something like that."

Anna felt a warm sensation spread pleasurably through her body, starting somewhere below her navel and working its way out to her fingertips. "Charlie Cobb. You should be ashamed." It was only a feeble imitation of a scold, and she was sure he knew it as well as she did. Her voice had a low, thick quality, a buttery sound that gave the lie to her words, even as she spoke them.

"I know, Anna. I'm not a good man, not really. I think things I shouldn't." He took her hand and looked her full in the face. "I'm sorry, Anna. I don't deserve to be in your presence, really. You're right to send me away. If I had an ounce of backbone, I'd get up from this swing right now and walk away, never looking back."

Her brow furrowed. "Oh, now, Charlie. Don't say things like that. You're not a bad man, not at all. You can't help it if—" She bit her lip and looked away.

"Can't help it if what?"

Now it was her turn to look guilty. "I was about to say something unkind . . . about Daisy."

"Oh."

They swung for a while in silence.

"She's a good woman," Charlie said, finally. "She does the best she can."

"She's very nice," Anna said. "I hope you all can come visit again, soon."

"Thank you. I really appreciate the way you talk to Daisy."

"Yes, well . . ."

Anna wanted to tell Charlie about the French nightgown. She wanted to tell him she had one much like those pictured on the page he'd looked at. She wanted him to see her in the nightgown, see that she was so much lovelier than Daisy, so much more appreciative of his charm, his imagination, his poetic spirit. Anna knew she could make Charlie happier than Daisy; she understood him in a way his own wife never could.

"Well . . . I guess I'd better be going," he said.

"Yes. But I'm so glad you stopped by. I hope you'll do it again."

"On a Thursday afternoon?" He gave her a little smile.

"That would be lovely."

"By the way, I have an answer for your original question."

"Which one was that?"

"The one about the *Argosy* magazine. Not exactly the question you asked, but the one you meant to ask, maybe."

"What was it?"

"What I thought of it. Of what you wrote."

"Oh. Well?"

"I think you're right about sunset."

Anna smiled.

"And you know what I think about Thursdays."

She smiled a little wider.

Charlie stood. "Well, Mrs. Dotson, I guess I'd better take my leave."

She offered him her hand, and before she knew it, he'd bowed and kissed her knuckles. "Oh!" she said, pulling it back.

He smiled down at her. "Until our next meeting." He walked across the backyard and maneuvered his bicycle through the gate. He turned for a last wave at her and rode off, whistling.

Anna watched him go. When she couldn't see him anymore, she closed her eyes, trying to memorize the way his lips had felt on the back of her hand.

CHARLIE COBB GRINNED BROADLY as he turned his bicycle out of the alley and onto Railroad Street. So she wanted to be friends? Oh, he wanted nothing more . . . for now. And that comment she'd made—what was it? "We're both married. We've made promises before God . . ." Well, who was thinking about doing anything against a marriage vow? Surely Mrs. Anna Dotson wasn't envisioning the dark pleasures of adultery, was she?

Charlie laughed out loud. *I didn't make any promises before God, only a sleepy justice of the peace in Herndon, Kentucky.* He was pretty sure that didn't count—at least, not in his books.

Oh, Anna, sweet Anna . . . I'll have you yet.

13

WALTER WAITED as Brother Olmstead finished shaking Charlie Cobb's hand. Charlie complimented the minister on his sermon and introduced Daisy and Alice.

"I'm so glad you visited our church today, Charlie," Walter said when the minister had finished his greetings.

"We're glad to be here, Doc. Thanks for inviting us."

"I hope you'll come back. Did Alice like it?"

"I think so," Charlie said, glancing at his daughter. "She still doesn't talk much, and never around folks she's just met, but I'll bet when we get home, she'll give Daisy an earful."

Walter smiled. "I don't know if you have plans this afternoon or not, but I'm going to set up our Graphophone a little later. I'd love for you all to come by and enjoy the music with us."

"Graphophone? Don't believe I've ever heard of that."

"Well, then you need to come by. It's the latest thing. I've got about a dozen music cylinders for it. It's like having an orchestra right on your front porch."

Walking home from church, Walter told Anna he'd invited the Cobbs to come listen to the Graphophone later that afternoon.

"Oh? Well, that's all right, I guess," she said.

"I really like Charlie Cobb," Walter said. "He has a very pleasing manner about him. I really hope I can get him interested in Masons. I think he'd be an asset to the lodge."

"I'm sure that's right, dear. He seems a nice enough fellow."

After they were finished with lunch, Walter carried the heavy Graphophone out onto the front porch. The device was housed in a wooden cabinet. A stylus tracked along the grooves of a six-inch wax cylinder that was turned by a spring-driven mechanism. The vibrations from the cylinder resonated along the stylus, then were amplified by a large brass horn, narrow at the bottom and opening up to fourteen inches wide at the mouth. The horn had a decorative, floral-shaped design. He set it up on a table on the front porch, then noticed a smudge or two on the lacquered finish of the horn. He rubbed the smudges with his shirtsleeve until he was satisfied with the result. Walter brought out another box full of cylinders for the machine and made his first selection, "The Washington Post" by Sousa. Soon, the music could be heard blocks away. Folks started gathering on the front porch of the Keystone Hotel, listening to the music as if it were a concert. Walter loved to entertain.

Sometimes he played along with the tunes from the Graphophone on his tuba or his violin. Today he was content to just listen and wave at passersby as they loitered along the sidewalk in front of the house or stood by the front gate.

Soon he saw Charlie and Daisy Cobb walking toward the house. Charlie tipped his hat.

"Anna, they're here," he called through the doorway. He turned and waved at Charlie and Daisy as they came up the front walk.

"I really like the music. What's this song called?" Charlie said.

" 'By the Light of the Silvery Moon.' It's pretty popular. The fellow who sold me the cylinder said it's sold over fifty thousand copies of sheet music."

"It is very pretty," Daisy said.

"Hello, Daisy," Anna said, coming onto the front porch. "But where's Alice?"

"She was playing with another little girl close to the house, so we just let her stay there," Daisy said.

"Oh, dear. Mabel will be disappointed. But never mind," Anna said. "Here, sit down, sit down. I'll get us some lemonade."

Charlie and Daisy settled into a pair of wicker chairs as Anna went to the kitchen to get the lemonade. Walter began explaining the mechanism of the Graphophone. "They've got hundreds of different cylinders nowadays, everything from classical music to church hymns. Even some ragtime—I wouldn't own anything like that, of course. And you can listen to it all right in your home, with one of these."

Charlie nodded and looked interested. Daisy fanned herself and smiled.

Anna came outside, bearing a tray that held four glasses filled with chipped ice and a pitcher of lemonade. She poured for everyone, then sat down next to Daisy.

"Well, that's quite a marvel," Charlie said, still admiring the Graphophone.

"I really enjoy it. I've even gotten some of the sheet music for a few of my cylinders so I can teach it to the band."

"What instrument do you play?" Daisy wanted to know.

"The tuba and the violin, mostly. A little piano. We've got a Steinway in the parlor, but I don't get to practice much."

"We want Mabel to take lessons, one of these days," Anna said.

"Put on another cylinder, would you, Walter?" Charlie said.

Walter slid "By the Light of the Silvery Moon" off the spindle and replaced it with another recording. "This is a new one, just came out last year," he said. He cranked up the mechanism and carefully placed the stylus on the spinning cylinder. A male voice, accompanied by a piano, began singing.

> *Let me call you "sweetheart" I'm in love with you.*
> *Let me hear you whisper that you love me, too.*
> *Keep the love light glowing in your eyes so true;*
> *Let me call you "sweetheart" I'm in love with you.*

Anna's eyes found Charlie's during the song; silent messages passed between them. Walter and Daisy, as far as she could see, were oblivious.

"That's a nice song," Charlie said when it was over. "I like it a lot."

"The woman who wrote it is from Tennessee," Walter said.

"Sure enough?"

"Fresh ice," Daisy said after a pause, admiring her glass. "That's so nice on a warm afternoon like this. Are you able to get deliveries on the weekends?"

"Oh, no. But the weekly delivery usually lasts us, even in the hot part of the summer," Anna said.

"You must have a real nice icebox," Daisy said.

"Would you like to see the kitchen?" Anna said.

"I sure would," Daisy said.

They went inside, and Anna took Daisy into the kitchen. She showed her the large, walk-in icebox. Next to the icebox was the pantry, with shelves lining both walls from the floor up to the eight-foot ceiling, laden with canned vegetables and canisters of flour, sugar, and other staples.

"That's the biggest icebox I believe I have ever seen," Daisy said. "You can keep so much in it . . . Do you like to cook?"

"I like to, but I'm not very good at it," Anna said. "Gertrude does most of the cooking. What do you like to cook?"

"Charlie likes fresh vegetables and fruit, and I like to cook fresh meat when we can afford it."

"Maybe you can come over and teach me how to cook some of the meals that you prepare for Charlie. I would like to learn to cook better for Walter and the children."

"I reckon I could do that, if you'd like."

They went upstairs and Anna showed her the children's bedrooms and bathroom, then her room and Walter's, separated by their bath.

"That's so nice, to have your own room like that," Daisy said. "Charlie and me have always slept in the same bed. But he snores so bad," she said, giggling. "I'd love to be able to close a door and not have to listen to it."

Anna smiled at her and tried to think of something to say. She was confused and momentarily speechless for she was beginning to take a liking to Daisy.

"CHARLIE, I'D LIKE TO ASK A FAVOR OF YOU," Walter said, setting his glass on the table and giving him a serious look.

"Well, sure, Doc, what is it?"

"You know how everybody talks down at the barbershop."

Charlie nodded, giving Walter a careful look.

"I think people like you and J. P. have a lot more influence, here locally, than you think."

"Well, Doc, I don't know. I'm still pretty new in town."

"Yes, but the fellows down at the barbershop like you. I can tell. And they listen to what you've got to say."

Charlie shrugged.

"So, I'd like to get you to put in a good word for Horace Oldham. He's up for reelection as judge, and I think we ought to keep him in office."

Charlie nodded. "If you say so, Walter. I'll do what I can. I try to stay out of politics, but if somebody asks me what I think, I don't mind putting in my two cents."

"Good enough. I'd sure appreciate it. Several of us on the Board of Aldermen are trying to talk to enough people to make sure Horace gets back into office."

"Suits me. But speaking of the Board of Aldermen . . . are you any closer to a decision on this suffrage business?"

Walter looked pained. "Charlie, I wish I knew what to tell you. But to tell the truth, I can't say I know my own mind on that."

"Is that so?"

Walter nodded. "Anna has gotten all caught up in it, and I guess I ought to say more to her about it, but you know how it is with wives. You can only talk them out of so much."

Charlie gave him a grin.

"I've been doing some reading on it, and honestly, I still don't know what to think."

"Well, I can't say I envy you the responsibility. You've got a lot on your mind these days. I honestly don't know how you fit in everything you're involved in. Your patients, your church, the Masons, all of it. You're on the go an awful lot, seems like to me."

Walter nodded. "True enough. A time or two, Anna has tried to get me to slow down, and I keep meaning to, but, to tell you the truth, I'm really interested in all these things. My music, and the Masons, and lecturing, and the Board of Aldermen . . . I don't know, I just . . ." He gave Charlie a sad little smile. "Here I am a doctor, and you're the one listening to all my complaints."

Charlie grinned and shrugged. "Well, Doc, it's the least I can do."

"YOU'VE GOT SUCH PRETTY THINGS," Daisy said, eyeing the dresses in Anna's closet. "Thank you for letting me see them."

"Well, of course. I'm so glad you asked."

"I'd love to have some time to make me a nice dress like one of these," Daisy said. "I think Charlie would like it if I could fix up a little."

"Oh, don't be silly! You're lovely as a peach, just like you are," Anna said.

Daisy blushed a little and smiled. "Well, thank you. But, well, sometimes, with Charlie . . ."

Anna gave her a careful look. "What, Daisy?"

Daisy gave her a guilty look. "Oh, I shouldn't say. It's just a feeling I get, sometimes."

"Please, Daisy. Tell me."

"Well . . . Charlie has what you might call a wandering eye."

Anna waited.

"I can see the way he looks at other women, sometimes. I guess maybe I worry about it . . . a little."

"Well . . . I don't think . . ."

"Oh, I don't reckon he does much about it," Daisy said. "I guess lots of men look; that's just their way."

Anna nodded.

"I just think if I could have some nicer things . . . Walter must like to see you fixed up all pretty, mustn't he?"

Anna looked out the window. "Oh, I . . . Walter is a very busy man, Daisy, you must understand. He's gone so much that . . ."

"Well, anyway. I don't need to rattle on about it," Daisy looked at Anna. "It's just that . . . I never really had a woman friend, before. It was just me and my mother and daddy and brother, and then Charlie came along, and now . . . I just wanted to talk to somebody about it. A woman."

"Well, I'm glad you did," Anna said.

WALTER WAS EXPLAINING some of the projects of the local Masonic lodge to Charlie when the two women came back out on the porch. Charlie and Walter stood and held chairs for their wives.

"Put another song on, Walter," Anna said. "Put on that last one: 'Let Me Call You Sweetheart.' I like it."

The cylinder was still on the spindle from its last playing. Walter cranked up the spring drive and set the stylus. The song floated out over the front yard and the neighborhood.

Walter sat back down in his chair and closed his eyes, swaying a little in time with the waltz tempo of the song. It was nice, sitting out on the front porch with friends, listening to the music. Walter felt himself softening, relaxing. He thought about what he'd just been saying to Charlie, about being gone so much of the time. Maybe it was the sentiment of the song, or the general mellowness of the afternoon and the pleasant passing of time, but he was feeling genuinely remorseful—a little ashamed of how he was neglecting Anna and the children. A man could win a popularity contest and lose his own family in the process, if he wasn't careful.

Walter thought about Horace Dobbs and his young wife, Savannah. Now there were two people who had just about nothing except each other, more so than just about anybody you'd likely meet. Last week, Savannah had gone into labor with their first baby. Walter had feared it was going to be a difficult delivery; he'd had two consultations with the young woman at the end of her first two trimesters. When the message came—a boy who lived down the rutted dirt road from the Dobbses had ridden bareback into Gallatin to fetch Walter—it was after five in the afternoon.

The shame of it was, the day was Mabel's birthday, and Walter knew Anna had planned a little family celebration that would start as soon as he got home from the clinic. He'd listened to the dirty-faced boy's breathless news, and sighed. Then he went to the phone on the wall and cranked it up, placing a call to the house. He told Anna that he had a patient who was in labor and likely to have some trouble, and he'd apologized. "But I have to go, dear. She could very well die if she tries to deliver this baby without some help." Anna hadn't said anything other than "I understand, Walter." He hung up, threw some obstetric instruments, a bottle of chloroform, and another of alcohol into his black bag, and rushed out the door, barely remembering to lock it behind him.

By the time he'd gotten to the Dobbses' little cabin up in the hills outside of Bethpage, Savannah was, indeed, in trouble. She'd been in hard labor for several hours, but the baby wasn't moving down into the birth canal as it should. She was gasping for breath, and her pulse rate was fluctuating wildly. He coached Horace to massage his wife's midsection while he employed forceps to help move the child. He delivered the seven-pound boy, held him up and spatted him, and was rewarded by a lusty yell from a brand-new, healthy set of lungs. He handed the baby to his father, then turned his attention to Savannah, who was hemorrhaging severely. Somehow, he was able to get the bleeding stopped.

He stayed with the Dobbses until he was satisfied Savannah was resting comfortably. "Have you got any family nearby that can help?" he asked the nervous young father. Horace nodded. "My maw oughta be here before morning, and Savannah's is coming up from McMinnville."

By the time Walter got home to Gallatin, it was nearly dawn. He didn't want to risk waking anyone, so he lay down on the couch in the parlor and dozed as much as he could until the sounds of the waking house roused him.

When Anna came downstairs, she looked a question at him. "Mother and baby ought to be all right," he told her.

"That's good," she said. "Mabel remembered you and your patient in her prayers last night."

"I'm grateful," Walter said.

WALTER LOOKED AT ANNA, smiling and talking with Charlie and his wife. She was so lively, so pretty. Walter remembered the influenza epidemic, back in 1896 in Lafayette, when he and Anna had labored side by side, round the clock, to care for the ailing. He wished there would have been a way to have her at his side last week, in the small, isolated cabin where he brought the Dobbses' son into the world and kept Savannah from leaving it. But their lives were more complicated now, and he had to make difficult choices. Walter took a sip of lemonade and wished things were different.

14

SCOTT WOUND UP and threw the baseball, its arcing trajectory carrying it to the dead center of the red-painted pie plate that was the target for the dunking booth mechanism. But the ball didn't have enough velocity; it bounced harmlessly off the plate, and Vestal Willits, the town constable, was still sitting high and dry above the trough full of water.

"Now, that don't hardly seem fair," said the red-cheeked, laughing man in charge of the dunking booth. "This here boy paid his nickel, just like everybody else, and he hit the target. I think old Vestal oughta go in the water, what do you folks think?"

The crowd cheered loudly and the man nodded, slapping his hand against the pie plate. The lever tripped and the constable fell with a loud splash into the trough.

"Attaboy, Scott!" said a man wearing a red, white, and blue garter on his sleeve that identified him as a member of the Chamber of Commerce. "He's got an arm, there, Mrs. Dotson," he said, smiling as he leaned down to shake Scott's hand. "This boy's liable to give ol' Ty Cobb a run for his money."

"The man had to hit the plate," Scott said, looking sideways.

"Well, you still hit the target, son," Anna said.

She strolled on, Scott and Mabel tagging along behind. The town square was draped with bunting everywhere she looked. There were booths set up on the streets and in the spaces between the places of business. Walter had permitted the women from their church to sell slices of pie from the stoop in front of his clinic; a watermelon-seed-spitting contest was underway on the street in front of the drugstore; and Elizabeth Jennings and several other women were passing out suffrage pamphlets from a brightly decorated stall in front of the Jennings Art Gallery. It seemed to Anna that everybody in Sumner County was in the Gallatin town square. The one person she knew that she hadn't yet spotted was Charlie Cobb.

"Mama, I want some corn on the cob," Mabel said. "Can we get some corn on the cob?"

"Yes, honey, just a minute." Anna peered at the knot of men gathered around the "Test Your Strength" kiosk, one of those affairs where you pounded a lever with a heavy mallet and tried to send a metal cylinder high enough up a pole to ring a bell mounted at the top. Several of the high school boys and young single men had their sleeves and collars unbuttoned, panting as they dug nickels out of their pockets to pay for one more chance at the teddy bears that would presumably guarantee the affections of one or another of Gallatin's young women. A few older men were watching the contest, offering free advice to the sweating contenders. But none of them were Charlie Cobb.

They made their way to the booth selling corn on the cob, where Anna bought an ear for Mabel and one for Scott. She looked up at the clock on the courthouse tower. It was nearly eleven o'clock—time for the band concert.

"Come along, children," she said. "Eat while you walk. We don't want to be late for Daddy's concert, do we?"

A crowd had gathered around the bandstand on the courthouse

lawn, where Walter was giving some last-minute instructions to the musicians. Anna looked for a seat near the bandstand, but because it was nearly time for the concert to begin, she had to settle for a place farther back, under one of the big elm trees. She was glad of the shade, but Scott wouldn't be happy, since he wouldn't be able to see his father very easily.

The band tuned up, then started in with Sousa's "Liberty Bell," one of Walter's favorites. Walter liked to play tuba on the marches. From here, all she could see of him was the gold-lacquered bell of the tuba, sticking up from the last row of musicians.

Next the band performed an arrangement of Ward's "Materna," with a guest soloist, an older woman Anna didn't recognize. There was nothing old about her voice, though. It carried quite handily over the cornets, the euphoniums, the flutes, and the clarinets. "Oh beautiful for spacious skies, for amber waves of grain," she sang. When she finished, she received a nice, enthusiastic round of applause.

Scott was restless because he couldn't see his father, and Mabel saw a girl from school, sitting close to the front with her family. She offered to take Scott with her and see if they could sit with the other people. Anna nodded, and at the next break between numbers, off they went, dodging between the rows of spectators.

Just as the band started its next selection, someone plopped down on the seat next to her, just vacated by Mabel. It was Charlie Cobb. He scooted in close; Anna could feel him against her, all the way from her shoulder to her knee.

"Happy Fourth of July, Anna," he said, with his trademark smile.

They were in a more sparsely populated part of the audience, but still Anna was nervous about Charlie sitting so close to her in public.

"Where's Daisy?" she said without looking at him.

"Who knows? I left her somewhere over on the other side of the crowd."

"She's here? Aren't you afraid we'll be seen?"

"I'm too crazy in love to care," he said in a low voice, close to her ear. Anna felt her heart break into a lope. Charlie's hand was crawling across hers where it rested, wedged between the outside of her thigh and his. His hand covered hers, and the backs of his knuckles pressed upward, into the lower part of her thigh.

Anna felt flushed, and not from the heat of the July morning. She felt an urge to grab Charlie's face and kiss him, right there and then. The warmth of his hand seemed to run all the way up her arm and into her chest. She wanted to guide his hand up to her breast and feel him touch her there, cup her gently, like a crystal goblet.

"We've got to be careful, Charlie," she said. "There are people all around."

"And they're all admiring our fine town band, being led by the good doctor. They're not paying a bit of attention to two people having a friendly visit, here under this nice shade tree."

Hearing the faint derision in his tone, Anna was simultaneously repelled and attracted. It was as if Charlie was saying about Walter what she wished she could. Walter was always out front, wasn't he? Always leading the meeting or directing the band or teaching the Sunday school class or lecturing the Masons. Well, he was missing something today, wasn't he? He had time for everybody in Sumner County except his wife. Anna didn't have to sit at home and wait for him. There were people who would pay her some mind, and one of them sat next to her right now, feeding flame into her veins with his touch, his words, his presence.

"How would I send you a letter, if I were to want to do such a thing?" Anna said, looking at him for the first time.

"That's easy, Mrs. Dotson. Just send it to post office box thirty-five, Gallatin, Tennessee. I'm the only one with a key, and the only one who ever picks up the mail there. What about you?"

"I don't know . . . Walter picks up the mail from our post office box. He says he doesn't approve of ladies going into the post office by themselves."

"What does he approve of ladies doing?"

"Stop it. Somebody is going to hear you."

"All right. But I want to write to you, too."

"I know . . . Just tuck the letter into the *Argosy* magazines. I can pick them up and drop them off at the barbershop, same as always."

"I'll do it, Anna my love." He was getting up to go, but before he did, he slid his hand, palm upward, between the back of her thigh and the park bench. He gave her leg a firm squeeze. Then he was gone.

Anna realized she was trembling. Never in her life had she felt such riptides of desire as she did for Charlie Cobb. It was as though he held some mystical power over her; he had but to appear, speak a few words in her ear, touch her, and she was ready to discard everything she'd ever been taught about fidelity, the sanctity of marriage vows, respectability . . . everything. All for the sake of a single hour in his arms, feeling his flesh against hers.

A part of her mind was able to stand back and take stock of the situation. There was a voice within her that urged her to have nothing more to do with Charlie: to quit walking past Person's window during the day just to see if he was there, to stop sending him *Argosy* magazines with handwritten notes in the margins next to the most provocative passages, to do everything she could to distance herself from the unaccountable magnetism he wielded over her heart and mind.

And yet . . . the other part of her—the womanly, feeling part—

wanted him desperately. That part of her relished the feeling of domination by a force she couldn't control. That part of her loved being desired by a man as virile and bold as Charlie Cobb.

The Gallatin Commercial Club Band was coming to the closing bars of its finale, Sousa's "Stars and Stripes Forever." The crowd on the courthouse lawn was rising to its feet, clapping in time to the music. Owen Pinkney, the druggist, was standing at the front, playing the piccolo solo that never failed to draw enthusiastic applause, despite his numerous missed notes. Anna stood and clapped with everybody else.

WALTER PLUNGED THE BUTCHER KNIFE cleanly through the crisp, green watermelon. It was so ripe it nearly fell open without cutting. The wet, sweet scent plumed out to Anna's nostrils, smelling of cool refreshment. She'd had the melon in the icebox all day, in preparation for tonight's dessert.

When she and Walter told the children at the dinner table that they'd be eating dessert in the backyard, they chorused, "Watermelon!" It was a special summer treat to eat cold watermelon in the backyard, the fireflies spangling the darkness above the grass with their tiny yellow beacons. Mabel and Scott were probably a little more careless with the watermelon than strictly necessary—they were eating in the backyard, after all—but Anna didn't mind so much. She smiled at them as they shoved their faces into the sweet, cool flesh of the melon, coming up with smears from chin to eyebrows. They spit seeds at each other, laughing and chasing each other around the yard.

"All right, now, you two. Time to clean up and go inside."

By degrees, Anna and Walter were able to coax the children over to the hand pump atop the cistern, close by the fence along the back alley. Walter pumped cool water into their cupped hands, and Anna supervised as they scrubbed the watermelon leavings from their faces.

"Go on to the back porch, and leave your wet things by the kitchen door," she told them. "Get into your nightclothes lickety-split, and maybe I'll come read you a story."

With only a little more playful splashing, Mabel and Scott did as their mother said. Anna went inside while Walter rinsed off the table where he'd sliced the watermelon.

Anna braided Mabel's hair while Scott finished fidgeting himself into his nightshirt. They piled up onto Mabel's bed and tucked themselves in on either side of Anna while she read to them from Mabel's favorite bedtime book, *Andersen's Fairy Tales*. To Anna's mind, some of the stories had a darkness and sadness about them that was worrisome, but Mabel and Scott didn't seem to see it that way. They never tired of hearing "Thumbelina" or "The Steadfast Tin Soldier." Anna suspected the brightly colored illustrations on every other page had something to do with it, also.

She finished the story and Scott rolled off Mabel's bed, padding barefoot to his room. She tucked in her daughter, kissed her slightly sweaty forehead, and reminded her to say her prayers. She went into Scott's room and repeated the process.

Anna went down the hall to her room. The windows were up, but on this midsummer night, there wasn't a breath of a breeze. She felt like taking a cooling sponge bath before going to bed. She started to call down to Walter to bring up a pail of water from the cistern, but then she heard him in the bathroom, making ready to go to bed. She decided to fetch the water herself.

She went downstairs and into the kitchen, grabbing the large wooden pail from the countertop by the door. She went out onto the back porch, then down the steps into the backyard. Stepping carefully in the darkness, she saw the whitewashed concrete of the cistern. She set the bucket beneath the pump spout and started working the squeaky handle.

There was a noise in the dark, on the other side of the alley fence. A cough—a male cough. Anna felt her nostrils flare with alarm. "Who's there? I can hear you, whoever you are."

"Don't call the constable, Anna. It's me. Charlie."

15

"WHAT ARE YOU DOING HERE?" Anna whispered hoarsely. "You like to scared me to death!"

"Shhh ... easy now, Anna. Don't be scared. I like to come here sometimes. Just to stand here and watch."

"Watch what? You're liable to get yourself shot, sneaking down people's alleys at night."

Charlie laughed, low and quiet in the darkness. "I don't bother anybody. And can you blame me, wanting to be close to the woman I love, in the cool of an evening?"

His voice was working its old magic, loosening her up and making her think of things better left alone.

"How long have you been standing out here in the alley?"

"You mean tonight, or—"

"No. How long have you been doing this?"

He rubbed his chin and stared up at the stars for a few seconds. "I guess since about the time Walter played his music doohickey for us. That Sunday evening was the first time."

"What do you tell Daisy? Doesn't she notice you being gone from the house?"

He shook his head. Even though it was dark, Anna would have

sworn she could feel him smiling at her. "I go for walks sometimes, Anna. I told you, I don't feel the need to tell Daisy everything, just like you don't tell Walter."

"Well . . . you'd better get gone, before somebody sics a dog on you." She grabbed the handle of her bucket.

"Can I carry that for you?"

"Have you lost your mind?" She yanked the bucket up, spilling a good bit of water down the side of her dress. "You'd better go, Charlie."

"Well, all right. But now that you know I come here sometimes, why don't you come out and talk to me once in a while?"

"I'll think about it."

Anna went back into the house. She lugged the heavy bucket upstairs and into the bathroom, and emptied it into her wash basin. Then she unbuttoned her shoes and her dress, and peeled off her underthings. It felt good to stand naked in the bathroom and let the air play over her skin; for the past few hours she'd felt sticky with the heat.

She stood in the bathtub and soaked a sponge in the wash basin, then squeezed it slowly over her shoulders, the back of her neck, her face. The cool water was refreshing.

Anna unpinned her hair and selected a cotton nightgown from her armoire. Turning down the gas to the bathroom light, she went into her darkened bedroom. She looked at the window by the head of her bed, the one that looked out onto the backyard. Anna went and stood by the window in the darkness, staring out at the place where Charlie had been, in the alley. She thought about him, standing out there in the dark, maybe night after night, just hoping for a glimpse of her. After a while, she lay down on her bed. She was still thinking about him when she finally drifted off to sleep.

"ANNA! ANNA DOTSON!"

Anna turned. Elizabeth was waving at her from across the

street, bouncing on her tiptoes. She leaned forward to step into the street, then had to jerk herself backwards as an automobile whizzed past, the driver honking his Klaxon as he barely missed her. When the way was clear, she hurried across the street to Anna.

"Have you seen the papers today?" she said.

"No, I guess not. What's happened?"

"The most wonderful thing. The women in California have finally convinced the Progressive Republicans to put a suffrage proposition on their statewide ballot in October. This is a wonderful day for the cause, Anna."

Anna smiled at her friend. "Yes, indeed. Are there any plans locally?"

"We're trying to organize a rally to publicize the California decision. I've gotten a telegram from some of the ladies in Nashville and other cities, and everyone's very excited."

"Well, I'm happy to hear it."

Elizabeth gave Anna a careful look. "Somehow, I thought you'd be a little more impressed with the news."

"Oh, I am glad, Elizabeth."

"Is everything all right?"

"Yes, we're all fine. Walter, the children . . . everybody."

Elizabeth just kept looking at her.

"Would you like to come over to the gallery for a little while, Anna?"

Anna let Elizabeth guide her across the street and down the side of the town square until they came to the Jennings Art Gallery. They went inside. Anna noticed that in the place where her Mary Cassatt used to hang, they'd put a reproduction of a Gainesborough portrait: a girl in a pink bonnet.

"Morning, Mrs. Dotson," Wallace said. Anna nodded and smiled.

"Come upstairs, Anna. I've got a fresh pot of tea."

The Jennings had a small sitting room on the second floor, above the gallery. When they were seated, Elizabeth gave Anna another measuring look. "Now, then. You look like someone who has a lot on her mind. And I'm your friend. Won't you tell me what's bothering you?"

Anna looked out the window for a long time. She had gotten to the place where the thought of Charlie Cobb was like a part of her. Though she was troubled by the conflict between what she wanted and what she knew to be right, she still felt the impulse to keep the secret safe and close. If she shared it with someone—even a friend like Elizabeth—she would lose something. Anna wasn't quite sure she was ready for that loss. But maybe it would be good to share her burden. A small corner of it, anyway.

"Elizabeth, I wonder . . . do you ever find yourself . . . weary . . . of Wallace?"

Elizabeth laughed. "Oh, my! Is that all it is? Of course I do, Anna. Show me a woman who's been married for any time at all that hasn't discovered her prince's armor isn't quite as shiny as she thought at first. You mustn't think badly of yourself for that. Walter is a fine man, I'm sure . . . but he's just a man."

Anna took a sip of tea. "Well, I know that's right, Elizabeth, but . . . I think, sometimes, that there might be someone else . . . someone besides Walter . . . who might make me happier."

Elizabeth carefully set down her teacup. "Is there someone specific you're thinking of, Anna?"

Anna nodded.

"Someone here in Gallatin?"

Anna nodded again.

"Do you want to tell me who it is, Anna?"

"Oh, it's probably nothing, Elizabeth. I'm . . . I don't think anything will happen."

"But do you want something to happen?"

Anna looked out the window again. "I don't know. Sometimes, maybe."

Elizabeth was quiet for a long time. "Anna," she said finally, "I don't know who this man is that has caught your eye, and I don't know what you have or haven't said to each other. But I have to tell you that I think you should think very, very carefully about what you're considering. A marriage vow isn't just words, Anna. And you have your children to think of, not to mention your reputation and your place in the community."

"But Walter doesn't even see me anymore! We haven't . . . been together as husband and wife for . . . I don't know how long. Is that any way to live?"

"I'm sorry, Anna. I know this . . . difficulty has been bothering you for some time. But it's not as if you're the only woman who has ever had to face the fact that her husband doesn't look at her the way he did when they were newlyweds. Marriage isn't always about romance. It goes through seasons, like everything else."

"Well, mine has been stuck in the dead of winter for quite some time now." Anna looked at Elizabeth. "Are you saying that Wallace doesn't ever . . . I mean, that you don't—"

"Anna, I don't keep up with that the way you do." Elizabeth's cheeks were flushed, and she wouldn't look Anna in the eye. "I just suppose I've become content with the way things are with Wallace and me. Except for our disagreement about the cause, of course."

"But isn't that part of what we're fighting for?" Anna said. "Don't we want men to see us as something other than objects for their convenience or charges that have to be guarded constantly, like children who can't take care of themselves? I want my husband to look at me and see *me*, not some caricature he's composed in his head and labeled 'wife.' Is it so wrong to want something just because I want it?"

"And what is it you want, Anna? Really?"

"I want to feel like a woman again! I want to feel desirable and cherished . . . and I want to desire on my own account. I want to long for someone so badly, be so deeply in love that I think I'm going to drown. It's not as though I'm making some unreasonable demand, Elizabeth. I'm not so horrid to look at, if I may say so."

"Certainly not, Anna. You're as lovely a woman as there could ever be."

"Well, why does my husband treat me as if I'm some homely drudge?"

"Oh, Anna. Surely you're exaggerating."

"Am I really? Let me ask you something, Elizabeth. That French nightgown I bought in Chicago, like the one in *Vogue*—like the one you ordered for yourself. Why did you want it in the first place?"

Elizabeth looked flustered. "Well, I . . . I suppose I thought it was pretty."

"And tell me: Didn't you imagine how you'd look in it, how you'd feel wearing it?"

"Well, yes, but—"

"And didn't you, just for a moment, wish someone else could enjoy that feeling with you? Someone you cared about? Someone you loved?"

Elizabeth stared at her. "Anna, I have no idea what to say to you right now."

Anna set down her cup and stood. "Thank you, Elizabeth. I very much appreciate your concern."

"Anna! I didn't mean to—"

"You didn't, Elizabeth. Everything you've said is perfectly sensible and proper. Just like Walter. And I'm sure I ought to just listen and be grateful and learn to keep my place, but—" Anna clenched her jaw, afraid to say more. She took a deep breath. "Well, I'll be going now, Elizabeth. Thank you for the tea. And for the talk."

She went past Elizabeth, doing her best to ignore the look of shock and hurt on her friend's face. Anna went downstairs and into the gallery. Wallace Jennings looked up as she entered the main showroom.

"Good day, Mr. Jennings," she said. "And thank you again for delivering the Cassatt. It looks lovely in my room."

He didn't say anything; he just watched as she strode to the door and yanked it open.

"WHY DO YOU HAVE TO GO TONIGHT?" Daisy said. "You used to read to Alice out of one of the books before she went to bed. Or make up a story in your head. But now every night you go for a walk, and by the time you come home she's asleep."

Charlie looked at his wife. She was staring at him in that way she had that always reminded him of a sheep. She'd just spoken as many words at a time as he'd nearly ever heard her use, and a small part of him knew he ought to be feeling at least a little bad, but he didn't. In fact, all he could feel right now was annoyed. Why now, of all times, did Daisy decide to find her backbone?

"Well, I'm going anyway. I'll read to Alice tomorrow night. I need some fresh air." There. And he hadn't even raised his voice. He knew men that wouldn't have used as much restraint. He reached for his black bowler. "Just leave a lamp on in the front room, would you?" She was still looking at him with her sheep face when he closed the door behind him.

Charlie took long, swinging steps down Railroad Street, looking up at the stars and thinking about Anna Dotson. No wonder Walter was so successful; with a woman like Anna at his side, what couldn't a man accomplish in this world? Charlie should have been more careful, he guessed. Daisy was a cute little thing, back in the days when he'd met her, but a simple woman like his wife just couldn't understand things the way Charlie needed her to. He tried to imagine himself reading one of the poems from *Argosy* to Daisy, tried to guess what she'd say about it. Most likely, she'd just stare at him, waiting for him to tell her what to think.

But not Anna. Anna Dotson was a woman with fire inside her, a woman whose passion burned close to the surface. Charlie could feel it when he was near her; he could smell it, just as he could smell the La Rose perfume that plumed in her wake each time she walked past him. Anna could give a man dreams so big he'd just have to go places, do things he'd never thought possible.

For as long as he could remember, Charlie had been around the edges of the good life. Like a late arrival at a banquet, he'd made do with the leavings of plenty that nobody else wanted. But Anna Dotson . . . she was the feast, the payday to end all paydays. A woman like that would make just about anybody sit up and take notice. Charlie imagined the look on his daddy's face, on the face of everybody in Big Rock, the day he came riding into town with Anna by his side. Then somebody would finally know who Charlie Cobb really was. Then they'd all see.

What Charlie couldn't understand was why Walter Dotson seemed so lackadaisical in his attentions. If Charlie had a wife like Anna waiting for him, you could bet your last brass button that he'd be taking care of his homework on a regular basis. But Walter didn't seem to know what he had. Well, it was too bad for Walter . . . but all the better for Charlie.

Charlie cut through the empty lot behind the freight depot, into the alley. So far, there were no barking dogs in any of the yards he passed on his way to Anna's back fence, which was a mercy. There was enough moonlight for him to make his way down the center of the alley, stepping around the cast-off lumber, broken wheels, and other refuse dragged out to the alley by the folks who lived in the big houses along North Water Street. Finally, Charlie came to the big elm tree that leaned into the alley from the corner of Anna's backyard, the tree that shaded the cistern. He eased up to the gate and stood there, looking up at the house.

Anna, come out to me. I'm here, and I'm waiting for you.

There was a light on upstairs, and Charlie imagined it was Anna's bedroom. He stared at the glowing window and called to her silently.

16

ANNA LISTENED AS THE SOUNDS of the house stilled around her. She tossed on her bed; in the heat of the August night even the silk of the French nightgown seemed clingy and annoying. She sat up on the edge of her bed and looked at the Cassatt painting, washed in the moonlight coming through her window. The woman in the painting looked so cool and comfortable, sitting outside reading. Anna got up and padded to the open window, staring out at the backyard. She wondered if he was out there. She couldn't decide for certain if she hoped he was or he wasn't.

Anna went to the bathroom and picked up the sponge beside her washbasin, but the basin was empty. Sighing in exasperation, she went to her room and grabbed the silk kimono that lay across the corner of the bed. She wrapped it around her and went downstairs, still in her bare feet, and into the kitchen. The wooden pail was in its usual place, on the counter. She picked it up and opened the door.

The grass of the backyard felt cool on her feet; out here there was at least a little bit of a breeze. Anna walked toward the cistern, watching where she put her feet, trying not to think about Charlie Cobb's whereabouts or her wishes about them. She set the bucket under the pump spout and began to work the handle.

She heard footsteps in the grass, coming through the gate. For some reason, Anna didn't look up to see him, she just listened to his approach. And then, as she'd somehow known he would, Charlie Cobb grabbed her hand from the pump handle and pulled her up to face him.

She looked at him and she didn't say anything. In this moment, neither of them needed words. He pulled her to him and kissed her fiercely, as she'd never been kissed ever before in her life. His tongue was in her mouth and hers was in his and the taste of it was sweet, oh, so sweet, and every ounce of resistance or hesitation in her washed away on the tide of her pounding heart, the onrushing wave of desire that rose up in her.

Anna felt his hands sliding up under the kimono, under the French nightgown, going places and doing things that made her breath come fast and catch in her throat. She heard a low, rising moan and realized it was coming from her own throat. She pushed herself into him and felt the hardness of his body. Her knees buckled with the wanting of him and he laid her down on the cool grass under the elm tree and raised himself over her. He was inside her and clinging to her like a lifeline and the only thing in all the world that Anna wanted was to get closer to him, to join herself with him, to wrap herself around him like a second skin.

She gasped and dug her fingertips into his back; he gave a sudden, hushing breath and buried his face in the crook of her neck. "I love you, Anna," he said in a hoarse whisper. "I need you. I've never felt about a woman the way I feel about you."

"I love you, too, Charlie," she said, running her hand along the thin washboard of his spine, up and down. "I love you, too."

They held each other as the moon and stars circled overhead. Anna thought maybe she even dozed a little. Charlie stirred and said, "I have to go, now."

"Yes."

He stood and buttoned his clothing. He looked at her as if he were about to say something, but finally just smiled and walked through the gate. Anna watched him go down the alley. Tonight, somehow, she didn't need to call out to him. She had something from him to hold his place with her, and for right now, that seemed enough.

Anna pumped water from the cistern into the bucket and carried it back to the house. She went upstairs and filled her washbasin, then sponged herself all over. She put the nightgown on, her body still moist from the sponge, and went to her bed. All around her, the house was still, silent except for the night creaking of the wood floors.

Anna realized she was smiling. Very soon, she was asleep.

SUMMER EASED INTO AUTUMN. For Anna, the days either crawled or sprinted past, depending on how long it had been since her last chance to be with Charlie. They met a few times near the cistern in the backyard, until, one night, a neighbor's dog started barking at the sounds they made. After that, they tried to limit their trysts to Thursday afternoons when Walter was at his office and the children were at school.

After a few times of being with Charlie, Anna felt guilt climbing into her thoughts, more and more. And yet, the passion she and Charlie shared was like some sort of delectable delicacy; now that she had tasted it, she didn't have the will to deny herself. Some part of her knew that one day she'd have to honestly face herself . . . but she was always able to convince herself the day hadn't yet come.

One day, as she was watching Mabel at her homework, Anna realized that her daughter would soon begin exhibiting signs of womanhood. Later that evening, she told Walter she thought they should put a doorway from Mabel's room into the bathroom she shared with her younger brother. He nodded and said nothing, but Anna kept at him until finally he agreed to see about what it would cost.

• • •

ON A BRIGHT AFTERNOON in mid-September, Walter found him-self with some time between patients. He decided to stroll down to Whitehead's and buy some of the supplies he would need for the doorway. He had a list, and Bobby helped him gather everything and bring it to the counter.

Walter hefted a sack of nails and gave Bobby a careful look. "You're sure I've got my full two pounds here, now? You wouldn't be giving me the brother-in-law treatment, would you?"

Bobby grinned. "Aw, Walter. Don't say things like that with my boss standing right behind me."

Emil Whitehead grinned over his shoulder. "Bobby, I sure hope you put your thumb on the scale when you weighed out the doc's nails. He can afford it."

Walter laughed and shook his head. "Come on now, fellas. Just be-cause I'm a doctor doesn't mean I can feed the whole town."

"I'll bet that's not what you say to those fancy patients of yours down in Davidson County," Emil said. "I'll bet you don't try that poor boy stuff on them."

"Shoot, Walter makes ten or fifteen dollars just for walking in the door with those folks," Bobby said. "He takes their pulse and has them stick out their tongue. Then he has them stick out their wallet."

The three men laughed. "What kind of project you getting ready to start, Walter?" Emil asked. "You must be planning something for all these nails and that lumber you ordered, and all."

"Oh, Bobby's sister wants another doorway added to the children's bathroom," Walter said. "I've stalled her about as long as I can, I think."

"Why does she think there needs to be another doorway?" Bobby said.

"Well, Mabel's getting up close to a certain age, and Anna thinks she needs a little more privacy," Walter said.

"Sounds like a lot of money and trouble for nothing, to me," Bobby said.

"Now, Bobby, you ought to know your sister better than that, after all these years," Walter said. "How about this: I'll let you go home with me and talk her out of it."

Emil gave a low whistle.

"No, sir, I believe I'll pass," Bobby said. "Now that you mention it, a second doorway for Mabel sounds like a fine idea."

Walter gave him a knowing nod.

"You fixing to do it yourself, Doc?" Emil said.

Bobby gave a barking laugh. "Walter, doing carpentry work? Oh, I don't much think so."

Walter gave Bobby a severe look. "You'd better watch yourself, whippersnapper. I might not let your sister invite you over for Sunday lunch anymore."

Bobby held up his hands in surrender.

"Seriously, though, I was going to ask if you knew a likely handyman here in town who I could talk to about doing the work. I think I've about got all the supplies bought that he'll need, and I don't mind paying for a good job."

Emil peered up at the ceiling, thinking. "Well, I've heard tell this new barber over at J. P.'s place is a pretty fair country carpenter."

"You talking about Charlie Cobb?" Bobby said.

Emil nodded. "Somebody I was talking to the other day—can't recall who, right this minute—told me he framed out and hung a window for him, did a real nice job and gave a reasonable rate."

"Well, I'll say. He's been cutting my hair for nearly a year now, and I didn't know that about him," Walter said.

"I'll probably see him over at the Keystone after work today," Bobby said. "You want me to say something to him for you?"

"Sure, if you don't mind," Walter said, picking up his sack of nails. "And I'll try to remember to stop by the barber shop tomorrow on my way to the clinic and talk to him. Well, I guess I've killed enough time in here with you two."

"But you haven't spent enough money," Emil said.

Walter gave Emil a sardonic grin and a shake of the head.

"Give Anna a hug for me," Bobby said as Walter walked toward the front door. Walter waved and nodded as he went out.

Walter walked down the sidewalk, smiling and nodding at the people he knew. He pulled in a deep breath; the air smelled of the turning of the season. Walter loved this time of year, when he could sense that the dull heat of the summer was really going to relent. The sky always seemed its bluest to Walter in the early autumn.

The county fair was in full swing, out at the old parade ground just outside of town. All the talk around the courthouse square and in the barbershop was of whose horses had won the pulling competition, who had the best-looking sheaf of wheat or ears of corn, and various opinions of the new farm implements on display. Earlier today, Walter had set a broken arm for a young man from the eastern end of the county who had fallen out of his saddle while practicing for the pleasure horse show this coming Saturday night. All he wanted to know from Walter was if the cast would fit inside the sleeve of the dress coat he intended to wear into the show ring. Walter supposed many of Gallatin's women were busy baking cakes and canning fruit and putting the finishing touches on quilts, hoping for a coveted blue ribbon from the judges—or a red, at the very least.

Walter decided to take Anna and the children to the fair tomorrow evening. It had been a long time since they'd done anything special as a family. Maybe he could help Scott win a tin whistle or some other prize at one of the booths; maybe he'd buy Mabel her favorite stuffed animal—even at the exorbitant prices the vendors would be asking. Maybe he'd see a glimmer of enjoyment in his wife's face, for a change. If nothing else, watching her children having a good time ought to be good for Anna, he reasoned.

Walter couldn't figure out what was wrong with Anna. Sometimes she'd be high as a kite, smiling her way around the house like someone who knew the world's best secret. But let him comment on her good mood, or ask her what was making her happy, and she'd close up tighter than a clam with a bellyache, and that would be the last smile he'd see on her face that day. Other days, she was as glum as an old woman with the gout, dragging herself from here to there with about as much enthusiasm as a horse on the way to the glue factory. In the same way, if he did or said anything to try to cheer her up, it was almost worse than if he'd done nothing.

Anna's widely shifting moods were worrisome to Walter. When they'd lived in Vienna, he'd had occasion to study some of the new work being done by Professor Freud. While Walter had severe reservations about some of the implications of Freud's psychological theories, he could appreciate the more practical diagnostic aspects of the Austrian's work. Walter was beginning to worry about whether Anna might be suffering from some sort of hysterical disorder. He wished he knew how to talk to her about it without putting her off.

At any rate, he thought, it would be good for all of them to go out to the fairgrounds and enjoy some variety. He could see the roofline of his house now as he turned onto North Water. Shifting the bag of nails to his other hand, he began to walk a little faster.

17

THE DOOR OPENED and Gertrude gave Charlie a sullen look. For a few seconds, he thought the maid was going to bar his way into the house, but she finally let the door fall open. She actually turned her back on him and walked away, the rude old hag!

"Good afternoon, Gertrude," he said as cheerily as if she'd given him a big smile. "So nice to see you."

Charlie grinned to himself as he trudged up the stairs with his step-ladder. Anna's maid didn't much care for him, he guessed. Well, that wasn't his problem. What did he care what the hired help thought? He was here to do a job—and more than that, if he got the chance.

This past weekend, he'd done the initial demolition work, tearing down the plaster covering the wooden slats in Mabel's room and on the other side, in the bathroom, then sawing through the slats to create the rough opening. It was hard and messy work, and he'd spent almost as much time sweeping up and removing the plaster as he had creating the opening for the new doorway.

Today he aimed to frame up the opening and hang the new door. If he had time, he'd set the latch in place.

Anna came upstairs. *About time*, he thought. He'd certainly made plenty of noise, letting her know he was here.

"Hello, Mr. Cobb," she said, giving him a demure smile. "So nice to see you again. The opening looks just right."

He grinned at her. "Yes, ma'am, well, I try my best to please, as you know."

She gave him a look that made him want to back her up against the wall, right where she stood. "I do indeed know. How far do you think you'll get today?"

"As far as I can." He felt a stirring below his belt; their little word game was having its effect. Good; she was in the mood today. Charlie never knew for sure which Anna he'd find when he was with her. Would it be the one who relished his touch and let him explore her with his hands and body, or the guilt-hounded one who demurred and drove him to distraction with the nearness of her, yet wouldn't allow him into her secret places? After that first night in the backyard, Charlie thought he'd gained permanent admission to the temple of Venus. As it turned out, though, Anna was prone to second thoughts. In a way, it whetted his appetite all the more to get her to the place where she was completely in his command—it was something to look forward to. On the other hand, it was frustrating, never knowing from one time to the next where he stood with her.

Last week, when Walter had approached him about doing the carpentry work, Charlie had had a brief thought of passing on the job. He was at a low point: Anna was remorseful and distant; Daisy was nagging him more than usual; and J. P., seemingly jealous of the clientele Charlie was cultivating, was talking about either charging him a percentage of his tips or reducing his salary. Still, he told himself, Walter was willing to pay, and the money would always come in handy. And then, that very afternoon, Anna had dropped off an *Argosy* for "Daisy." Tucked inside was a note that read, "Walter out this evening, children fast asleep by eight. Please come to me."

It was annoying last Saturday, having Walter as well as Anna's brother hanging over his shoulder nearly every minute he was here, asking him questions about how he intended to proceed and whether he needed anything else to complete the job and generally making nuisances of themselves. But today, the good doctor was safely at work, healing the sick. Little brother Bobby was in his clerk's apron, behind the counter of Whitehead's Hardware, preoccupied by the local young women walking past his window and making eyes at him. The kids were at school, Anna was in the mood for love, and Charlie was in the mood for Anna. If only they could keep snorty old Gertrude downstairs where she belonged, everything would be just fine.

Charlie whistled as he measured and cut the two-by-fours he would use to trim out the jambs and lintel. His saw bit into the grainy yellow pine and released a pleasant, resin-laden scent. He nailed the boards into place and went downstairs to fetch the one-by-nine planks he planned to use for the facings. As he passed through the kitchen on his way to the backyard, Anna held out a fried apple pie, dusted with powdered sugar and still warm from the pan. Charlie took it from her and bit into the half-moon-shaped pastry, making appreciative noises. She smiled at him. Charlie saw Gertrude watching over Anna's shoulder, wearing a look of the strictest disapproval. He winked at her and she turned away in disgust.

He went out and laid the planks across his sawhorses in the backyard, cutting them into the lengths he'd premeasured. Then he mitered the corners. Tucking all three pieces under his arm, he went back upstairs and nailed the framing pieces into place, then stood back for a moment and admired his work. All that was left before hanging the actual door was nailing in the door stops on the inside of the jambs and lintel.

As he was measuring the lengths for the jamb stops, Anna came upstairs. "How's the project going, Mr. Cobb?" she said, holding a glass of cool water out to him.

"Thank you, ma'am," Charlie said. He took a few swallows of the water and set the glass on a table. "Making good progress. What do you think of it so far?"

She inspected the doorway. As she looked, Charlie eased up behind her and put his arms around her. She leaned back into him and his heart moved into a higher gait as he felt her body press against him, from his chest all the way down to his groin. He stroked her stomach and cupped his hands beneath her breasts. He breathed in the scent of her hair, a mixture of lavender and La Rose perfume.

"It's looking good," she said in a low, throaty voice. "I think Mabel will be happy. Do you think you'll hang the door today?"

"Oh, I don't think so," he half-whispered. "I want to string this job out as long as I can. I like the company here."

She twisted around in his arms to face him, offering her lips to him. He kissed her.

"You're salty," she said, wrinkling her nose. He moved to kiss her again, but she turned her head and pushed away from him. "Don't," she said. "Gertrude will hear."

"Don't you need to send her to the store, or something?"

"Not today, Charlie," she whispered. "All right?"

He gave her a surprised look. "Really? But I thought you were sending all the right signals, just a little while ago."

She wouldn't look at him. "Charlie, we . . . I've got to be careful."

"I love you, Anna."

"I know, Charlie. I love you, too."

"You sure?"

Now she was watching him. "Yes. But it isn't as easy for me as it is for you."

"What are you talking about? I've got people at home to worry about, too."

She looked at him for several seconds. "Yes. I've thought about that."

"What's that supposed to mean?"

"I don't know. Nothing. I've got to go back downstairs now. You need anything else?"

"Just you."

She looked at him a few seconds, then smiled. "Well, then." She went downstairs.

Charlie cut the strips for the door stops from pieces of the one-by-nine and nailed them into place. He put a coat of paint on everything, so it would have a chance to dry overnight. Then he loaded his tools into his toolbox, swept up the sawdust from the day's work, and went downstairs.

"I'll be leaving now, Mrs. Dotson," he said as he reached the bottom of the stairs. He continued on toward the kitchen and the back door, hearing her footsteps clicking along the wood floor of the hallway from the parlor.

"All right, Mr. Cobb, and thank you again," she said.

"If you think of it, you might ask Dr. Dotson or your brother to put another coat of paint on the woodwork I put in today," he said. "That way, everything should be ready for me to put on the hardware, next time I'm back."

"When do you think that will be?"

He studied her face carefully. They were speaking as though they had an audience—which, in a manner of speaking, they did; Gertrude was most likely lurking around some corner or other. But what Charlie was hoping to see or hear was some indication that Anna wanted him to come back for some reason other than getting Mabel's doorway finished.

"As soon as I can, Mrs. Dotson," he said. He smiled at her. Something went loose and relaxed in her face when he said it, and Charlie was glad. He touched the brim of his derby and let himself out the back door.

• • •

ANNA STOOD AT THE KITCHEN WINDOW, hugging herself as she watched Charlie Cobb cross the backyard and go out the alley gate.

What in the world am I doing with you, Charlie Cobb?

Anna knew, deep within her, that this business between Charlie and her couldn't end well. She had crossed a forbidden line, and it didn't make any difference what she said to Elizabeth Jennings or anybody else, the line was real and the consequences were liable to be real, too. A day of reckoning was coming; she could feel it all the way down in the bottom of her soul.

But how in the world could she get by without Charlie in her life, now that she'd let him in as far as she had? Their lovemaking was like rain in the desert to her. She thought about him all the time: how his arms felt when he was holding her, how his breath tasted when they kissed, the way her heart sang inside her when their bodies were joined. Thinking about turning away from that, never again feeling the way she felt when Charlie took her in his arms, made life seem like a bleak, dusty road to nowhere. Charlie was all she looked forward to—and he was like an ache in her side that wouldn't go away. She needed him desperately, and at the same time she knew that every day she kept on with Charlie Cobb brought her closer to the time when everything that she treasured in life would come crashing down around her ears.

She turned around. Gertrude was looking at her.

"What is it, Gertrude? Is something wrong?"

Gertrude didn't answer for a few seconds. "Ain't for me to say, missus."

"Whatever do you mean?"

Gertrude just walked away.

18

"Eighteen . . . nineteen . . . twenty. Ready or not, here I come!"

Scott thumped down the front steps and tore around the corner of the house toward the backyard. He was pretty sure he'd heard either Mabel or Alice giggling over that way. Girls were so silly; if you just stayed still, they'd nearly always make some kind of noise so you could find them. Mabel would, anyway. She was about the worst hider Scott had ever seen. She was so bad, he looked forward to being "it," just so he could show her how bad a hider she was.

Sure enough, he'd barely rounded the corner of the house when he saw a slip of blue calico, fluttering in the wind from behind the trunk of the big elm tree. Careful to keep himself between his prey and the straightest line to base—the front porch steps— he eased closer and closer to the tree. He was about ten feet away when he heard Alice start to giggle. Silly old girls.

"I see you, Alice, behind the tree. And I hear you, too."

She came out, her face pink like it always was anytime she was a little bit embarrassed. "All right, Scottie."

Scott hated it when anybody called him "Scottie," especially silly, pink-faced baby Alice. But Mama had told him he should be patient with Alice and be nice to her, so he didn't say anything. Instead, he peered carefully around the backyard, thinking about where Mabel might have hidden. Mama and Mr. Cobb said it was against the rules to hide inside the house, so she'd better not have gone in there, he thought. She probably hadn't. Mabel might be a silly, giggly girl, but she wasn't a cheater . . . most of the time. He looked up in the branches of the elm tree. She probably wasn't up there, either, because ever since her last birthday, Mabel said she was too old to climb trees. Scott was pretty sure he wouldn't ever be too old to climb trees, even if he lived to be a hundred.

He walked over to the cistern and there she was, all humped over in a ball, like a big bunny rabbit wearing a purple dress with a bow in the back. "I see you, Mabel, behind the cistern!" Two down and four to go: the grown-ups.

You could never be sure about grown-ups. Sometimes, they would hide in a really easy place so you could find them quick, because they were only acting like they wanted to play and really just wanted to get it over with. And then sometimes, they would trick you and hide so well you could almost never find them. Scott sometimes wished grown-ups knew how to be in-between about something, instead of all the way at one end or the other.

Scott tried to think about which kind of grown-up Mr. Cobb was. He was a nice man, Scott guessed. He smiled a lot, especially at Mama. And getting a haircut from him wasn't so bad. At least he didn't scold the way Mr. Person did, and didn't pop you on the head with his comb if you wiggled the least little bit. Maybe Mr. Cobb knew how to hide good, but not too good. Mama sure didn't; she would almost always be somewhere so that Scott couldn't miss her, even if he was trying.

Scott wandered across the backyard, looking carefully behind the hedge near the swing in the side yard and behind the bushes up close to the house. The bushes and the hedge were good hiding places, even in the winter, because they kept their leaves all year round. For a second, Scott thought he saw somebody's shoes sticking out from under part of the hedge, but it was just a root.

He continued on up the side of the house, toward the garage. And then, he saw a sliver of color, near the ground by the garage door—the same color as Mama's dress! He tiptoed toward the garage, staying far enough to the side so that anyone inside the open door where Daddy drove in his automobile wouldn't be able to see him coming. He stuck his head around the corner and inside the opening. "I see you Mama, in the—and Mr. Cobb, too!"

Mama and Mr. Cobb were in the corner, in front of Daddy's car, and they had their heads together, like they were telling secrets to each other. Mr. Cobb stepped back real quick when Scott called them out, and Mama threw her hands in the air and said "Oh!" like somebody had startled her.

"Well, I guess you found us, Mr. Walter Scott Dotson Junior," Mr. Cobb said, giving Scott a big grin. He always called Scott that; Scott didn't like it so well, but it was sure better than "Scottie."

"I guess we have to go to base now," Mama said. She was smiling too, but to Scott it seemed like she was smiling a little too much—like when he used to tell baby jokes and everyone would laugh, but the jokes weren't as funny as everyone was pretending. At least, Mabel told him so. She never laughed at any joke he told, no matter how funny it was.

Scott found Daddy crouched down by the front steps, on the side opposite where he had taken off to look for Mabel and Alice. Scott called him out, and that only left Mrs. Cobb to be found, but Scott didn't feel like playing anymore. Something about the way Mama and Mr. Cobb were acting was bothering him. He didn't know why, exactly, but there was something wrong about it, and it was making him feel bad inside.

"Ollie, ollie, in free," Scott called. Daddy gave him a surprised look.

"Aren't you forgetting someone, son? You haven't found Mrs. Cobb yet."

"I can't find her. I give up."

"What's the matter, honey?" Mother said. She was giving him a worried look, like she did when he had a cough or a fever.

"Nothing. I just can't find her, that's all."

About that time, Mrs. Cobb came walking around the side of the house opposite the garage. "I'm surprised you didn't find me, Scott," she said. "I was down behind the rain barrel, by the kitchen steps. You walked right by me."

Scott didn't care. He just wanted to go up to his room and look at books, or play with his toy soldiers, maybe. "I'm tired of playing hide-and-seek. I'm going in the house."

ANNA WATCHED HER SON trudge up the steps. Despite herself, she couldn't help giving Charlie a worried glance. What had Scott seen? And what would a boy his age think about what he'd seen? She should've known better than to run to the garage with Charlie.

"Well, is anybody ready for some dinner?" she said in her best imitation of a bright, cheery tone.

"Why don't Scottie want to play no more?" Alice said.

"It's all right, sweetheart, it's about time for dinner, anyway. And then, don't forget about the ice cream."

Alice grinned and ducked her head. Daisy took her daughter's hand and they all trooped up the front steps and through the parlor, into the dining room. While everyone found their seats, Anna went into the kitchen to tell Gertrude to bring out the food. Gertrude gave her a sour look, but Anna was already on her way upstairs to see if Scott had gone to his room—and to see if she could find out anything about what he thought he knew.

She tapped on his closed door. "Scott, honey. Come down to dinner. Everyone is waiting for you."

"I'm not hungry."

She went inside. He was sitting on the floor at the foot of his bed, staring at a red-painted top he held in his hand.

"What's the matter, honey? Aren't you feeling well?"

"I'm fine."

"Well, why don't you come downstairs? It wouldn't be nice to sit up here in your room when we have company. Is something bothering you?"

He shrugged. Anna looked at him closely. *You're a horrible mother, Anna Dotson, bringing your sin out in full view of your innocent child! You're a pitiful excuse, is what you are . . .*

"Are you sure you don't feel sick?"

Scott shook his head. "No."

"No what?"

"No, *ma'am*. I'm not sick. I just don't like the way Mr. Cobb was playing, that's all."

Her heart climbing up her rib cage, Anna said, "What did he do that bothered you, sweetheart?"

Scott shrugged. "I don't know. He just shouldn't be telling you secrets in the garage, maybe." He looked up at her. "What was he telling you, anyway?"

Anna's mind whirled. Telling secrets was better than if Scott had said "kissing," which is what they were doing. It could be worse. "Well, honey, I'm so sorry that worried you. We were just laughing about having found the same hiding place, and wondering if you were going to find us. That's all." *Liar! And to your own child!*

He looked at her for several seconds. "That's all?"

She nodded and smiled at him.

He looked back down at the red top in his hand. "Well . . . Maybe that's not so bad, I guess."

"Maybe not. I'm sure Mr. Cobb didn't mean to upset you. Now, won't you come down to dinner?"

"I guess so." He stood up and shoved the top into his pocket. Anna followed him downstairs, wondering how she was ever going to be able to stop despising herself.

AFTER DINNER AND ICE CREAM for dessert, the adults set up a small table for pinochle in the parlor, while the children played. Mabel and Alice made a beeline for Mabel's room. "Come on, Alice. I'll show you the new door your daddy made for my room," she said, grabbing Alice's hand and half dragging her toward the stairs. Scott went upstairs, too. Anna thought he was still giving Charlie doubtful glances, but maybe he'd forget about the garage incident in a few days.

"Charlie, I want to thank you again for the fine job on the new door," Walter said when the four of them were seated around the table. "It looks just grand. I told Anna it looks like it was built with the rest of the house."

"Well, like I told Anna, I aim to please." He grinned at Walter, seated just to his left, then across the table at Anna. She tried to return his smile, but couldn't quite manage it.

Daisy shuffled the cards. "I sure am glad my daddy ain't anywhere close by," she said, "me playing with spot cards and all. He'd have me up in front of the church next Sunday, confessing my sins."

"Daisy, your daddy would have something to say about most anything, if he thought somebody was having a good time," Charlie said.

"Charlie." Daisy gave him an admonishing look. "You ought not say things like that."

Charlie shrugged. "All right, sorry. Why don't you deal the cards; you're about to wear them out."

Charlie was partnered with Anna against Walter and Daisy. Charlie won the bid and called hearts as trumps. Anna made a sound of annoyance.

151

"Oops, sounds like I missed my partner with the hearts call," Charlie said. Anna gave him a chagrined look.

"Now, no talking across the table," Walter said, grinning. "Or else Daisy and I will have to start communicating, too."

"Well, we can't have that," Charlie said. "Guess I'll try to keep quiet."

They played out the hand, and Charlie and Anna barely made their bid. "I sure thought we had you," Walter said. "Didn't you think we were going to catch them on that last trick, Daisy?"

Daisy smiled and shrugged. "Charlie's real good at cards. He always has been lucky."

"That's right, and don't you forget it," Charlie said. "Let's see . . . my shuffle, isn't it?"

They played on as full dark settled outside the windows. Charlie kept up a steady line of patter, and he and Anna also kept winning. He would grin at her and compliment her play and Anna would smile back and pass it off as simple luck. A few times, she thought Daisy was looking at her strangely. She decided she'd be glad when the Cobbs went home for the evening.

19

December 1911

Anna picked up the hat. It was a nice, heavy felt—a derby, like the ones Charlie usually wore. But this one was much nicer than anything she'd ever seen him wear. The Nashville haberdashery where she was browsing was one that catered to a clientele a bit above the one to which Charlie, with his barber's wages would belong.

She carried the hat to the register, looking over her shoulder toward the front door. With her luck, Walter would walk by and see her through the window, then come in to investigate. "I'd like this hat, please," she said to the clerk, "but please give me something to carry the box in so my husband won't know what it is."

The clerk smiled knowingly. "Yes, ma'am," he said. He took her money and put it in the till, then carefully placed the hat down in a box, packing it in with plenty of tissue paper. He reached under the counter and found a large, plain paper sack and put the box inside it. "Think that'll do?"

"Yes, that's fine," Anna said, quickly grabbing the sack. "Thank you so much."

She went out onto the sidewalk and quickly walked away from

the haberdashery. She reminded herself that she didn't need to be so nervous; Walter was busy with his own errands, and besides, what could be more normal near Christmastime than a woman buying her husband a new hat? But the hat wasn't for Walter, and Anna didn't want him to expect to find one under the tree on Christmas morning. *What a tangled web we weave*, she thought.

The windows of the stores in Nashville, decorated for Christmas, put her in mind of this time a year ago, in Chicago, and her sad attempt to breathe some life back into her marriage. Anna thought about the past twelve months, and to her it seemed as if twelve years had passed, so different was her life now from then. Maybe she had thought that Charlie's love would fix things, somehow. What a mistake! Now, she had not only the dull burden of her anger at Walter's insensitivity and general disregard of her needs, but also the moment-by-moment anxiety over keeping the secret of her clandestine affair. And the secret was bound to leak out, sooner or later.

Elizabeth Jennings was still looking at her askance. And there was no telling what was going around in Scott's mind—though, Anna had to admit to herself, he had said nothing about the incident in the garage since that evening, nor had he acted in any way that gave Anna concern. But, Gertrude! Anna had thought more than once about dismissing her, so palpable was her air of disapproval. If she didn't know Walter was bound to ask questions, she would have probably let her go by now. Anna wished her conscience was a little less tender; she could plant something in Gertrude's coat pocket—a piece of silver, maybe—and accuse her of stealing. But Anna didn't think she could pull off such a dirty trick, and her load of guilt was already close to what she thought she could manage without losing what was left of her mind.

She went into a few more stores and picked up some things for the children and Walter, adding enough to her bundle to easily camouflage Charlie's hat, nestled down in the center of the lot. She walked back up Broadway, climbing the hill up from the river toward Union Station. She decided to just wait there for Walter and the train back to Gallatin; she was suddenly tired of shopping and ready just to get home as soon as she could.

The next day, Wednesday, she tucked a note into an *Argosy*. "Be sure to come by tomorrow afternoon. I've got a surprise for you." By now, most of the men at Person's barely gave her a glance when she walked in to leave the magazine behind Charlie's chair. She hoped that was a good sign.

The next day she decided to give Gertrude the afternoon off. "Go home and rest," she told her. "It's nearly Christmas; you ought to spend some time with your family." Gertrude looked at her for a long time, and Anna could easily imagine all the words going back and forth behind those dark, tired, brown eyes. "Yes'm," she said, finally, and gathered her things and left.

Charlie knocked on the kitchen door at about two o'clock and Anna opened to him with a smile.

"Hello, my darling," he said, and leaned in. Anna kissed him, but broke the contact earlier than he wanted. "Come upstairs, let me show you what I've got."

"Oh, I can hardly wait to see what you've got," he said with a leer.

"Charlie! I wish you wouldn't talk like that every time we're alone."

"Sorry."

She led him up the stairs to her bedroom and made him turn around while she opened her armoire and got out the hat. She had wrapped the box in white tissue paper, trimmed with a wide, red satin ribbon. "All right, you can turn around," she said, holding the box out toward him.

"Why, thank you, Anna," he said, taking it from her. "Should I open it now, or wait?"

"You might as well open it," she said. "I don't imagine you're going to want to take it home and put it under the tree."

"Maybe not." He smiled at her, then slid the ribbon off the corners of the box. Tearing back the paper, he smiled wider when he saw the "Bee" printed on the lid of the box. "Is this a hat?" he said. "It is! And a very nice one, too." He took it out, untangled it from the paper packing, and put it on his head. "And a perfect fit! Thank you, my dear." He stepped to her and gave her a kiss on the cheek.

"You're welcome. I hope you like it. It looked like the style you prefer."

"Sure is. And I've got something for you, too—but I didn't bring it with me. Can I get it to you in the next day or two?"

"That would be nice. What is it?"

"Ah-ah. Can't give away the surprise."

"I guess not."

He came close and took her in his arms. "Say, it's been a long time since we . . . enjoyed each other's company. The kids are at school and I didn't see old Gertrude downstairs anywhere. What do you say?"

Anna laid her head against his chest. A part of her wanted to do what Charlie was asking; something always came uncoiled in her when his voice got that warm, husky tone it had right now. And she'd been contemplating the possibility ever since dropping off the *Argosy* at the barbershop yesterday. But somehow she couldn't get the consent of herself this afternoon. She looked up at him. "Charlie, I—"

He pressed his mouth to hers, and despite her reservations, Anna felt herself responding. Before long they were lying atop a pile of discarded clothing on the floor of her bedroom, slaking their appetite for each other. Anna's pulse sang in her ears, her body arched toward its crescendo.

When it was over, Anna suddenly wanted desperately to be by herself. She pushed Charlie off of her and quickly gathered her garments, then went into the bathroom. While she was dressing, he rapped on the door.

"Anna? Are you all right? Is something the matter?"

"No . . . I'm fine. I . . . you'd probably better go now."

"You sure nothing's wrong?"

"No. I just want to be alone for a while."

She dressed, then waited in the bathroom until the sounds from outside told her he had gone down the stairs and out the front door. She went out and down the stairs, watching as Charlie walked away across the backyard. She went back upstairs and threw herself across her bed, holding her face in her hands.

CHARLIE WALKED DOWN THE ALLEY, his body still tingling from the session with Anna. *Not a bad little early Christmas present. And I got this hat, to boot.* He grinned to himself, then tried to figure out what sort of gift he could find for Anna, so as not to make himself a liar. It would have to be something he could locate in Gallatin, since he didn't have time off for the rest of the week until Sunday, when the stores would be closed. And it couldn't cost too much, or Daisy would ask all kinds of questions. No, something quick and easy that he could leave at the barbershop, then take to Anna at a convenient time.

He thought about the issue of *Argosy* that Anna had just given him, the one containing her note. There was a poem in there titled "Lover's Light," about a woman who left a candle burning in her window to signal her lover that she wanted to see him. But a jealous suitor discovered the arrangement and waited in the bushes near the woman's house one evening when the candle was lit. He killed the unsuspecting lover as he was entering the yard and dragged him away, burying him in the woods. But the woman kept lighting the candle, night after night, year after year, pining away for the beloved she would never see again.

That was it: Charlie would buy her a candle, and maybe a cut-glass candle holder, if he could find one that wasn't too expensive. He'd tell Anna to use it as a signal for him to come to her. She couldn't miss the poetic reference; she'd probably get all sentimental about it. Charlie nodded to himself. Yes, a candle was just the thing. *Merry Christmas, my little Anna.*

Charlie wondered what had gotten into her, at the end. Why had she pushed him away so abruptly? She was probably having second thoughts again. Well, she'd just have to get over it. He wasn't going away so easily. And Charlie had a feeling that Anna didn't really want him to. She was worried about getting found out, sure, but she needed him in some way. After all, the good doctor wasn't taking care of her needs, was he? Anna needed a real man in her life. Charlie decided to give it a rest for a few days, try to figure out which way the wind was blowing. He figured, the breeze had to blow his direction sooner or later. After all, as Daisy had said, he'd always been lucky.

WALTER PLAYED THE OPENING CHORDS, ending with an arpeggio, then gave everyone an expectant look. Stumbling a little bit at first, the crowd finally began to sing "Auld Lang Syne" as he played along. At the end of the chorus, everyone shouted, "Happy New Year!"

It had been a good party. Most of Gallatin's leading businessmen were here, along with their wives. Walter enjoyed playing the host, and Anna had been as close to her old self as Walter could remember in a while, gliding in and out among their guests, making everyone feel welcome, insuring that everybody had a good time. Even without the alcoholic beverages often customary at such gatherings, Walter believed their guests had had a wonderful evening.

He and Anna stood on either side of the doorway, bidding everyone goodbye and "Happy 1912." When they had waved to the last guests as they descended the front steps, Anna said, "I'm just going to run upstairs and check on the children."

Walter puttered around downstairs, picking up the dishes and cups that had accumulated on most of the house's horizontal surfaces during the course of the evening. He carried the things to the kitchen and stacked them carefully on the counter near the sink. Gertrude would have a full day of work tomorrow.

Anna came back downstairs and helped him finish picking up the odds and ends left from the party.

"It was a nice affair, don't you think?" Walter said.

"Yes, I think it was. Folks seemed to be having a good time."

Walter nodded. "Say, Aloysius Hix said he's been seeing a lot of you, lately."

"He did?"

"Yes. Says the last two times he's been in J. P.'s waiting for a haircut, you've come in and left a magazine or something with Charlie Cobb . . . What's the matter, Anna?"

She was giving him a strange look. "Oh, yes, now I remember." She gave a little laugh and shook her head. "For a bit there, I couldn't imagine what Mr. Hix was talking about. But I give my old issues of *Vogue* and *Argosy* to Charlie to give to Daisy. That's all it is."

Walter studied her for a moment. "Well, that's nice, dear. I'm sure she gets a lot of enjoyment from reading them."

Anna nodded. "Why don't you go on upstairs, Walter? I'll finish up the little bit that's left down here."

As he went upstairs, Walter tried to put his finger on what it was about Anna's response just now that was vaguely troubling. For the merest instant, she'd looked at him the way a cornered rabbit might look at a fox. What was the line from Shakespeare?

The lady doth protest too much, methinks.

ANNA SAT ON THE EDGE OF HER BED and stared at the candle on her windowsill. She wondered if it had come from the department store downtown; she was pretty sure she had seen some cut glass knickknacks made in the same style there the last time she went shopping. Charlie had probably picked up the first thing he'd seen. He'd probably spent a total of five minutes finding, selecting, and buying this for Anna's Christmas present. Hardly a match for the Bee derby she'd chosen for him in Nashville.

When the party guests had shouted "Happy New Year" awhile ago, Anna's first thought had been "Not likely." Walter had given her a chaste kiss with pursed lips and Anna had compared it with the breathless, deep, searching kisses she shared with Charlie.

What a mess her life had become. Shaking her head, Anna pushed herself up from her bed and began undressing. She put on her woolen nightgown and turned down the gaslights in her room, except for the one over her bed. She turned back the quilts and crawled between the sheets, then reached beneath her pillow for the *Argosy* Charlie had given her with her candle. He had circled the poem about the woman who lighted a candle for her secret lover. She read the poem again, then reached up to turn down her light.

How pathetic: lighting a candle, night after night, for a lover who was never coming back. It might be even more pathetic than the mess Anna had managed to get herself into. "Happy New Year," she said to herself, then settled into her pillow and tried to go to sleep.

20

Bobby Dennis locked the front door of the hardware store and pocketed the key. He pulled his watch from his vest pocket and flipped open the cover: nearly five thirty. He made a sour face. A lady had come into the store just minutes before closing time and asked him an interminable list of questions, then wound up buying nothing more than a dime's worth of nuts and bolts. And today, of all days! He was supposed to meet a certain young lady at the Keystone's restaurant, and he was already late.

Bobby began walking at a brisk pace down North Water. Maybe she would still be waiting for him when he got there. He'd been talking to Mary Caine, off and on, for several months now, always angling for an opportunity to spend some time with her somewhere other than the sidewalk in front of Mr. Matthews' store. And alone, instead of with the bevy of friends she always managed to have around her. Oh, she was a fine filly, Mary Caine was! And she could be so delightfully vague, yet promising at the same time. But finally, two days ago, he'd managed to wring from her an agreement to allow him to buy her dinner at the Keystone restaurant . . . and then this old biddy came in and dawdled around and made him late!

Bobby took the steps onto the Keystone porch two at a time

and hurried inside. He peered around the lobby long enough to satisfy himself that Mary Caine wasn't there, then went into the restaurant.

No luck. She wasn't there either, a barmaid told him, and she hadn't been there, as far as she could recall. Mary Caine had stood him up!

Thinking about what a fine how-do-you-do this was, Bobby ordered a mug of beer from the bar and paid his nickel. He went outside onto the porch and plopped down at a table, reflecting on the general flightiness of women and the transitory nature of their interests.

"Hello, Bobby. Mind if I join you?"

It was Arch Graham. Arch was about Bobby's age, but Bobby wouldn't normally have chosen to share a table with him. Arch was a big mouth, almost as bad a gossip as some of the girls. But it would have been rude to tell him he couldn't sit, so Bobby nodded toward one of the empty chairs. "Help yourself, Arch."

Arch sat down and set his beer in front of him. He hooked another chair with the heel of his shoe and dragged it over to prop up his feet. He gave an expansive sigh and took a long draught of beer, then clumped it down on the table and wiped his mouth with the back of his hand.

"Well, Bobby, how's the world treating you?"

"About the same, Arch."

"Bit warm for this time of year, wouldn't you say?"

Bobby nodded.

"Say, isn't that your sister's house, across the way, there?"

"Yep. Why do you ask?"

Arch scratched his chin. "Oh, nothing."

Bobby nodded and took a sip of beer.

"Just that my cousin and her husband live behind it there, across the alley, and she says there's been a lot of commotion going on there lately."

Bobby gave Arch a puzzled look. "Is that so? I don't know anything about it."

"Yeah, says that new fellow, barber ... what's his name? Works at Person's?"

"You mean Charlie Cobb?"

"That's the one. Says he comes and goes through the back gate, all hours of the day and night."

"Well, there must be some mistake, I'd say."

Arch looked at him, a smile playing around the corners of his lips. "I don't think so. My cousin, she keeps a pretty good eye on things, and she says Charlie Cobb comes around pretty regular."

"What are you trying to say, Arch?"

Arch held up his palms. "Hey, now, don't get riled at me, Bobby. I'm just telling you what I hear, is all."

"Well, how about you keep it to yourself, then? I don't care for the direction you seem to be heading." Bobby drained his beer and stood. "I'll be going now. Good day to you."

"Sorry, Bobby," Arch called after him. "Just telling you what I hear."

Bobby wasn't one for trouble, and he wasn't about to sit still and listen to the likes of Arch Graham poor-mouthing his family. Or Charlie Cobb, for that matter. As far as Bobby knew, Charlie was well-liked around town. He didn't see any reason to let Arch Graham's loose talk change that in his mind.

But the next day, as he was helping a customer up by the nail bins near the front of the store, he happened to glance out the front window and see his sister walking toward the square. Though he hated himself for it, the first thing that jumped into Bobby's mind was the memory of Arch's insinuations of the evening before. He watched Anna cross the square, and it looked to Bobby as if her bearing would take her directly toward Person's.

Nope. It's just Arch's loose jaw, is all it is. My sister wouldn't do something like that.

He put it out of his mind for the rest of the day, which wasn't too hard; the store was busy. Spring was coming on and everybody had little projects they were doing around the house. Add to that the farmers coming into town for this and that, and Bobby had plenty to keep himself occupied.

WALTER FELT HIMSELF SINKING into Charlie's barber chair. There was something very relaxing about being here in J. P.'s shop with its smell of bay rum, laced with tobacco smoke; the low, casual talk of the other men; and the expert way Charlie Cobb trimmed his hair. And it probably also had to do with the late-night house call Walter had made the night before, to one of his ear, nose, and throat patients. He'd been a little on the sleepy side all day, and now he kept having to fight his eyelids back open. It was a good thing Charlie could sense when his customers wanted to chat and when they just wanted to sit quietly for their haircut and shave. That was another thing that annoyed Walter about J. P.: no matter what, the garrulous older man would want to make conversation with anybody he had in his chair. So Walter had taken to only having Charlie cut his hair, even if it meant waiting a bit.

"Hey there, Doc. Just the man I wanted to see."

Walter cut his eyes around to see who had spoken to him. It was Bill Suggs, a fellow Mason. Walter suppressed the grimace he felt. "Hello, Bill."

"What time we leaving tomorrow evening?"

Oh, yes. Walter and Bill were scheduled to travel to the Claiborne lodge in Nashville to present guest lectures. Walter sagged with disappointment. Counting Bible study tonight, Thursday evening would have been the only night he'd have had at home since last Sunday. Oh, well . . .

"Let's see, Bill. How about if I pick you up in my car at about three? We need to be there by six to be in time for the dinner."

Suggs nodded. "What time do you think we'll be home? Mary'll ask me that, first thing."

Walter calculated. "If we don't have any bad luck, we ought to be back here by midnight, I guess."

Bill puffed out his cheeks. "Late night. Mary won't be happy."

Anna won't either, most likely.

"All right, then, Doc. I'll be ready. Three o'clock." Suggs nodded at J. P. and Charlie, then left.

"You sure do stay busy, Doc," Charlie said. "I don't know how you find time to do all you do."

Walter gave a little shrug. "I probably do too much."

BOBBY SMILED. Mary Caine was standing just inside the door of the Keystone lobby, and she was giving him that shy, happy look that he especially liked. Only this time she wasn't doing it from the center of a bunch of her friends. She was here to meet him for dinner, just the two of them, after which she'd promised him a walk around the courthouse square before he escorted her home.

"Hello, Mary," he said, tipping his hat to her.

"Hello, Robert."

"I'm sure glad we could find another time for this. And I'm sorry again about the other day."

She brushed his arm with her fingers. "That's all right. I understand."

"Well, would you like to go in and sit down?"

"You know what? It's so nice out today, why don't we sit on the porch?"

Bobby was a little disappointed; he'd been looking forward to the darker, quieter atmosphere inside the restaurant. "Well, sure," he said. "That sounds just fine. Let's go find a good table and then I'll go tell them we want to eat outside."

The porch wasn't too crowded today, which was good. Bobby located a table for two, well back under the wide porch, but still with a good view of the street. He had to admit, it was a very pleasant spring day. As long as Mary Caine was happy, he guessed he didn't have any reason to complain. Bobby really liked her. He'd been thinking about asking Walter if he could borrow the Winton Six sometime, to take Mary for a drive in the country.

He held her chair for her, then went back into the hotel to notify someone in the restaurant that he wanted to be served out on the porch. He came back and sat down across from Mary Caine. Out of habit, he'd given himself the chair that looked out toward the street.

"Well, how have you been?" he said.

"Just fine. My mother wasn't too happy about me meeting you down here, like this, but I told her 'Mother, I'm twenty years old and I know how to behave myself, and besides, Robert Dennis is a very nice young man.'"

"Well, my goodness! I hardly know what to say. I didn't know it was so hard for you to—"

"What? What is it, Robert?" Mary twisted around in her seat, trying to see what had suddenly distracted him.

"Oh, it's nothing, Mary. Never mind . . ."

But for the rest of the meal, Bobby worried over what he'd seen: Charlie Cobb, walking up the front sidewalk of Anna's house, knocking on the front door, and disappearing inside. After a few minutes, he came out, touched the brim of his derby, and went off north down Railroad Street.

What was Charlie Cobb doing at his sister's house? It was probably nothing, Bobby told himself—he was probably still stinging from Arch Graham's comment a few days ago. He tried his best to keep his mind on what Mary Caine was telling him about this and that, and he thought he mostly succeeded. But when they'd finished their meal, he had more than half a notion to cut short their stroll around the courthouse and take her straight home, then go to Anna's house and find out firsthand what errand had brought Charlie Cobb around.

ANNA TOOK the *Argosy* and quickly flipped through the pages. What was Charlie thinking, leaving it with Gertrude? Did the man know nothing? Fortunately for them both, Gertrude couldn't read, but what if she hadn't given the magazine to Anna, as Charlie had apparently told her, but to Walter instead? Ah . . . there it was.

> *Walter is speaking at an out-of-town Mason's meeting tom. nite. I must see you. All my love, C.*

21

"OH, I HOPE MRS. HICKERSON still has some of those ribbons,"
Mabel was saying. "They were so pretty in Dorothy's hair, and
I'm afraid they'll all be sold. Can't you hurry, Mama?" Mabel tugged
on Anna's hand as they neared Gladys Hickerson's fabric and notions
shop. "Hurry, Mama, please."

"Mabel, now just settle down," Anna said, smiling. "If they don't
have that ribbon, they'll have something else, and maybe Mrs. Hickerson can even order it for you."

Mabel made an impatient face at her mother and pulled the door
open. She started inside, then quickly stepped back and held the door
as Mrs. Baskerville came out of the store.

"Oh, hello, Mrs. Dotson," the attorney's wife said. "And Mabel,
how nice to see you," she said, smiling down at Mabel and cupping
her chin in a gloved hand.

"Good afternoon, Mrs. Baskerville," Anna said. "Lovely spring
weather we're having, isn't it?"

"Yes, quite nice. Mabel, are you helping your mother with shopping today?"

"Yes, ma'am. We're buying some ribbon. At least, I hope we are."
Mabel gave her mother a worried look.

Anna laughed. "Mabel has her heart set on something one of her friends wore to school today, and nothing would do except for us to come down here today."

Mrs. Baskerville gave Mabel an indulgent smile. "Well, sometimes we girls get in our heads what we want, don't we, Mabel?" She looked at Anna. "By the way, my husband mentioned to me the other day that he saw you in the barber shop, of all places."

Anna hoped her face didn't display the sudden drop her stomach had taken. "Person's? Oh . . . yes. I take my old *Argosy* magazines to the new man there. He takes them home to his wife."

"Mr. Cobb?"

"Yes, I believe that's his name."

Mabel gave her mother an odd look.

"How thoughtful," Mrs. Baskerville said. Her eyes lingered a few seconds on Mabel. "Well, I'd better be getting along. I hope you find your ribbon, dear," she said, giving Mabel a quick smile.

"Yes, good day, Mrs. Baskerville," Anna said.

They went into the store. Mabel hurried to one of the glass display cases. "Oh, good. Here it is, Mama. Come see. Mama? Mama! Why aren't you coming?"

Anna realized she was peering out the shop window, watching Mrs. Baskerville walk away. She quickly turned toward her daughter. "Sorry, dear. Show me the ribbon."

WALTER PUSHED BACK from the table and patted his belly. "My, my. Anna, that was the most delicious pork chop I've had in a long time."

"Thank you, Walter. It was one of the recipes that Daisy gave me. She's a real good cook."

"Daisy Cobb?" Bobby said, giving his sister a quick look.

"Yes. Mr. Cobb from the barbershop—his wife."

Bobby looked away.

"Well, I believe I'll lie down for a little while before the business meeting," Walter said, stretching lazily. "Bobby, sure glad you could join us."

"Thank you, Walter," Bobby said, still looking somewhere else.

"Mabel, Scott . . . time for Sunday afternoon naps."

"But, Mama, I . . ."

Anna lifted an index finger and gave her son a no-nonsense look.

"Yes, ma'am," he mumbled.

"Come on, Scottie," Mabel said. "I'll read to you until we get sleepy."

"Don't call me 'Scottie,'" he said, slouching after his sister.

Anna picked up the meat platter and turned toward the kitchen. "I'll help you, Sis," Bobby said, pushing back his chair.

They cleared the table, stacking the plates beside the sink. Anna removed the tablecloth, carried it to the backyard, and shook the crumbs into the grass, then came back in and smoothed the white, embroidered linen back into place on the table. She went into the kitchen and Bobby was leaning against the counter by the sink with his arms crossed, looking at her. She gave him a questioning expression.

"Anna, I have to talk to you about something."

"Well, all right. What is it?"

"It's just that . . . I've been hearing things around, and . . ."

"What kinds of things." Anna could feel her pulse quickening. She told herself to settle down and not do or say anything foolish. She picked up a plate with what she hoped was a casual air and turned on the water. She picked up a cloth and started scrubbing in circular motions.

"A little while ago, when you said Daisy Cobb's name . . ." Bobby began.

Anna's scrubbing motions quickened, became smaller.

"I see you going into Person's sometimes," Bobby said, not looking at her. "Without Scott. Why do you do that?"

Anna realized she was rubbing the plate so hard her fingernails were white. She took a deep breath and made herself give her brother a puzzled, slightly hurt look. "Why are you acting this way, Bobby?

Yes, I go into Person's. Mr. Cobb's wife likes to read my old *Argosy* magazines, and I drop them off there when I'm finished with them, so he can take them home to her. The Cobbs are our friends, and Daisy doesn't know many people in town yet. I'm trying to be nice to her. Why should that be anyone else's concern?"

He held her eyes a few seconds, then looked at the floor. He shoved his hands into his pockets. "I don't know. I just . . . People say things, and you're my sister, and . . ."

"And I appreciate you coming to me," she said, turning back to the plate. She ran water over it, rinsing it, and set it facedown on a clean dish towel she had spread on the other side of the sink. "But you really can't allow yourself to let people's loose lips make you so suspicious." She picked up another plate and started scrubbing. "It's unbecoming," she said.

Bobby nodded. "I'm sorry, Anna. I just . . ."

"I know, Bobby. It's all right."

"Well. I guess I'll go on home now."

"All right, Bobby. Glad you could come over."

"Um-hmm."

"And don't forget Mabel's recital on Thursday. You are coming?"

"Yeah, I'll be there."

Anna heard him shuffle out of the kitchen, then heard the front door open and close. She washed the lunch dishes, trying hard to think about something besides the lie she had just told her younger brother. How much longer could this go on? How much longer before she or Charlie made a fatal slip, and their illicit affair was out in the open for all to see?

Anna's head was starting to hurt. She decided to finish the dishes, then go lie down herself for a while.

MABEL WAS STANDING at center stage, fidgeting a bit as her teacher consulted her program. "And now, ladies and gentlemen, Mabel

Dotson will give a recital of Mr. Henry Holcomb Bennett's poem, 'The Flag Goes By.'" She gave Mabel a smile and an encouraging pat on the shoulder, then moved aside.

> *"Hats off!*
> *Along the street there comes*
> *A blare of bugles, a ruffle of drums.*
> *A flash of color beneath the sky:*
> *Hats off!*
> *The flag is passing by . . ."*

Mabel said her lines, staring the whole time out one of the side windows of the school and fiddling with the sash of her dress. She stumbled over one or two words, and her delivery was more deadpan than anything else. Still, Bobby had to admit, his niece got through all six verses of the poem without losing her place. When she finished, the audience of parents and relatives gave her a nice round of applause. She started back to her seat, but then, catching her teacher's eye, she stopped herself long enough to give a quick curtsey.

"She did just fine," Bobby said to Anna. She nodded, smiling. On the other side of her, Walter was beaming.

Someone across the aisle was leaning forward, face turned in their direction. Bobby realized it was Charlie Cobb. He saw Bobby looking at him, pointed toward the stage and mouthed the words, "Smart girl." Bobby nodded his thanks and Charlie sat back in his seat.

Cobb's wife was beside him, fanning herself with the assembly program. Bobby looked at the two of them for a moment, then consulted his program. Next was a group of very small girls, who would be singing "Mary Had a Little Lamb." Bobby was most interested in the name of the accompanist for the piece: Miss Mary Caine. He looked up at the stage and, sure enough, Mary was taking her place behind the big, dark upright piano. He smiled, hoping she'd look out and see him watching her, but she was too busy arranging the music in front of her and adjusting the piano bench.

The girls filed out and lined up unevenly, waiting for their teacher to lead them. He felt Anna moving beside him and saw something out of the corner of his eye; it was Charlie Cobb again, leaning forward to look across the aisle and motioning toward the stage. Anna and Walter were nodding and smiling at him, and Anna leaned over to whisper to Bobby that the Cobbs' daughter, Alice, was standing in the front row, about to sing with the group.

Anna pointed Alice out to him, and Bobby thought the poor little girl had a stricken expression on her face, as if she were about to cry. But the teacher came and stood in front of her, Mary played the introduction, and the girls started to sing.

When the program was over, there was a reception outside on the school lawn, which stretched beneath a stand of large elms, hickories, and chestnuts. A table was set up, and some of the parents had set out cups of lemonade and plates of cookies. It was a nice evening, and not quite dark yet. Bobby stood with Anna and Walter and made small talk with the parents and relatives who had come to the program. He kept hoping Mary Caine would happen along, but so far it was only relatives and parents—aside from the handful of boys that kept raiding the cookie tray when nobody was looking.

"Well, summer is almost here," someone said.

"Seems to me like it's already arrived, hot as it's getting," Walter said, to general agreement.

Charlie Cobb came strolling up, his wife trailing a step or two behind him. "Real nice program, wasn't it?" he said, shaking hands with the men in the group. "Real nice. Our kids all did just fine, I thought."

Bobby watched Anna, but she didn't act any differently at Cobb's approach than she had with any of the other men who were standing around. Maybe it really was all in his mind, he told himself. He hated himself for even suspecting his sister of such things.

Daisy Cobb looked a little uncomfortable, over on the edge of the group, and Bobby decided to try to make some conversation with her. As the main group continued exchanging comments on the program, the weather, and whatnot, Bobby moved around toward Daisy and gave her a smile. "I thought I saw Alice running with my niece a few minutes ago, chasing some boy."

Daisy smiled and ducked her head. "Oh, there's no telling. If Mabel told her to jump off the top of the courthouse, Alice would probably give it a try."

Bobby chuckled. "Her group did a nice job on the song, tonight."

"Yes, I reckon."

A quiet moment slid past. "Say, Anna told me she's been bringing you some of her magazines to read. I guess you've been enjoying those?"

Daisy got a puzzled look. "Do what, now? Magazines? Sometimes Anna sends me postcards, but never magazines."

Bobby nodded. "Anna says she takes them to Charlie, down at the shop to bring to you."

"No . . . I don't . . ." She looked like someone trying to do hard arithmetic in her head. In a moment, she gave Bobby a weak grin. "Knowing Charlie, he either took a notion to read them all himself first or just plumb forgot to bring them home."

Bobby did his best to give her an agreeing laugh, but he had a sinking feeling in his chest. He made a few more attempts at small talk, then excused himself from the group. He walked quickly away across the schoolhouse lawn and he didn't look back.

The next day, Bobby saw Walter walking across the town square, headed for his office. Hating himself for what he was about to do, he asked Emil to watch the counter for a while, then walked out to intercept his brother-in-law.

"Hello, Bobby. How's the hardware business today?" Walter said.

"Walter, I have to talk to you."

Walter looked at him closely once they were in his office. "What's the matter, Bobby? You look like you just heard some awfully bad news."

Bobby opened and closed his mouth a couple of times, then dragged his eyes toward Walter's. "It's Anna, Walter. I think she might be carrying on behind your back. With Charlie Cobb."

Walter looked at Bobby as if he'd just been slapped.

"What in the world are you talking about, Bobby?"

"Walter, this is hard for me, too, can't you see that? It's my sister we're talking about."

"Anna . . . and Charlie Cobb? How is that possible?"

Bobby groped for words. "It . . . it just is, Walter. I didn't believe it either, at first, and then I started to notice all the times she went into Person's. What business does my sister have, going into a barbershop three or four times a week?"

Walter remembered Aloysius Hix's comment at the New Year's Eve party. "Going in to J. P.'s . . . She takes magazines to Charlie so he can give them to Daisy."

Bobby told Walter about talking to Daisy after the end-of-school program, and about how she knew nothing about any magazines. Walter started shaking his head slowly from side to side.

"Yes, and that's not all, Walter. Ask her about the candle."

"Candle? What candle?"

"The one she burns in her window on nights when you're away. Arch Graham's cousin lives across the alley from you, Walter. She's seen it. I've talked to her, myself."

Walter shook his head. "I knew she wasn't herself for a while, but lately she's been better . . ."

"She's playing you for a fool, Walter." Bobby felt tears stinging his eyes. "You've got to talk to her. You've got to lay down the law."

• • •

WALTER WORRIED OVER BOBBY'S WORDS for several days. He didn't want to believe his brother-in-law was seeing things the right way, but something was nagging him inside, like a sore tooth that wouldn't go away.

On the first Saturday after the end of the school term, Walter, Anna, and the children were driving down North Water Street, on their way to Westmoreland to visit his parents. It was a beautiful day and not too hot, and the twenty or so miles on quiet country roads seemed like a treat for everyone—especially Scott, who didn't get to ride in the car nearly as much as he wished.

As they neared downtown, Walter saw a familiar figure walking along the side of the road; it was Charlie Cobb. He slowed the car and pulled over to the curb beside Charlie, who looked over his shoulder and gave them a friendly wave.

"Hello, Doc," he said, leaning his elbows on the top of Walter's door. "Nice day for a drive."

Walter smiled and nodded. "Yes, we thought so. We're taking a little outing to Westmoreland, where my parents live."

Charlie touched the brim of his hat and smiled across at Anna. "Mrs. Dotson," he said.

She's playing you for a fool . . . Going into J. P.'s . . .

"Say, Charlie, I don't suppose you'd like to ride with us?" Walter heard himself say.

Charlie looked surprised. "Well, I . . . You know, I believe I would! If it wouldn't put you to any trouble."

"Of course not. Climb in . . . No, don't sit in the backseat. Come up front with Anna and me. I want to show you how this automobile works."

Anna was uncharacteristically quiet as they drove out of town. They reached Westmoreland in a little over an hour, and Walter's parents, though a bit surprised to see someone with Walter and Anna besides the children, soon were laughing at one of Charlie's jokes as if they'd known him for years.

After a lunch of cold fried chicken, corn bread, and chowchow, they all loaded back into the Winton Six for the drive back to Gallatin. As they came out of a curve at the bottom of a hill, Walter braked the car.

"I heard this little tract here might come up for sale sometime soon," he said. "I'd like to stretch my legs a little bit, anyway. How about it? Anybody want to come look at some real estate with me?"

Scott and Mabel were eager for any chance to escape the confinement of the small backseat, but Anna demurred. "It looks muddy," she said. "I've got on my new shoes."

"That's fine," Walter said, "You can just wait in the car."

"I'll stay with Anna," Charlie said. "This stretch of road is kind of lonesome."

Walter nodded. He got out of the car and set off behind the children, who had already jumped the small roadside ditch and were kiting across the rolling pasture that fronted the road.

When he judged he'd walked far enough, Walter called to Mabel and Scott. "You two run on for a little bit. I need to find some bushes."

Mabel giggled. "You should have used Grandma and Grandpa's privy before we left," she said.

Walter smiled and waved at her; she spun to catch up with her younger brother.

Walter doubled back toward a small tree line at the edge of the field closest to the road, behind the car. Reaching the copse, he slipped along as quietly as he could until he had the Winton in view.

Charlie and Anna were kissing.

Walter felt his heart leaving him. So it was true. He tried to look again, but couldn't bear it. Besides, there was no mistaking the passion between the two of them.

His wife was betraying him. Walter was a cuckold. *She's playing you for a fool . . . a fool . . . a fool . . .*

Somehow, he collected himself and got the children back to the car. For the rest of the drive, he had to fight the constriction in his throat—part rage and part utter desperation. He did his best to keep up a stream of small talk, but found it harder and harder. For some reason, though, Anna had now found her tongue. She chattered like a schoolgirl. In a way, Walter was glad, since he had no stomach for talking to either Charlie Cobb or his adulterous wife. *Maybe her little dose of Charlie loosened her reserve,* Walter thought angrily.

22

THE HEELS OF ANNA'S NEW SHOES clicked up the walk toward Mrs. Baskerville's front door. She hadn't meant to be late today, but she guessed the other women were already here. *Oh, well . . .* She tapped at the door and Mrs. Baskerville's servant let her in. Anna could hear the other women's voices coming from the parlor, and she hurried across the foyer at the foot of the stairs, hoping she hadn't missed too much gossip.

When Anna stepped through the doorway into the parlor, a sudden hush fell. The other women all looked at her, and their expressions were exactly like that of the cat who'd swallowed the canary. After a few awkward seconds, Mrs. Baskerville forced a little smile. "Mrs. Dotson. We weren't sure you were coming."

"Well, why would you think that?" Anna said, moving toward the tea service and selecting a cup and saucer. "I'm sorry to be late, but I decided to get caught up on my letters after the children left for school."

She poured herself some tea and sat down, but something was wrong. The other ladies weren't looking at her anymore, but the way they weren't looking at her made her feel as if they were still staring at her. Anna looked at Elizabeth, but even her best friend wouldn't meet her eyes. Instead, Elizabeth looked as if she'd just tasted something foul.

"Anna," Mrs. Olmstead said finally, "I . . . that is, we—the other ladies and I—feel it is our duty to ask if there is any basis in fact to the disturbing rumors about town concerning you and Mr. Cobb, down at Person's Barbershop."

Anna felt her mouth dropping open. "I'm not sure I know what you mean," she said.

"Not sure?" she heard someone mutter.

"It is being said that you and Mr. Cobb are . . . involved. Romantically. In an illicit relationship," Mrs. Olmstead said, pronouncing the words as if she were afraid speaking them might taint her lips. "Is it true?"

Anna closed her eyes and took several deep breaths. "Absolutely not," she said in as firm a voice as she could manage. "Mr. and Mrs. Cobb are our friends. We frequently have them to dinner at our house. Our children play together. Such talk is preposterous."

Mrs. Baskerville was looking at her as if she smelled something disagreeable. "Preposterous?" she said. "Why, my husband says you're in the barbershop two or three times a week, making cow eyes at that Cobb man."

"Mrs. Baskerville, let's keep our speech ladylike," Mrs. Olmstead said.

"How many times must I say this?" Anna said. "Not that it's anyone else's business, but I take back issues of my magazines to Mr. Cobb so that he can take them to his wife, who enjoys reading them but can't afford the subscription."

"Why don't you just take them to her at her house during the day?" Mrs. Oldham said. "That would be more seemly."

"Person's is conveniently located," Anna said.

"No doubt of that," Mrs. Pardue muttered. Mrs. Olmstead gave her a hard look.

"Anna," Mrs. Olmstead said, "I sincerely hope that it's as you say. But I must tell you that several sources in our town contradict your story. It's our Christian duty to—"

Anna stood. "I will not stay here and listen to any more insinuations! Good day, ladies." She half-flung her cup and saucer at the low table, spilling most of the contents. She strode out of the room, biting back the sob that threatened to spill from her throat.

Elizabeth caught up with her on the walk outside. "Anna! Wait! Anna, please."

Anna wheeled around. "What is it? Are you going to follow me home?"

"Anna, is it true? You have to tell me; I'm your friend."

"I'm quite sure I have no idea what they're talking about in there."

Elizabeth Jennings stood with her arms crossed and a wary expression on her face. "Anna, the ladies in the tea aren't the only ones talking about it. People are talking about it when they come into the gallery. It's all over town. Why, my husband even hears the men discussing it. They say you're in J. P.'s barbershop every other day, passing things to him."

"Magazines that I've read, and I'm giving them to him to take to his wife! Weren't you listening?"

Elizabeth shook her head. "They say you look at him, Anna. They say it's not just a casual glance when you do it."

Anna shook her head. "I cannot believe my best friend is actually believing such lies."

"Are they lies, Anna? I want to believe that, I truly do. But after some of the things you said to me last summer, the way you reacted, I . . . I just don't know."

"If I was carrying on an affair, would I talk so openly to you about it?"

"No, you wouldn't Anna. You'd deny it. Just as you're doing now."

Anna couldn't think of anything else to say. She simply turned and walked away.

So ... this was behind the strange looks she'd been getting in town lately. This was behind the cool tone of Mrs. Olmstead and Mrs. Baskerville, the way they looked at each other every time Anna said something, as if agreeing again on something they'd previously settled. Anna had been tried and convicted in the silent court of their opinion. It infuriated her, all the more so because there was nothing she could do about it.

Anna wondered what Walter knew, or suspected. She tried to figure out what she ought to do. She walked home, and every time she passed people on the street, she felt as if they were staring at her behind her back, pointing and snickering to each other. *That's Charlie Cobb's whore! That's the doctor's wife, the one who's carrying on with that barber!*

She went inside and straight up to her room. She paced back and forth, frantic to think of a way to get herself out of this mess. She stopped for a moment and studied the windowsill beside her bed, stained with the wax of the candles she'd lit to summon Charlie to her bed on the nights when Walter was away.

Anna went to her writing desk. She found some paper, a pen, and ink, and scribbled a note to Charlie. She told him that things were getting out of hand; that people all over town were starting to talk, and what would they do when word got back to Walter, as it surely must, very soon? She informed him that she intended to strictly stay away from the barbershop until things quieted down, and advised him to avoid being seen anywhere near the vicinity of her house. She folded the note and put it in an envelope, then scrabbled through her desk for a postage stamp. She would walk down to the post office and mail this to Charlie Cobb's box, and pray that for once, he would listen to her.

CHARLIE READ ANNA'S NOTE, leaning up against the wall in the post office. He grinned, and pushed his bowler back on his head. Well, well, well! His little bird was singing a different tune, wasn't she? So folks in town were starting to talk. Wasn't that just too bad?

Charlie knew what Anna was thinking. She was all worried about fouling her nest with Walter, about losing the way of life to which she'd become accustomed. She wanted to rid herself of the inconvenience of Charlie, now that things were getting a little hot.

Well, we'll just have to see about that. I may not be ready to just fold my tent and ride off into the desert. I may decide I like what I've got, and I might be willing to do something about it.

Charlie looked at the note one last time before crumpling it in his fist and dropping it into the wastebasket. He walked out of the post office, whistling.

"THANK YOU," Anna said, dropping the embroidery thread into her pocketbook. She walked out of the store, ignoring the smirk on the clerk's face.

She needed to get home. It had gotten so that she could hardly stand to show her face in town. But Anna's stubborn streak wouldn't allow her to just lock herself away in her room. No, if she did that it was as good as an admission of guilt. She had to keep up her normal routine, and look people in the eye, and dare anyone to say anything to her face. Besides, she hadn't seen Charlie Cobb since mailing him the note, a few days ago.

Her heart began to betray her, causing her to contemplate the rest of her life without Charlie's passion, his adoration of her body, his lovemaking. But she firmly closed the door on that line of thinking. *I have to get on with my life—for my children's sake, if nothing else.*

As she approached the house, someone got up from one of the tables on the porch of the Keystone Hotel and began sauntering across the street to intercept her. It was Charlie Cobb!

"What are you doing?" she hissed, keeping her face turned away from him as she neared her front gate. "Get away from me. Everyone will see."

"Will they, my darling? And what will they see? Two people, talking in the middle of the street, in the full light of day. What could be more innocent than that?"

"You know what I mean. The whole town is talking."

Charlie Cobb laughed—actually laughed! "Oh, yes. That must be terrible for you."

"Get away from me," she said, and turned toward her gate.

He stepped in front of her, barring her way. "Listen to me, Anna. You want me, and you know you do. And I want you. And Dr. High-and-Mighty Walter isn't doing his duty by you, and you damned well know it. I'm not going away, Anna. I'll have you . . . and you know I'm telling you the truth." He held her eyes for a moment, then turned and walked away.

Anna could hardly breathe. The insolence! The callous disregard! And yet, as she walked toward her front porch, a part of her mind relished the sound of his words: "I'm not going away . . . I'll have you . . ." *What is wrong with me? I must actually be losing my mind!*

She went inside, unpinning her hat and laying it on the side table in the vestibule. She went upstairs to her room.

Walter was sitting on the side of her bed, staring at her windowsill. At the stain left by night after night of melted candle wax.

He looked up at her like someone who had had a piece of flesh cut away with a dull blade.

"Anna, is it true?" he said.

"What's the matter, Walter? You look terrible."

He gave her a tired smile. "You know, those are the first words of concern you've spoken to me in . . . oh, I can't remember how long. Isn't that interesting?"

"Walter, what are you doing home at this time of the day? Don't you have patients?"

"Do you want to tell me about this here?" he said, aiming his chin at the windowsill.

"What?"

"Looks like there's been a candle burning here, Anna." He looked at her. "Some kind of signal?"

"Why would it be a signal? I just like candlelight, sometimes. It helps me relax."

"Anna, your eyes are looking everywhere in the room but at me. Either you're making up lines to say, or you're lying. Or both."

"Walter, I don't know what you're talking about."

"Don't you?" He got up from the bed and walked toward her, and Anna realized that for the very first time in her life, she was afraid of him.

"I forbid you to have anything further to do with Charlie Cobb." A pained look crossed his face when he said Charlie's name. He looked away. "And to think I befriended him! Wanted to have him join the lodge . . ." He tugged his eyes back to her. "You've disgraced me, Anna, and disgraced yourself. The only thing for you to do now is to admit your sin and ask forgiveness. And never see Charlie Cobb again."

"I don't need forgiveness, Walter. I haven't done anything wrong." Anna surprised herself; the way she said the words, she almost believed them herself.

He looked at her, and for a moment, she thought maybe he was going to hit her. But he didn't. Instead, he slumped away from her, past her, through her doorway. "The children will be home soon," he said. "I expect you'll want to be ready for them." He walked away, down the hall. Anna heard his footsteps descending the stairs, as slow and dragging as someone walking behind a coffin.

WHEN CHARLIE ARRIVED HOME, the first thing he saw was Daisy, standing on the other side of the kitchen table, staring at him and holding the last issue of *Argosy*.

"What's this?" she said in her dumbfounded, bleating voice.

He paused for a second or two, then stepped past her on the way to their bedroom. "What does it look like? It's a magazine. You ought to read it, sometime. It's got some good stories in it."

"I been reading it. There's things in here in your handwriting. And someone else's."

"Well, what gives you the right to be pawing around in my personal things, anyway?" he said, rounding on her and half-shouting. He saw Alice, cowering in the corner behind her mother, but right then he didn't care. "That was put up among my underthings. You had no call to go snooping around in my things."

"Anna's brother, Bobby, he told me back before school was out. He said Anna was bringing magazines to you at the shop—for me. He said she told him you were bringing them home for me to read. But you ain't, are you, Charlie? You never meant for me to know about them, did you?"

"Daisy, what in the world are you—"

"It's Anna, ain't it, Charlie? I seen the way you look at her. I know you, Charlie. I know you look at other women, you always have. It's Anna, ain't it?"

"I don't know what you're talking about!" He slammed the bedroom door. He yanked the hat off his head and threw it into the corner. He stomped around the room with his hands on his hips. First Anna, and now Daisy! That was the thing about women: Either they didn't want to have anything to do with you, or they thought they owned you.

He went to the corner and retrieved his hat, jamming it onto his head. He flung open the bedroom door and stalked past Alice and Daisy. "I'm going out for some fresh air. I don't know when I'll be back."

Charlie walked quickly into the night air, trying to decide whether he was angrier at Daisy or Anna. He thought about the note Anna had left in the last magazine—probably read by Daisy. *So Anna wants to let things cool off awhile? Well, she might find out she'll have a harder time waiting for me than I'll have waiting for her.* Charlie felt a grin starting across his face—a hard grin. He wasn't ready to quit the game—not by a long shot.

23

"WHEN GOD CREATED ADAM AND EVE and instituted the sacred bond of marriage," Brother Olmstead said, "he intended that both parties in the covenant regard that relationship as sacred. And when our Lord walked among us, he held up no less a standard. 'If any man looketh on a woman to lust after her,' he said in the Sermon on the Mount, 'he hath committed adultery already with her in his heart.'"

Anna felt her face burning. If every eye in the church wasn't on her, she felt certain every mind was. Brother Olmstead might as well have gotten down from the pulpit, walked down the aisle, and pointed at her in her seat as he preached.

She didn't know how much longer she could hold on, with things the way they were. Everywhere she went, she felt accused, stared at, and ridiculed. Walter wouldn't as much as look at her, except to assure himself, several times a day, that she was where she said she'd be and that she wasn't within a hundred feet of Charlie Cobb. She hadn't been to a meeting of the ladies' tea since the fiasco just before midsummer, and she had been put on notice that her presence wasn't welcome. Mrs. Olmstead had come to the house, her back and her expression as stiff as a ramrod, and given Anna a sermonette about confession being good for the soul, and how the best thing to do when we'd made a mistake was to admit it and move on with life in a suitably contrite manner. Anna thanked her for her concern and assured her that if she had anything to confess, she'd let her know. Since then, none of the ladies would have anything to do with her, except Elizabeth Jennings. And even Elizabeth's company wasn't the balm it used to be. There was so much unspoken between them that they could hardly converse around the shouting silence.

The only time Anna felt anything approaching peace was when she was with Mabel and Scott. Mercifully, her children didn't seem to know anything about the scandal surrounding their mother, or if they did, they gave no evidence. Helping Mabel with her homework or reading to Scott in his bed at night, Anna realized how precious her children were to her. If anything happened to take them away from her, she knew her life wouldn't be worth living.

Because of her work with the women's suffrage movement, Anna knew she had virtually no rights if Walter decided to divorce her. If she could be found to have had an adulterous relationship, no court in Tennessee would permit her to keep custody of her children. Since the house was titled in Walter's name, she would be forced to rely on whatever he chose to give her.

And so, Anna continued to deny everything in public and berate herself in private. And the maddening thing was, she still missed Charlie Cobb. Though it was certainly true that he had helped her reduce her life to a shambles, it was also true that he was maybe the only person in the world who was in no position to judge her. Shame and guilt were corrosive when pent up in a human heart, as Anna knew all too well. With Charlie, she didn't need to feel shame or guilt—or at least it could be shared. That was better than nothing.

Brother Olmstead preached on, and Anna did her best to allow the words to go past her ears without stopping. She kept her face composed and her eyes straight ahead; she wore her denial like a suit of armor. It was about all she had left. Anna hoped it would be enough.

BOBBY GRUNTED as he turned the crank of the Winton Six. The engine tried to catch, but died. He rested a few seconds, then gave it another go. This time the engine caught well enough for him to hurry around to the driver's side and switch the ignition from the battery to the coil. He got in and wrestled the automobile into reverse gear and started backing out of Walter's driveway.

It was a little cool for a drive in the country, maybe, but he had finally talked Mary Caine into the notion and he wasn't about to postpone the outing. With all the gossip in town surrounding his sister, Bobby was surprised Mary would still have anything to do with him. If the novelty of motoring was what it took to stay in her good graces, then Bobby was just grateful his brother-in-law, amid all the worry over his errant wife, was still kind enough to loan the use of his car. In fact, it was almost as if he wasn't really thinking about it when Bobby asked him. He had sort of glanced at Bobby and waved in assent, as if somebody else driving his car wasn't worth considering for more than a few seconds. Which, with everything going on in his life right now, it probably wasn't.

Bobby was upset, too. He had always admired his older sister. He remembered the first time she'd brought Walter to their parents' home, in Lafayette. He'd viewed Walter with mistrust at first—how could he be good enough for Anna? But he'd come to admire his brother-in-law very much over the years. It was so hard to imagine that his sister, who had the same parents and the same teaching Bobby had, could do something so crass and bring such shame upon herself.

Well, maybe a drive in the country with Mary Caine was just what he needed, too. Anything to take his mind off the mess his sister was in. Bobby eased the stick into low gear and cautiously let out the clutch. After a lurch or two, the Winton Six set off down the street toward Mary Caine's house.

CHARLIE REACHED his hidden vantage point just as Walter's car backed out of the driveway. He quickly crouched down low so a random glance from Walter as he drove away wouldn't betray Charlie's presence.

Good. He'd been waiting for a chance like this for a while now. Looked like the good doctor was off again on one of his Masonic junkets. Just the time for Charlie to go in and remind Anna of why and how much she still needed him. She could give him the public cold shoulder all she wanted; he could see in her eyes that it was just an act. She was afraid of what Walter would do, or what the community would do, maybe. Charlie didn't care about any of that. He wanted Anna Dotson, and he'd gotten used to having her, and nobody was going to dismiss him until he was good and ready to go on his own account.

Charlie pulled his overcoat closer around him. The north wind was a little more crisp than was strictly comfortable. A litter of fallen leaves covered the backyard underneath the big elm tree beside the cistern. Glancing once more up and down the alley and all around to make sure no prying eyes were about, Charlie opened the back gate and crossed the yard toward the back door.

He knocked, hoping the meddlesome maid wouldn't be the one who answered. And when the door opened, he smiled. His luck was holding; Anna stood there.

"Hello, my love. I've been missing you, and I just had to see you."

"Don't you think you've done enough damage already?"

He imitated a hurt look. "Damage? I thought we loved each other, Anna."

"Do I have to draw you a picture, Charlie? Everyone knows. If anyone sees us, even talking together like this, I'm ruined."

"No, you aren't. Come away with me, Anna. We'll go somewhere—Texas, maybe. We'll start a new life, our own life. We'll have children. We'll be together, as we should be."

She looked at him, and Charlie convinced himself there was something like interest behind her eyes. "You'd do that? Leave Daisy and Alice and run away with me?"

Charlie nodded. "Just say the word." *Uh-oh. Might have gone a little too far with that last bit. Oh, well. Let's just see what she says.*

She turned her head, took in a deep breath and let it out. She shook her head. "It won't work, Charlie. I can't leave my children. You can surely understand that, at least. And besides, how could I ever trust you, or you me? Every time I looked at you, I'd have to remember that the only reason we were together is because we both broke promises we made to other people."

He gave a disappointed look. "I've always trusted you, Anna. How can you say I haven't? But, listen . . . can't we try again? What we have is so amazing, so wonderful. We can be more careful. Nobody will ever have to know."

And then, they both heard the sound of the front door opening, followed by Walter's voice: "Anna? Where are you?"

Her eyes rounded with fear. "Get out of here!" she hissed.

Charlie ran toward the back gate and down the alley. What was Walter doing here? Hadn't he seen him pull out of the driveway?

WALTER CAME INTO THE KITCHEN just as Anna was closing the door and turning around. "What are you doing home, Walter?"

He stared at her, then took a quick look into the backyard. "I took a break; I was tired. I was going to come home and lie down for a minute, and . . ." He gave her a close look. "Anna, something is going on. I can tell by the way you're looking at me, the way your eyes are darting back and forth."

"No, Walter. I just went into the backyard for some fresh air. I was coming back inside when you walked in." Even she could hear the tremor in her voice.

"You're lying." He strode toward her and grabbed her by the shoulders. "Tell me the truth, Anna! He was here, wasn't he? That damned bastard was back here, in my house, and you let him in, didn't you? After I forbade you."

"No, Walter, I—"

Yes, you did!" He pushed her away from him and it was all Anna could do to keep her feet. Walter ran to the vestibule and pounded up the stairs.

"Walter! What are you doing?"

He came back down a few seconds later, and Anna's heart froze when she saw the gun in his hand. She grabbed his arms. "Walter, no! No! Don't do this, you can't do this!"

He shoved her against the banister. "Get away from me, you whore. You're not in any position to tell me what I can and can't do." He strode to the front door, pulled it open, and was gone.

Anna fell in a heap in the middle of the vestibule. Her husband was on his way to kill her lover and very well might come back and finish her, as well. Her children would be rendered as good as orphans.

Oh, God! There must be some way out of this.

She wept until she had no tears left. She pulled herself upright and dragged herself to the settee in the parlor to wait for Walter's return and whatever it might bring.

There was only one thing left for her to do, she finally decided: Tell Walter the truth, convince him of her sincere resolution to change, and beg him not to commit any violence that might get him sent to prison. She was so weighted down with guilt and remorse; she didn't think she could live if she also had to bear responsibility for driving her husband to commit murder.

• • •

CHARLIE WENT INTO HIS HOUSE and closed the door. His heart was still pounding from the close call, but he was talking to himself, settling himself down. *No harm done. He never saw me. Just lie low for a while, and then—*

Daisy came into the front room. "What's wrong, Charlie? You look like you've had a fright."

Charlie was about to answer her when he heard the sound of feet pounding on the front porch, quickly followed by a fist hammering at the door. He opened the door to find Walter Dotson with a gun pointed at Charlie's chest. Charlie raised his hands, and fought the instinct to back up.

"Walter, now listen. You don't want to do this."

Walter grabbed the front of Charlie's shirt and dragged him out onto the porch. He shoved him against a post and jabbed the cold, blue barrel of his pistol up under Charlie's jaw.

"Give me one reason why I shouldn't blow your brains all over the front door of your house," Walter said from between clenched teeth. "You've been fornicating with my wife, and you've ruined her reputation and probably mine, too. I ought to kill you right now, you son of a bitch."

Charlie fought to control his breathing. "You don't want to do that, Walter. You've got it all wrong. There's nothing—"

Walter savagely thrust the gun barrel upward. "Shut up with your lies, do you hear me? At least have enough respect for me not to think you're going to sell me any more of your lies."

The muzzle of the gun made it impossible for Charlie to talk. All he could do was give a little, quick nod.

"All right." Walter eased the gun away from his neck, but kept it pointed between his eyes. "Now you listen to me. You've got until tonight to get out of Gallatin. I'd shoot you now, but you've got a wife and daughter who deserve some consideration. But come dawn, if I see you, I'll kill you. Do you understand?"

Charlie nodded again. His eyes flickered toward the crowd of on-lookers that was starting to gather in the street behind Walter. He hoped they were listening to the threats coming out of Walter's mouth. He wished somebody would go call a constable.

"I want you to get out of here and go somewhere a long way from here, somewhere out of reach. I don't ever want to cross paths with you again, or hear of anybody I know crossing paths with you. You're a no-good, low-down, cheating bastard, and you'd better listen to me when I tell you I'll kill you if I run into you again. I know the sheriff in this county, and he'll believe me when I tell him I acted in self-defense to kill a sorry, wife-stealing scum. I won't even spend the night in jail. Understand?"

Charlie nodded, his eyes moving steadily from the dark circle at the opening of the gun barrel to Walter's face.

"This will be the last conversation you and I will ever have. Next time I see you, I won't say anything. I'll just shoot you."

Walter backed away from Charlie, keeping him covered with the pistol. When he reached the sidewalk, he turned after giving Charlie a final, glaring look, and walked away. The crowd parted to let Walter through. Charlie watched him until the slope took him out of sight.

"You all heard what he said to me! You're witnesses. He threatened to kill me."

The people started walking away. No one would look at Charlie.

"You're my witnesses, I said!"

He went inside. Daisy and Alice were in the middle of the room. Alice was crying into her mother's apron, and Daisy was comforting her daughter as best she could. She was staring at Charlie with a stricken expression. "I told you, Charlie. I knew it was Anna. I knew it. What are we going to do now?"

"Be quiet and let me think," Charlie said. He paced the width of the room a few times, running his hands through his hair. Daisy watched him with big, fearful eyes.

"You and Alice better go to your folks," he said finally. "I'll put you on the train this afternoon."

"What are you going to do? You're not going to fight Walter, are you? Don't get yourself killed, Charlie. Don't make me a widow, not now."

"I said be quiet! Who said anything about you being a widow? Now, go in the back of the house and get your things together. And take Alice with you. Just leave me alone for a little while, so I can hear myself think."

24

ABOUT TWENTY MINUTES after he left, Anna saw Walter coming up the front sidewalk, the gun still in his hand. With her heart freezing in her chest, she pulled herself together and waited for him, standing in the center of the vestibule. He walked in, gave her a glowering glance, and started to go around her, toward the stairs. She grabbed at his arm, but he pulled away from her and continued upstairs. He went into his room, slammed the door and locked it, and ignored her pleas to let him in.

When the children came home, she told them their daddy was sick and was in his room. She drifted through the rest of the afternoon, hardly able to keep herself from screaming. Waiting for Walter to come down the steps, waiting for a knock at the door with news of what he had done. Waiting to see what new horror she had brought her family.

BOBBY TUGGED ON THE HAND BRAKE and stopped the Winton Six inside the garage at Walter's house. He smiled; he owed Walter a big "thank you." Not only had his drive in the country with Mary Caine succeeded—it had succeeded beyond his wildest dreams. On an old covered bridge on a quiet road just outside town, Bobby had actually stolen a kiss from her. He could still taste the softness of her lips. Yes, things with Mary Caine were definitely looking up.

He went into the house. Anna was sitting in the parlor, listening to Mabel recite her spelling words.

"Where's Walter?"

"He's gone upstairs to lie down. He wasn't feeling well."

He nodded and went back outside. He decided to go sit for a while in the Keystone lobby and maybe see a few of his cronies. He wanted to savor his success with Mary Caine this afternoon . . . though he wasn't about to share his enjoyment with any of his friends. No, he was keeping Mary Caine all to himself. He didn't want to give any of his friends any ideas that might be aimed in her direction.

Anna's face looked more dour than usual, Bobby thought as he crossed the street. He shook his head. He hoped Walter had talked to her, and he fervently hoped she'd decided to have nothing else to do with that no-good Charlie Cobb.

He went into the hotel lobby and the first thing he saw was a handful of his friends, standing near one of the tables, evidently involved in an animated discussion. But when one of them saw Bobby come in, he said something to the others and motioned toward Bobby with his head, and they all fell silent, staring at him. Bobby gave them a quizzical smile.

"Hello, boys. What's wrong? Do I have horse manure on my shirt, or what?"

"He doesn't know," somebody said.

"Where have you been, Robert?" somebody else said.

"Why, just out for a little drive on my afternoon off. Is that a crime?"

"Then you haven't heard the news? About your brother-in-law?"

Bobby's face went stiff with apprehension. "What news?"

"Doc threatened Charlie Cobb with a gun," Arch Graham said

with obvious relish. "Told him he was fornicating with another man's wife, and he was going to—hey!"

Bobby lunged at Arch, drawing back to punch him squarely in the nose. But two or three of the others grabbed him and wrestled him back.

"Easy now, Robert," somebody said. "Arch is telling the truth. I heard the same thing myself, from somebody who was there and saw the whole thing."

Somewhere in the middle of Bobby's mind, he knew that it was probably true, all of it. After all, Anna had lied to him about the magazines, hadn't she? And Bobby had told Walter of his own suspicions himself. But something about hearing the likes of Arch Graham talking about his sister made him want to punish somebody. He took deep breaths, trying to settle himself down.

"All right, then. Tell me what happened."

His friends looked at each other with wary faces; Bobby was still panting and both his hands were balled into fists.

"It's like Arch was telling you. Doc had a pistol, and just he went to this Charlie Cobb's house and braced him up against the front porch and told him if he didn't leave Gallatin by morning, he'd be dead."

"Why . . . what . . ."

"Sorry, Robert. Where you going?"

"I . . . I have to go. I have to go."

His hat flew off his head as he dashed through the hotel door, but he didn't care.

WHEN THE CHILDREN WERE IN BED and asleep, Anna went into her room and dressed for bed. She stared for a long time at the door to Walter's room. With her blood cold in her veins, she decided to try one more time to say to him what she could hardly believe she was going to say. She tapped at his door and called to him. To her surprise, the latch clicked and the door opened. Walter went back to his bed and lay across it, still fully clothed. His arm was over his face.

"Walter, please listen to me. The children are in their beds asleep, and I have things to tell you I don't want them to hear."

Walter moved his arm and studied her carefully. "What do you have to say to me that I don't already know?"

"Did you kill Charlie?"

He made a twisted face. "I thought that might be your first question: asking about your sweetheart." He said the last word as if it were the worst insult he could imagine. "No, I didn't. I told him he had until dawn to get out of Gallatin and far enough away that I won't ever see him again. If he's not gone tomorrow, then, by God, I'll kill the bastard."

Anna felt an instant of relief, even as she shuddered at hearing Walter speak words the likes of which she'd never heard come from his lips. She began steeling herself for what she had to say. "Walter, I want to tell you the complete truth. I'm doing this because I want to prove to you that I want to change, and that I regret, more deeply than you can imagine, how I've violated our marriage and disgraced us both."

He peered at her for a long moment. "Is that so? All right. Give me your filthy story."

"Walter, I . . . yes, it's true. I . . . had relations with Charlie Cobb."

His jaw clenched. He kept looking at her.

"It was wrong, it was sin, and I don't expect you can ever forgive me," she said. "I could go into all the reasons . . . at least, in my mind, they were reasons. But that wouldn't do any good, especially now. All I can say is that Charlie led me on, and to my shame I was more than willing to be led."

"How long has it been going on?" Walter said, his voice barely a croak.

"Just over a year—since last summer."

"Here? At our house?"

Anna nodded. Tears of shame were stinging the corners of her eyes.

Walter covered his face with his hands. She could hear his breath, panting in and out as he struggled with his rage. He turned back toward her. "How many times?"

Anna struggled to control her voice, but lost. She kneeled by his bedside, as if in prayer. "A lot," she said, and the syllables came out as sobs. "More than once a week, usually."

Walter grabbed his head as if he'd been stricken. His eyes squinted shut and his face was locked in a grimace, like someone having red-hot irons pressed against his flesh. "Oh! God in heaven! I can't believe my ears."

"Walter, you must listen to me. I'm telling you this, confessing my sin to you, because I really want to change. Look here." Anna tugged off her wedding ring and laid it on Walter's bedside table. "I've defiled my vows, Walter, and I don't blame you if you want to send me out of your life, but listen to me. You mustn't kill Charlie. You mustn't! Our children need you. They need you more than they need me, most likely. At least you've never betrayed their home and their innocence, as I have. Walter, please control your anger. Not for my sake, but for Mabel's and Scott's."

While she was saying this, she felt the bed moving. She looked up just in time to see Walter grabbing the pistol out of the drawer of his lamp table and pointing it at her head. She screamed and grabbed at the gun, knocking the barrel upward just as Walter pulled the trigger. The pistol roared and Anna screamed again, then sprang up and fled downstairs.

She didn't know what she was doing or where she was going; she only felt the need to run somewhere. She went outside; a cold north wind had begun to blow after sunset, and the frigid air tore at her lungs. Anna ran, barefoot and clad only in her nightgown, down North

Water Street away from the lights and the people at the Keystone, toward the town square, empty now that it was dark and the stores were closed. She fell down in a heap in front of Owen Pinkney's drugstore, curled up in a wretched ball.

Anna was shivering and sobbing at the same time. Maybe she would just stay here until she froze to death; that would solve the problem. She'd be gone and finished with her miserable life. Walter would have no more reason to kill Charlie or her.

WALTER LISTENED to the brief silence after the back door opened and slammed. A few seconds later, he heard the children beginning to wail.

What was he doing? He had almost murdered Anna, right here in this room. The gun was still in his hand. He stared at it; the fingers curled around the grip seemed like someone else's. He felt as if he were falling outside himself, as if he were ceasing to inhabit his own body.

Mabel and Scott were coming down the hall toward his room. Quickly, Walter slid the pistol into a drawer in his bedside table and ran his fingers through his hair. The children . . . he had to think about the children . . .

ANNA DIDN'T KNOW how long she sat on the cold brick sidewalk. Not long enough for anyone to happen by and notice her. She decided to go back to her house. She could freeze herself to death in her own backyard just as well as she could do it here. She pulled herself to her feet and started shuffling toward home, her teeth chattering as she clutched herself against the cold.

She went into the backyard and curled up at the base of the elm tree where she had first given herself to Charlie Cobb. This was fitting, wasn't it? She would die in the place where she had put herself irrevocably on the road to hell.

As she lay there shivering, she heard footsteps, then breathing, somewhere above and behind her. She looked up and saw Walter's figure silhouetted against the night sky. He was holding a blanket in his hand.

"I was coming to look for you. Anna, come back inside. You'll make yourself sick."

Mabel and Scott were standing in the kitchen, in their bedclothes, holding onto each other and whimpering. Anna and Walter talked to them and did their best to soothe them. "The gun woke us up," Scott said.

"All right, son, all right," Walter said. "Come on. Let's go back upstairs."

Comforting the children was having a calming effect on Walter; his breath was still coming in ragged gasps, but he was trying to gain a purchase on himself.

"You're right about one thing, I suppose," he said, when he and Anna were back in his room. "That low son of a bitch isn't worth killing. He's not worth the cost of the bullet it would take to send him to hell."

Anna waited a few moments, then said, "If you can find it in your heart, Walter . . . I'd rather not tell Mabel and Scott any more than we must. I don't want to hurt them any more than they may already have been."

He stared at the floor for a long time, then shook his head slowly from side to side. "No. They're completely innocent. They should be spared."

"Thank you."

A few more moments passed. "What will you do next?" he asked her.

Anna shook her head and shrugged. "Go to Elizabeth Jennings, I suppose. She at least tried to warn me. Maybe some of the others." After a few seconds, she said, "Walter, do you think you and I ought to talk to someone? Together?"

"Who?"

"I don't know . . . Brother Olmstead, maybe. We need help, Walter. He's our minister. Will you go with me to talk to him?"

"Maybe so. I don't know how much good it will do. I don't know if I can . . . What you've done has . . ."

"I know, Walter. We don't have to decide that right now. Let's take this one thing at a time, all right? For now, I just want you to promise that you won't do anything rash or violent about Charlie."

He looked at her. "I gave him until morning. That's all I can promise, right now."

Dear God, please get Charlie Cobb out of this town, and please keep my husband away from him until he's gone.

"DON'T GO DOWN THERE, CHARLIE! They'll see you! They'll kill you!"

"Will you be quiet, Daisy? I need that money to get us out of town. And besides, Dotson's not the only one who owns a gun," Charlie said, checking the chambers of his .32-caliber revolver.

"Charlie, don't do it! Let's just go, right now. Let's take our things to the station. Nobody ain't going to bother us if they can see we're fixing to leave."

Charlie flicked his wrist, snapping the cylinder in place. Daisy ran to the door and tried to block his way out. "Don't, Charlie! Please!"

He grabbed her shoulder and shoved her out of the way. "I said move, Daisy!" Alice was wailing in the background.

He jammed the revolver into the pocket of his coat, keeping his finger on the trigger. If Walter Dotson thought Charlie was scared of him, he ought to think again. Charlie had been handling guns since he was old enough to walk, just about. He could knock a tin can off a fence post with his .22 before he could read. Just let Walter start something; Charlie would finish it for him.

Oh, he'd leave town for a while, let things cool down. No harm in that. But sooner or later, he'd come back this way—just to show everyone he could, if for no other reason. Charlie wasn't about to let himself be pushed around by somebody, just because the other fellow had more money and knew people. No, sir. If somebody pushed Charlie, he'd push back. In his own time and his own way, but he would, and you could bet your bottom dollar on that.

Charlie thought about slipping down the alleys, but decided that wasn't his style. He walked down Railroad Street, keeping his hand inside his coat pocket and on his gun. His eyes roved both sides of the street and all the crossings, watching for any sign of Dotson or somebody who might be helping him.

It was well past midnight, and the bank and stores were closed. There'd be people he knew over at the Keystone. He figured someone would make him a loan there. He was crossing the square when he noticed a faint glimmer of light from a building in the square. Someone was working late. Charlie went around to the back door and knocked. J. H. Bingham, the butcher, opened the door a moment later, wiping his bloody hands on his already stained apron.

"We're closed at the moment. I was just getting this beef ready for the morning."

"I just need to cash a check; got to the bank just as it closed. I don't suppose you have any cash in the till?"

The butcher rubbed his jaw, a frown between his eyes as he measured Charlie. "S'pose I might. Wait here a minute." He disappeared into the shop, and Charlie glanced around the alley. A mutt with matted fur was eyeing him from behind a stack of crates, and the faint stench of slightly rotting meat wafted over from that direction.

"All I got to spare is eleven dollars. Have to make change in the morning," the butcher said as he returned.

"That would be fine, just fine." Charlie stepped inside, using the corner of the wooden butcher block to hurriedly write the check. Thanking the man, he stuffed the cash in his coat pocket, and left.

He still didn't have enough, but maybe he could talk his way into a ticket—promise to wire the rest of the money.

Charlie stayed alert and as inconspicuous as he could, keeping his field of vision moving. He was just across the street from Person's when he spotted a man walking briskly by the courthouse in his direction, and from the way he had his right hand hidden beneath his coat, Charlie guessed he probably had a gun. Charlie stopped still, moving his own gun inside his coat pocket slightly in front of him to convey the unmistakable message that whoever it was had best think twice before doing anything threatening.

"Charlie Cobb!" the man called. "What are you doing out and about at this hour of the night?"

It was Will Hall, one of Charlie's regulars, his coat collar turned up against the cold.

"Was that the two o'clock that just pulled in?"

"Sure was. I'm just getting back. Wish it wasn't such a long walk home. Sure is a cold night."

"Say, I don't suppose you have any money on you," Charlie asked.

Will looked surprised by the blunt question. "Well, a few dollars."

"It's just, I'm taking my family on a little trip and realized I'm a bit short for the tickets. I'm good for it."

"Well, sure you are, Charlie." Will set down in his bag and dug in his pockets, producing five dollars and change.

"Much obliged, Will, much obliged."

"Have a good trip, Charlie. Let me know when you get back, we'll have a beer over at the Keystone."

"Sure thing. Goodnight, Will. Thanks again." Charlie walked quickly on into the night.

He took the alley until he calculated he was about even with Railroad Street, then rounded the corner of the building at the intersection and took the street the rest of the way home, keeping a careful watch all the way.

That night, he and Daisy packed their belongings into their steamer trunk and the wooden crates they'd used when they moved from Big Rock. Alice whimpered the whole time, clinging to her mother's skirts and asking when she was going to see Mabel again. Charlie had to do some pretty hard talking to himself to keep from shaking her; the girl's constant whining was getting on his already-frazzled nerves.

In the morning, he would put Daisy and Alice on a train bound for Kentucky and her parents' home. He would stay at the station long enough to arrange for a drayman to pick up their belongings for shipment to Herndon, and then he would head for Big Rock and his family. Charlie needed some time to be in a safe place with no one around to harass him or ask him questions he didn't want to answer. And he was pretty sure Daisy's folks wouldn't exactly be glad to see him, anyway.

I just need a little time to get on my feet and make a plan. Then I'll be back. Oh, yes, my sweet little Anna—I'll be back.

25

J. P. PERSON LOOKED UP when the door to his shop opened. It was early for Walter Dotson to be in. He usually came around lunchtime.

"Good morning," he said, nodding to J.P. "Don't suppose you have time for a quick shave?"

"Sure I do, Doc, but don't you want to wait for Charlie? He's not in yet. I suppose he must be running late, but I expect him any minute now. Not like him to be late."

"Charlie won't be here."

"Why do you say that? Did you see him?"

"Yes, I did. Saw him early this morning at the depot, getting on the train."

"That's a strange thing. He didn't mention to me about taking time off. Did he say where he was going?"

"No, I didn't speak to him. I was some distance behind."

"Well, that's just a right strange thing. He was here just yesterday playing checkers with Harry Orman and having a right good time, and he didn't say one word about a trip. Anyway, have a seat, Doc, and I'll get you fixed up."

Walter seated himself in the chair. He knew J.P. wanted to ask more, because he was as quiet as he'd ever been for the whole shave. And when he was done and Walter had thanked him and paid, he asked Walter if he might have a brief word in private.

Walter followed him to the back room, past the watchful eyes of the other men in the shop, who had been unusually subdued.

When they were alone, J.P. said, "You seem to know more about Cobb than you've told me. Will you tell me what's happened to make him leave town?"

"No," Walter replied curtly.

"I beg your pardon," J.P. replied, and, giving Walter a long look, he turned and walked back into the shop.

Walter followed, and continued through and out the front door, giving only brief nods. He headed directly for his office. He had only wanted to reassure himself that Charlie Cobb was well and gone. As he passed Whitehead's Hardware and Dry Goods, Bobby rushed out.

"Walter!" he called. "Please, I need to speak to you. About what happened. About what people are saying."

Walter sighed. "Come with me to my office, Bobby. We'll talk there."

ANNA LOOKED UP from the magazine she was trying to tell herself she was reading. Walter was coming in the front door, and Bobby was with him. Bobby looked as if he'd been crying.

"Anna, I want your brother to hear it from your own lips," Walter said. "You told me you wanted to change. Prove it. Tell it to your brother, just like you did to me."

"Walter, why? Is this really necessary?"

"I want to hear it, Anna," Bobby said. His voice sounded raw. "I want to hear it from you. I've already heard it from everybody else, including Walter."

"Are the children at school?" Walter said. Anna nodded.

"All right, then. Your brother has made a request."

As best she could with shame and grief choking off her voice, Anna told him. "Yes, Bobby, it's true. I was unfaithful to Walter. It was horrible and sinful, and I beg you to forgive me, if you can."

Bobby sat heavily in one of the upholstered chairs. He was shaking his head slowly, staring at the floor in front of the chair. "Even after everything I've heard, I didn't want to believe." He fell silent for a moment, then said in a voice that was almost a growl, "I'll kill him."

"No, Bobby! Don't say that. You mustn't dirty your hands in this; that would only make things worse. I beg you, don't think of avenging me. I have no honor left to avenge."

Bobby just stared at the floor, and the dead expression on his face was torture to Anna. He had always looked up to her. Now, he was having to face the fact that his big sister was an adulteress of the most sordid kind.

Bobby finally left. Walter walked out onto the front porch with him, then came back inside and went upstairs without so much as looking at Anna. She sat in the parlor and stared at the magazine in her lap. Futile thoughts chased each other around in her mind like a mob of fighting cats. Finally, she went upstairs and fell across her bed, still fully clothed.

CHRISTMAS CAME AND WENT, but the gaiety of the season was completely lost on Anna. She forced herself to go through the motions for the children's benefit, but she felt like a hollow imitation of a person. It was almost as if she were standing outside herself, watching someone pretending to be her.

Walter wasn't any better. He never spoke to her and rarely even looked at her. When he did, his expression was full of hurt and suspicion. The only time he said anything was when he told her he was considering taking the children and moving to Chicago, saying they were sure to hear the gossip at school, or in town. As yet, he hadn't acted on it, but Anna felt as if she were constantly under inspection, and constantly failing to pass muster.

When she went about in Gallatin, it wasn't much better. She was attending the ladies' teas again, but the other women generally talked over her head, as if she weren't there. When they spoke to her, they did so with all sorts of looks at each other, as if to say, "Look at me, now. Listen to what I say to the fallen woman."

Only Elizabeth Jennings came anywhere close to making Anna feel like a real person. Anna could tell Elizabeth pitied her, but even that was a relief from the judgment and disdain she felt from everyone else. They mostly talked about the cause. Elizabeth was very excited about the plans for the coming March: thousands of suffragettes from all over the country were traveling to Washington, D.C., to march in a demonstration, demanding the passage of laws to give women the vote. Anna did her best to act interested in what Elizabeth was telling her, but most of the time that's all it was: an act.

Anna was having difficulty sleeping most nights. It was hard to imagine, because she felt close to exhaustion most of the time. But as soon as she'd lie down at night in the stillness and dark, her mind would start up, replaying all that had happened—including the times when she and Charlie had made love. And deep down inside herself, Anna knew she missed him. Even after the disaster her life had become, there was a part of Anna that couldn't turn loose of Charlie Cobb. Anna prayed to be delivered from the thought of him, the need for him that still clung to her, but it seemed her prayers went no higher than the ceiling of her bedroom.

She wrote Charlie two letters. One she addressed to Herndon, Kentucky, where Daisy's people were, and the other she sent to Big Rock. She told Charlie that they must never see each other again, that if he tried to come back to Gallatin, Walter and Bobby had promised to kill him. She carried the letters to the post office herself, dropped them through the brass slot. She wondered if it was the last communication that would ever pass between the two of them.

One afternoon Anna was at home, too tired to make even the pretense of keeping up her normal activities. She took to her bed and tried to sleep, but as usual, her restless mind wouldn't allow the mercy of slumber. After a while, she sat on the edge of her bed and suddenly remembered the French nightgown. It had lain undisturbed in the bottom of the drawer of her armoire since sometime last summer. She got up and went to the armoire, taking the nightgown out and holding it up. She went back to the armoire and found the last *Argosy* Charlie had sent back to her with notes in the margins. The magazine was still in its place, at the bottom of the same drawer that held her nightgown. She sat in a chair with the nightgown bunched in her lap and flipped through the pages of the *Argosy*, looking at Charlie's handwritten notes and remembering.

And then she looked up and realized Walter was standing in her doorway, glaring at her. How long had he been there? Anna froze, afraid of what might happen next.

"What are you looking at?"

"Nothing. Just one of my magazines."

He strode across the room and before she could react he snatched the *Argosy* from her grasp. She watched as his face clenched tighter and tighter, forming a mask of dark rage.

"So this is how your lover communicated with you, is it? What does this say?" He tilted the magazine and peered at it. "'Dearest one, I cannot wait to hold you in my arms like the lovers in this story.'" He flipped a few more pages. "'My Anna, this poem made me think of you, sitting in the garden, like the woman in the picture over your bed.'"

He flung the magazine across the room, making an inarticulate sound of rage.

"You filthy woman! What is that thing you've got in your lap? Give it to me." He snatched up the French nightgown and held it out in front of him. "What sort of lewd thing is this? Did you wear this while you were defiling your vows with him?"

Anna was too afraid to move or speak. Wadding the nightgown in one fist, Walter grabbed her wrist and yanked her out of the chair. "Come on. I'm going to show you something." He hauled her into his bedroom. Still clamping her wrist in one hand, he pulled open the drawer of his nightstand and retrieved his pistol. Holding the pistol and the nightgown in the same hand, he dragged her down the stairs and into the backyard.

"Stay here," he said, jabbing a finger at the back steps. He retrieved a board and placed it against the trunk of the large elm tree in the corner of the yard. Then he draped the nightgown on the board, the delicate fabric catching on the rough bark. He walked about fifteen paces away, then took aim at the nightgown. He looked over his shoulder at her. "This is what I think of your filthy nightgown. This is what I'll do to Charlie Cobb if I ever lay eyes on him again." He turned and sighted, then fired three times. The first bullet struck the nightgown where Anna's heart would have been. "That's what you and Charlie Cobb did to me," he said. He fired again, and the slug pierced the nightgown lower down. His third shot was close to the first.

Somewhere nearby, a dog started barking, alarmed by the gunshots. Walter turned to Anna and said, "Why don't you try it, Anna? You keep saying you want to repent, you want to change. Prove it." He held out the gun toward her. "Kill this damned nightgown. Put it to death, and put to death everything it stands for."

Trembling, Anna stood. She walked toward Walter, not sure whether he might not suddenly decide to do to her what he'd just done to her nightgown. He reached out and grabbed her, thrusting the gun into her hand. "There," he pointed. "Shoot it. There are two bullets left in the cylinder."

Holding the gun with both hands, Anna aimed and squeezed the trigger. The recoil caused her to stagger back a step. She wasn't sure whether she'd hit anything or not.

"Well, I'm surprised! You did hit it," Walter said. "Again! Shoot it again!" Walter's eyes were wild. Anna was afraid not to do what he said. She aimed the gun again and fired.

"Give me that," he said. He grabbed the gun from her and ejected the spent cartridges, then put in five more. "Now. Shoot it again. Shoot it, damn you!"

Anna was beginning to weep. She held up the gun, but her grip was loosening. She fired twice more, thinking she'd hit the nightgown each time. Then she dropped the revolver and ran toward the house, wailing with fear.

"Run away, that's right," Walter called after her. "But you can't hide from what you've done. You're still pining for him, aren't you? Up in your room pawing through your magazine and lusting for him. You haven't changed. You're still the same."

His words followed her inside, going round and round in her mind: *still the same, still the same, still the same*... Anna ran upstairs, screaming just to drown out the maddening voices in her head. She fell across her bed and wept until she fell into an exhausted sleep.

26

March 1913

THE BARBER MOTIONED toward the chair, and Arch Graham pushed himself up from the waiting bench. "Little off the top and pretty close on the sides," he told the man. The barber nodded. "Shave?"

Arch told him yes, easing himself into the barber chair.

"Say, J. P.," said the customer in the next chair over, "have you ever heard any more from that Cobb fellow that used to have the first chair by the window?"

"Yeah," J. P. said. "Why?"

"Well, I rented him a house when he was living here, and he skipped out of town owing me a month's rent. I need to get a hold of him so I can get my money. Reckon he's working somewhere round about?"

"He told me he's got a job at a place in Nashville . . . Jackson's Barbershop, I think he said it was."

"Oh, yeah. I know that place," the man said. "On Broadway. Not too far from Eighth Street."

"Maybe so," J. P. said. "I just hope he stays there. I don't need any trouble, and I don't think Doc Dotson has gotten over that business between Charlie and his wife, from last winter."

"Well, maybe not. But I'm still going to see about getting my money."

Arch Graham thought this was all very interesting. He wondered how Robert Dennis would feel about it. He decided to find out, first chance he got.

"HE'S IN NASHVILLE!" Walter's face was inches from Anna's; she could feel his spittle hitting her forehead and cheeks. "The son of a bitch has come back! He thinks I didn't mean what I said."

"Walter, please—"

"And you're still protecting him, aren't you? You're still trying to keep your lover alive, so you can disgrace yourself some more, so you can go away with him and fornicate to your heart's delight."

Anna shook her head.

"Do you see this?" Walter brandished his revolver in front of her face. "This is what he's going to get from me. After everything he's done to me, to our home, this is what he deserves."

"Don't say that, Walter."

He whirled and paced away from her, strode back and forth across the room, muttering and scowling. Anna was afraid of him, afraid for him.

"Will you please put down the gun, at least?"

He walked over to a table near her chair and placed the revolver there. The muzzle was pointing at her. Watching him carefully, Anna pivoted the gun so that the barrel was aimed away from her and from Walter.

"Walter, I'm going to ask you a question, and I want you to think carefully before you answer."

He stopped pacing and looked at her.

"Will you tell me where Charlie is in Nashville?"

His jaw dropped. "You actually expect me to give you that information, after what you've done?"

"I want to go see him, Walter, and tell him that he must leave Nashville, never to return. I mean it, Walter. My life is worth nothing to me now, but we still have two children to raise. They need a father who is with them, not one locked up in the penitentiary, or hanged for murder. Let me go to him and tell him to leave. I'll do it however you say, as long as you stay away. I'll . . . I'll take Scott with me, if you like. Charlie and I can't very well do anything if Scott is there, can we?"

He was studying her as if she were some sort of animal that he'd never seen before. "You mean to warn him away? Not carry on some liaison with him?"

Anna kept her eyes on him. She nodded.

"And don't let him touch my son. I don't want that miserable scum putting his hands on Scott." He looked at her; Anna thought he was still measuring her, trying to decide if he could believe her. "I can find out, you realize," he said. "I know people in Nashville. If you're lying to me, I'll learn about it."

She continued to hold his gaze. After a few seconds, he gave a small nod. "All right. We'll see. He's working at Jackson's Barbershop, on Broadway, near Eighth. When will you go?"

"Tomorrow."

He let out a sarcastic laugh. "Can't wait to get to him, can you?"

Anna said nothing. After a moment, Walter shook his head and walked out of the room. When Anna was certain he was gone, she scooped up the pistol and put it in a place she knew Walter would never think to look.

Just in case . . .

"WHAT DO YOU THINK SHE'LL DO, Walter?" Bobby said. "Do you want me to follow her?" The two men were sitting in Walter's office at the clinic. After his conversation with Anna, Walter had gone to the hardware store and asked Bobby to come down to the clinic as soon as he finished work.

"No, she might see you, Bobby, or else Cobb might, and know they were being watched. I've got a cousin who's in Nashville now, on business. His name is Jent. I'll get in touch with him and tell him what's afoot. He can observe them and remain undetected."

"What will you do if she . . . goes with him?"

Walter clenched his jaw. "I don't care what Brother Olmstead or Anna or anybody else says. I'll kill the bastard."

ANNA STEPPED OFF THE DIXIE FLYER into the bustle of Union Station, tightly gripping Scott's hand.

"Are we going to buy some candy, Mama? Do we have time to go look at some toys or something?"

"I don't know, son," she said, barely registering his words. "We'll see."

Anna and Scott walked down Broadway toward the Cumberland River. The day was gray and cool; to Anna, it had seemed the weather so far this year wasn't paying the least attention to the calendar. Here it was March, and as far as she could tell, it might as well still be January.

The striped barber's pole was impossible to miss. The shop was on the south side of the street, and as Anna walked through the front door, she could tell it was a busy place.

And there, working at the chair on the far end, was Charlie Cobb.

CLARENCE JENT HAD SEEN ANNA when she got off the train at Union Station, holding her little boy with one hand and keeping the other inside a fur muff. She looked exactly as Walter had described her on the telephone; he could probably have picked her out of a crowd, even without the help of knowing she was traveling with her young son. She was a fine-looking woman, Jent had to admit; in the right circumstances, she could offer temptation to just about any man.

He stayed well behind them as they made their way down Broadway toward the river. Jent had already reconnoitered the barbershop and knew where they were headed, but he had decided to pick up the trail at the train station, in case Walter's wife and her lover had made some sort of plan for misdirection in connection with their liaison. Walter had told him that she might suspect being followed, but as far as Jent could tell, if she did suspect something, she didn't care. She walked right down the middle of the sidewalk, turning neither to the right nor to the left. And when she came in view of the barbershop, she made a beeline across the street, walking in without as much as a backward glance, like she owned the place.

Pretty bold, missy. Pretty bold.

Jent found a deep, arched doorway into a bank, directly across Broadway from the barbershop, and stationed himself so he could see the front of the place. Though the glare on the plate glass window made it a bit chancy, he could make out Anna's form as she walked from one end of the shop to the other. She stopped in front of the last chair. Jent guessed she must have arrived at her destination. He hoped the two would come outside; he wanted to see the man who had his placid cousin Walter ready to commit murder.

As best he could tell through the glass, when Cobb's customer got out of the chair, the little boy got in. He guessed Cobb was trimming the boy's hair. Anna stood beside him as he worked, no doubt planning something underhanded. Well, Jent would see to it that Walter got a full report.

After a while, the front door opened, and here came the three of them: Walter's wife, the little boy, and Cobb. Jent studied him. He had a dark, shifty look about him that Jent instinctively mistrusted.

What in the world did Walter's wife see in this lout, with everything that Walter had given her?

They stood on the sidewalk in front of the glass window and talked. The little boy didn't seem to be paying much attention, which was a mercy, as far as Jent was concerned. Better not to fill his ears with the lascivious filth passing between his mother and her paramour. Jent felt his lip curling with distaste. This woman didn't deserve his cousin!

The conversation went on for a good while, and by the angle of their faces and their expressions, Jent could tell they were pretty serious about it. Once, Anna put her hand on Cobb's arm, her face wearing an expression of pleading. She was doing most of the talking, it seemed. Cobb would shake his head or nod and get in a few words, then she'd go at it again. Sometimes she appeared to be pleading, and other times she'd be smiling at him. Jent couldn't get the drift of it, watching from across the street. But he couldn't very well do anything else.

After ten or fifteen minutes they parted. Anna's hands were inside her fur muff, and Jent watched as Cobb reached out and took them, inside the muff, and gave them a parting squeeze. Anna smiled at him, then turned and walked back the way she'd come with her son, toward Union Station. Cobb stood staring after them for a moment, and Jent felt his disgust rising as a big smile spread across the face of the louse.

Well, if he's not grinning like a pig in mud! I'll wager he just heard her tell him she'd find a way to come to him again—maybe for good!

As soon as Cobb went back inside, Jent hurried after Anna and the boy. He tailed them into Union Station and watched them until they boarded the train for Gallatin. They were still on the train when it pulled out of the station.

Jent hurried back to his hotel, digging in his coat pocket for the scrap of paper on which he'd written the number Walter had given him yesterday, the phone in his clinic. Jent had things to report to his cousin.

ANNA SAT IN HER ROOM, her Bible in her lap. Maybe it was true; maybe God really did sometimes send guidance when you least expected it. At least, it seemed so to her from the words she had just read in the Old Testament book of Judges:

> *And Jephthah vowed a vow unto the Lord, and said, If thou shalt without fail deliver the children of Ammon into mine hands, then it shall be, that whatsoever cometh forth of the doors of my house to meet me, when I return in peace from the children of Ammon, shall surely be the Lord's, and I will offer it up for a burnt offering . . .*
>
> *. . . and Jephthah came to Mizpeh unto his house, and, behold, his daughter came out to meet him.*

Anna read the story several times, and each time she read it, it made more sense. Sometimes, to win the victory over your enemies, you had to give up something precious.

Anna went to sleep that night, thinking that maybe there were worse things than death.

27

WHAT ARE YOUR plans for today, Anna?" Walter said. He was sitting in the parlor, drinking a cup of coffee when she came downstairs. He studied her carefully; she looked different—calm, somehow. She had made some sort of decision, he guessed.

After hanging up the phone on his cousin's call last night, he had decided to see what Anna would do. His cousin had told him he believed Anna and Cobb had made plans to be together, and what did Walter want to do about it? Walter had told Jent he would contact him as soon as he made a decision. It seemed as if maybe that moment was fast approaching.

"Oh, not much of anything," she said, looking everywhere in the room but at him. "I may try to get some cleaning done, maybe a little shopping."

He nodded, giving her a tiny smile. Of course she was lying to him. *Keep giving her rope.* "Well, I have to go see a patient out in the country," he said. "I expect I'll be gone all afternoon." He waited to see what effect this news would have on her. Sure enough, she gave him a quick, interested look. "Really?" she said. "You don't have patients in the clinic?"

"Not this afternoon. I imagine I'll leave around two, two thirty. Something like that."

She nodded and went into the kitchen. He heard her bustling around, clattering plates. He finished his coffee and reached for his overcoat, draped over the back of a chair. He put it on, then carried his cup and saucer into the kitchen.

"We have an appointment with Brother Olmstead tonight, remember," he said.

"What? Sorry, I was thinking of something else."

Yes, I guess you were. "I said, remember our meeting with Brother Olmstead tonight."

"Oh, yes. Yes, I'll be ready for that, whenever you get back from your patient."

"Well. Goodbye, then."

She gave him a flickering little smile and he left, thinking of the best way to be prepared for whatever the day might bring. He drove to his office, parking his automobile in its usual, conspicuous place, in full sight of the town square. He went inside, locked the front door, and hurried to his office. He picked up his phone.

"Clarence, I need your help again today." He told Jent what he suspected and outlined a plan.

ANNA LEFT HER HOUSE at one thirty, dressed in her warm coat and with her hands in her fur muff. Today wasn't any warmer than yesterday, she thought. She walked down North Water Avenue and rounded the corner, looking up the street toward the town square. Walter's car was in its usual place, so he hadn't yet left for his appointment.

Anna went into the hardware store to say hello to her brother, but for some reason, Bobby wasn't at work. She went down the street and into a few stores, browsing among the goods and displays, looking at whatever clock she could find in order to keep close track of the time.

When it was just after two o'clock, she stepped onto the sidewalk and glanced toward Walter's clinic. His car was gone. As soon as Anna saw this, she turned and walked quickly toward the train station.

She bought a ticket to Nashville and stepped aboard the Dixie Flyer when it came wheezing and hissing up to the platform. She found a seat in an almost-empty car and sat as low as she could, hoping not to be seen or spoken to by anyone. It worked; the train pulled away from the station at a quarter past, and Anna was still alone in the car.

Forty-five minutes later, when the train began slowing for Union Station in Nashville, Anna felt panic rising in her. She was trembling and her breath was coming in short, shallow gasps. What if Walter suspected she was coming to meet Charlie again? What if Bobby was here? So many things could go wrong.

But she was here, and this was the only way, she had decided. She could no longer exist in a world so crowded with conflicting desires and needs. It was time to act.

She exited the train and walked down Broadway toward the river, as she had the day before. Without Scott to worry about, she was able to keep both hands inside the muff, which was a mercy. She neared the barbershop, but looking at the clock tower rising above Union Station, she could see that it was barely past three o'clock. Four, Charlie had said. The shop closed at four, and they could go somewhere and talk, he said. Somewhere private.

She walked on past the barbershop, wondering if Charlie noticed her through the glass window. She thought about the first time she'd walked by J. P.'s shop, back in Gallatin, much as she was doing right now. She didn't look, didn't try to see him. Not yet. That would come later.

She continued on down the street, weaving in and out of the crowds, taking deep breaths and trying to think about mundane things. She walked to the intersection of Broadway and Eighth, then kept going, around the corner, to the next intersection. She rounded the block and again approached the barbershop. She looked over her shoulder at the station clock tower: it was now a quarter past three.

She decided to go on inside. Anna leaned against the revolving door, then another man, in a hurry, came through behind her. The door pushed against her, almost causing her to lose her balance. Pressing her hands, still inside the muff, against the glass pane of the door, she regained her equilibrium, and entered the barbershop.

The man in Charlie's chair was finished. Charlie swept the towel from in front of him and he dug in his pocket, then handed Charlie some coins. Charlie looked up and saw her. He smiled.

Anna returned the smile and started toward him. He watched her approach, and the look on his face told her that he was seeing everything he expected to see. She waited until she was close, maybe four feet away, then pulled her right hand out of the muff, bringing Walter's revolver with it. She shot Charlie once. Then again. He fell, writhing in pain. Noise erupted all around her. Anna stood over Charlie and watched as his blood pooled on the floor beneath him.

Goodbye, Charlie. I'm sorry, but this was the only way.

PART TWO

The Trial

28

THE PHONE RANG and Walter snatched the mouthpiece from its cradle, bringing it close to his lips. "This is Walter."

"Walter, this is Clarence. My God, Walter, she shot him!"

"What?"

"Anna shot Charlie Cobb. I saw the whole thing from across the street. She walked into the barbershop, went right up to him, pulled a gun and shot him, in full view of a whole roomful of witnesses."

Walter groped with the idea for a few seconds. "Is he dead?"

"If he's not, he's missing a good chance. I ran over there just after it happened and looked through the window. He was on the floor and blood was pooling all around him. He wasn't moving. I don't think he'll make it."

Riptides of emotion were coursing through Walter. First came the fierce joy that the cheating scum Charlie Cobb was dead or close to it; then unbelieving shock—of all the courses Anna might have pursued today, this was the one Walter never saw coming. Then came a sudden, intense fear for Anna's future, followed by guilt over having left his gun out on the table a few days before—he never doubted that his Smith and Wesson .32 was what Anna had used to commit her crime. Finally, there was the anxiety over how he was going to explain this to Mabel and Scott, followed by deep sadness for the suffering and uncertainty their innocent children were about to endure.

When he could form more words in his mind, he said, "Have they taken her away yet?"

"The paddy wagon just now rolled up," Jent said. "Some detective or other is in there with her now."

"All right. If you can get a message to Anna, tell her that I'm on my way. I'll post her bail and we'll get the best attorney in the state to represent her."

"You're going to back her in this?" Jent said.

"As God is my witness," Walter said, his voice cracking with emotion, "I will move heaven and earth to help Anna. She is my wife, and the mother of my children."

He hung up and reached for the list of telephone numbers he'd written out earlier in the day. The first number on the list was for Bobby, who was waiting at Anna's parents' house. Within the hour, Walter hoped, all of them would be converging on the police station in Nashville.

DETECTIVE SIDEBOTTOM burst through the door of Jackson's Barbershop and the first thing he saw was a man in a barber's apron, holding a pistol and standing over the body of a man on the floor who looked to be busy bleeding to death. Sidebottom covered the barber with his service revolver. "Put down the gun!"

The man looked at Sidebottom with wide eyes, and very deliberately pointed the pistol at himself, then took hold of the barrel. He held out the gun, grip first, toward the detective. "Here you go, officer. I'm not the one you want. It's her," he said, pointing toward a petite blonde woman in a stylish dress and overcoat, sitting quietly between a barber and a man in a railroad uniform.

"I'll get it, Detective," someone said. Sidebottom looked at the speaker and realized it was a patrolman he knew, a fellow named McGarver. "I was downtown," McGarver said, "and I saw a bunch of people boiling out of the barbershop, onto the sidewalk. I came in and found her with the gun still in her hand. Witnesses said she tried to walk out after shooting the victim, as calm as you please."

One of the barbers nodded vigorously. "She shot him, and I jumped in front of her, holding up my hands, and said, 'Lady, what's the matter with you?' She said, 'My husband is Dr. Walter Dotson. This man ruined my marriage and my life, and I've done what I came to do. You can send word to my husband.'"

"Yeah, and then Charlie made a noise on the floor there behind them," another barber said. "She turned around and said, 'I don't believe he's dead yet.' She was fixing to shoot him again when this fellow—" he nodded toward the railroad employee—"grabbed her from behind and took the gun."

One of the men asked her what was wrong with her, and Sidebottom listened as she calmly repeated her story: "I am Anna Dotson from Gallatin, Tennessee. My husband is Dr. Walter Dotson. This man here destroyed my marriage and my life, and I've done what I came here to do . . ."

Sidebottom observed Anna for a few moments, sitting there as cool as a cucumber. He asked her what she had to say for herself.

"Is that thing dead yet?" she replied, looking over at the man on the floor.

Witnesses told Sidebottom that four shots had been fired. He examined the victim, who was still alive, but barely. "Where's that blasted ambulance?" he said. McGarver assured him it was on its way. The detective thumbed open the breech of the weapon used in the assault, and found three unspent cartridges still in the cylinder. The

Smith and Wesson revolver had a five-round cylinder, so that meant only two shots had been fired from this pistol. But the witnesses said they heard four shots. Sidebottom filed this inconsistency away for future reference.

The ambulance screeched to a halt outside the barbershop and the attendants came in and hurriedly gathered the bleeding victim onto a gurney. As they were leaving, Sidebottom gave them explicit instructions: when removing the victim's clothing, they were to make certain there were no concealed weapons, especially a pistol, as that might explain why the witnesses heard four rounds when, as far as Sidebottom could see, only two were fired. Sidebottom watched them hurry out the door, judging that by the victim's appearance and the amount of blood on the floor, this assault was likely to turn into a murder case.

Anna asked him again, "Is it dead?"

The detective glanced at her and began to suspect the sanity of a woman who could preserve such a calm demeanor under such circumstances. She was either in emotional extremity, a very good actress, or the most cold-blooded criminal he had witnessed in many years. Given her appearance and where she was from, the last possibility seemed far-fetched.

Sidebottom handcuffed her and escorted her to the paddy wagon. Sirens blaring, they drove to the station house. It was just after four o'clock in the afternoon when Sidebottom escorted her in. The steel handcuffs clasping her wrists in front of her were in jarring contrast to the rest of her appearance. If she was upset by her circumstances, she surely didn't let it show. She stood quietly and patiently as Sidebottom gave her name to the booking officer, went obediently with him to the holding cell and sat down inside.

PAUL CHRISTIAN HAD EASED UP behind the detective and listened carefully as Sidebottom gave his description of the events to the booking officer, but after a while he decided to drift back over toward the holding cell, where Anna Dotson was. She was sitting by the steel-barred door, her hands in her lap now free of the handcuffs, and she seemed to be trying to overhear as much as she could of what was being said by Sidebottom and the other officer.

By degrees, the reporter moved closer, watching her without her knowledge. She was a pretty woman, by any measure; her blue eyes, fair skin, and attractive figure could inspire just about any crime of passion on the books. Christian found a chair and moved it over close to her. After a while, she noticed him sitting there.

"Who are you? Are you a policeman?" she asked.

"No, ma'am. I'm a news reporter. May I ask why you're here?" Sometimes the simple approach worked best, Christian knew.

"I think I've killed someone," she said.

"Why do you think that?"

She looked at him, and it was as if a dam burst inside her. She started telling him things about her husband, her children, the ladies' social circle in Gallatin, Tennessee . . .

Christian was grabbing for his notebook and pen and trying to catch up with her when he noticed Sidebottom looking at him. He winced inside; the detective looked angry. But Anna Dotson was spilling her story, and Christian wasn't about to leave her side unless somebody physically dragged him away. Within a few seconds, he knew he had the makings of a sensational headline—four or five sensational headlines, in fact. As he scribbled madly, he was trying different ones out in his head: "Gallatin Socialite Shoots Paramour in Front of Witnesses," "Violence in Downtown Barbershop Leaves One Dead," "Doctor's Wife Goes on Rampage" . . . There were so many angles to this thing it was all the eager reporter could do to just keep up.

He began to notice that Sidebottom was keeping the other officers away while Mrs. Dotson was speaking to him; apparently, the detective decided that the flow of information coming from her shouldn't be interrupted. A little later, Sidebottom even came over and offered her a glass of water. She drank it, and as she handed it back to him, he said, "Would you like to tell me what happened?"

She looked away and wouldn't answer. Giving Christian a surreptitious wink, Sidebottom moved away, and in a few seconds, Anna Dotson resumed spilling her insides, like a sinner at a confessional. He didn't even have to ask her questions; it was as if she'd had this story penned up inside her for so long, and now it had to come out—but for no ears but his, it would seem.

At one point, there was another commotion up by the booking desk. "He's gone," Christian heard an officer say. A few minutes later, Sidebottom came back out and the reporter heard him tell the booking officer to change the charge from assault to murder.

When Christian had filled every blank sheet in his notebook and begun writing on the backs of his paper, Anna ran out of things to tell him. Christian felt wrung out; it was like grabbing hold of an electric wire and not being able to let go. Sidebottom stepped into the room and looked at him, then motioned with his head for the reporter to step outside.

"What have you got?" he said as soon as Christian came out.

"I . . . can't tell you," Christian said. "The, ah, confession was given to me in confidence."

Sidebottom's eyebrows went up at the word "confession," but he wasn't satisfied. "What's the matter, Paul? Cat got your tongue?"

Christian was a little intimidated by him; Sidebottom was famous around Nashville for his ability to solve cases no one else could. Not to mention that he had done some bare-knuckles boxing in his youth, by all reports. Still, Christian held his ground.

"I really can't tell you, detective."

"Well, Paul, my boy, we'll see about that. You'd best have a careful talk with your editor. You may have just scribbled yourself into a place as the state's primary witness in the first capital murder trial of a woman in the history of this state. You're about to become almost as famous as Mrs. Dotson in there. You might even help us put a rope around her pretty little neck."

Christian took a deep breath. He knew Sidebottom was right, but he still couldn't say anything—not yet. He nodded. "I'll talk to my editor."

Sidebottom walked away, and Christian ran to find the closest telephone.

29

ANNA STARED OUT THE WINDOW of Walter's car, watching the still-bare trees crawl slowly past. Walter had posted her bond at the police station, and since they released her to him he had not left her side. She couldn't remember a time since the early days of their marriage when he had been so solicitous.

"Anna, we're going to find a way to get through this together. I promise you."

"It doesn't matter, Walter," she said. "I don't want to live. I made Jephthah's vow, and now God can take me as punishment for my sin."

"Don't talk like that, Anna. You did what you did out of loyalty to our family. Charlie Cobb seduced you, and now he has paid for it. You did what I should have done."

"No, Walter. I was the one who did wrong. I'm the one who has to pay for it."

"Don't say that. We're going to get you out of this, I swear it."

Anna never even looked at him. She just stared at the trees, wondering why nobody had told them it was spring.

They got home well after dark. Walter helped her out of the car and into the house. Anna told him she was tired and just wanted to rest. He nodded and helped her up the stairs, cupping her elbow as if it were a piece of fine china. He told her he was going back downstairs to see off Bobby and her father, who had also driven to the police station, in support of Walter. A little while later, Walter brought Mabel and Scott to her to say goodbye; Bobby was taking them to stay with his and Anna's parents for a few days, until some of the furor died down. Anna kissed them and held them long in her arms. "Be sweet children for Grandmother and Granddaddy, all right?" she said. They both nodded.

When Walter went downstairs with the children, Anna got up and locked her bedroom door. Standing in front of the full-length mirror in her armoire, she began removing her clothing. She unbuttoned her dress and let it fall in a crumpled pile at her feet. She stepped out of her shoes, then her petticoats. She peeled her camisole up over her head. Last, beneath everything else, right next to her skin, was the French nightgown. She had worn it to Nashville today, like a sacramental garment, special to the purpose that had called her. She studied the neat bullet holes that perforated its front. She pulled the nightgown up and over her head, wondering what Charlie would have thought if he could have seen her wearing it this way, with the bullet holes as small, concise symbols of the rage their affair had engendered. Would he have even cared? she wondered. Or would he have just been eager to get at what was underneath?

She crumpled the nightgown in her fist; the fine, semitransparent silk compacted into a single handful. What a very slight thing it was! And to think how much trouble it had started.

Anna walked over to her fireplace and dropped the nightgown among the smoldering coals there. It popped and sizzled and flared yellow, and then it was gone, its last traces vanishing up the flue in a few wisps of smoke.

Next, she padded to her armoire and retrieved the *Argosy* magazines she had kept, the ones with Charlie's notes in them. She sat cross-legged and naked on the floor in front of her fireplace, turning each page as carefully as if it were a centuries-old manuscript. As she came to a page with his writing on it, she read it slowly, lingering over the shapes of his letters. She tore each page precisely along the fold and dropped it atop the coals, watching it catch flame, curl, blacken, and disintegrate into red-edged fragments.

When she was finished with the magazines, she went into the bathroom and found Walter's shaving razor. Anna carried it back to her bedroom and sat down on the edge of the bed. She held the razor in her right hand and stretched out her left arm, looking for the place in her wrist where her veins stretched bluish against her pale skin.

From somewhere far away she heard a sound—someone calling her name? It didn't matter. Anna touched the edge of Walter's blade to her wrist and began to press.

There was a crash and a splintering and Walter came through her bedroom door. "Anna! Don't!" He rushed to the bed and grabbed her right wrist, wrenching it away from her arm.

"Leave me alone, Walter! Let me end it! I made a vow!"

He fell on her, pinning her beneath his weight, clamping her right wrist in a tight grip, then prying the razor from her fingers and throwing it across the room.

"Let me die, Walter," Anna said between sobs. "I want to die. I'm too sinful to live, and now I'm a killer. Let me die."

"No, my Anna. I can't let you do this. You've already taken one burden that should have been mine. Don't take your own life, too. Think of your children. Live for them."

She stopped struggling. After a few moments, Walter slowly raised himself off of her. Watching her carefully, he went to her armoire and found one of her cotton flannel nightgowns. He brought it to her and helped her put it on and then, his arm around her waist, led her to his bedroom and put her in his bed.

"Sleep now, Anna. Gather strength. In the morning, we'll think about what we need to do next."

He sat in his reading chair, near the foot of the bed, and watched her. Anna closed her eyes and became still.

Walter's evocation of the children had found its mark. She wasn't sure what benefit it would be to Mabel and Scott to have a mother such as she, but Anna decided to put aside the idea of ending her own life.

But she still had to face a trial for murder. She could very well be the first woman in Tennessee history to be hanged. Though the thought of the rope around her neck made her shudder, Anna didn't think she was afraid to die. A judge and executioner could just as easily aid the culmination of her vow as Walter's razor, she reasoned. If God chose to take her that way, she would not protest.

Walter barely slept that night; each time Anna shifted on the bed, he was instantly alert, ready to intercept her if she tried again to do herself harm. The long, silent watches crept by, and he had only his tired, bruised mind to keep him company.

Walter thought about everything that had happened, going all the way back to the night Anna had tried to interest him in intimacy as he sat in his chair, downstairs in the parlor. Though he could scarcely fathom it, he had lately come to the conclusion that the despicable Charlie Cobb understood something about his wife that he had completely missed. Walter had always known Anna was passionate, stubborn, and inclined toward impatience, but until these last fateful days he hadn't fully grasped the implications of those attributes.

Walter remembered the influenza epidemic, all those years ago in Lafayette. Anna's stubbornness, her determination to stay with him and help in tending the patients, had flown in the face of her parents' anger and even the hospital administrator's better judgment. For that matter, the very fact that they were able to court at all during that winter season was because of Anna's immoveable resolve to have her own way where Walter was concerned.

Why, then, hadn't he been able to understand her need for his touch? When they had lost the baby, something had gone out of Walter. The thought of another pregnancy, of placing her at risk—not to mention the possibility of losing another baby—turned him, somehow. And then, when Anna would ask him about it, he'd give some offhand, dismissive answer. "I'm a doctor, Anna . . . I know best." She was longing for his affections, and he was too proud, or too afraid, to permit himself to be vulnerable to her.

Well, he was paying for it, wasn't he? Not only did the whole of Sumner and Davidson Counties—and maybe beyond even that— know that his wife had been involved with a calculating, opportunistic rascal like Charlie Cobb, Walter was sure that at least some of them suspected the reason. He could just imagine the talk at Person's, when he wasn't there: *Couldn't keep her at home . . . Didn't take care of her needs, if you take my meaning . . .* He was ashamed, and he wished he could blame it all on Anna, but in his heart of hearts he knew that if he had only paid a bit more attention to her, been slightly more considerate, this whole wretched business might have been avoided.

Walter thought about the women's suffrage movement, about Elizabeth Jennings standing in front of the Board of Aldermen and an angry crowd of onlookers, demanding to be heard. Maybe the notion of women demonstrating and marching in the streets was indecent, like some people said. Maybe the idea of equal rights for women really did violate God's created order, as some seemed to believe. But, Walter wondered, if the majority of men were as inattentive and uninterested in their wives' ideas and thoughts as he had been, what choice did the suffragettes have, really?

As the gray of the predawn started to seep through the curtains of his room, Walter stretched and rubbed his face. His eyelids felt like someone had used sandpaper on them; the skin of his face felt stretched and taut. He looked at Anna, her shoulders rising and falling with the rhythm of deep sleep. He thought she'd be all right, at least long enough for him to stretch his legs.

He slipped quietly from the room and walked down the hallway. He went into the children's bathroom and ran a little water into his palms, splashing his face. He raised his arms above his head and grimaced. He would likely have a resounding headache later, from lack of sleep.

Walter went down the stairs. He paced to the front door and glanced outside, then stared. There were people outside, standing on the sidewalk, looking at his house. They were staring, hoping maybe to get a glimpse of the famous criminal, Anna Dotson.

Walter sank down in a chair and held his face in his hands. His family had become a curiosity, something for people to gawk at. How would they ever explain this to the children?

NASHVILLE TENNESSEAN

and The Nashville American

Vol. 6–No. 310.	March 16, 1913

WOMAN SUFFRAGE – SENSATIONAL KILLING

"He ruined my home and wrecked my life," declared Mrs. Anna Dotson, the wife of Dr. Walter Dotson, a prominent physician of Gallatin, after she had fired four fatal shots into the body of Charlie Cobb, a barber, at Jackson's barbershop, 819 Broadway, Saturday afternoon, about 3:30 o'clock. Cobb died within a few minutes after reaching the city hospital, where he was rushed in an automobile, while Mrs. Dotson calmly waited until Lieutenant Sidebottom, chief of detectives, and Automobile Detective McGarver arrived on the scene and placed her under arrest.

While the shop was crowded with the usual Saturday afternoon customers, the woman, without a word, walked up to the man whom she claims caused her ruin, while he was shaving a patron, drew a pistol from her muff and fired four times. Cobb sank slowly to the floor and lay crumpled in a heap, while Mrs. Dotson, clutching the revolver, watched him with fascinated eyes.

The crowd who had witnessed the tragedy broke terror-stricken from the shop. Men ran in every direction. Mrs. Dotson, without a tremor, walked over to C. A. Hodges, who has charge of the chair next to Cobb's, and asked him what she should do. "I have done just what I came here to do," she said. "He ruined my home and my life. My husband, Dr. Dotson of Gallatin, knows you, will you kindly notify him?" Mrs. Dotson, on the advice of Hodges, sat down to wait until the police station was notified and looked on while the man she had shot was taken to an automobile and hurried away.

Mrs. Dotson was taken to the police station in the patrol wagon where she was registered on the blotter as Mrs. Anna Dotson charged with murder and carrying a pistol. She was then taken to the women's department and locked up. When seen shortly after the shooting took place, she was pacing the floor nervously, tears streaming down her cheeks. She again said that she accomplished just what she came to Nashville for. "I did not do it for revenge. I shot him to protect my brother and husband. I was afraid that they would kill him, and I did not want anyone to suffer for my sins."

Mrs. Dotson is a pretty blonde of 32 years. Beautifully dressed in a dark brown street dress, she presented a strange contrast to the dark interior of her cell. After a few minutes of broken conversation, she regained her composure and told the tale of events that led to the tragic death of the barber.

"I met Mr. Cobb about a year and a half ago under very peculiar circumstances. One Sunday afternoon while my husband was away, I was sitting on the front porch of our home in Gallatin reading the Sunday morning paper. My sister, who was then Miss Flora Dennis, was sitting in the yard in a swing with a young man, while my two children were playing near the porch. The gate opened and I saw a young man, quite handsome, walking up to the porch.

"He raised his hat and asked me if I would let him have the paper for a few minutes. I gave him the paper and he went away. Shortly afterward he returned it and stood and talked to me. He said that he lived across the street at the hotel and had often seen me and even declared that he had met me, but I know that he had not.

"When my husband returned I told him of the strange conduct of the man, but Dr. Dotson knew him and said that it was Cobb's manner, and that he was known to be very familiar. Picking out those times when my husband was away on a visit to a patient or in Nashville, Cobb continued coming to the house. In a few months we had become very good friends.

"I thought that my husband did not love me; he did not show any sympathy or seem to care, and that is the reason I let Mr. Cobb come to see me.

"I never had an engagement with him outside of my home the whole time that I knew him. He always came there. A short while ago I found that it was all over. I had forfeited my home and my life was ruined, and while walking down the street with my husband I could not face the people who at one time were my friends. They knew, and I could not look them in the face. I thought about it all the time, and finally, unable to hold it in any longer, I confessed all to my husband and brother.

"My husband did not show any sympathy, and my brother said that he would rather the whole family was dead than have this disgrace. Dr. Dotson is a good man or he would have killed me on the spot, but after hearing my confession, he began planning to go to Chicago and take the children with him. He told me he loved me enough to stay with me, but I could not live with my two children, for some time they would find out my disgrace, and would not have any respect for me.

"I knew that something had to be done or someone else would suffer besides myself. I knew that my brother would kill Mr. Cobb, and so I had to do it myself. Friday afternoon I came to Nashville to have my little boy's hair cut, and I went to the shop where Cobb was working. While he trimmed the child's hair, I told him that I had told my husband everything, and he seemed angry, but declared that he was not afraid, and

I became frightened then, for I thought that should he meet Dr. Dotson when he came to the city he might kill him.

"Some time ago my husband had given me a revolver which someone had given him, and I decided to come to Nashville today. I kept the pistol in my muff, and as soon as the train reached Union Depot I went to the shop and shot him. I did not do it to revenge myself, only to protect those that I love."

Mrs. Dotson frequently halted during her story, her voice choking with emotion. Tears streamed down her cheeks, but toward the end she was calm, and talked freely of her relations with the man she had killed.

C. A. Hodges, barber, employed at the Jackson shop, declared that he was working on a customer when Mrs. Dotson entered the door. Cobb was shaving a man and glanced around. Staring at each other without making a sign of recognition, the man stood dumbfounded in his tracks, while Mrs. Dotson continued advancing. Not a word was spoken and when Mrs. Dotson was within three feet from the barber, she drew her hand from her muff and opened fire.

Hodges declared that the man whom Cobb was shaving leaped from the chair and made for the door. His face was covered with lather, while a towel was tucked in his shirt collar. He left his collar and necktie in the shop and up to a late hour Saturday night had not returned for his possessions. Where he went is not known and other attendants in the shop could not give his name.

After the wounded man had fallen, Hodges said that Mrs. Dotson walked over to his chair and asked him what she should do. He told her to wait a few minutes, and she sat down. She did not even seem excited but stated that her purpose was accomplished. Hodges stated that Cobb had only been at work in Nashville during the past week and that little was known about him.

After the shooting Cobb was taken to the city hospital. He was unconscious and the new pulmotor was put into service to resuscitate him, but he succumbed within five minutes. The remains were turned over to the undertaking establishment of Gupton-Sweeney Co., to be prepared for burial, and his family was notified.

Messages of the tragedy were sent to Gallatin, where both the victim and the prisoner were well known. Dr. Dotson was soon located, and when told of his wife's trouble, immediately started for Nashville in his automobile. He arrived at police headquarters at 6:30 o'clock, and was ushered into the office of the chief of detectives. He was accompanied by Robert F. Dennis, Mrs. Dotson's brother, and attorney J. T. Baskerville of Gallatin. Immediately after the arrival of her husband, Mrs. Dotson was brought out of the prison. Her face pale and hands trembling, she walked into the private office. Mr. Dennis stepped back, while his sister walked up to her husband and without a word slipped her arms about his neck. The husband clasped her tenderly in his arms. Both were crying. No words were spoken for some time.

Mrs. Dotson sank into a chair, almost prostrate with emotion, while Dr. Dotson leaned over her, talking in low tones. Robert Dennis sat near his sister, but said little. Steps were quickly taken for the release of Mrs. Dotson. Mr. Baskerville communicated with Judge Neil, and her bond was set at $6,000. It was several hours before the bondsman arrived and about 10 o'clock Mrs. Dotson was released from custody. Accompanied by her husband, brother, and attorney, she left for Gallatin in Dr. Dotson's automobile. The following men signed the bond: Dr. Walter Dotson, Judge W. L. Oldham, J. M. Dennis, Sr., B. H. Hix and Dr. Richard Barr. Mrs. Dotson will be given a preliminary hearing Monday morning at 9 o'clock in the city court before Judge Neil.

Dr. Dotson, when seen Saturday night, declared that he was sitting in his front yard when the message of the tragedy was delivered to him. He said that he was preparing then to take his children to the railroad station to send them to his father at Westmoreland, Tenn. He said that as soon as he learned of his wife's trouble he started at once for Nashville. He would not make any statement in regards to his family affairs, having been advised not to do so by his attorney. Mr. Baskerville would not give out anything for publication. He declared that the trial would speak for itself.

Cobb had been working in Gallatin for

the past two years. He came to Nashville about a week ago and obtained a position in Jackson's shop. He boarded with Mrs. Crutcher, 131 Sixth Avenue, North. Cobb's father, who resides at Big Rock, fourteen miles from Clarksville, is a blacksmith. Cobb's wife and child are in Henderson, Ky., with her mother, but on account of the telephone wires being down she has not been told of her husband's death.

The dead barber was about 28 years of age. He was a handsome man. According to the undertaker, four bullets took effect in his body, one striking him in the head, just behind the left ear, another in the left side of his neck, a third entering his neck just below the ear, and a fourth striking him in the left side, lodging near his heart.

At his boarding house, it was stated that Cobb had been in excellent spirits during his week's stay, and Saturday morning joked with those who sat at the same table with him. C. C. Cobb, the dead man's father, will arrive here this morning and will complete the funeral arrangements.

A peculiar incident connected with the shooting of Cobb was that C. C. Jent, a cousin of Mrs. Dotson, was passing the scene when the killing occurred, and stopped only to learn that Mrs. Dotson had killed a man. According to Mr. Jent, whose home is in Hopkinsville, Ky., he was on a Broadway car en route to catch a train for Kentucky, when he noticed the crowd at the entrance to the barber shop. When he reached the depot, curiosity impelled him to walk back to the place. He was told that Mrs. Dotson had killed Cobb. Jent said he went to the telephone and called Dr. Dotson and told him of his wife's trouble. The husband told him to go to the police station with her and stay until he arrived; that he was leaving at once for Nashville in his automobile. Mr. Jent, when told of Mrs. Dotson's statement in regard to her home being wrecked, declared he had never heard of any trouble in the Dotson household. He stayed at police headquarters until Dr. Dotson and his party arrived.

30

PAUL CHRISTIAN WAS UP bright and early that Sunday morning; he bought the first copy of the *Tennessean* the boy on his block untied from his bundle. The kid didn't even get a chance to look at it before the reporter was grabbing it from his hands. He started to protest until Christian flipped him a dime and told him to keep the change.

"WOMAN SUFFRAGE—SENSATIONAL KILLING" the paired headline read. Christian had tried to talk his editor out of the suffrage bit; in his mind, a woman shooting her paramour in front of a shop full of witnesses during broad daylight was more than enough to sell as many Sunday papers as anybody cared to print. The editor wouldn't listen to him, though. Later, Paul Christian would realize why it made sense. The two stories were related in more ways than anyone could see at the time.

Christian held up the paper and read his front page story right there, on the street corner in front of his apartment. In a couple of hours, he guessed, most of Davidson County would be doing what he was doing. The story was just too juicy to pass up; the headline practically begged to be read.

As he read the words Anna Dotson had given him, sitting in the holding cell of the police station, he felt a twinge of guilt. Her confession to Cobb's murder was spread all over the front page of the newspaper. Even if she had Houdini for a lawyer, Christian didn't see any way she could escape the gallows. She had thought about her reasons for killing Charlie Cobb, carefully planned the shooting, and carried it out in front of dozens of eyes. This was about as premeditated a murder as there was, and he'd helped her tell the world all about it. "Mrs. Dotson," he murmured as he read, "you'd better make your peace with God." The only thing for her to do to avoid hanging, he thought, was plead guilty and beg for clemency.

ANNA WAS CONFUSED about a great many things, she realized, but of one thing she was quite certain: she wasn't crazy.

On that first Sunday, the day after the shooting, she and Walter had gone to J. T. Baskerville's office, just across the town square from Walter's clinic. Baskerville had met them at the door, then locked it behind them. They went into his high-ceilinged office with its dark leather furniture and walls lined with bookshelves. Anna and Walter sat in armchairs facing the desk, and the attorney seated himself in his high-backed chair. He put his palms on the desktop and looked at them, and Anna thought he looked more like an undertaker than a legal advocate.

"Walter, Anna . . . I can't tell you how sorry I am to be meeting with you in this situation," he said, confirming the funereal image even more in Anna's mind. "After reading this morning's *Tennessean* . . ."

"J. T., Anna hasn't been herself, not for quite some time," Walter said. "I wonder if that gives us an angle to go at this thing."

The lawyer looked at Anna. "What do you think, Anna? Is Walter right? Have you been feeling quite well, lately?"

Anna met his gaze evenly. "Mr. Baskerville, I'm very sorry about all that has happened. I'm sorry for the shame I've brought on myself and my husband. But what I did yesterday was in fulfillment of a vow.

It is true that I'm responsible for the death of Charlie Cobb. But I did not murder him."

Baskerville's face tilted. "Excuse me? How is it that you accept responsibility for causing his death but don't think you're guilty of murder?"

Anna saw the way Mr. Baskerville and Walter were looking back and forth at each other. *They don't understand; they think I'm talking nonsense.* "If the law makes no distinction between killing someone and murdering them, then I accept the consequences. I knew what I was doing. If that makes me guilty, then maybe I should just plead guilty and—"

"Anna, you must put up some sort of defense," Walter said. "You have to try, at least. For your children."

Once again, the thought of her children made Anna pause.

"Why don't we at least see what the grand jury does?" Baskerville said. "I think it's likely they'll vote to indict, but they might not. And even if they do, we have options."

"Like what?" Walter said. Anna was both saddened and warmed in her heart to see the pitiful way her husband was pouncing on any scrap of hope he could find.

"Well, temporary insanity is a recognized—"

"I'm not insane." *How many times do I have to say it?*

"All right, then. There's the seduction defense . . . although that's usually brought by a husband who has committed violence, rather than the wife . . ."

"It should have been me," Walter said in a low voice. "Anna just beat me to it."

Baskerville took on a worried look. "Anna, the prosecutor will probably ask this question if we go to trial. I know what that reporter claims you told him, but I need to hear answers from you. First, where did you get the gun that you used?"

"It was Walter's gun."

The lawyer's brow creased deeper. "I see . . . And did Walter give you the gun?"

"No! Walter had nothing to do with this. I acted on my own."

"Yes, well, I understand, Anna, but please give me a direct answer. Did Walter give you the gun?"

"No. The gun was on a table and I took it away, so Walter wouldn't be able to find it."

Baskerville sat back in his chair, seeming a tiny bit relieved. "All right, then. So, Anna, it's your contention that Walter didn't send you to shoot Charlie Cobb?"

"Absolutely not."

"How did you know where to find him, then?"

Anna stared into a corner for a few seconds, then looked at Walter. He nodded.

"Walter . . . told me."

Baskerville was nervous again. "I see . . ."

"I told Walter that I would go to him and tell him to leave Nashville. I told him I wanted to end it with Charlie, once and for all."

Baskerville nodded. "Yes. Go on."

"And I did. I went to Nashville last Friday, and I took Scott with me, so Walter would know nothing was going to happen between Charlie and me. I told him to leave."

"And is that all you told him?"

She shook her head. "No. I agreed to come back the next day."

"And did you inform Walter of this?"

"No. I told Walter I was going shopping the next day. It . . . was a lie."

"Never mind that now. You are saying that Walter had no knowledge you were going to Nashville on the day of the shooting?"

Anna nodded. "That's right."

"I suspected," Walter said. "I even had a cousin of mine watching for her. That's bound to come out."

249

"But I think we must demonstrate that Anna acted without your prompting or encouragement, at least on Saturday," Baskerville said. "Otherwise, Walter, you could become an accomplice."

"That must not happen!" Anna said. "I did what I did to protect Walter, to keep him from . . . doing something drastic. Our children must keep at least one of their parents. Please, Mr. Baskerville, you have to understand!"

"I do understand, Anna," the lawyer said. "At least, I think I do. But we have to make sure the legal system understands, as well. That's why I'm asking all these questions now, as your counselor. I don't want you to have to face this for the first time when you're being interrogated by a prosecutor."

There was a silence, then Baskerville said, "Walter, Anna, I want to make a recommendation. I think we need some help with this case. I think we need to talk to J. M. Anderson, in Nashville."

"I've heard of him," Walter said. "The retired judge?"

Baskerville nodded. "Judge Anderson left the bench in 1901, and since then he's made quite a name as a criminal attorney. He doesn't work cheap, and I can't even guarantee he'll take the case, but I know him a bit, and I'm willing to ask him to consider it. If he wants to meet with you, I presume you'd be agreeable?"

Anna and Walter nodded.

"All right, then. Leave that to me, for now. But tomorrow we have to go back to Nashville for the preliminary hearing and arraignment. And as your lawyer, I want you to observe one rule above everything else: don't talk to anyone except me, do you understand? Anna, this Paul Christian fellow with the *Tennessean* has dug a mighty deep hole for you, what with the story that ran in this morning's paper. Anybody who reads it is going to have a hard time believing you could be anything except guilty. So tomorrow, and from now on until the trial, if this goes that far, you must keep silent about the case." He punched his desk with his knuckles to emphasize the last phrase. Anna nodded again, looking at Walter.

"All right, then. Now, I imagine a little bit of a crowd has gathered out along the walk in front of my office."

Walter's shoulders sagged. "Yes. They were in front of our house before sunrise, and they keep coming. They followed us here."

Baskerville nodded in sympathy. "Well. I want the two of you to slip out this back door, to the alley. The less you have to be in crowds and listen to what they say, the better. Besides that, I imagine there's at least half a dozen newspaper reporters out there. We don't need any more attention from them than we've already gotten."

J. M. ANDERSON HUNG UP the phone and leaned back in his chair, studying the pressed tin ceiling of his large, sunlit office. Baskerville had only given him a few details, but this could be an interesting case. Too bad it wasn't one he thought he could win—at least, from what he knew right now. The biggest trouble was, not only he, but anybody who had read yesterday's *Tennessean,* knew from Anna Dotson's own lips that she had come to Nashville on the Dixie Flyer with a pistol hidden in her muff, that she had walked from Union Station down Broadway, entered Jackson's Barbershop, stepped right up to Charlie Cobb, and put at least two bullets in him. And yet she said she hadn't murdered him . . .

Anderson shook his head. Anybody who could say such a thing with a straight face ought to be a shoo-in for an insanity defense. He wondered if he could persuade Baskerville's friend to at least consider it. With that, he thought he could probably keep the noose from around Anna Dotson's neck, and that would be a better outcome than the woman had any reasonable right to expect. Anderson had his reputation to think about, of course. Since leaving the bench, he'd assembled a pretty fair string of victories in court, and though he certainly didn't mind the notoriety such a famous case would bring, he also didn't want a famous loss on his record. Well, it would be interesting to talk to her, at least. Like everyone else in this part of the country, J. M. Anderson was more than a little curious about this attractive, cultured woman who had done the unimaginable. He pushed himself from behind his desk and went out front to tell his secretary to rearrange his schedule for the afternoon.

31

NASHVILLE TENNESSEAN
and The Nashville American

Vol. 6–No. 311.   March 17, 1913

MRS. COBB TO BE STATE'S WITNESS

According to Mrs. Charles Cobb, the widow of the young barber who was shot to death by Mrs. Anna Dotson, the wife of a prominent physician, Saturday afternoon in Jackson's barber shop on Broadway, a vigorous prosecution will be instituted against her husband's slayer. She declared Sunday that she wanted to appear as the prosecutor in the case, and instructed her attorney, G. Bibb Jacobs, that she wanted her name to appear on the warrant that was sworn out against Mrs. Dotson. Attorney Jacobs immediately began active steps against the accused woman, and in consultation with Attorney-General A. V. Anderson and

Assistant Attorney-General J. Washington Moore, agreed to have everything in readiness this morning by 11 o'clock to present the case before the grand jury.

Attorney Jacobs, in discussing the case, stated that his client had instructed him to leave no stone unturned, to push the prosecution with all possible speed. Before leaving Nashville Sunday afternoon, Mrs. Cobb declared that she would leave no loophole for Mrs. Dotson to escape; that she wanted the heaviest bond possible set for her, that she might be kept in custody until the law could take its course.

According to Mr. Jacobs, he will have

the eyewitnesses to the shooting summoned this morning before 9 o'clock, and everything will be in readiness for Attorney-General Anderson to have the indictment prepared for the grand jury at the required time. During the short interval since the shooting occurred much evidence has been procured by the attorneys.

This morning at 9 o'clock Mrs. Dotson will be given a preliminary hearing before Judge Neil in the city court. Little or no testimony will be taken, and it is thought that she will merely be bound over to the criminal court. She will probably arrive in the city early today.

Assistant Attorney-General Moore declared that the grand jury would probably report on the case at an early hour this afternoon.

Mrs. Cobb arrived in the city Sunday morning, having come from Herndon, Ky. where she had been staying with her mother. She was told over the long distance telephone of her husband's death, and hurried to Nashville. Dressed in deep mourning, the bereaved woman could talk but little of the circumstances that led to her husband's tragic end. Frequently her voice would shake with emotion, and tears streamed down her cheeks.

Mrs. Cobb said that when she lived in Gallatin, she and Mrs. Dotson had been very good friends. They had often visited each other, going riding together and attending card parties at the latter's home. Both she and her husband were on good terms with the Dotson family, she declared, and it was only recently that she knew of the difficulty that finally led to the shooting.

ON THE DAY Anna Dotson came to Nashville to enter her plea, Christian woke up wondering how much money was going to change hands in various newspaper offices by the end of the day. His office had a lively little betting pool, with odds running two-to-one in favor of a guilty plea. He was inclined to go with the majority on this, just because he couldn't see any way she could hope to rescue herself by going through with a trial. She'd confessed to the killing in the newspaper, and not only confessed to the act, but to the planning that led up to the act. The state's prosecutor had been telling everyone that he would be asking for the maximum penalty. The way Christian saw it, if Anna Dotson pleaded not guilty, she was a lead-pipe cinch to be the first woman in Tennessee hanged for murder.

The only mitigating factor in Anna's favor was that she had retained J. M. Anderson, a retired judge and one of the most respected criminal defense attorneys in the state. When rumors started flying around that the Baskerville fellow had been having conversations with J. M. Anderson, Christian couldn't believe it. Why would a successful lawyer and former judge like Anderson risk his reputation on a no-win situation like this? And right after that, the reporter started wondering if there was an angle to this case he hadn't thought about. So much about Anna Dotson didn't go according to plan; the possibility of some kind of surprise outcome seemed less far-fetched with her than it might have with another case.

So on Monday morning, as Paul Christian watched Anna sit with her husband and their attorneys while they waited for their case to be called, he was doing a lot of thinking. And one thing he was thinking, a worry that was lodged in his mind like a blackberry seed between his teeth, was that if Walter Dotson, the jealous husband, had shot Charlie Cobb, this whole thing might easily have ended with a no-bill from the grand jury. Christian measured the likelihood of a bunch of Tennessee men looking at and listening to a respected doctor, a community leader whose wife had gone astray, and then indicting him for doing what just about any one of them would have done in the same situation. In his mind, it seemed about as likely as the devil starting a snowball fight.

In doing his research for the story over the weekend on Anna's suffragette background Christian had gotten an earful or two from people like her friend Elizabeth Jennings. And, of course, he'd been writing stories on the women's movement for quite a while. He had to admit, though it made him uncomfortable to do it, that if all the tables in the whole world were turned, and somebody like himself were sitting in front of a grand jury full of women, he wouldn't much care for his chances, either.

Christian figured that with all the notoriety this case had, Judge

Neil would call it ahead of his other business, but the judge took his sweet time, finishing up the trial he was in before admitting the Dotson case. They all cooled their heels for three hours, waiting on A. B. Neil's pleasure. Christian spent most of the time alternating between scribbling notes on his pad and avoiding Walter Dotson's glare. He guessed Anna had identified him as the person she talked to while she was in the holding cell; he was pretty sure he wouldn't be getting a Christmas card from the Dotsons or any of their friends.

Christian had been there early, Johnny-on-the-spot, and he had the *Tennessean*'s best photographer in tow. Not that he had to do much arm-twisting; after his Sunday article, everybody at the paper wanted in on what promised to be a very juicy, protracted story. It was the kind of thing that could make a person's career. Tomorrow would be the third day in a row his words would appear on the front page.

At last, Judge Neil called the case of the *People of Tennessee v. Anna Dotson*, then asked the accused and her counsel to stand. He read the entire indictment, not skipping a single word, pausing every so often just to make sure it was all soaking in: "That Anna Dotson . . . on the 15th day of March, 1913, with force and arms . . . unlawfully, feloniously, willfully, deliberately, premeditatedly, and maliciously did make an assault upon the body of one Charlie Cobb . . . and, with malice aforethought, did kill and murder, against the peace and dignity of the State of Tennessee."

Judge Neil put down the piece of paper he was reading and stared at Anna with eyes like razor blades. "How does the defendant plead?"

"Not guilty," Anna said from underneath her veil. The photographer Christian had brought with him turned to the reporter sitting next to him and held out his hand. Christian saw the reporter grimace as he started digging in his pocket.

Christian had bought a copy of this morning's edition, and had it tucked under his arm as he hurried from the courthouse to the newspaper office. It was cool that day, as it had been for most of the spring, and Christian's pace was brisk. The arraignment had taken longer than he expected—aside from the judge's leisure, Anna Dotson had arrived late, much to the irritation of the spectators who had crowded together hoping for a glimpse of her.

He had hoped for another interview with Mrs. Dotson. But this case was going to sell a lot of papers, Christian thought with a grin, solely based on what she'd already confessed to him. When the Dotsons left the building, both they and their attorney looked haggard, but Anna appeared, to Christian at least, to be at peace. He had the feeling that she was about to break out into a smile. What was going on in that pretty blonde head?

NASHVILLE TENNESSEAN
and The Nashville American

Vol. 6–No. 312.   March 18, 1913

INDICT COBB'S SLAYER

After taking testimony from 11 o'clock until 3 o'clock Monday afternoon, the grand jury sitting in the case of Mrs. W. S. Dotson, wife of a prominent Gallatin physician, who shot and killed Charlie Cobb, a barber, in Jackson's barber shop Saturday afternoon, returned an indictment charging her with murder in the first degree. It was agreed between the attorneys on both sides that the woman's bond should be $20,000, and after some delay the necessary signatures were procured and Mrs. Dotson was released shortly before 5 o'clock, leaving immediately for her home in Gallatin. Her trial was set for May 20.

Standing just within the bar of the criminal court, K. T. McConnico, one of her attorneys, at her side, Mrs. Dotson heard the indictment read without showing the slightest sign of emotion or fear. When the reading was finished she calmly walked over to her husband's side, and the pair hurried from the room.

The sensational shooting of Cobb Saturday afternoon caused a large crowd to gather at the police station early Monday morning, several hours before the arrival of the defendant and her party. Her arrival caused considerable excitement, the crowd following her wherever she went.

The case was set for 9 o'clock Monday morning and long before that hour many people congregated at police headquarters. The court room was crowded, standing room being at a premium. When court convened, and Mrs. Dotson's case was called, disappointment could be read in every face when it was announced that on account of the trains, she would not arrive until 10:10 o'clock. Judge Neil stayed in the courtroom even after he had cleaned up the docket, while in the halls and around the doors of headquarters hung a crowd of the curious. As the minutes slipped by, rumors began to spread and considerable excitement prevailed. According to one rumor, Mrs. Dotson's bond had been declared forfeited and a state's warrant had been sworn out. But Judge Neil declared that he was assured that Mrs. Dotson would appear in court and he waited.

Shortly after 10 o'clock a large delegation of Gallatin people who had come in on the accommodation could be seen coming up Second Avenue. In the center was Mrs. Dotson, her husband, and J. T. Baskerville, their attorney. The crowd craned their necks and Wiles, the photographer who was on the scene, advanced to meet the party, trying to get a photograph of Dr. and Mrs. Dotson.

The photographer put his camera in readiness and as the defendant passed he snapped the picture. Dr. Dotson, hearing the click of the lens, whirled around and said: "You dirty scoundrel." Mr. Baskerville, in attempting to shield his client, rushed at the photographer and struck at the camera, but he was too late, and despite the efforts of the attorney and those surrounding her, several pictures were snapped of Mrs. Dotson before she entered the police station.

Mr. Baskerville, in speaking of the affair, said that he did his best to break the camera, as Mrs. Dotson objected to the publicity and he was trying to carry out her wishes.

As Mrs. Dotson ascended the steps to the courtroom the crowd rushed ahead of her, seeking a vantage point from which they could stare at the prisoner. As she entered the room Clerk Wasserman immediately announced that the court was in session and Mrs. Dotson was called to the stand.

Arraigned before Judge Neil, the charge of murder and carrying a pistol was read to her. She never moved a muscle, but continued staring at Judge Neil in a cool manner. Mr. Baskerville entered a plea of "not guilty" and the defendant was bound over to the criminal court.

When Mrs. Dotson was called to the stand the crowd climbed up on the benches to hear what she would say, and several policemen had to be stationed around the room to keep order. Accompanied by Grand Jury Officer Rice, the defendant was taken promptly to the jail. The crowd followed. A policeman stationed at the jail door kept back the curious, while Mrs. Dotson was registered on the jail blotter.

Walking closely by her side, Dr. Dotson was in constant attendance and sat with her in the jail office while she answered the questions. She gave her age as 32 years, her weight as 103 pounds. She declared that she was 66 inches in height. She was dressed very plainly Monday morning, being clad in a brown morning dress and white-top shoes. A large black hat and heavy veil hid her face while a heavy motor coat and black muff, in which she had brought the revolver to Nashville on the afternoon of the killing, kept out the biting morning air.

As Mrs. Dotson answered the questions of the jailer, she smiled several times, as did Dr. Dotson. Through the courtesy of Jailer William Longhurst, she was placed in a private room, just off the main office, and there allowed to stay until the grand jury had reported on her case. During the interval, many Gallatin people, who had come to Nashville to witness the preliminary hearing, came to see her.

After luncheon Attorneys McConnico, Seay and Baskerville, representing the defense, and Attorney-General Moore and B. Bibb Jacobs for the state and the Cobb family, held consultation in regard to the bond to be set for Mrs. Dotson's appearance in the criminal court for trial.

While the lawyers conversed, the crowd still hung about the hall, trying to get a look at the woman. They jammed back into the court on which the private room opened, and many climbed up on the grating to look in at the windows.

At 1:45 o'clock the grand jury filed into the court and foreman R. D. Marshall handed the findings to Judge Neil. Dr. Dotson was in the room, and sat laughing and talking with his lawyers while the report was being read by the court. A special ruling by the court permitted citizens of Gallatin to sign Mrs. Dotson's bond, after it had been announced that $20,000 had been the sum agreed upon.

The bond was quickly written out and signed and an order for the prisoner's release was sent to the jail. On account of the crowd at the doors and the fear, Mrs. Dotson was taken to the courtroom through the rear of the building. When she entered the room it was practically empty, with the exception of attorneys and newspaper men.

Without a tremor, she walked within the bar. K. T. McConnico met her midway and standing before Judge Neil she listened attentively to the reading of the report of the grand jury. Mr. McConnico immediately entered a plea of "not guilty" to the charge set forth in the indictment, and Mrs. Dotson, after a few preliminaries, was released.

Closely surrounded by her husband and lawyers, she walked to Union Station, a few blocks distant, where she boarded a train for Gallatin.

When seen Monday by a representative from the *Tennessean and American*, the lawyers for the defense declared they had nothing to say, that the trial would speak for itself.

Those who signed Mrs. Dotson's bond were as follows: Tom Bradley, $10,000; W. P. Freeman, $500; Ed S. Anderson, $1,000; Walter Dotson, $4,500; B. H. Hix, $500; V. C. Walden, $1,000; H. J. Dotson, $2,500. The latter bondsman is the father of Dr. Walter Dotson.

CHRISTIAN'S STORY RAN on Tuesday, the day after the arraignment, accompanied by the blurred picture of Anna's appearance there. In fact, there was a succession of stories in various papers about the Dotsons, covering everything from Walter's medical practice to Anna's activity with the Sumner County suffragettes. It was the only topic of discussion in the newspaper office. In fact, Christian was starting to get a little tired of being summoned to conversations willy-nilly. It was hard to get his work done.

Detective Sidebottom collected a few column inches, too. He was widely interviewed about his views on the case, and much was made of his trips to Gallatin, during which he interviewed people who knew the Dotsons, the Cobbs, or who had any information to offer about the case. He even located a neighbor who claimed to have heard pistol shots from the Dotsons' backyard not too many days before the crime. Sidebottom seemed very interested in this; he said he had a hunch it might explain something about Anna's motivation. "I believe the husband might have been a conspirator," he told Christian. "I'll bet he had something to do with the gunfire in the backyard. At first, I suspected there was more than one shooter. All of the witnesses said they heard four shots. But after meeting with the coroner and after he described the exit and entrance wounds on Cobb's body, I now think there was only one shooter: Anna Dotson. Though I still think Doctor Dotson had something to do with Anna going to the barbershop with the intent to kill Cobb."

• • •

ANNA AND WALTER RETURNED to Nashville for a meeting with J. M. Anderson not long after the arraignment. Anderson had a fine, leonine countenance, with graying hair and a strong chin. He smiled at her as she entered his spacious office and removed her veil, and came around from behind his large desk to hold her chair as she sat. He shook hands with Walter and Mr. Baskerville before returning to his tall-backed, oak-framed leather chair. As he seated himself and bridged his fingertips, Anna could easily imagine him on the bench, presiding over a trial.

"Well, I'm glad we could all sit down together," he said. "Anna, I sincerely hope I can be of assistance to you in this trouble. How did things go with Judge Neil?" he said, looking at Mr. Baskerville.

"As I feared, Anna was indicted for first-degree murder," Baskerville said.

Anderson nodded. "I was afraid of that, too. I want you to know from the outset, Anna and Walter, that this is going to be an uphill battle. I took the liberty of meeting with Attorney General Anderson, who'll be prosecuting the case—no relation, by the way," he said with a little smile. "I called him up and asked him to have a cup of coffee with me over at a café on Demonbreun. From our informal conversation, I could tell he believes the state's case is very strong. He gave me every indication he plans to ask for the maximum penalty."

Anna swallowed and nodded. "I understand, Mr. Anderson. And I'm prepared to accept the consequences for my actions."

"Well, but let's not get ahead of ourselves," Anderson said. "We've got some time before the trial, probably?"

"The twentieth of May," Mr. Baskerville said. "About two months."

"Well, then. Let's talk about that. You entered a plea of not guilty. That would guarantee a jury trial and as I've already said, the state thinks it has a rock-solid case."

"Mr. Anderson, I didn't murder Charlie Cobb," Anna said.

Anderson glanced at the two other men in the room, then studied the backs of his hands for a few seconds. "Well, Anna, I hear what you're saying, and I believe you're sincere in saying it, but I don't know offhand how we'd convince a jury to make such a fine distinction." He looked at Walter and Mr. Baskerville again, then back at her. "I wonder, Anna, if you'd consent to being examined by a psychiatrist?"

"I'm not insane, Mr. Anderson."

"And your demeanor bears that out, I must admit. But Anna, I want to save your life, if there's any way possible. Will you let me make an appointment for you with Dr. J. W. Stephens? He's the director of the City View Sanitarium, and the best psychiatrist in Nashville. I'd like his opinion on your mental state."

"I've heard of him. He's a fine doctor, Anna," Walter said.

"Well, if it will prove to you and everyone else that I'm not crazy, I'll go see him," Anna said. "But I tell you, I knew what I was doing."

"Fine, then. I want you to see Dr. Stephens. And Anna, Walter, listen to me: I must, in fairness, tell you that if you won't at least consider temporary insanity as a defense in the case, I don't see how I can represent you."

Walter nodded quickly. Anna just stared at him for a few seconds, then shrugged.

TWO DAYS LATER, Anna stepped out of Walter's Winton Six onto the grounds of City View Sanitarium, on a hillside overlooking the Murfreesboro Pike. She walked toward the building, her apprehension building with each step. What if, somehow, Dr. Stephens concluded she really was insane? Would he lock her up here, in a padded cell, bound in a straitjacket? Would she ever see Mabel and Scott again?

Anna tried to force these thoughts out of her mind. She wasn't crazy, and she knew it, and of course Dr. Stephens, if he was as good as everybody said he was, would see that soon enough. She glanced at Walter, walking beside her with his palm on her elbow. He was looking straight ahead. Anna could tell he was worried, too.

They were met at the massive front doors by a very pleasant-looking orderly, dressed in white. He took them up a flight of stairs and down a very clean hallway, to a solid-looking door made of some dark wood and set with panes of frosted glass. He motioned them inside into a waiting room, then crossed the room and tapped on a smaller door. The door opened, he said a few words to whoever was inside, then smiled at them and left.

It was quiet here. Anna was relieved; she'd been prepared to hear the wails and cries of the inmates, to see someone running half-naked down a hall, pursued by orderlies. But as far as she could tell, the City View Sanitarium was a well-kept, orderly place.

Dr. Stephens came into the waiting room and greeted them. He told Walter he wanted to see Anna alone, then took her back to his office.

"Do you know why you're here, today?" he asked when they were both seated.

"You're supposed to examine me and determine my sanity in the matter of the killing of Charlie Cobb."

Dr. Stephens nodded and then sat back in his chair. "Tell me your version of what had happened that day, and how you feel about it."

She told him.

"I knew what I was doing, Dr. Stephens. I killed Charlie Cobb, but it wasn't murder—at least, as far as my vow to God was concerned. I killed him to protect my husband and my brother, to keep them from committing violence or being killed themselves. I did it for my family, Dr. Stephens. There was no other way."

32

ANNA SAW THE PSYCHIATRIST two more times, during the weeks between her pleading and her trial. Stephens told J. M. Anderson that he believed Anna suffered from a mental condition he called "monomania," in which the subject was perfectly sane in all areas of life except one; with respect to that single area or topic, a monomaniac was so fixated as to be incapable of rational thought. He said that he believed Anna Dotson exhibited the symptoms of monomania with respect to Charlie Cobb. From that perspective, he said, she might very well have been functionally insane when she committed the crime.

Anna didn't believe a word of this, but since it seemed to give Mr. Anderson, and especially Walter, a ray of hope, she kept her thoughts to herself. She had agreed to be examined, but only on the condition that she was allowed to speak on her own behalf at the trial. J. M. Anderson told her that in most cases involving temporary insanity, the jury wanted to hear the defendant anyway, so he thought this was a good idea. But Anna knew what she meant to say if certain questions were asked. Anderson's plan for an insanity defense was all well and good, but Anna had already decided she was going to tell the truth as far as she knew it, and the consequences would just have to take care of themselves.

• • •

IN THE WEEKS PRECEDING THE TRIAL, Anna, Walter, and J. T. Baskerville made dozens of trips into Nashville to confer with J. M. Anderson. Every time, Anderson would try to persuade Anna to plead guilty to a lesser offense so that he could offer the prosecution a sure conviction in exchange for a lighter sentence. And each time, Anna would quietly and firmly refuse. One day, about two weeks before the trial was set to begin, Anderson, exasperated, said, "Confound it, Anna! You're painting yourself into a corner with your stubbornness." He looked around at Walter, who was smiling. "What on God's green earth have you got to smile about, Dr. Dotson?"

Walter looked at Anna and shook his head. "That's my Anna. Stubborn as a mule when she gets a notion into her head. I couldn't ever change her; her mother and daddy couldn't, and they tried for years before me. I don't think there's a lawyer, judge, jury, or court in the state of Tennessee that can, either."

"Well, your stubborn wife is going to get up in front of a jury of twelve stubborn Tennessee men, and then we'll see whose mind gets changed."

ANDERSON WAS WORRIED. He had a two-part strategy: First, he would attempt to convince the jury that Anna Dotson was not mentally competent, using Stephens' expert diagnosis of monomania; next, he hoped to show that Charlie Cobb had seduced her, exerting such force of will as to emphasize or even bring about her mental instability, then exploiting it for his own gratification. He had notified the prosecution of his intent to amend Anna's plea to not guilty by reason of insanity, and they would presumably call their own experts to refute Stephens' diagnosis. Still, it was as good a defense as he thought he could mount, under the circumstances.

But what kept J. M. Anderson awake nights was the character of his client, the way she presented herself. On the one hand, she was forthright, confident—and much too good-looking for her own good.

Her candor could be disarming, and he suspected a jury of men would be as subject to her charm as anyone else. But would they believe she was insane? Would they really permit themselves to buy into Charlie Cobb's emotional power over her? Anderson just couldn't convince himself that they would. Furthermore, he was all too aware that Anna, once she got up on the witness stand, might say just about anything. With a single sentence, she could knock his defense strategy galley west. There was just no way to predict how she was going to respond; even her husband admitted as much, for pity's sake! About twenty times each day, Anderson regretted having promised her she could take the witness stand.

In the meantime, he moved for a continuance, on the basis of "adverse and prejudicial publicity." The trial had already been rescheduled for mid-June, but the public interest hadn't waned. Judge Neil reviewed his motion until just after the first of June, when he denied it. Next, Anderson made an emergency appeal to the Tennessee State Supreme Court, asking for either a continuance or a change of venue to another county. He cited the extensive and unflattering newspaper coverage of the crime and claimed that it was highly unlikely that an impartial jury could be chosen anywhere in Davidson County. Infuriatingly, the court ruled against him, stating that "a prospective juror could not be automatically disqualified simply because a particular potential juror had read newspaper accounts."

J. M. Anderson had run out of cards to play. Anna Dotson was going to go on trial, that trial would be in Nashville, and it was going to begin on June 17, 1913. There was not a thing in the world that he or anyone else could do about it.

33

IT WAS SHORTLY AFTER EIGHT in the morning on June 17 when Paul Christian went over to the press office located in the police department. He usually shared the newsroom—and the type-writer—with the courthouse beat newsmen from the other papers, but not this time. Tacked to the door was a cardboard sign that read "Paul Christian." Underneath the sign was another cardboard notice tacked to the door: "No other reporters will be allowed entry with-out permission of Paul Christian, by order of the Nashville Police Department." It was signed "Sidebottom." The room contained one hard bed with enough room for one reporter to stretch out on, two rickety chairs, a desk, and a typewriter—Spartan accommodations at best. But the small room was convenient to the courthouse, police department, and jail; it was an amenity all the reporters had come to appreciate. And, apparently, it was to become Christian's exclusive home away from home for the seven-day trial.

He went over to the courthouse and up to the second floor. A court officer was waiting for him; the bailiff took the reporter into the courtroom and up to the first row of spectator benches. A card was attached to the back of that section of the long oak bench, and it read, "Paul Christian, *Tennessean and American.*"

Folks were sure going to a lot of trouble for him, he thought. Of course, he was the prosecution's star witness.

From the scowls and mutters he was getting from the fellows from the other papers, this special treatment wasn't sitting well with them. Christian had to admit, if he'd been in their shoes, he'd have grumbled, too. As far as anyone could remember, no one reporter had ever been given an exclusive reserved seat in a criminal trial.

Just before nine o'clock, one hundred adult men residing in Davidson County answered their subpoenas to appear as prospective jurors in the case of the *People of Tennessee v. Anna Dotson.* Twelve men from the pool of over one hundred would be chosen to decide her fate.

The courthouse was crowded. Besides the hundred men who were summoned there were many others: curiosity seekers, attorneys, reporters, and interested citizens. Surprisingly, given the generous coverage the trial had been receiving for nearly three months now, the officials were neither prepared nor equipped to accommodate such a large crowd.

As the prospective jurors began to gather outside Judge Neil's courtroom, located on the second floor, the massive crowd was spilling out and down to the ground floor; some of the subpoenaed jurors were sitting on the low walls along the sidewalk cut into the hillside, outside the side doors of the building.

Christian saw the defense team and the state's entourage, led by Attorney General Anderson, hurrying into a side conference room, just off the main courtroom. Later, the lead prosecutor would tell the press that he had made what he characterized as his "first and last offer" to the defense team: a plea of guilty and a recommendation for a life sentence with possibility of parole after twenty years.

Christian could tell from their faces that Anna's lawyers thought it was a good offer. Defending someone who had already confessed had to be weighing heavily on their minds. Anna's lawyers approached her as she stood beside the entrance to the courtroom, next to her husband, Dr. Dotson, and their two children.

Anna was wearing a long brown dress with a brown mesh veil covering her face. Her dress was conservative and though her veil hid her face, nothing camouflaged her attractive figure.

J. M. Anderson came out of the conference room and walked briskly toward Anna, Walter, and their two frightened children. He said something to her and then ushered them all outside for a few minutes. When they came back in, the defense attorney's face was more grave than ever. Christian guessed he'd given Anna some advice related to the impromptu meeting he'd just had with the prosecution, and she'd refused it.

"Wouldn't even discuss it with her husband," the reporter heard Anderson say to E. T. Seay, one of the assisting defense attorneys.

"Life in prison with parole after twenty years sure beats the noose," Seay said.

The men in the crowd that was milling around the courthouse were mostly studying Anna when they could; the few women there looked like they were doing their best to avoid having anyone think they were noticing her.

Judge Neil's bailiff stepped out into the hallway and told the attorneys to come inside. As the attorneys entered the courtroom, the court officer stood guard at the door.

After the attorneys, Anna, Walter, Daisy Cobb, Detective Sidebottom, and Christian were also allowed inside. Anna's attorneys took up their positions at the defense table, facing the judge's bench and at right angles to the jury box. Anna sat in the center of the table, with Anderson on her right, and Seay and Baskerville on her left. The lawyers each presented a calm exterior, but Christian knew they had to be churning on the inside.

Across from the defense bench and still facing the judge, but farther from the jury box, sat the stern-faced prosecution team. Christian was seated behind them, on the other side of the wooden rail separating the judge and the attorneys from the rest of the courtroom. Attorney General Anderson was assisted by attorneys "Bibbs" Jacobs, Washington Moore, and Woodall Murray. To Christian's left, also in the front row, was Daisy Cobb, dressed in a plain black dress.

There was a lull in the proceedings while everyone waited for the judge to enter. Attorney General Anderson, a small, feisty forty-year-old, leaned toward the defense table and said to J. M. Anderson, "The offer is withdrawn." The prosecutors were obviously confident and anxious to get the trial underway.

Judge Neil entered and took his seat and asked, "Is the state ready?"

"Yes, your Honor, we are ready to proceed."

Judge Neil turned to the defense table. "Is the defense ready?"

"Yes, your Honor, we are ready."

"Then we shall proceed to choose a jury. I suppose the best way is to first bring into the courtroom the prospective jurors, and I will ask some general questions. Then I will retire to my office, and each juror shall be brought into my chambers, one by one, and asked additional questions by counsel. If both sides accept the juror, he will be taken to the jury room; if a juror is challenged and is dismissed, we will escort him out with instructions to stay away from the courthouse until a jury of twelve men is ultimately chosen. Each of you has eight challenges for any reason. Any objections?"

"That is acceptable to the state."

"It is suitable to the defense."

And with that, the trial was underway. Even though he knew it was going to happen, Christian couldn't suppress a wince when the bailiff motioned him out of the room. Only the principals and their counsel would be allowed to observe the voir dire. As he walked slowly from the courtroom, Paul Christian took a long look at the back of Anna Dotson's head. She sat as straight as any school teacher. Christian couldn't help wondering how she'd maintain her posture when the jury sentenced her to the gallows.

J. M. ANDERSON LISTENED CAREFULLY as Judge Neil ordered that the jury pool of one hundred men be brought into the courtroom. The clerk went out into the hallway and began to call out the names. It took half an hour, since some of the prospective jurors were on the floor below and outside the courthouse. The officers of the court had to walk down the hallways and down the stairs until they'd located and summoned each man whose name was on their lists. Finally, they were all in the courtroom, seated in the spectator seats, along the walls, and in the balcony.

Judge Neil ordered the prospective jurors to stand and be sworn. They raised their right hands and swore to "truly answer the questions posed to them." The judge then explained the purpose of voir dire: "to pick a fair and impartial jury."

The judge asked the first, compelling question: "If you have not read in the newspapers or heard any conversation about this case, the *People of Tennessee v. Anna Dotson*, please raise your hands." Only five or so men raised their hands, confirming to the judge and to the lawyers that the case carried substantial notoriety, since the news coverage of the murder was so widespread.

Judge Neil summoned the lawyers to the bench, and in a low voice he said, "There is no reason to ask any prospective juror whether he has read about the case. Reading the newspapers is not grounds to disqualify a juror, and the Supreme Court of Tennessee has so ruled." He peered meaningfully at the defense counsel.

The prosecution agreed readily; J. M. was far from enthusiastic, but decided to say nothing. Still, he could tell that things were already not going his way. The publicity factor was something he had planned to question the individual jurors about, for the purpose of creating a record for a possible appeal. But now, if he went that route, he risked offending Judge Neil.

The individual questioning of jurors began. One by one, the prospective jurors were called into the judge's chambers and each took a seat in the middle of the room. After the judge had asked his questions, both sides followed with their own.

The prosecution mostly asked each man if he believed in the death penalty, and whether, if the evidence supported it, he could sentence a woman to die on the gallows if she were convicted of murder in the first degree. A handful of men answered that they did not believe in the death penalty. The prosecution moved to excuse them, but Anderson quickly objected to this being a valid reason for their exclusion. Judge Neil ruled in favor of the state, though, and he excused for cause those who did not believe in the death penalty. Since it was for cause, these challenges did not count against the total number of regular challenges the prosecutors were allowed—another blow to the defense.

In his questions to the prospective jurors, Anderson at first concentrated on whether a prospective juror, having heard conversation about the case, could still be fair. He asked each, "Will you keep an open mind and give the defendant a fair shake?" Then, as a follow-up question, the defense counsel handed each prospective juror a partial copy of the March 16th *Tennessean and American.*

Anderson was careful not to discuss the part of the article describing the murder, lest he draw the ire of Judge Neil, who had already announced that asking questions along that line would not be tolerated. Instead, he showed the men the portion of the double headline that read, "WOMAN SUFFRAGE." He asked each of the prospective jurors, "What is your feeling about the suffrage movement by women?"

The prosecution looked confused by this line of inquiry, which suited Anderson just fine. Judge Neil seemed irritated by it, and that was a little more worrisome, but since the "SENSATIONAL MURDER" headline was not shown to a single prospective juror, he let the questioning about women's suffrage continue, over the objection of the state. J. M. Anderson excused eight men who were adamant about their opposition to the right of women to vote. It was a good idea, but it used up all eight of his peremptory challenges; the defense had no way to exclude anyone else from the jury.

Anderson also would have wanted to exclude from the jury any man who stated skepticism about insanity or monomania as a valid basis for a plea of not guilty. Unfortunately, the suffrage issue used up all his options. He knew as well as any first-year law student that the case is often won or lost in voir dire. The most important thing an attorney can do for his client is to try to empanel a jury that will be most sympathetic to the point of view he wants to present. Anderson had done his best, but now he was out of ammunition.

So, as it turned out, there were an equal number of men on the jury on both sides of the women's suffrage question. Amazingly, though, for such a notorious trial, by noon, twelve jurors had been chosen from the original batch of one hundred. The average age of the panel was about fifty. These men would decide Anna Dotson's fate.

34

Aₙₙₐ ₗₒₒₖₑD ᵤₚ as the jury filed into the courtroom. Her
life now lay in the hands of these twelve strangers. When Mr.
Baskerville returned from the judge's chambers to their table in the
courtroom, he had made a reassuring face, but Anna could tell from
the way he shuffled his papers this way and that that he was far from
relaxed about her prospects. She closed her eyes and said a quick
prayer. Whatever happened was up to the Good Lord and J. M. Anderson—along with the twelve men now staring at her from the jury
box.

The other Mr. Anderson, the lead prosecutor, gave the state's opening statement. The attorney general portrayed Anna Dotson as "an
intelligent and sane woman who had entered the barbershop with the
intent to kill, after considerable aforethought." He suggested that the
jury would "agree that she was a mean woman who simply committed adultery for her own gratification, and then committed murder as
an act of vindictiveness." Attorney General Anderson asked the jury
to "assess the ultimate penalty, death by hanging." Anna felt her chest
tightening each time he mentioned the death penalty. Though she
thought she had clearly understood all the possible consequences of
her actions, the possibility of execution had suddenly become much

more real to her. She could feel it in the denouncing tone of the prosecutor's voice; she could see it in the closed faces and staring eyes of the jurors.

Anna was thankful she had worn a hat with a veil; she didn't think she could have endured that harsh scrutiny any other way.

J. M. Anderson gave the opening statement for the defense. He portrayed Anna in a different light. "Anna is a person who was driven to this act by the deeds of the deceased. Anna was temporarily insane; you, the jury, will hear expert testimony that will prove Anna was suffering from monomania, which means she is a sane person in all respects except in relation to one person or thing . . . Anna is, sometimes to her own detriment, an independent woman." The defense attorney paused and made eye contact with each member of the jury as he spoke his next words. "Anna killed Charlie Cobb, but in her own, infirm mind, she believes she did not murder him."

At this, several of the jurors reacted with visible expressions of doubt. *She killed him, but she did not murder him?* It was the truth; it was exactly what Anna had said herself, in Mr. Anderson's office, and elsewhere. But stated here in the courtroom, and coming from the mouth of J. M. Anderson, even she thought it sounded far-fetched. Anna felt her hope dimming from moment to moment. Despite her best efforts to rein in her imagination, she began seeing visions of Mabel and Scott standing at the graveside of a mother who had first disgraced them, then left them bereft.

The first witness for the prosecution was Davidson County Coroner L.W. Gupton, who testified as to the path of the two gunshots that struck Cobb: "One in the left ear area, and one in the left side, near his midsection." The coroner continued, "The shot to Cobb's head went down into his body, severing arteries and leading to his death from bleeding." He continued, "The second bullet entered Charlie Cobb's body in the upper midsection . . . either of the two would have killed him." Apparently, the coroner's testimony was supposed to lay to rest any lingering doubts about whether two or four shots had been fired. Then the prosecutors introduced into evidence Charlie Cobb's clothes. As the gray, blood-soaked garments were being passed around among the jurors, there was silence in the courtroom, similar to the hush that accompanies the shoveling of dirt on a dead man's grave after the preacher has said his last words. The jurors, as well as the audience, were visibly affected. All the while, Anna continued to sit staring straight ahead, her face still covered by the veil. She made herself hold absolutely still. She was surprised at how little emotion she felt, seeing Charlie's ruined clothing.

The next called were the eyewitnesses who were inside the barbershop when the shots were fired. The prosecution began questioning with the direct examination of barber C. A. Hodges. "Immediately after the shooting, and while she was still holding the gun, McCurdy—he's another barber—he asked her, 'Lady, what is the matter?'" Hodges testified. "She told him, 'That man wrecked my home and broke my husband's heart. This thing has ruined my life and will not ruin another.'"

Staring at the jury, Attorney General Anderson said, "'This thing'? Is that what you said, Mr. Hodges? Anna Dotson, the smoking gun still in her hand, characterized the man she had just killed as a 'thing'?"

"Yes, sir," Hodges said.

Still staring at the jury, the attorney general said, "No further questions, your Honor."

Hearing her own words in Hodges' mouth, Anna realized how she must be appearing to the jurors. But how could they understand what Charlie Cobb, had taken from her? How could any man understand?

ON WEDNESDAY, the state picked up where it had left off. Another witness who was in the barbershop testified that after Anna shot Charlie Cobb, she said, "I am Mrs. Dotson of Gallatin. You know my husband. I did what I came here to do and you can send him word. This man wrecked my home and broke my husband's heart."

Anna had to make a conscious effort to keep herself from nodding in agreement to her own words.

The prosecutor carefully crafted the questions he asked the eyewitnesses, continuing to pile up testimony intended to corroborate the state's point that Anna was cold and callous, even after the two fatal shots were fired. The eyewitnesses testified that she appeared prepared to fire more shots into the body of Cobb as he writhed in pain on the floor. One witness insinuated that had it not been for Mr. Dunn, who, with the help of Mr. Jackson, the proprietor, grabbed the gun when Mrs. Dotson pointed it down at Cobb, she would have fired more shots into his body.

One of the barbers, who did not see the shooting but was there at the time, testified about events surrounding the previous day's visit by Anna Dotson. He stated that on that Friday, he overheard Charlie Cobb telling Anna Dotson, who was standing next to him while he was cutting Anna's son's hair, "I am moving my family back to Nashville within two weeks." The purpose of this testimony was to buttress the state's assertion of premeditation; it clearly showed that Anna planned to kill Charlie Cobb if he attempted to move back to Gallatin, Nashville, or anywhere close.

Witnesses testified that Anna had brought the gun into the barbershop after hiding it in her muff. The prosecutor was painting Anna as a calculating killer, since she concealed the pistol all the way from her home in Gallatin.

The state showed the jury the photograph taken of Anna, published in the newspaper the Tuesday after the murder, depicting Anna Dotson with the same muff when she appeared at the preliminary hearing. "Gentlemen of the jury, this woman was more interested in her attire than the life of Charlie Cobb," the prosecutor said, further cementing in jurors' minds her supposedly coldhearted attitude.

Some of the jurors were starting to look really angry, but Anna held herself in check and continued to sit as still as a stone, staring straight ahead. They could put a noose around her neck, and they probably would, but she was determined to hold onto what was left of her dignity.

Barber L. H. McCurdy testified, "I had the next chair to Cobb. I knew him for about a week. Cobb was a pleasant, agreeable man. I first saw Mrs. Dotson the day before the killing. She had passed the shop a time or so before she entered with a little boy accompanying her. She went in the direction of Cobb's chair, toward the rear of the shop, and the boy was placed in Cobb's chair to have his hair cut. Mrs. Dotson stood beside the chair and talked to Cobb while he was cutting the child's hair. When the work was finished, Mrs. Dotson walked with the child to the front of the shop. Cobb followed them, and he reminded her that she had forgotten to pay for the work. She asked his pardon and Cobb told her to pay him and he would settle for it. Afterward, Cobb and Mrs. Dotson walked out of the shop to the vicinity of the barber pole. They stood there and talked for about ten minutes."

Mr. McKinley, a city fireman, said, "I was getting a shave when shots were fired. Mrs. Dotson's back was toward me at the time. Mrs. Dotson later appeared very calm. I asked her what was the trouble, and Mrs. Dotson replied, 'He broke my husband's heart, wrecked my home, and I am the mother of two children.'"

Anna watched the juror's faces, but if they had any shadow of sympathy for a woman's plight, they did a good job of hiding it. This was hopeless; how could twelve men be expected to understand what was in her heart and mind?

Officer H. P. McGarver testified next. He acknowledged making the initial arrest and identified the revolver that was exhibited. He said, "There were two empty shells in it when I examined the pistol a few minutes after the shooting."

The judge recessed the trial for the noon hour. Anna, Walter, and the defense attorneys went to Mr. Anderson's office for a bit more privacy. J. M. Anderson sent out for sandwiches, but Anna wasn't hungry. She couldn't get out of her mind the way the jurors had looked at her.

As if reading her mind, Walter asked J. M. Anderson, "It seems the prosecution is doing quite a bit of damage. Are we going to be all right?"

Anderson didn't answer for a few seconds. "All they've really done so far is establish the facts. We aren't disputing the facts—we can't. When it comes time to make our case, we have to show them the 'why' behind the facts. That's what we're counting on."

Walter didn't look convinced. And, as far as Anna could see, the other defense lawyers didn't, either.

Just after the recess, the state called Jordan Warren, a neighbor from Gallatin. Anna wished she could have looked at Walter without raising her veil and turning her head; what in the world could the prosecutors want with Jordan Warren?

Under questioning from the prosecution, Anna began to understand, and her dread ratcheted higher.

"On the Monday or Tuesday before the killing," he testified, "I heard several shots fired in the backyard of the Dotson home. I was eating dinner at the time and heard two or three shots, but was unable to see anyone. When I finished dinner and was standing in front of the Keystone Hotel talking to a gentleman, I heard more shots and saw Dr. Dotson set up a board, which I presumed had been used as a target. I did not see Mrs. Dotson. I thought there was probably six or seven shots altogether. I did not see who was doing the shooting."

The prosecution was still hanging on to the possibility that Walter had put Anna up to the shooting. They were trying to use Jordan Warren's testimony as a link between Walter and the target practice in his backyard, which could, in turn, imply that he had a hand in planning the crime. *Oh, Walter! This is what I was trying to protect you from!*

Attorney General Anderson asked Jordan Warren a few more questions, then he was finished. He turned toward the jury and announced his next witness: "The state calls Daisy Cobb to the stand."

35

Daisy was wearing the same plain black dress as the day before, Walter noticed. On the witness stand she displayed a particularly meek and sad demeanor; the jury and the audience were clearly sympathetic to her. And why shouldn't they be? She was as much a victim as anyone—not only of Anna's actions, but of her husband's infidelity.

The first question from the prosecutor was "Do you know Anna Dotson?"

"I do." Slowly, her head turned until she faced Anna. Their eyes met and held. The room was silent—not a cough or a shuffle to be heard. Anna, in contrast to Daisy, was dressed in a fashionable outfit with a matching hat. A blue veil covered his wife's face; she sat motionless, as she had throughout the trial thus far. Walter didn't know how she could possibly remain so outwardly calm.

The state pressed on. "Do you want Anna Dotson to be found guilty of murder for the death of your late husband, Charlie Cobb?"

Tears began trickling from Daisy's eyes. "Yes, I do."

"Do you want Anna Dotson to pay the ultimate price for what she did to your husband and for what she did to you and to your child, Alice, seated over there?"

"Yes, I do," Daisy said, her shoulders beginning to shake with sobs.

Attorney Seay rose from his seat beside Anna. "Your Honor, with all due respect, it is not up to Mrs. Cobb; it is up to the jury to decide the fate of this remorseful defendant."

The attorney general jumped out of his chair. "When counsel gets his chance he can certainly cross-examine Mrs. Cobb! It is not his time to make a speech on behalf of his so-called remorseful client, who murdered Charlie Cobb in cold blood!"

Judge Neil pounded his gavel. "Mr. Prosecutor, stop yelling, and both of you, stop arguing to the jury through your objections! I sustain the objection."

Walter studied the jury; how could they just ignore what the prosecution had said? The state's attorneys were taking every opportunity to paint Anna as a cruel, cold-blooded killer. It made Walter angry, but there was nothing he could do about it except sit with his hands in his lap, balled into fists, and pray that J. M. Anderson knew what he was doing.

Judge Neil turned to the jury. "Gentlemen of the jury, it is up to you to decide the fate of the defendant. It makes no difference what anyone else thinks; you will make the final decision." The attorney general sat down, grumbling under his breath, but from the expressions on the faces of the jury, Walter wondered if the objection had served any purpose other than highlighting the difference between the emotionally overwrought Daisy and the seemingly cool and collected Anna.

Daisy's testimony was heart wrenching. She testified about having a "loving relationship" with her husband. She did qualify that by stating that lately she "did indeed think something was amiss" in their marriage. "I began to suspect that there was something going on between my Charlie and Anna Dotson." Daisy Cobb talked about the friendship she and Charlie had with Anna and her husband, Walter.

She related that they "were quite intimate" and had "been thrown together often," that she saw Anna Dotson almost every day. "I considered her my best friend and dismissed any thought that I might have that she and my husband were carrying on. I trusted her." Daisy's lips trembled, and she covered her mouth with a hand and tried to compose herself.

It was strange for Walter to realize that in many ways, he and Daisy were co-victims. And yet he wanted, more than anything, for Anna to have a second chance—and Daisy wanted Anna to die.

"We used to play hide and seek in the Dotsons' yard with the children, and I noticed that Mrs. Dotson and Charlie were always the last ones caught," Daisy continued. "One day I pinned a rose on his coat and she took it off. However, during that time I never saw any improper relations between the two."

These words gave Walter a sharp pang. He thought of all the times he should have suspected something. If only he'd paid attention to his wife, as a husband should! Surely he'd have seen . . . something.

"Anna and I had written to each other on many occasions when I was out of town, visiting my family in Kentucky," Daisy said. "We exchanged letters and cards expressing words of endearment." The state then introduced as evidence and exhibits several postcards Mrs. Cobb identified as having been written by Mrs. Dotson to her while she was on visits to her parents' home in Herndon, Kentucky.

Daisy testified about the night she and Charlie decided to leave Gallatin on short notice. She said, "Charlie told me he had gotten into trouble with Anna Dotson . . . I took that statement by Charlie to mean he and Anna had been having relations." She continued, "Charlie told me the truth about the affair after Walter had left our front yard—after Walter had made the death threat. The last letter that I received from Charlie was dated the day before his death."

Daisy said, "That night, when Walter came to our house, I was convinced that Walter would kill my husband if Charlie did not leave Gallatin as soon as possible. I decided to forgive Charlie that night after he confessed to me, and I wanted to try to make our little family work. We left very hastily, leaving much of our furniture and belongings behind. Me and Alice went to Kentucky to my parents' house ... Charlie was not welcome by my family when they found out the truth of the situation ... Charlie went to his pa's home in Tennessee.

"I wanted to have a talk with Anna. I wanted to know how my best friend could find comfort in sleeping with my husband, behind my back, pretending all the while to be my friend. She pulled the wool over my eyes and Dr. Dotson's too. Maybe I could have forgiven her. It would have been hard, but I could have forgiven her. But I cannot forgive her for ruining my baby's life, my little girl who has harmed no one, and who now has no father." Daisy broke down and sobbed uncontrollably.

Walter was having a hard time controlling his own emotions; in Daisy's words he could easily recall many of his enraged reproaches of his wife. He felt whipsawed; his compassion for Daisy's tragedy was at war with his need to protect Anna. He looked at the jury and calculated that every one of the twelve men would have offered Daisy a handkerchief and knotted a rope around Anna's neck in the same moment.

Next, Daisy identified nine postcards written to Charlie from Anna. "I found the letters in Charlie's dresser and had kept them, waiting for the opportunity to question Charlie about the letters and cards." She said that the real answer to the meaning of the letters and cards came after she was able to get the spoken truth from Charlie. She compared the handwriting on the intimately worded cards and letters sent to Charlie with the other letter and cards sent to her by Anna, stating, "It is the handwriting of Anna Dotson."

One of the notes read, "That party will be gone for a while after

Monday. Come. Want to see you. Important." Another note from Anna to Charlie read, "Gee, I am lonesome, need you." Still another read, "Mustn't be too blue." And another: "Saturday afternoon at home . . . I will be home all the afternoon alone. All have gone to the fair but me . . . I am so lonely. P.S.: No one suspects anything."

The nine cards and letters from Anna to Charlie were circulated to the jury, along with cards from Anna to Daisy, expressing words of endearment. The handwriting clearly matched. As the jurors' eyes scanned the two sets of notes, one practically begging for intimate visits from Charlie Cobb while the other offered endearments to his wife, Walter could see jaws tightening and gazes hardening. The prosecution was quickly alienating from the jury any thoughts of clemency for the defendant.

"While he was in Nashville," Daisy went on, "I received a letter from him most every day. He was always kind and affectionate and he said that he wanted me to come to Nashville and live with him. We never had a cross word. The last letter I received from him was postmarked March 14, and I did not get it until after he was buried." Daisy began to cry then, audibly.

"Did you love your husband?" Anderson asked.

"I did," she sobbed.

"And did he love you?"

She could only nod.

"I have no further questions."

Walter realized his face was burning with shame. Once again, he felt the rage of a man betrayed, held up for public ridicule by a cheating wife. He clenched his jaws and reminded himself that his first duty was to his family. Anna had repented . . . and Scott and Mabel needed their mother.

The defense chose not to cross-examine Daisy. "No questions, Your Honor," Anderson said. He had likely concluded that Daisy

Cobb's testimony was damaging enough; to cross-examine her would only further inflame the jury against his client.

"FOR ITS NEXT WITNESS, the prosecution calls Paul Christian."

It was late in the evening when Christian walked toward the witness stand. As he looked around he noticed the courtroom was filled to capacity, and there were as many women as men. In the back part of the upper gallery he saw a conclave of suffragettes seated together, wearing white dresses with the characteristic yellow sashes around their waists. He could only imagine what they might be thinking. He found himself hoping he didn't run into a group of them outside the courthouse.

Christian was sworn in and sat down. The attorney general asked him his name and then asked if he was a voluntary witness.

"No, I was served a subpoena."

"Were you at the police station on the day of the murder, March 13, 1913?"

"Yes sir."

"Did you happen to meet the defendant?"

"Yes."

"And where did you meet her?"

"She was in the holding cell inside the booking room of the police station."

"Please indicate to the court the person that you are was referring to?"

Christian looked at Anna Dotson, still wearing her veil, then pointed to her.

"Did you have the occasion to talk to her about the events that had transpired earlier in the day?" the prosecutor asked.

"Yes."

"Did you write down any information that you obtained from her?"

"Yes, I did."

"Do you have your original notes?"

"Yes."

"How long did you talk to her?"

"Off and on, for over an hour."

"Did she admit to you that she killed Charlie Cobb?"

"Yes."

"Could you read the exact words to the jury?"

Counsel for the defendant objected to Christian's reading his notes. But Judge Neil conditionally overruled the objection. "The witness can read his notes and refresh his memory before testifying as to what the defendant said to him, if he cannot recall the events independently. If he cannot remember, he can relate to the jury the exact words as he wrote them down at the time."

Christian knew very well he didn't need to read his notes; he had thought of nothing but this case ever since that first phone call that summoned Sidebottom to Jackson's Barbershop on Broadway, back in March. But he acted as if he needed to, anyway—no sense risking a misstatement, after all—and he took a few minutes to shuffle through his papers.

While Christian was pretending to read his scribbled notes taken down that fateful day, he noticed out of the corner of his eye that Anna was pulling the veil up over her hat. She was staring at him. From what had been reported to him, it was the first time during the trial that she had revealed her face. He noticed that all of the jurors were suddenly, intently studying her. It was as if she had just made some sort of debut.

Finally, after a few moments of silence, Christian proceeded to testify about the interview, including the admission of the shooting by the defendant, the reason she said she had shot Cobb, her state of mind, her admitted premeditation, and her tale of the turbulent matrimonial history between herself and her husband.

As Christian testified, he occasionally looked over toward the table where Anna and her lawyers were sitting. Anna would slightly nod her head up and down, as if in agreement with every bit of his testimony. It was unnerving. Here he was, putting a noose around her neck, and she was acting like his personal amen corner.

Christian knew he would never forget the look on her face during his testimony. It was as if she were trying to assure him that everything was all right, that he shouldn't worry, that she wasn't angry at him. *I told you the truth and you printed the truth*, her eyes seemed to be saying. Her gaze was soft, almost fragile. She sat with her head high and her shoulders erect. Even as he condemned her to death, Christian was thinking to himself, "Damn it, I actually like this woman."

Anna's attorneys had their heads down through most of his testimony. Christian guessed J. M. Anderson wanted to lean over and ask Anna to quit nodding along with his version. He probably surmised, though, that appearing to coach her would only draw more attention to her reactions. And even though Christian was the one doing the talking, nobody in the place was looking at him, and he knew it.

"That's all we have, your Honor," the prosecutor said, after Christian had been on the stand for about an hour. He walked back toward his table. "Your witness, Mr. Seay," he said as he went. And now, Christian knew, he had to face the cross-examination.

36

Did you ever tell Mrs. Dotson that you would be testifying against her in court while you were taking notes of her supposed confession?" Attorney Seay said.

"No, I did not."

"Don't you feel like you took advantage of her?"

"No, I do not."

Seay leaned against the witness stand and gave Christian a sort of conspiratorial little smile. "You really want Mrs. Dotson convicted, don't you, so that your story will gain more national notoriety? You could be a big-time reporter after this, couldn't you?"

The question got under his skin. He paused for a couple of seconds and took a couple of deep breaths. "No, she talked to me without any prodding. She simply volunteered her story without any insistence from me. I just listened and copied down her words. That is my job—it's what I do. I report. I don't have any desire to have anybody convicted until proven guilty beyond a reasonable doubt, and that includes Anna Dotson."

But at the same time, Mr. Seay, I don't much want my name associated with the first court-ordered hanging of a woman in Tennessee. Of course, he couldn't say that part out loud, could he?

Seay gave him a long, measuring look. "Did you think she was in possession of all her faculties when she proceeded to implicate herself in this case without even knowing who you were? I mean, didn't you think it was a little strange, her telling all that to someone she'd never seen before?"

The defense was taking a gamble. Too bad Christian didn't have the cards they were looking for.

"She appeared perfectly sane. It is true that at times she seemed nervous and even cried a few times, but mostly she kept her composure and seemed quite an intelligent and well-bred woman. My impression was that she sincerely believed she would spare her husband and possibly her brother from being charged with murder, by murdering Charlie Cobb herself . . . but I am not an expert on insanity."

For once, the men in the jury were looking at Christian, not at Anna. It seemed like he'd struck some sort of nerve. He thought about it for a few seconds, then looked at the jury and said, "I had not known Mrs. Dotson before, or since, the murder, but I am genuinely puzzled by the terrible deed committed by such an intelligent and likable woman."

"Objection!" the attorney general hollered, bouncing to his feet. Christian might have been the state's star witness, but he'd clearly just ventured over the line. Judge Neil sustained the objection and charged the jury, "What Mr. Christian thinks or supposes about the defendant doesn't count and cannot be considered."

Now it was the defense's turn to object. Judge Neil overruled them and instructed Christian, "Son, please do not answer with your personal thoughts, just answer with the facts."

"Yes sir, I understand. I am aware it is not for me to say whether she is guilty or not, and I am not interested in seeing anyone hung. That is up to the jury, not me." *What's gotten into me, all of a sudden?* he thought.

Attorney General Anderson was bellowing again. The court sustained it. "Young man, I have warned you," Judge Neil said, giving him a hard look. "I will find you in contempt of court if you don't just answer the questions."

By now, Christian could tell both sides wanted him off the witness stand as soon as possible—and the judge, to boot. *At least I don't have any blood on my hands.* He'd done what he had to do for the state, and all he could do for Anna Dotson. Depending on the way a person looked at it, his testimony either drove the nail into Anna's coffin or gave her a first ray of hope. Of course, the judge had told the jury to disregard his suppositions, but once words see the light of day, you never know where they'll stick and where they won't.

In the end, Christian was satisfied his testimony was accurate and truthful. Whether it helped the state or the defense was up to the individual jurors. He was willing to let it rest with them. When he left the stand and walked back to the front row, where his place was reserved, Anna gave him a tiny smile. He would never forget that smile and those eyes, even if he lived to be two hundred.

The judge adjourned the case for the day. Christian shuffled out with the rest of the crowd. Sidebottom was out in the hallway and Christian went up to him.

"Detective, I hope you're not mad about anything I said in there."

He patted Christian on the back. "Son, you got the confession that let us close the case and hand it to the court. I just try to make sure we get the right person on trial, and I did that. What happens from there isn't up to me. You did your job . . . and mine too, in a manner of speaking. How can I complain?"

"I know, but I mean . . . Would it bother you if I said that I kind of like Anna Dotson?"

"Well, there are a lot of likable folks who commit bad crimes. Let's just say it's up to the jury now."

"What do you think they'll do?"

"Who knows? It's a tough case." He gave Christian a wink. "If I could predict what twelve men in a jury room will do, I'd quit working for a living." He nodded and scratched his head, looking into the distance. "Right now, though, I have my doubts, too. Looking at her and listening to everything, and thinking about what she did and how she did it . . . I don't know. Maybe she is some brand of crazy or other."

Attorney General Anderson came striding up to them. "Detective, I wonder if you've got a few minutes to go somewhere with me? There's a matter to be discussed, and I'd like your opinion on it."

Sidebottom gave him a surprised look. "Well, sure, Mr. Prosecutor. Anything you say."

Anderson gave a quick, tight nod and took Sidebottom by the elbow, leading him off toward the stairway to the street entrance. The detective looked back over his shoulder at Christian as he went and gave him an expression that said, "Who knows?"

J. M. Anderson stood as the attorney general and Detective Sidebottom came into the café on Demonbreun. The three men shook hands and Anderson motioned the chief prosecutor and the detective toward the empty seats at the small table.

"Now, Leonard, I think we ought to be able to settle this right now," J. M. said, bringing into play his most magisterial bearing as he studied the attorney general. "What can you give me?"

The state's prosecutor glanced at Sidebottom, then at his opponent. "Mr. Anderson, I appreciate the position you're in. But you have to appreciate mine. You've got a client who's guilty as sin, and she says so herself—Lord o' mercy, did you see her nodding while the newshound was talking?"

J. M. did his best to keep a poker face.

"Meanwhile," the attorney general said, "I've got a grieving widow, an orphan, a full and voluntary confession, and a boxful of jurors that are ready to start building a gallows." He paused, leaned back in his chair. "But . . . I'll tell you what. I've been talking with Detective Sidebottom here, and he thinks your Mrs. Dotson ought not hang. I haven't asked him why." The attorney general snickered and Sidebottom gave a little guilty grin and a shrug. "So, here's what we can do. If Anna pleads guilty to second-degree murder and goes to the women's penitentiary for twenty years—and no parole, mind you—we'll call off the dogs and drop the first-degree charge. What do you say?"

J. M. Anderson let them think he was pondering for a few seconds, then nodded. "Well, Leonard, I appreciate it. The state is making a generous offer. I'll talk to my client and let you know."

"Call me at my home," the attorney general said. "You've got my number. But remember this," he said, laying a hand on Anderson's arm, "once the jury finds her guilty—and they will—then sentences her to hang—and they'll do that, too—you and I never had this little talk. Understand?"

J. M. ANDERSON LEFT THE CAFÉ and went straight to his office, where Anna and Walter waited. He sat down and told them about the prosecution's final offer.

"Anna, as your counsel, I must tell you that I believe in the strongest way possible that it's in your best interest to accept this offer. Twenty years sounds like a long time, but you have to set that over against what I believe is a very real possibility of hanging. Our strongest case was for an insanity plea, and this Christian fellow did some serious damage today with his testimony."

Anna's hand was clasped in Walter's and the two of them looked at each other for a long time. "I didn't murder Charlie Cobb," she said finally. "I'll tell the jury my side of the story, and then it will be in God's hands what happens to me."

Anderson looked at Walter, hoping for some help. But the doctor shrugged. "This must be Anna's decision. I fully support whatever she says."

After the two left his office, Anderson opened the bottom drawer of his desk, reached into the back, and brought out a bottle of Jack Daniel's. He uncorked the whiskey, took a long pull straight from the bottle, then picked up the telephone to call the attorney general.

37

O N THE FOURTH DAY OF THE TRIAL, the defense presented its first witness: Dr. Stephens, the director of the City View Sanitarium. The psychiatrist took the stand and stated that in his opinion, Anna was of unsound mind when she committed the deed.

"I do not believe she was able to distinguish right from wrong."

In an answer to a question from Attorney General Anderson during the cross-examination, Dr. Stephens stated, "The fact that she was able to plan and execute and afterward relate her action with perfect calmness is no evidence that she was not of unsound mind at the time the crime was committed."

"Can you enumerate your reasons for believing the defendant suffered from a delusion?"

"As it appeared to me, the first clue was Mrs. Dotson's assertion of her vow to God. When she interpreted Cobb's return to Nashville as evidence of God's answer to her prayer, and considered this circumstance as proof that God had placed him in her hands to kill, I found evidence of irrationality."

"Could you please define the condition that was your diagnosis for the jury."

"Monomania is a condition that makes a person insane with regard to one particular thing, even though entirely rational in every other area of life. A monomaniac might be perfectly normal in appearance.

"With respect to her children, her husband, her ability to plan and carry out actions, Anna Dotson looks and sounds like any other person. With respect to her thinking about Charlie Cobb, it is my professional opinion that she was incapable of rational thought." When Stephens was finished, the defense called a second psychiatrist, Dr. Glenn; he confirmed the diagnosis of monomania.

Christian watched the jury while the psychiatrists testified, but he couldn't tell exactly how they were responding. Some of them seemed to be interested in the testimony, and some of them just seemed bored. He wasn't sure what to think. On the one hand, how could somebody's mind become so unhinged about a single person that the person could walk into a crowded barbershop and commit murder? On the other hand, Anna's talk about Jephthah, his vow, and its unintended consequences sounded like the ravings of a lunatic, especially so when stated in the psychiatrist's calm, measured voice.

The prosecutors decided not to call any experts in opposition to the two psychiatrists, because they didn't think the jury was giving the insanity plea any credence. Later, Christian learned they'd reached this conclusion mostly because they considered his testimony about Anna's mental state would be more convincing to the average person. They calculated the jury would give more weight to Christian's observations of Anna than those of the trained specialists.

When the second psychiatrist left the stand, J. M. Anderson made the announcement that everyone in the courtroom had been wondering about. "The defense calls Anna Dotson."

A low buzz filled the chamber as Anna stood from the table and walked, head up and shoulders straight, to the witness stand. Christian took a glance around the packed courtroom. There was Daisy Cobb, sitting with her family, right behind the prosecution table. On the other side of the aisle was Walter Dotson, sitting with his arm around Mabel and Scott, who looked very small and helpless as they watched their mother raising her right hand to take the oath. Reporters and courtroom artists scribbled away at their pads, trying to capture the mood, the electric sense of anticipation for those who would read their words and view their pictures in just a few hours.

In the upper balcony, as they had been throughout the trial, sat the women's suffrage contingent. Their presence was coming to seem to Christian almost like a silent rebuke: *What right do twelve men have to consider the guilt or innocence of this woman, whose situation they can hardly comprehend?* He was thinking about the news from Washington about their recent demonstration, about the way the police had scarcely intervened when angry crowds hurled projectiles at them, along with the inevitable insults. Kate Warner, Anne Dallas Dudley, Louise Herron ... these women kept right on writing and speaking, despite the opposition of influential men. What gave them such quiet determination? Was it possible that they were all as crazy or misguided as some believed? Christian thought again about how he'd feel if he were in Anna's position right now, looking into the eyes of twelve women in the jury box.

Anna had taken off her hat and veil, revealing for the first time in the trial to the entire courtroom her complete countenance. As she sat, calmly waiting for the first question from her lawyers, Christian couldn't decide if she made him think more of Joan of Arc ... or Lizzie Borden.

Anna would be on the witness stand all morning and most of the afternoon. As she spoke, Christian sometimes had to remind himself to take notes. He foolishly thought he knew everything she was going to say, but as she told her story, he realized there was so much he had never guessed.

Attorney Seay looked nervous as he approached Anna to begin her testimony; Christian could guess why. Just from the time he'd spent with Anna Dotson, he knew she almost customarily did and said the unexpected.

She told about her early married life, about how happy she and Walter had been. "I never ever had any occasion to doubt my husband's love for me," she said. That didn't ring true to Christian, based on some things Anna had said to him that afternoon in the holding cell. She told of meeting Charlie Cobb, of his growing attentions toward her. "He sometimes came to my house when I was there alone," Anna said. He began to try to persuade her to enter into an intimate relationship with him, she said, and she resisted his advances for some months. But, at last, she testified, she yielded.

After she had finally confessed the affair to Walter, she said things became increasingly desperate, between her husband's rage and her own shame and remorse. She related how Walter left their house with a gun, saying he was going to find Charlie Cobb. "That was when Charlie and his family left Gallatin," she said.

"We began seeing our pastor, Brother Olmstead," Anna testified. "He urged us to remember our Christian commitments, to do things only in the Bible way. But things were so far gone between Walter and me, it seemed to do little good." Anna told of an occasion before the shooting where she kneeled beside her children's beds and begged God to keep them safe, even if it cost her life and the life of someone else precious to her. She told about reading the story of Jephtha from the Old Testament, and how it had seemed to her that God was speaking directly to her through this scripture, assuring her that killing someone in obedience to a sacred vow was not the same thing as murder. She spoke of her desperation and how she begged Walter not to commit violence, to keep himself safe for their children's sake. For several periods during her testimony, Anna was overcome with emotion and had to pause to collect herself. As she spoke, it seemed to Christian that Anderson and Baskerville visibly shrank within themselves, listening to their client implicate herself in premeditated murder.

Christian could see the prosecution leaning forward, obviously itching for Seay to finish so they could pounce on the defendant. An hour or so before the noon recess, they got their chance. Before he could even get out of his seat, Attorney General Anderson started talking. It was as if the words were forcing themselves out of him, as if they'd been bottled up while he listened to her.

"Mrs. Dotson, what did God tell you after you made this vow?"

"God didn't speak to me in audible words. I don't think he does that, this day and time."

"I see. And so, how was it that you were so strongly convinced the good Lord wanted you to carry out this criminal act?" he said, looking at the jury.

"Because he gave me the opportunity I had prayed for."

"Mmm-hmm. Did you have some sort of dream, some sort of vision about all this?"

Was he trying to make her sound crazier than she already did? Christian wondered. If that was his plan, it seemed a strange one. But Anna, if she perceived any opportunity in the question, completely ignored it. "No sir," she said.

"You read the Bible a good deal, do you, Mrs. Dotson?"

"Yes. I read the Bible a lot. I think it is God's word."

"And in your reading, have you happened across the Ten Commandments?" he said, practically smirking at the jury.

"Yes, I have."

"Are you familiar with the commandment 'Thou shalt not commit adultery'?"

"Yes," Anna said in a small voice.

"How about 'Thou shalt not kill'? Did you think maybe that God repealed that particular commandment, just for your convenience?"

"No. But I think I was in the right."

After the noon recess, the prosecution hauled out the letters and notes addressed to Charlie in Anna's handwriting that had been introduced as part of Daisy's testimony. "Is this your handwriting on this note, Mrs. Dotson?" the attorney general asked her. "This one that says, 'All have gone to the fair . . . I am home alone'?"

"Yes."

THE NEXT DAY, Anna was questioned about the shooting in the backyard. "It was a nightgown," she said. "On one occasion when Charlie . . . when Mr. Cobb and I were intimate, I had been wearing it. I came to hate it . . . it represented everything that had gone wrong in my life. I put the nightgown up on a board in my backyard and I shot it with the pistol—three times." She disputed the date that the shooting occurred, as presented by Jordan Warren, her neighbor. "I was the only one who shot the nightgown," she said. "Walter wasn't there."

Christian saw Sidebottom shaking his head at this, and he agreed with the detective. Anna was trying to protect Walter from any connection with the shooting, including his "target practice" in the backyard. Christian knew the detective had tried to obtain the nightgown, hoping that the number of holes would confirm or deny Anna's repeated assertions that she had acted alone, with no encouragement from Walter. Christian expected the prosecution to press her on this, but for some reason, even though her testimony conflicted with that of another witness with nothing to gain or lose, they let it go. Christian could tell this troubled Sidebottom; later, he heard him arguing with the prosecution about it.

Anna related that after the Cobbs had left Gallatin under threat of violence by Walter, she had posted two letters to Charlie: one to Daisy's family address in Herndon, Kentucky, and the other to Charlie's family home in Big Rock. "I didn't know where he was. I was just trying to warn him to stay away."

She said that she finally learned of Cobb's whereabouts from her husband. "He had written the address of the barbershop on a piece of paper. When I asked him, he gave it to me. I told him I was coming to Nashville the next day, to tell Charlie to leave. I brought my son with me, as a way to assure my husband that nothing improper would occur.

"I told Mr. Cobb that my husband knew everything, and I asked him if he wasn't afraid to stay in Nashville, so close to Gallatin, since Walter had warned him to stay far away. 'I'm not afraid of him,' Charlie said. 'I'm ready for him.' I wanted to kill him right then, and I had the pistol with me, but Scott was there, and I was afraid."

Christian couldn't believe his ears. He didn't think there was any way that this woman would have carried a gun with her at the same time she had her little boy. Other than damning herself even more decisively, he decided, she was just trying to further remove any speculation that Walter knew she intended to kill Charlie Cobb. What woman in her right mind would willingly take her child to a shooting?

"The next day, I told my husband that I planned to do some shopping and some errands. When he left for his medical office, I took the afternoon train to Nashville. I had the gun in my muff. I went to the barbershop, walked up to Mr. Cobb, and shot him. And then, I was free of my vow to God."

As Anna finished speaking, the courtroom was completely silent. It was eerie, Christian thought, sitting among so many people and hearing not a single sound except his own breathing. But what they were hearing was so compelling, so riveting, that he guessed no one—not even the prosecution—could think of anything to say. Anna Dotson was handing the state everything it needed to convict her. Christian truly believed he was watching and listening to one who would be the first woman sentenced to death by hanging in the state of Tennessee.

"No more questions, your Honor," Attorney General Anderson said at last. Judge Neil, frowning like someone waking up from a bad dream, said, "The witness may step down."

38

Anna finished her testimony on Friday morning. That afternoon, the defense called an assortment of character witnesses from Gallatin, including the sheriff of Sumner County. Everyone assured the court that Anna Dotson had always been known as a bright, intelligent, and pleasant person.

Then a man named Olmstead, the minister of Anna and Walter's church, took the stand. He testified about the apparent mental and emotional condition of both Anna and Walter when they came to him for counsel, after Anna's confession of her affair. "Dr. Dotson told me that he thought he ought to kill Charlie Cobb. On one occasion, he said to me, 'That man as good as burned down my house and destroyed my family. I wish he had just gone ahead and cut my throat while he was shaving me.' Of course, as his minister, I urged him against such thoughts and actions."

"Did you ever hear Mrs. Dotson mention Jephtha's vow?" Attorney Seay asked.

"Yes. She discussed it with me on one occasion. I told her that Jephtha's vow should not be a guide for her actions, that killing Charlie Cobb was unjustified except in the event that he was attempting to force himself on her. I told her that even in the Bible, Jephtha's vow was presented as a rash action, more as a warning than a recommendation to similar behavior."

Christian wasn't sure if the minister thought he was helping or hurting Anna. The minister's account made it sound as if she'd been given every chance to reconsider the wisdom of her thinking.

"Through most of our meeting, Mrs. Dotson sat on the floor with her head on a chair. She asked me if she had the right to kill Mr. Cobb and I told her that should the man come back, invade her home and attempt to renew the old relations, then she had the right to kill him, but under no other circumstances.

"She then arose from the floor, and went and got a pistol. I'll never forget this. She pointed it at the chair as though she were seeing something. Then she laughed queerly and pointed the gun at herself. I managed to wrench the weapon away from her grasp. I tried to calm her, to convince her that Jephtha's vow was a rash one. I wanted her to promise not to carry out her intentions, but she would not promise to break the vow she had made to God."

Attorney General Anderson did his best to discredit Olmstead. He shot question after question at him in quick succession, attacking him as "a preacher of the gospel sanctioning the killing of Cobb by this woman." Mr. Olmstead responded to most with skill, but several seemed to hit a nerve and riled him.

The next morning, the defense put Anna's sister, Flora Lambert, on the stand, followed by her brother, Robert Dennis. Both said they had always known Anna to be a sincere, energetic person, but never violent in any way—until she got mixed up with Charlie Cobb. Robert's testimony was especially poignant; several times, he wept openly, describing the difference in his sister's demeanor after she met Cobb. "When I found out what was going on, I could hardly believe it," he said. "Anna was like a different person. She was despondent, listless. She ate little or nothing."

The final witness for the defense was Anna's father. He told about her life as a child at their home in Lafayette, that she was always "pleasant and sunny of countenance."

"We taught all our children the Bible from the time they were old enough to listen," the minister said. "When her brother Bobby first told me of her difficulties, I was devastated. I was planning to take her to Texas, to my brother's home, when . . . all this happened."

Christian surmised the defense was doing its best to counter the prosecution's portrayal of Anna as a selfish, calculating, coldhearted murderer. From the faces of the jury, he wasn't sure the testimony was having enough of the desired effect.

At 4:10 on Saturday afternoon, the defense rested its case. The state then asked for a recess, and returned in a few minutes to announce that they would not offer any rebuttal to the defense. Apparently, they'd decided the faces of the jury indicated their readiness to begin deliberation. The prosecution calculated the jury had heard enough and was ready to convict. The court was adjourned until nine o'clock the following Monday, when the state would commence its closing arguments. Christian looked at Anna Dotson and her husband and children; this would probably be one of the longest weekends of their lives.

ON MONDAY MORNING, Assistant Attorney General Moore was the first to speak to the jury. He asked the jurors to "seek out evidence and act fearlessly on it. Forget categories of 'man' and 'woman' and deal out justice based on truth."

"Gentlemen of the jury, you must decide whether the defendant was a lunatic or whether she was engaged in adultery that was mutual, happy, and joyous." He argued, "It is human nature for conscience to smite a young, intelligent, refined, virtuous wife upon the first occasion that she transgressed and committed adultery. But consider: would she not have been more apt to have gone crazy after her first act of illicit relations with Cobb than after weeks and months of intimacy with her lover?" He added, "A woman of learning with children cannot be seduced."

Upon hearing these words, Christian glanced up at the balcony. It appeared that the women with the yellow sashes were displeased by such a sweeping characterization.

Next, Attorney General Anderson took up the attack. "Note, gentlemen, that Anna Dotson did not voluntarily confess until after her husband had questioned her with increasing intensity, even resorting to threats of driving her away from home. He asserted that Anna should have seen through Charlie Cobb's intentions much earlier. Any decent woman would have kicked him out for making such advances."

Curiously, Anderson made a vigorous attack on Dr. Dotson, charging him with conniving with his wife in writing the letters to Cobb, mailed with the intention of luring Cobb back to Gallatin in order that Anna might kill him. Christian thought the prosecution was overreaching with this line of reasoning. He couldn't help noticing that Anna was shaking her head after he made this statement. The jury noticed it, too.

The chief prosecutor went on. "And what about this husband, giving his poor, supposedly deranged wife a piece of paper with the Jackson's Barbershop address on it, when he knew she had vowed to kill him? He ought to be thankful that the law forbids a wife from testifying against her husband."

The attorney general next addressed the insanity plea. "Gentlemen of the jury, the defense has presented few facts and an abundance of invention and theory." He pointed out that if Anna Dotson were delusional, "she would have killed him on Friday, without regard for the presence of her little boy. Instead, like a truly calculating murderer, she awaited her better chance, the next day."

He concluded by telling the jury that Cobb had been the instrument, not the cause, of Anna's lust. "The time has come when there must be a stop put to this business of women going around and shooting down men just because their dresses are wrapped around their legs. Do not be influenced by pity." There was another rustling in the balcony when he said this.

After Attorney General Anderson sat down, the lawyer named Murray, hired by the Cobb family to help with the prosecution, argued, "Charlie Cobb was welcomed with open bosom by Anna Dotson. She was not some helpless, weak-willed damsel. No, gentlemen, she sought out opportunity to be with Charlie Cobb; she was his willing accomplice in the illicit relationship." Murray scorned Anna for holding the vow to kill as being "more sacred than her marriage vows." He looked at each juror as he spoke.

"This murder was premeditated, with malice aforethought. Anna Dotson, who had betrayed not only her husband, but also her friend Daisy Cobb, decided she simply had no more use for Charlie Cobb. Remember what she said to the officers of the peace at the scene of her crime? 'Is that thing dead?' Those were her very words, gentlemen! There is only one answer to such coldhearted violence and immorality. You, the jury, should convict her for first-degree murder. Indeed," he said, moving back toward the prosecution table and pointing at Anna as he went, "hanging is too good for her!"

Judge Neil looked at the defense. "Mr. Anderson, is the defense ready to present its closing arguments?"

There was a long pause, and Christian actually wondered if Anderson was going to pull a white handkerchief from his pocket and wave it above his head. Finally, though, he stood slowly and said, "Yes, your Honor."

He walked around the end of the defense table like a man going to the wall in front of a firing squad. He paced deliberately toward the jury box. Every eye in the courtroom followed him until little Scott clambered over the railing and crawled into his mother's lap. The old defense attorney, hearing the commotion behind him, turned and watched with everyone else as Anna stroked her son's head and hugged him close. As Anderson turned away from those seated in the courtroom to face the jury, it was easy to imagine his expression: *Look at this child. Look at this mother.*

"Gentlemen of the jury," he said in a slow, heavy voice, "consider the little bird that hovers over the serpent, mesmerized by its eyes until, having chanced too near, it is consumed with one snap of the fanged jaws. That little bird cannot tell you why it is so held by fatal fascination. No more can my client, the mother whom you now see comforting her innocent child, tell you what it was about Charlie Cobb that rendered her so susceptible to his illicit charms.

"Can you truly not imagine what she might do to protect her own? Recall how many times she spoke of her remorse, when she was finally, despite the fog of her delusion, able to realize what she had done to her home in her sin with Charlie Cobb. Think of her husband, gentlemen. Think of your own wives! Which of you, hearing a confession similar to that which Walter Dotson experienced, would not want the same thing he wanted, would not want to kill the man who had participated with your spouse in such infamy? And yet, what did she tell him? 'Don't do it! Think of your children!' This poor woman, who had already despaired of her own life in her shame and confusion, was trying to prevent yet another tragedy, one that would rob that little boy, along with his sister, of a father. She was trying to protect her husband in the only way she knew!"

By now, sobs were easily audible, not only from Anna, Walter, and their children, but also from the audience. It was a masterful performance from the veteran lawyer. He seemed to gather himself as he went, seemed to draw strength from the emotion in the courtroom. The jury watched him, seemingly as entranced as the little bird with which he had begun his remarks.

"Was it the right thing to do? Was it the wise thing? The sane, reasoned thing? Of course not, gentlemen! Anna Dotson, quite simply, was driven beyond the edge of reason by her own guilt, by her fear for her husband, by her anxiety for her children's future. And in that extremity, that singleness of mind, that obsession, that monomania, to use the respected Doctor Stephens' word . . . she did the only thing she could think of. She took some words from a terrible, bloody old story out of the Old Testament, and she clung to them, and with nothing in her mind but ending her troubles the only way she could imagine, she carried a gun into Jackson's Barbershop and shot the man who represented danger to everything she held dear.

"Charlie Cobb held a terrible fascination for this woman, and he used it to his own ends. Well, he paid the ultimate price for his folly. But now, gentlemen, will you spread the carnage further? Will you condemn not only Anna Dotson, but also her children, whom she did such awful things to protect? Think of that little boy there, peering through prison bars at his mother, dressed in the drab clothing of the penitentiary. Think of that little girl, probably the same age as some of your daughters or granddaughters, placing flowers on the grave of a mother who died at the end of a rope.

"Will you put that rope around her neck, gentlemen? I pray that you will not. I pray, instead, that you will look into your own hearts, and find my client not guilty by reason of insanity."

39

JUDGE NEIL ORDERED A RECESS of fifteen minutes before taking up the delivery of his charge to the jury. It was four o'clock on Monday. When the judge reentered, the courtroom was filled to its capacity; people were even standing along the walls at the back.

The judge looked at the twelve men in the jury box. "You are about to deliberate upon the evidence that has been presented to you. In your deliberations, you must first determine whether Anna Dotson was insane at the time of the killing. If you find the defendant insane then you must stop any further deliberation and report back to the court. If you find the defendant not guilty by reason of insanity, the defendant will be immediately committed to the Tennessee State Asylum for the Insane, where she will be held and treated for an indefinite period of time, to be released only after a determination by this court that she has regained her sanity.

"If you find Anna Dotson to have been sane at the time of the killing of Charlie Cobb then you, the jury, must decide whether she is guilty of murder in the first degree. Such a finding of guilt would impose an obligation upon the jury to then determine her sentence—in this case, either life imprisonment or death by hanging."

When Judge Neil finished his charge, the jury was excused to discuss whether they wanted to go back to the Hermitage Hotel, where they were being sequestered, in order to get a good night's rest before returning at nine the following morning, or immediately begin deliberations. When the jury filed out of the courtroom, most of the spectators left the courthouse, assuming that the jury would surely opt to go back to the hotel.

Only a few minutes later, though, the jury came back into the courtroom. The foreman, a man named Smith, said, "Your Honor, we have decided to deliberate in the courthouse until a verdict is reached."

The judge looked a little surprised. He announced to those who remained in the courtroom, "If the jury reaches a verdict, it will not be announced until tomorrow morning at nine." With these words, the courtroom emptied of its few remaining spectators, led by Christian's fellow newspapermen, rushing to get their stories filed.

When jury foreman Smith made his announcement, Christian saw guarded smiles on the faces of the prosecution. Christian could tell what the attorney general and his team were thinking: the jury sensed a quick verdict among themselves.

As midnight approached without the jury having returned a verdict, Christian started to question his earlier assumption. He realized he was wrung out; he left the courtroom and went over to the press office in the police station to get a little sleep.

Unfortunately, though, his mind wasn't ready to turn loose of the case. He tossed and turned on the narrow cot, snatches of testimony running through his head. He mulled over the discrepancies between Anna's nightgown testimony and the account of the shooting presented by her neighbor; he thought about the inaccuracies regarding her relationship with her husband as she had presented it to the jury; he thought about what he had begun to view as Anna's other "little white lies" to the jury, realizing that he had already forgiven her for the untruths, since each was intended to protect her husband and children. Though Christian understood her motivation, he feared that the prosecution—and Anna's own admissions—had already dug her grave. And then, he realized with a bit of a start that somewhere along the line, he had actually started rooting for Anna, hoping for her to escape the fate that seemed all too certain.

About four o'clock in the morning, Christian got up from the cot and walked through the dark streets to the courthouse to see if the jury had finished its deliberation. He was stunned to find that they were still in their conference room, still trying to make their decision.

The bailiff was propped up in a chair outside the jury room, dozing with his arms across his belly. Christian touched him on the shoulder and his eyes fluttered open. He yawned and told him that Judge Neil was in his chambers, sleeping on a couch. Christian thought about trying to talk to the judge, but decided instead to go back to his office and attempt at least a catnap.

When sunrise started creeping through the police station's windows, Christian got up and went back to the courthouse. Later, around eight o'clock, the court officer found him and said, "Judge Neil would like to see you."

Christian entered and the judge invited him to sit down. They made small talk for a few minutes, but eventually got around to the case at hand.

Christian asked, "What do you think the jury will do?" He really didn't expect Neil to answer; he never had before when asked the same question in other trials. Really, Christian was just trying to make conversation.

To the reporter's surprise, he said, "Christian, there is one thing I have learned the hard way: You usually cannot predict a jury. I think they're having a difficult time deciding to hang a woman. Besides, I think maybe your testimony got her the life sentence. I think you like the woman, and you let the jury know it."

Christian shrugged. "Sorry, your Honor."

He made a dismissing motion. "I think the decisive question is whether the defendant was not guilty by reason of insanity. This monomania business is the first thing they've got to tackle. If they find the defendant sane at the time of the killing, then there's not much way around them finding her guilty of premeditated murder, and once they do that—and you know better than anyone, the defendant admitted to it—they'll just about have to impose a severe penalty: death by hanging or life imprisonment." He paused a moment, staring out the window. "If I were on the jury, I would have to seriously consider first-degree murder with life imprisonment."

"Do you not think this is an appropriate situation for the death penalty?"

Another long pause. "I personally think the death penalty would be too harsh under the circumstances. But it really doesn't matter what we think, Christian, does it?" the judge said, looking at him. "It is solely the decision of the jury . . . not me, not you."

He looked out his window another long time. "Christian, if I were a betting man, I would bet the jury will impose a life sentence."

BY NOON ON THAT TUESDAY, the courtroom was as hot as Hades. Nashville was sweltering in ninety-degree June weather; the three large fans attached to the courtroom's fifteen-foot ceiling did little but stir the stifling air. Despite the stifling heat, the spectator section and the gallery were filled to capacity. Incredibly, the jury had deliberated all night and was now into its twentieth straight hour.

People actually waited in line at the courthouse door, starting before sunrise. It was powerfully fascinating, this case of the *People of Tennessee v. Anna Dotson*, and the whole population of Nashville was under the sway of the unfolding drama. They wanted to be there to see firsthand what would happen.

Christian sat in his front-row seat and tugged at his collar, feeling like a wrung-out dishrag. The courtroom was aflutter with the cheap paper fans sold by the hucksters along the sidewalk; Anna Dotson's trial was turning into a commercial event, as well as a legal one. Though it was miserable inside, the people in the courtroom probably considered themselves lucky; plenty of other would-be spectators were turned away at the door by the court officers, once the seats were filled.

Christian could hear the babble of conversations going on all around him: "I'll bet you a dollar to a doughnut hole they find her guilty . . ."

"Why, that woman's as crazy as a loon! They'll let her off—I'd be surprised if she don't do it again, some day . . ."

"Well, that husband of hers sure ought to get some of the blame . . ."

"Did you see that little boy? So precious . . . such a shame . . ."

As the noon hour passed, the heat started to wither the air of expectancy. People were complaining, wondering out loud when the jury was ever going to finish this business. Christian even heard a few speculate about a hung jury. Wouldn't that be something, he thought. Among other things, it would be a testimonial to old attorney Anderson's skill in his closing oratory. To Christian, a hung jury looked like an answered prayer for Anna Dotson.

He decided to take advantage of his reserved seat; with the note from the court tacked to his chair, he wasn't worried about finding a place to sit if the jury suddenly returned. Christian started moving around the courtroom, interviewing spectators to get the reaction of the general public. It would make some good copy. Many women in the courtroom, he soon found out, were mightily upset over the total dominance of the proceedings by men. "It's a man's world!" one of them said. "What chance has a woman got?" Christian noted her response, and he couldn't help glancing up in the balcony at the suffrage women, sitting there like a Greek chorus in their white dresses and yellow sashes, watching from above. If he'd had the guts to go up there and talk to them, he calculated they'd tell him that the fault of the men involved in this case would be whitewashed, swept under the carpet, and otherwise ignored by the jury. An annoying little voice at the back of Christian's mind told him they'd be right. He constructed a quote from one of them for his imaginary interview: "What justice can be done for women in a country where none but men are permitted to decide their guilt or innocence?"

Christian continued to speculate on what the jury was thinking. He decided that the most intriguing part of the murder trial involved the differences in perception between men and women over the misguided quest for independence by this solitary woman, Anna Dotson. Curiously, women seemed to rally around the beleaguered defendant; men mostly scorned her. Once again, he thought about the implications of having none but males on the voting rolls—and in the jury box. He looked at the twelve empty seats, eventually to be occupied by the men who were now deliberating Anna Dotson's fate. After taking this long, their decision would be seen as controversial—no matter the outcome.

Sometime toward mid-afternoon, as his notepad was getting soggy with the perspiration from his hands, and the people in the courtroom were getting louder and louder, the bailiff was roused from his chair by the door of the jury room. He went down the hall to Judge Neil's chambers and knocked on the door. Judge Neil listened, nodded, and sent him to the courtroom. The bailiff came in through the door behind the judge's bench, unnoticed by anyone in the noisy courtroom except Christian. He cupped his hands around his mouth and shouted, "Please be seated. The jury is ready to return a verdict! Folks! Settle down! The jury is ready. Please be seated, and please do not demonstrate after the verdict is announced!"

There was a hushed scurrying as people reclaimed their seats or

315

stood against the walls. Christian took his seat in the front row. The courtroom became unnaturally quiet.

The prosecuting attorneys soon came back into the courtroom, led by the attorney general. Anna Dotson came next, white-faced and clutching her husband's gold vest watch, which he'd given her as a good luck piece. She was followed by Walter and the children, followed by the team of somber defense lawyers, led by J. M. Anderson. Finally, the family and relatives of the deceased followed, though maintaining a careful distance from Anna and her party.

The bailiff announced, "Court is in session . . . all rise!" Judge Neil entered from his private door, directly behind his bench. He stood behind his chair and nodded to the bailiff.

The bailiff went over to jury entrance, next to the jury box, and opened the door. The twelve men slowly entered the deathly quiet courtroom. To a man, the jurors looked exhausted, completely used up. Large half-circles of perspiration stained their shirts beneath their arms; their sleeves were rolled up. Whatever they were about to announce, it hadn't come easy.

"Please be seated." Judge Neil said.

The benches creaked, and there was the soft scuffling of leather-soled shoes on hardwood, and then, again, complete silence.

"Has the jury reached a verdict?" Judge Neil said.

The foreman, Mr. Smith, stood up and gave a tired nod. "Yes we have, Your Honor."

"Will the defendant please rise?" the judge said.

Anna Dotson stood up, a bit unsteadily, looking intently into the eyes of the jurors, still clenching the gold watch. Most of the jurors' faces were bowed, avoiding eye contact with her or with anyone else. Christian wasn't sure if this was from sheer fatigue or their feelings about what was about to happen. Most likely, it was both.

"And what is the verdict?" the judge said.

The foreman took a long look around the room, then looked directly at Judge Neil. He took a deep breath. "Your Honor, we, the jury, find the defendant guilty of involuntary manslaughter, and sentence her to five days in the county workhouse."

40

BEDLAM BROKE LOOSE in the courtroom. Judge Neil pounded his gavel and the bailiff and other officers shouted. Finally the place calmed down enough for the judge to make himself heard again. He polled each member of the jury, asking each man if he concurred with the sentence. When he had satisfied himself that the jury wasn't going to budge, he shook his head in apparent disgust, then ordered the bailiff to take Anna into custody so that she could begin serving the terms of the sentence the jury had just pronounced. It was the first instance of jury nullification Christian could remember in all the trials he'd covered, and Judge Neil looked fit to be tied. Judges didn't even like to have their cases overturned by the normal appeals process; to have a jury decide to ignore or modify the instructions the judge had given them was even more galling. It happened sometimes, but it was very rare.

When the foreman read the sentence, the other reporters jumped up and sprinted from the courthouse, each vying to be the first to communicate the unbelievable news to his newspaper. But Christian sat there, trying to gain control of his tumbling mind. He knew that the *Tennessean*, as well as the newspapers in Atlanta, Knoxville, Chattanooga, and elsewhere that were running his stories about the trial, wouldn't publish anything unless it was under his byline. He hadn't been sitting in the police station during Anna's arrest for nothing, after all. So, there wasn't that big a hurry. Christian wanted to talk to the jurors, the judge, or anybody else that could help him explain to the public how the most publicized murder case in recent years had come down to such a bizarre ending.

What gradually emerged from Christian's conversations with the jurors was that J. M. Anderson's voir dire tactics about the suffrage movement, combined with his closing arguments, had found their mark. Some of the jurors, at least, gave serious consideration to Anna's motivation. They also began thinking about how things would have been different if it had been Walter Dotson as defendant, rather than his wife.

None of this held water with Judge Neil. When he was interviewed after the trial, he characterized the sentence as a "miscarriage of justice." This phrase was even repeated in the next day's banner headlines.

From the jurors' views, though, things looked different. As Christian found out from his interviews, the first issue taken up as the deliberations began on Monday afternoon was the defense of monomania. After lengthy discussion, six jurors remained convinced that Anna was sane at the time of the shooting, while six thought she was insane. Neither side would budge.

Around eleven o'clock that Monday evening, the exasperated jurors tentatively voted to report the impasse to the judge. However, the foreman, J. D. Smith, convinced the jurors to temporarily set aside the debate over the monomania defense and deliberate as if Anna Dotson were sane.

So, the jury turned to the charge of first-degree murder, and what the punishment should be if the defendant was sane. They meticulously went back over all the testimony, concentrating on Anna's own words. The jury agreed that the murder was premeditated, but even so, there was still another irreconcilable split amongst the jurors with regard to the punishment.

Three of the jurors felt strongly that the prosecution had made a case for the death penalty and reminded the other jurors, who didn't feel so strongly about it, of the judge's final charge. If they determined she was sane at the time of the murder and they found her guilty, they must sentence her to life in prison or to be hanged.

Periodically, the jurors told Christian, the discussion turned to the side issue of women not being able to sit in judgment of one of their own. The jurors knew firsthand from the suffragettes that women openly questioned how a "men only" group could possibly carry out justice in this case. Some of the jurors said they felt pressure from the looks of the suffragettes in the balcony.

Christian began to realize that J. M. Anderson's tactics had amounted to a brilliant move. The defense attorney was able to plant the notion of women's rights in the mind of each juror, and to ask them questions about it during voir dire. At the time, it seemed like a side issue. But as the trial wore on, Anderson's strategy came more and more to the front—in the juror's minds, at least. Christian reflected that this was the way history worked sometimes. What seemed irrelevant today might turn out tomorrow to be the deciding factor. By assuring the presence on the jury of at least six men who had an open mind toward women's suffrage, Anderson guaranteed that the prospect of a woman's fate being decided by an exclusively male jury would come under discussion. Sure enough, the six pro-suffrage jurors made their opinions known.

One juror commented, "You know, every time we left the Hermitage Hotel to come to court in the mornings, and when we went back to the hotel when the judge adjourned for the day, them suffragettes would always be there near the front door, dressed in them white dresses with them yellow sashes. And the way they looked at us . . . they wanted our attention."

Another juror said, "How could we miss the message on that sign one of the suffragettes held up outside the front door of the hotel every day: 'No right to vote, no right to sit on juries, no right to judge our own.' I think they wanted to let us know we ought to consider the fact that a woman was not allowed on the jury to judge Anna Dotson."

Yet another juror pointed out to Christian, "The headquarters of the Tennessee Equal Suffrage Association is in the Hermitage Hotel . . . That's why we seen them all the time . . . What do you expect?" Indeed, Christian found out later that several of the suffragettes who had attended the trial had also participated in the Washington, D.C., protests.

After another polling of the jury by the foreman during the wee hours of Tuesday morning, three of the jurors still remained in favor of the death sentence. Five others favored a life sentence. Four of the men recommended a lighter sentence, a conviction on second-degree murder with a twenty-year prison sentence.

The jury appeared to be once again hopelessly deadlocked, this time on the issue of the punishment. Again they voted to announce a hung jury to the court. But J. D. Smith once more convinced the jurors to continue deliberations. Since none of the jurors really wanted to announce an impasse, they reluctantly agreed to strive for a verdict they could all live with.

By late morning, even the foreman was about to throw in the towel. Then one juror, a Mr. Peebles, came up with an idea: "Why don't we deliberate as if Walter Dotson had shot Charlie Cobb?" The jurors agreed to look at it that way.

The jurors went around the table, each stating his own views about the case had Walter Dotson been on trial for the murder of Charlie Cobb. The first thing they agreed upon was that if given the chance, Dr. Walter Dotson would have certainly shot Charlie Cobb, and he would have been on trial for murder, not Anna Dotson. This was when, Christian suspected, J. M. Anderson's final arguments were ringing most strongly in their ears.

Then, in a very interesting development, the jurors decided to discuss the general range of punishment as if Walter Dotson had killed Charlie Cobb. In the process of considering what they would have done with Walter Dotson, the jurors began to realize that they had been applying a double standard to Anna Dotson.

As a result of looking at the case in a different angle, the jurors began to reluctantly discard some of their views of women. The concept of equality began to control their deliberations. "If Anna Dotson were a man, on trial under the same circumstances, what would we do?" they asked. And their answer would begin to reshape the perception of equality between the sexes in Tennessee for years to come.

Epilogue

NASHVILLE TENNESSEAN

and The Nashville American

Vol. 7–No. 45.   June 25, 1913

VERDICT OF JURY IN FAMOUS MURDER CASE DELIVERED TUESDAY AFTERNOON

"She shall serve every minute of it," declared Judge A. B. Neil, of the criminal court, when the jury, after deliberating more than twenty-one hours over the fate of Mrs. Anna Dotson, charged with the murder of Charlie Cobb, brought in a verdict of involuntary manslaughter Tuesday afternoon at 2 o'clock, with a sentence of five days in the Davidson County jail. From the evidence produced, Judge Neil expressed himself as being thoroughly dissatisfied with the finding of the jury, declaring that it was a miscarriage of justice.

When the twelve men, worn and tired with their long fight that waged all through the night, walked into the courtroom, a dead hush overspread the crowd that packed the room. Mrs. Dotson was sitting with her husband and attorneys, and when the door opened she became deathly pale.

When the stentorian tones of the foreman announced the verdict, she stared straight ahead of her as though she did not understand and suddenly laughed quietly to herself, while the attorneys jubilantly congratulated Dr. Dotson and his wife.

The court was thunderstruck at the

verdict. Never before, declared the judge and attorney-general, had they heard of such an opinion in the case of murder like this one.

After a consultation the attorneys for defense announced that the defendant would serve the sentence, and she was taken in charge by Jailer Will Longhurst and taken to the woman's department and locked up. Dr. Dotson accompanied his wife to the jail office, where tender farewells took place between the prisoner, her young son, daughter, and brother. The scene was affecting.

When the jury reported the verdict there was no demonstration. According to several attorneys the criminal court had set a precedent in the settlement of murder cases.

Mrs. Cobb, the widow of the dead barber, sat quietly by the side of her father-in-law, when the jury returned and when the verdict was announced, leaned her head on her hands in dejection. She declared that she did not wish any one harm, but further than that would say nothing in regard to the case. "Of course I am disappointed, but I don't care to say anything else."

Attorney-General Anderson, when seen shortly after the announcement, declared that the jury had grossly failed in its duty. He said that Judge Neil specifically charged them that if they found the woman was not insane, a verdict of murder in the first degree should be returned. He declared that by sentencing her they found that she was not insane and had, therefore, failed to carry out the instructions of the judge and had also failed in their duty to the state at large.

Monday morning a large crowd assembled at the courtroom, thinking that the jury would report at 9 o'clock. It was learned that an agreement had not been reached, and court was adjourned at 10 o'clock until 2 o'clock. The halls were crowded during that interval and the telephone in the office kept the clerks busy. When court convened the crowd was even larger, standing several deep against the walls and blocking the windows and doors.

Immediately after the verdict was announced Judge Neil dismissed the jury. In speaking of the case afterward, Judge Neil declared that he was thoroughly disappointed with the verdict. "Are you going to let her serve the sentence?" he was asked. "That I am. Every minute of it," he declared emphatically. "Of course, I have no criticism to make of the case, but I am disappointed."

An incident that was only brought to light Tuesday morning was the fact that Monday, during the closing of the argument a group of local suffragettes were present in court, lined up near the defendant, when Judge J. M. Anderson made his eloquent appeal for the prisoner, and wept during the whole time that he spoke.

Later in the evening Mrs. Dotson was taken by automobile to the county workhouse, where she was housed at the home of Frank Graham, assistant superintendent. Mr. Graham stated Tuesday night that she would be made to work like the rest of the women who are sent to serve sentences at the place. She is the only white woman now under sentence at the workhouse.

It was later stated at the criminal court that the jury was tied on Monday night, nine standing for acquittal and three for murder in the second degree, with a twenty-year sentence. It was rumored that a large number of the jurors were Masons, as was Dr. Dotson.

Judge J. M. Anderson, who led the defense, when asked for a statement in regard to the verdict, declared that he had nothing to say.

AFTER THE TRIAL, Walter Dotson resigned from many of his extra activities in order to spend more time with his wife and family. The following year, Walter and Anna moved to Lebanon, Tennessee, where he resumed his medical practice.

World War I came and Dr. Dotson volunteered for the Army Medical Corps; he ended his stint in the United States Army with the rank of major and was bestowed with several military awards and citations. After returning home from the war, Walter Dotson signed a petition that called upon the Tennessee legislature to vote for ratification of the Nineteenth Amendment to the United States Constitution, the amendment that would grant women the right to vote—and to sit on juries.

Walter and Anna's daughter, Mabel Dotson, continued to adore her mother until her untimely death from tuberculosis in 1919. She was nineteen. Their son, Walter Scott Dotson, became a successful physician like his father, practicing medicine in Westmoreland, Tennessee, but also died at a relatively young age.

After Walter's relatively premature death in 1926, Anna moved to Westmoreland, close to her childhood home, in a house on the Lafayette-to-Westmoreland road. She lived out her life in virtual solitude, occasionally being seen downtown, usually accompanied by two large dogs on leashes.

Anna Dotson remained unmarried after the death of her husband, and died in 1948 at the age of sixty-eight. The Dotson family is buried together in a simple plot in the Gallatin cemetery, marked by a center monument with the Masonic symbol engraved on the top.

PAUL CHRISTIAN DID SEE Anna Dotson once more. It was almost a year after the trial, on a pleasant Saturday in May 1914. He was covering another news story: an account of the first suffrage parade in the South, held in Nashville. Suffragettes from all over the nation started the parade from lower Broadway and were marching westward up the street, four miles to Centennial Park. Leading the parade was the famous Nashville suffragette, Anne Dallas Dudley; she was going to be the lead subject of Christian's story.

Ironically, the parade went past Jackson's Barbershop. Christian was standing on the southwest corner of Broadway and Eighth Avenue, a few doors up from the place, observing the suffragettes. As the long lines of women marchers passed by, all wearing white lace dresses with yellow sashes around their waists, many carrying signs and placards proclaiming support for an equal suffrage amendment to the United States Constitution, he noticed one particular woman. There was no mistaking that blonde hair, those blue eyes. In his wildest imagination, he would have never dreamed he would ever see Anna Dotson again, let alone walking down Broadway, although he had spent many a day and night thinking about her. Well, there she was, marching with the gait of a queen, strolling next to her best friend, Elizabeth Jennings.

As the women passed by, several men behind Christian were shouting. "She-males!" they hollered. "Why don't you stay home, where you belong?"

And then suddenly, Anna looked over toward the corner and noticed him standing there, not far from the barber pole in front of Jackson's. She stumbled a bit, but quickly regained her balance. And then, she smiled. Christian smiled back. Not exactly having journalistic distance from the subject, he didn't include that memorable encounter in the story that ran the next day. Instead, he focused on Anne Dallas Dudley. But in a strange way, Anna Dotson had probably affected the course of women's lives as much as Mrs. Dudley—though she certainly never intended to.

As Anna turned away and marched up Broadway with the other demonstrators, Paul Christian kept watching her. A few seconds later, with the men around him still yelling their epithets and insults, he tipped his hat.

Author's Note

The central characters in this 1913 murder story are real, as is the text of the newspaper articles. Although much of this novel involves actual historical events, I have taken certain storytelling liberties in order to fill in gaps circumscribed by the actual 1913 trial testimony as reported in the three local newspapers: *The Tennessean and American,* the *Nashville Banner,* and the *Nashville Democrat.* In the parts where the story fictionally connects the testimony I have tried to portray things and events that would reasonably have occurred, remaining faithful to the characters and to the events as they actually happened.

This tragic murder occurred during the worldwide, tumultuous struggle as women sought rights historically denied to them by men. In America, women were demanding the right to vote (and thus the right to sit on juries). As the suffrage movement grew, World War I broke out and women's suffrage went on the back burner. Soon after the hostilities subsided, the movement reappeared with renewed zeal and the attempt to amend the U.S. Constitution to allow women the right to vote eventually centered on the state of Tennessee.

The amendment that would grant women the right to vote required approval by three-fourths of the (then) forty-eight state legislatures, or thirty-six states. The postwar attempt had garnered approval from thirty-five states; nine states had voted against and three other states did not appear prepared to vote on the issue. Tennessee became the battleground for the friends and foes of women's suffrage. By a margin of one vote, the state of Tennessee became the linchpin state that ushered into law the nineteenth amendment to the U.S. Constitution, granting women the right to vote.

Although my research did not reveal any overt suffrage activity by Anna Dotson, there is nothing to indicate that she did not have an interest in the women's suffrage movement. The desire for independence and recognition are two common denominators connecting Anna Dotson and the women's suffrage movement. In this novel I have attempted to weave the actual events surrounding the movement during the early years of the twentieth century as essential elements for an independent-thinking woman of the times. Anna Dotson, it seems to me, was such a female; indeed, her independent proclivities might be characterized as a microcosm of this contemporary women's revolt against repression and perceived insignificance.

On the other side of the coin, this story also reflects the conflict men of the times were experiencing through their own struggles in accepting women on equal footing. The conflict was particularly manifested by the landmark verdict of the all-male jury in Anna's case; the verdict jolted conventional thinking anchored in the Victorian past.

Many observers of the trial said that the verdict was a "miscarriage of justice," while many others thought the perpetrator of the murder got only what was deserved. The opinions were closely divided, akin to the one-vote margin of victory for the suffrage movement in Tennessee that led to the ratification of the Nineteenth Amendment to the United States Constitution.

Was this a "miscarriage of justice?" I invite you to be the judge.